BLUE
RAIN

TESS FARRADAY

QuestMark
CONTEMPORARY
ROMANCE

Questmark Inc.

Published by the QuestMark Book Group
QuestMark Inc., 15 Paradise Plaza, #351, Sarasota, FL 34242
www.questmarkinc.com

BLUE RAIN

A QuestMark Romance / Published by arrangement with the author.

Cover design and interior text design by Jeanie James | Shorebird Media.

Cover photos: © Jerry Horn | Bigstockphoto.com
                © Kris Vandereycken | BigStockPhotos

ISBN: 978-0-9798856-4-8

PRINTED IN THE UNITED STATES OF AMERICA.

10 9 8 7 6 5 4 3 2 1

Dear Readers,

Born and raised in the city, I dreamed of a place where blue skies were endless and horses ran free. I found that home in Nevada, and so does Kasey Wildmoon, the heroine of *Blue Rain*.

Kasey Wildmoon is an investigative reporter set on finding the killer of the West's wild horses. During her search, she discovers magic in the antique necklace inherited from her Native American birth mother and love with the stubborn cowboy standing in her way.

Cowboy Bronc McDermitt saved Kasey's life when they were teenagers. Her girlhood crush hasn't gone away. Around Bronc, behaving like a cold, logical reporter is quite a chore.

The idea for *Blue Rain* came to me while I was riding in the Black Rock Desert. My horse shied at something hidden in sagebrush. It turned out to be a sun-bleached horse skull pierced by a bullet hole. It was a chilling discovery.

Blue Rain features a touch of magic and that's what I wish for all of you.

Here's to embracing everyday magic and dreaming dreams to help us celebrate tomorrow,

— *TESS FARRADAY*

PROLOGUE

SCOLDING ROCK RESERVATION
BLEEK COUNTY, NEVADA

HER INDEX FINGER JABBED one station button, then another. Kasey trusted the radio to keep her awake. She'd waited sixteen years for her driver's license and this day.

At six-thirty A.M., minutes after her parents left for work, she'd backed down the driveway and pulled away from home. Since then, she'd chalked up seven hundred miles on the old Toyota. Now, she could see nothing except desert night and the patch of dirt road illuminated by her headlights.

She felt slightly sick, a little drowsy, a lot cranky and she had no idea where that last turn had taken her. Adventure wasn't all it was cracked up to be.

An indistinct voice quaked beneath the radio static. All right. Kasey looked down to adjust a knob. She had no worries over taking her eyes off the road. Since the last gas station, she'd seen one red-and-white cow, two jackrabbits, and a deceased snake. Since sundown, nothing.

When she looked up, silver lightning glinted in the sky far to her right. Cool. The skies over Los Angeles were never dark enough to show summer lightning.

The Toyota shuddered at the boom of thunder. Lightning flashed once, then three times in a row as if a gigantic hand shook a silver spear close, closer, then dead ahead. At the lightning's last flare, the sky swirled indigo.

Kasey swallowed hard, gave up on the radio, and searched for the windshield wiper knob. If it started raining, she'd be ready.

A low rumble made her glance up. The car shook. The road wavered like melting wax and fissures hunted across its bone-white surface. Light seeped through one widening crack as Kasey pressed the brake. Nothing happened. Except that the radio went dead. The car kept rolling.

She took a deep breath and tried to think, but the air she sucked into her lungs felt hot and oxygen-free.

The brightness from the crack whirled into a cone, spinning just yards from the Toyota's bumper. In its heart, Kasey made out a horse, then a human form.

No way. It had to be cactus or maybe a mirage.

Kasey pumped the brakes with sensible slowness, though her hands trembled on the steering wheel.

She shaded her eyes against the glare on her windshield. She should have slept in Reno. Now she blinked, forcing the apparition to vanish. It didn't.

Instead, a silver and blue stallion reared up amid a corona of heat snakes. His front hooves reached for the vast Nevada sky.

"There's nothing there," she insisted, but her voice shivered and a rider took shape.

An Indian maiden wearing shell-studded deerskin sat astride the stallion. She beckoned, though Kasey saw right through her.

"Because she's imaginary," Kasey said, then clamped her lips together. She refused to talk to a hallucination.

Her mother might know what to make of this. Not her real mother, although Det. Maggie Harrigan would book this specter for disturbing the peace and question her own sanity later.

But Kasey's biological mother, the Paiute mother who'd abandoned her, *she* might understand.

Wouldn't that make a fairy-tale ending to her search? Except for one thing. Kasey was alone in the middle of the desert with no one—biologically related or otherwise to help her.

She swallowed and refused to panic. Her best option was the one she used on roller coasters: just hang on and wait for the madness to stop. The car crept forward, crunching rocks to gravel, gravel to dust.

Damn it, she would not cry and she was not nuts.

Kasey yanked on the emergency brake. The car stopped.

She closed her eyes and sighed. The lightning stopped and the thunder moved away. Blood vibrated through her veins. Spots swam behind her eyelids, but she managed to dominate her fear until a weird heat pulsed through her necklace.

What—? Kasey shifted the necklace off her nape, draping it over the shoulders of her tee shirt, and lectured herself. This Native American light show had materialized because she was seeking her birth mother. Or because it really was a mirage.

Slowly, she opened her eyes. Wind gusted and in her headlights she saw tumbleweed bounding through the stallion's hind legs.

So, it was a mirage. Her fluttering pulse slowed. In Earth Science class at Martin Luther King High School, she'd learned mirages appeared as light passed through substances of differing densities. That explained the Appaloosa with night showing through his ribs, except for one thing. The only light shone from faraway stars.

Kasey was too smart to believe in magic and she had no time to waste on delusions. She wet her lips and put the car in gear.

Mom and Dad believed she'd slept over at Cookie's house. Only Cookie knew Kasey had driven all night toward the Scolding Rock Reservation.

More afraid of chickening out than a collision, Kasey stomped on the accelerator.

One second before she hit the shimmering stallion, heat from the necklace seared her breastbone. The shrilling of a flute pierced her eardrums and she wrenched the steering wheel hard right.

Her Toyota spun three times, like a dog chasing its tail, before a black volcanic rock with a glassy point stopped it dead.

⚡ ⚡

BRONC DIDN'T LIKE THE WAY things had shaped up. He glanced across the truck cab, past his buddy Cal, and watched the new kid. The guy's eyes narrowed as he aimed the truck toward the stranded driver. He cruised slow, like a vulture circling dinner.

All morning, the new kid—who claimed he went by Fox at his old school—had promised them some fun. Spotting the girl, he figured he'd found it.

As the truck eased closer to the lopsided yellow Toyota, Bronc made out a license plate frame stamped with the name of a California car dealer. Then a leggy girl came around the front bumper and Bronc didn't have the urge to look at much of anything else.

Sun glinted off dark glasses and a glossy bottom lip as she smiled. Trust a city girl to blow out a tire twenty miles from the nearest ranch, then face three hard cases like them and not have brains enough to worry.

Their truck slued sideways, blanketing her with dust, but she didn't flinch. Fox killed the engine and climbed out. He cast a quick glance over the desert, then turned back to give Cal and Bronc a quick thumbs-up.

Bronc felt himself getting riled. He'd only asked for two things out of high school graduation: a new Stetson and a day without cows. He'd planned to spend today lying in the shade, chugging a beer while he watched the sky turn from blueberries and cream to purple, then black. But he'd been outvoted.

"Hey, sugar." As the new kid moved toward her, the girl squared her shoulders. She looked ready to run. "How d'ya come to break down way out here?" He feinted a boot toe at her license plate and grinned as if being from L.A. made her fair game. "Lost Springs is a mighty long way from home."

Bronc climbed out of the truck, figuring he'd stand close enough to rein in Fox in case he turned loco. Bronc supposed the kid's nickname shouldn't gall him. Folks had started joking, calling *him* "Bronc" McDermitt after two winning seasons riding rough stock. They called his partner Buck because it was his last name: Cal Buck. But "Fox" seemed kind of forced, if you asked him. Which the kid hadn't.

The girl tugged the bill of the blue L.A. Dodgers baseball cap she wore with her ponytail poked through the back. Her hand shook a little.

"I'm not broken down, but thanks for stopping. I blew a tire last night and decided to wait until daylight to hike out. I guess I overslept." She squinted at the sun, then tossed her sassy ponytail and gestured toward the deflated tire. "I'd fix it myself, but I'm missing a jack handle."

He and Buck kinda laughed. Fox didn't.

"What brings you out this way? I know I'd remember seein' you in town." Fox shot an elbow toward Bronc's ribs, then advanced on the girl as she pushed her sunglasses up her nose with one finger.

Bronc slumped back against the truck and crossed his arms over his belt buckle. The truck's fender was hot from the noon-day sun. Stetson shading his eyes, Bronc watched Fox's lizard-skin boots spread wide, bracketing the girl's fussy white sandals. Somehow, the move just seemed dirty. On the other side of the truck, Cal shifted. He didn't like this, either. Why did they let Fox have his way? The kid's power was hard to pin down as smoke in a bottle. Three tough cowboys shouldn't ambush a city girl. It wasn't fun and it wasn't right. Bronc stared at the desert floor, half ashamed.

"I'm Kasey Harrigan." Her smooth voice gave a good imitation of being unruffled, but when Fox didn't return her introduction, she faltered. "I'm, um, driving to my mother's."

Don't show it, honey. Bronc felt the hot fender burn through his shirt. *Don't let him see you're afraid.* Bronc's fist clenched tight when her hesitance lured Fox closer.

"Why, sugar, we'll take you to your mama! We know every living soul around here, don't we, boys?"

Bronc flattened his hand against sheet metal hot enough to raise a blister. He refused to be part of this.

When the girl removed her sunglasses and tucked them into her back pocket, the cutoff jeans banding the top of her brown, athletic legs shifted, showing a thin strip of lighter skin.

If she ran, Fox would jump her. Bronc took a personal inventory. Was he too drunk to bulldog Fox if he tried?

Then, Fox's boots scuffled. The girl gasped and her alarm jolted down Bronc's spine.

"Give me my hat!" she snapped.

"How 'bout you come and get it?" Fox waved the cap out of reach, baiting her. "We got a truck fulla good times. Just share a couple brews with us, sugar, and soon's the sun goes down—"

Well, *hell.* Bronc slammed his fist against the side of the truck hard enough to make Fox look. This had gone far enough. "Easy," Cal warned.

Bronc bumped up his hat brim, squinted at the bleached disk of sun, and breathed deep. No good. He straightened his legs and lurched, sudden as the dead reborn, right toward them.

"Shep Fontana, ma'am, from Greasy Spur, Idaho." Bronc had

long believed he could only lie with a drawl. "At your service."

He doffed his Stetson in a downright courtly flourish.

The girl looked damn cute and scared spitless. One beer ago, he might have studied the weird necklace she wore, or puzzled out the print on her reddish tee shirt, there where it disappeared into the waistband of her shorts. Her black hair shone almost silver. As she continued speaking, one hand shaded her eyes. That hand trembled, but her voice didn't.

"We've been … separated for a while, me and my mom." She talked too fast, too high-pitched. Fox snorted like he'd scented blood. She added, "Her name's Leticia Wildmoon."

Cal sucked in a breath and the girl's eyes swung away from Fox. "You know her?"

Cal shook his head, leaving a silence brittle as glass.

The hell you don't. Bronc frowned at his buddy. Letty Wildmoon was Cal's renegade sister. Letty had been gossip fodder and had two fatherless kids before Cal had been born, an embarrassment to his mom's middle-age. Believing crazy Letty could be mom to a beauty like this was tough to swallow.

The girl tightened her ponytail and gritted her teeth. As she sidled away from Fox, Bronc noticed she stood basketball tall, up to his chin.

"Shep?" She repeated the name dubiously.

"Aw, now you went and remembered!" Bronc hoped she'd keep quiet long enough for him to help. "Lady'll be wanting her hat back." He snatched it from Fox.

"Shep's not your name," Fox snarled.

"Shh." His loud shush made Fox grimace and Bronc saw his reflection shiver in the kid's clear gray eyes. "Shoot, yeah. Me 'n' Kasey, here, why, our uncles are half-cousins." Bronc winked, as if they'd both pulled something over on the city girl. Fox looked ticked off and confused as Bronc turned away to watch the girl's mind work.

Her fingers wandered over her necklace as she wondered if she should play along, wondered if he was a savior or she was a sucker. Up close, the necklace looked like pink shells and blue-gray beads threaded on latigo. It hung loose around her neck, swaying back and forth across her breasts.

Well, now. That kinda thinkin' just wouldn't do.

"We, uh," Bronc steadied his nerves by shoving his Stetson back on. With Fox primed to fight, Bronc needed to watch his own back. He couldn't do that while he watched her front. "We just ain't seen each other since the family reunion in Boise. Ain't that a fact, Kasey?"

Bronc glanced into her lopsided Toyota. His feeble optimism died when he saw a litter of green glass Coke bottles, an unfurled sleeping bag, and nothing more. No guard dogs, no hulking brothers, no assist for designated hero Bronc McDermitt, who was just sober enough to stand.

He slung an arm over her shoulder. She stiffened as he aimed her toward Fox's truck.

"Gents." Bronc faked a misstep and jerked his thumb toward the lamed Toyota. "Me 'n' Cousin Kasey are gonna get reacquainted. Just tend to her tire, hear?"

"Listen, Bronc—" Fox said.

"Yeah?"

"Nothin'." Fox spat and took up his own tire iron.

Bronc kept the girl tight under his arm as he wheeled. He set his jaw hard as Clint Eastwood's. Then, he scowled and walked past Fox, headed for the kid's new graduation truck as if he owned it. Prickles like centipedes' feet went ticking down his neck.

This time, he'd out-toughed Fox. As long as the kid stayed scrawny as a stick of beef jerky, Bronc would have the upper hand. But he didn't like wondering what would happen if Fox ever developed the muscle to back up his rank attitude.

⚭ ⚮

THE TRUCK REEKED OF BEER.

"Now, what?" she demanded, though her hands shook. *"What?"*

"It's okay." He soothed her like he would a spooked colt. "He's mainly harmless and I can handle him. It's just, he's a godawful mean drunk." Bronc gave her a peek at the healing rip on his temple. "That's from the last time."

She didn't look too distressed over his misfortune.

"But he gives me no sass where women are concerned." Bronc left off studying the scenery and glanced to see if she was buying it. "If he comes back—" By God, she was. She'd given the faintest nod. Though he hadn't stuttered since second grade, Bronc stuttered now. "—j-just, go for broke."

"What do you mean?" She pronounced each of the four words and lifted her chin.

"Pretend you know me, r-real well." Bronc leaned back against the driver's side door and watched her. She stared right back and he couldn't manage another word. A vibration like bacon in a skillet sizzled between his eyebrows.

He didn't suffer long. As the door gave way behind him, jerked open by Fox, Bronc pitched backward. He would've fractured his skull, if her hand hadn't clamped on his wrist. She must play ball. "Hey! Is she really your cousin?" Fox accused.

Whether surprise or Fox's menace decided her, Bronc saw it happen.

"Kissin' cousins," she said, then licked her bottom lip, waiting for nerve to kick in. When it did, she butted her lips against Bronc's and added, "We're a real close family."

With that, her mouth hit Bronc's again and her shaky hands skittered up and down his back like little white mice. He should've laughed. As passion went, her act was pitiful. Truth was, though, her sweet Coke kisses turned Bronc McDermitt inside out.

Later, he kicked the patched tire and double-tightened the nuts on the wheel. As she squatted beside him, he whispered directions to Hannah's Hen House café. As she drove off, the wind snatched her ponytail out the window. He hollered, "See ya later, cuz!" and hoped she'd believed his promise to tell her the truth about Letty Wildmoon.

Later still, when Dad smelled beer on his breath and pocketed the car keys, Bronc telephoned Hannah's. He held the black receiver so hard, his fingers leaked sweat.

"She just took off, Bronc, honey," Hannah mumbled past her trademark Camel cigarette. "Left her hat, too. Let's see if I can catch her!"

But when the phone clattered on the counter, when the screen door slammed and the rasp of tires skittered down miles of phone line, he knew he'd called too late.

She'd gone, leaving Bronc with the last two things he'd got for graduation. He got grounded for stealing Dad's Ford to chase after her, while the old man stood yelling at him from the gate, and he got Kasey Harrigan's blue baseball cap.

He kept that cap under his pillow until summer's end. Then it spent time in suitcases, in dresser drawers and backseats. Finally, when things went bad, Bronc nailed it over the barn door like a horseshoe. There it served as a reminder that once, when he was young, good things had come out of nowhere.

ONE

TEN YEARS LATER...

LUSH FERNS, STAINED GLASS, a gold-maned harpist, and watery green light made Kasey feel she'd entered a Victorian rain forest. This restaurant, Magnifique, oozed ambiance.

"Ms. Wildmoon? Ms. Hodges has reserved a table in *le petit salon.*" The maitre d' gulped the French phrase like a goldfish. "However, she awaits you, below." He gestured toward the lounge sunk an entire floor beneath the foyer.

"Kasey!" Cookie hailed her from a stool at the hammered copper bar.

"Thank you. I see my friend." She should have tipped him, Kasey thought, girding herself to descend. A shaft of amber light played on the spiral staircase. New Brighton might be thir-ty freeway minutes outside Hollywood, but lunch remained a game of see and be seen.

Dressed in taupe suede, with ropes of turquoise jewelry and a single strand of shells, Kasey felt the stares of recognition. Billboards heralding her transformation from *Sun-Times* reporter to *Dare* magazine star had guaranteed her celebrity. *Celebrity instead of credibility.* At least Mark had left her that.

Eyes fixed on her roommate, Kasey passed the whispers and rustling. "Creep." She hugged Cookie's bony shoulders and Kasey breathed in shampoo and tequila. "You know I hate these places," she muttered into Cookie's mass of Orphan Annie curls. Kasey took a seat two down from Cookie. The stool between them held a fortune in Nikons.

"Welcome home. I missed you, too." Cookie repositioned her round-lensed glasses. "I saw your stuff on the computer desk and your backpack in the corner, when I got in this—" Cookie broke off as the bartender at her elbow loomed closer, grinning.

"Miss Wildmoon? I wake up to your face every morning." He delivered Kasey a mineral water and lime, then explained. "My apartment's on Wilshire Boulevard."

"Thanks." Kasey sipped the drink and swallowed. Along the bar, patrons jockeyed forward and back to stare.

Kasey avoided looking at them. *And* the new billboards, whose red letters proclaimed "Wildmoon Rising" above a color photograph big as two boxcars. Capitalizing on her heritage and equestrian skills, it showed Kasey, hair streaming behind, astride a racing Appaloosa.

The irony should have made her smile. After years of denying her desert hallucination, after a hundred nights filled with dreams of a Paiute princess who never lived, bad luck positioned reminders of her secret at freeway interchanges all over town.

Although she considered herself a writer, not a star, *Dare* was a watchdog magazine that covered personalities and politics, and believed K. D. Wildmoon's celebrity had catapulted them into the big time.

"Isn't this place precious?" Cookie asked.

"Precious—" Kasey broke off as a Viking-tall executive crossed the dimness. "Is that Mark?"

Cookie turned and they watched him duck to enter a fern-draped doorway. "Alone? Get serious."

Cookie was right. For Mark Savage, lunch meant corporate conversation and eye contact with important advertisers who financed Southern California's richest daily newspaper. Relaxation, escape, and food occurred later, in the silence of his glass and chrome penthouse. Still, the man's blond assurance, and her jittery response, reminded her of Mark.

"No, just another Ken doll in pinstripes." Cookie downed the rest of her margarita and licked salt from her lips. "Hey, have you checked in with your folks? Your dad called twice. 'Expected word from her by now,'" Cookie mimicked the grim tone of Lt. Mike Harrigan.

"Police work makes you paranoid." Kasey shrugged. Of course she'd checked in. At twenty-six, she maintained a rare closeness with her parents and Cookie fielded calls when their schedules caused spates of phone tag.

"Let's go." Cookie nudged Kasey to stand, navigated the path to their table, and settled down to study the gold-tasseled menu. "Help me eat something sinful."

"I shouldn't eat at all." Kasey pushed the menu away.

In-depth personality profiles meant eating what her subjects ate. In the Yukon, that meant stream-fresh trout. In Tijuana, she'd subsisted on a day's handful of rice and a *frijole*-smeared tortilla. This time, as the guest of a barrio gang, she'd feasted on three days of food-stamp bounty, followed by shoplifted candy bars and street-corner burritos.

Kasey scratched a bug bite on her forearm. Her work also meant sleeping where her people slept. That was how her stories developed texture and won awards.

Her success had nothing to do with her good luck charm.

Kasey closed her fingers before they could rise to touch her age-patinated shell necklace. As a teenager, she'd considered the bauble too "ethnic" for words.

She'd only worn it into the Scolding Rock desert so Leticia Wildmoon would recognize her.

Under no circumstances could the necklace have influenced the appearance of that desert mirage. Mere chance accounted for the necklace hanging around her neck during the ten minutes she'd shared a stalled elevator with Harrison Ford. And it was nothing but coincidence that the resulting interview had earned her a Daybook Award and a desk in the *Sun-Times* newsroom. After that, silly superstition made her conceal the necklace under her suit and silk blouse for her next big story. And the next.

As good-luck charms went, it wasn't smelly like lucky socks nor macabre like a severed rabbit's foot. But she owed her success to research and good writing, not magic.

"What about Chicken Wellington?"

Kasey shook her head. "I need to talk with you." She patted her battered briefcase meaningfully. "Needed to before this, but I called the paper when I got home and they said you'd left for the day." Kasey lowered her voice. "That was two nights ago."

"Lighten up, Kasey, I was freelancing."

"Right. I hope your guardian angel has more patience than I do!"

"I shot some stuff for *Soldier of Fortune,* the mercenary magazine." Cookie slammed her menu and regarded Kasey closely. "After two weeks in the barrio, you can't be eager to get lost again. You only fret over my love life when you're buggy to get back in the field."

Cookie had her pegged, but this time Kasey wasn't eager. Her next assignment made her edgy.

"Where are they sending you? To a rival gang?" Cookie brightened. "Hey! Did you let them give you that initiation tattoo?"

Kasey narrowed her eyes, declaring the topic closed. She extracted a folder from her briefcase, just as the waitress, wearing show girl makeup and a sarong, arrived.

"Two bleu-cheese burgers with bacon, and home fries," Cookie ordered. "With a side of sour cream."

"Don't expect me to—" Kasey laughed.

"And two real Cokes, no ice."

The waitress turned to Kasey.

"What she said," Kasey surrendered, but she only waited for the waitress to retreat two steps before opening a folder amid Cookie's silverware. "Now, not another word 'til you look at this." Kasey arranged a sheaf of newspaper clippings so that one—headlined "Federal Mustanger Pleads Not Guilty in Horse Deaths"—lay on top.

The article had been snipped from the *Los Angeles Sun-Times* and showcased a thee-column photograph credited to Cookie.

"A little grainy." Cookie examined the shot as Kasey's nails clicked on the tabletop. "So?"

"It's him." Kasey waited.

" 'Him' who?"

"That cowboy you photographed last week—"

"Last *month,* you mean. Yeah, I recognize my own name. Did you interview him or something?"

"Lord, Cookie." Kasey closed the folder and leaned back in

the booth. "You know I don't do cowboys."

"Ohhh." Cookie opened the folder again. "So you think it's ol' Mick Montana?"

"Shep Fontana."

"It's been a long time since you saw him." Cookie studied the photo. "And the court record said 'Gabriel McDermitt.'" Cookie pulled out a second clipping. "Gabriel 'Bronc' McDermitt."

"So he lied about that, too."

Cookie tapped the photograph. "I remember him now. He had these blue eyes. And black hair. High coloring in his cheeks, that kind of Black Irish look, and"—Cookie rubbed the curve of her jaw—"beard shadow.

"He was nerved up, like he didn't belong indoors. I got the feeling he'd plead guilty to anything, if they'd just throw open the doors and set him free. In fact, I told him he should talk to you."

"Why would you do that?"

"Instinct." Cookie winked and lunch arrived.

Sighing with exasperation, Kasey piled her other folders atop the one holding his picture. She matched Cookie bite for bite, trying to quiet the tension grating on her nerve endings.

It didn't help. Kasey's fingers had worried the edge of the folder ragged by the time Cookie brought the conversation back to the cowboy.

"And *Dare* wants you to do—what? An underdog feature?"

"My trademark stuff: coax the wild man to spill his guts." She shook her head. "Only I'm not so sure he fits the profile."

"If I remember right, his attorney hinted it wasn't him, but the Indians, who'd mowed down horses with an Uzi." Cookie removed her glasses. "Can you handle that?"

Kasey's heritage was public record, but she counted her copper skin as a cosmetic, just part of her professional persona. Like her jewelry.

"Of course I can handle it, but that's not the story. I'm supposed to go for a political edge. Profile him and do some digging on the entire Bureau of Wildlife system."

Cookie didn't look up from polishing her glasses with a linen napkin. "An exposé?"

They both knew how important Kasey's first investigative assignment since the *Sun-Times* fiasco could be.

"I'll start at the jail, tomorrow." Kasey turned a turquoise and silver ring on her finger. Anything to keep her hands off her necklace. "The *Sun* didn't follow up on this, right?"

"A hundred slaughtered wild horses, and cattlemen, hunters, and Paiutes versus the federal government?" Cookie blinked owlishly. "Gee, Kasey, we've worked the handsome cowboy angle. That aspect was the most *meaningful* to our readers."

"*Dare* would hire you tomorrow."

"We aren't having this conversation again." Cookie replaced her glasses. "I'd make half the money and work twice the hours. I sell my 'art' for money, honey." Cookie's voice softened. "And because I haven't slept with my publisher, he hasn't thrown me to the wolves. Yet."

Kasey slid the folders back into her briefcase and tried to laugh off her short engagement to Mark. "Undoubtedly the stupidest move of my life."

"A flaw to keep you human." Cookie patted her friend's hand. "And, about this Bronc guy? Unless you've been keeping secrets all these years, all he did—if it *is* him—was help a teenage girl fend off some drunks. Right?"

"You're right." Kasey scanned the restaurant, suddenly uneasy. She folded her napkin and glanced toward the staircase. Forty-eight caffeine-charged hours at the computer had left her high-strung and full of girlish memories. So what if the best kiss of her life had occurred when she was sixteen? It was a shame, but not a tragedy. She'd grown up and left romantic fantasies behind. Adults knew heroes were sadly temporary.

The remembered scent of Mark's aftershave warned her an instant too late for escape.

"*Dare* will get more than it deserves." Mark Savage's cool chuckle matched the ease with which he sauntered up. "Kasey will show her readers a straight-shooter and McDermitt will come out sounding like a good man, falsely accused." Arms crossed, head cocked to one side, he asked, "May I?"

It wasn't really a question.

Mark slipped into the booth beside her and Kasey's skin tightened. As always, Mark had planned well. Suave and perfect, he looked as if his valet had groomed him at the restaurant door, for this, their first encounter since he'd humiliated her on national television.

"My work is *my* business, Mark. I don't appreciate eavesdroppers. If you'll excuse me?" Kasey reached for her briefcase, but the confining booth forced the intimacy of his thigh against hers and she stopped.

Looking at his cool profile, she couldn't believe she'd agreed to marry him.

Why hadn't she seen the end coming before it became a professional disaster? At their champagne and crystal engagement party, for instance, when Mark bragged Kasey was only the third person of color allowed past Glenside Country Club's wrought-iron gates. He credited his mother, Beatrice, with that coup, and chuckled at Kasey's ire when they'd overheard Beatrice's jibe to a sapphire-laden dowager.

"A striking Native American woman, *striking*. We think so highly of Kasey," Beatrice had confided, behind a potted palm.

"What a pity the years will make her thicken, like those people always do."

Mark wasn't laughing now. He turned toward her. Manners dictated Kasey must return his look. As she examined Mark's styled hair and baby-smooth skin, her tension uncoiled. She felt no tug of interest, no threat, nothing but a shiver of victory.

"I want to talk journalism," Mark's voice rumbled with practiced sincerity.

"How refreshing."

"Kasey, I want you to come back and work for the *Sun-Times*. Just hear me out." Mark held up his palm, as if she'd bawled a protest. "I think there's something to this Bronc McDermitt story."

"Wow. There's no pulling the wool over your eyes. All it takes is the barest hint of scandal: a hundred-odd skeletons, felony charges and"—Kasey snapped her fingers—"'Scoop Savage' is on the trail."

Cookie covered her snort of laughter with a cough.

"It's always sarcasm, isn't it, princess? It keeps a lid on that hot reservoir of feelings, I suppose." His voice thickened and his buffed nails glinted as he reached for her.

Mixed metaphors, she wanted to tell him. Instead, Kasey folded her hands beyond his reach.

Mark loosened his tie.

"You take the dullest story and make it sparkle, like spinning straw into gold." He circled his index finger over the rim of her empty glass. "Passion makes your work unique. Everyone knew you were nipping at the heels of a Pulitzer . . ."

. . . before he told CNN that "Ninja's Boy" was fiction. Before he declared K. D. Wildmoon's heart was in the right place, but she hadn't done her homework, didn't have her ducks in a row. . . .

"That sounds nice, Mark, and it worked. Once." Kasey

heard her own bitterness as she remembered just how well. The first night he'd used that "straw into gold" line to a packed Press Club Awards audience, she'd gone home with him. "But you're wrong.

"In this case, for instance, I'll have to go into the desert on horseback and ask questions no one wants to answer. Someone's killing the West's wild mustangs, and I'll find out who. But it won't take magic." Thank God she'd never told him about the necklace. Kasey lifted her chin and met Mark's eyes. "It will take research and sweat."

"You can't do it," he said, gently. "Although you'll look good trying. Those *Dare* billboards were a stroke of marketing genius, by the way." Mark winked, then resumed his sober smile. "What I *do* think, is you'll write one hell of a Sunday story about this cowboy."

Mark cussed as if he'd memorized the words. The cadence didn't fit. Once, she'd thought the habit endearing. Now she knew Mark never reached the level of frustration required for truly eloquent profanity. Money kept him so well insulated.

"Would you like to wager something on that?" Kasey rested her crossed arms on the table.

"On—?" A tiny frown of confusion creased Mark's brow.

"Kasey finding the horse killer," Cookie interrupted.

As Mark rubbed his hands together and laughed aloud, Kasey felt a twist of misgiving. She quelled it; she could do this. "My stakes would be high," Mark warned, smiling.

"So would mine."

"If you don't nail who did it, to my satisfaction—"

"To the satisfaction of the law," Kasey amended.

"Even better. If you *don't*, you come back to work for me, at your old salary."

On your knees, he might have added.

Since no grandfather clock presided over the elegant salon, Kasey decided the sound ticking in her ears must be an emotional time bomb.

"Done." This time, when she reached for her briefcase and her hip bumped Mark's, she didn't recoil. She waited. Finally, he slid from the booth.

"And if you should win?" Standing, Mark repositioned the knot in his tie.

"Your mother sponsors a fun day at Glenside—you know, swimming, tennis, and games—for kids from my favorite charity."

"Simple enough." Mark shrugged. "What's the catch?"

"No catch." Kasey's eyes followed Mark's as he watched her hands smooth her suede skirt, then trailed them up as her fingers forked through her heavy hair, which had fallen forward at her temples. Only when she stepped past him, making for the spotlighted staircase, did Mark frown.

"Which charity?" he asked.

Kasey basked in the gold illumination as if it were sunlight, then she faced Mark and smiled.

"Las Gatas, Mark. Tell Beatrice they're the toughest girl gang in Los Angeles County."

֍ ֎

SOME NEIGHBORHOODS NEVER CHANGED. Kasey drove directly from Magnifique to Del Rio and parked. Del Rio had always been a slum. It sat on the verge of a concrete channel encasing the muddy trickle that had been the Los Angeles River. Shacks crowded between factories too odious for "industrial parks." Buried alive like the river, Del Rio was ruled by repo men and handguns. There was no pizza delivery, no twenty-four-hour convenience stores, no cops willing to patrol alone.

And it was here, one night last year, that she'd gone searching for a certain vendor who'd run afoul of the health department so often, he only came out after dark. Hungry and foolhardy, she'd cruised the street looking for the man who wore a platter of homemade tamales like an accordion. That's what she would have told anyone she met. In fact, she was restless for a good story.

She found it, one block south of Heron Metallurgical. Under a malfunctioning streetlight, strobe flashes revealed a dead dog and the adolescent boy mourning him.

"Is he—?" Kasey had been out of the car and talking before she caught the scent of decomposition and chemicals.

Her stomach still gripped at the thought of how easily she'd been duped. Maybe the smells hadn't really been there. Maybe her brain had painted the memory with information that came later.

"Ninja," moaned the boy. "Oh, Ninja."

Homeless, parents dead, one sibling in a foster home, the mourning kid told her he'd lost his best friend to convulsions after the dog had scrabbled down the concrete side to lap at the river.

At first, Kasey blocked out the sobbing boy. Ghetto cats and dogs often died of garbage intoxication and she tried to believe that of Ninja. But it didn't take a biochemist to see industrial vapor condensing over the river.

The boy refused to give his name. Afraid Social Services would return him to the abusive foster home he'd fled, he'd begun edging away when she asked him to help her load the dog in the backseat.

"You can't do nothin'." His face had contorted in horror.

"You're right, but I can find out what killed him, so this doesn't happen again."

In spite of her motives and the offer of all he could eat a

McDonald's, the kid vanished. When a vet's autopsy verified the dog had died from ingesting benzine, she wrote a hard-hitting news feature on the plight of street children and the role industrial pollution played in destroying lives and neighborhoods.

"Ninja's Boy" had been a risky story, but the editorial board had backed her. Even when Heron Metallurgical filed suit, an instant nomination for Kasey's second Daybook Award kept Mark in her corner. Publicly.

Privately, he'd told her to watch her step. Heron Metallurgical was one small tentacle of Kaiser Industries, famous for "dairy fresh" HomePride buttermilk products from bread and puddings to soups and salad dressings. They were less famous for ChemStar Detergents and the million dollars they spent annually, advertising in Mark's paper.

And then, Kasey found out the little sociopath had lied. The kid wasn't homeless, but a runaway from parents who imposed middle-class ethics and curfew on their fifteen-year-old's freewheeling, drug-dealing life. Though he'd never been in a foster home, he had spent time in juvenile facilities for purse-snatching.

Kasey wrote a follow-up story. Mark refused to run it. Kasey asked Mark to notify Daybook that the story had been inaccurate and should be withdrawn from competition. When Mark declined, saying he didn't want the notoriety of such a move, Kasey did it herself and wrote a retraction, which he refused to run.

When it became clear that the *Sun-Times* would receive public attention for the story a second time, Mark chose advertising revenue over affection.

Although Mark did his best to avoid it, they'd created a scene in the newsroom. Mark had suggested, then insisted he, Kasey, and the managing editor conduct the "last straw" discussion in his cherrywood-paneled office suite three floors above the newsroom, but the argument had escalated before they reached the elevator.

"Try to get a grip by the time I return," Mark had said, ducking into the men's room.

Instead, she'd followed. Two male reporters and a pressman spattered with ink and stripped to the waist had spilled out of the restroom as Mark strode back out with Kasey on his Gucci heels. By the time he wheeled and told her, through tight lips, that freedom of the press belonged to the man who owned the press, Kasey had tucked her four-carat engagement ring into his pinstriped vest pocket and flipped his diamond "slave bracelet" at him like a Frisbee.

Things went downhill from there. Mark called a regional press conference. With somber regret, he declared K. D. Wildmoon a promising reporter who'd made the mistake of writing with her heart, not her head. He fired her in time for the evening news.

Kasey's notoriety had only made her more attractive to *Dare*. They admired her combination of logic and instinct and turned her loose on any story—political, environmental, or social—that included strong personalities and controversy.

Kasey shook off memory's trance when she felt a surge of uneasiness. She scanned the street. Though no one stood watching, though nothing but a crumpled newspaper scuttled down the cracked asphalt, she returned to her car.

Staring blindly through the windshield, she tried to believe this new assignment was just one more story. But it wasn't.

Amid the interviews and facts and research, there'd be resentment toward Mark Savage and the cowboy named McDermitt. Spite wasn't a very lofty emotion, but both had broken faith.

Kasey sat up straighter, turned the key in the ignition, and slammed the car into gear.

Now it was payback time.

§§ §§

HE WATCHED HER DRIVE AWAY before dropping coins into the pay telephone. Modern inventions proved handy when dealing with mortals.

In ancient times, women carried their tribes' power and bested him until failure gnawed his entrails. Always he craved revenge. The last shaman should not be so shamed.

Then one woman, Blue Rain, staked all on the love of a man. He, the last shaman, had assumed that man's shape and betrayed the woman most grievously. Thus weakened, she battled him and lost. The tale traveled around cooking fires, counsel fires.

Across two states, the telephone rang.

Since then, he'd vanquished a dozen descendants of Blue Rain. This one was "modern." She'd lost the People's beliefs. Though she possessed a necklace of magical power, she didn't trust it. She thought logic made her strong.

He smiled. Fox, his spirit guide, gave him the talent to humiliate enemies by turning their "strengths" against them.

Each time Kasey Wildmoon trusted logic over instinct, she'd step closer to disaster. What sport for the last shaman.

"Yeah?"

"Make sure you've covered your tracks," the shaman said. "A journalist has decided there's more to McDermitt's story. She believes he's the guilty one."

"Give me a break. The feds can't find enough to hold him."

"Nonetheless, I want her arrival met with enough violence to send her home." Across the miles, he heard a screen door blown by summer wind. *"You know who to ask."*

"Shit. The kid's had enough trouble."

"He's the perfect choice. I'll send details of her itinerary. You

understand what's at risk."

He let silence do the persuading. Once he pushed her past mortal selfishness, threats would be enough. Forcing her to use the boy would require magic.

"I know what's at risk. If the stakes were any lower, I'd say no."

He chuckled and replaced the telephone receiver. By the time his cohort did the same, she'd forget his call had ever come.

TWO

FORTY-EIGHT HOURS after she'd faced him down, Kasey decided Mark might win. Not because she lacked the journalistic skills to beat him, but because she'd be forever lost in Nevada's Scolding Rock desert.

Kasey lifted her Coke from the rental car's cup-holder and steered with one hand. How could she tell if she'd headed in the right direction when the desert stretched away from her, cracked and white as an old flour tortilla?

A shiver of memory chilled her, or maybe it was the car's overtaxed air-conditioning. Déjà vu was nothing more than a mirage in the brain. Today, she was no sunstruck, lonely kid. Even if a hallucination horse came up and nibbled her earlobe, she wouldn't believe in him.

Kasey sipped her Coke and tried to accept the desert as her homeland. For centuries, these sands had mixed with the bones of her Paiute ancestors. How comforting.

She replaced her drink can, fingered her sun-warmed necklace—and heard a piercing trill. Haunting and urgent, it warned her an instant before the glimmering stallion materialized.

"Oh, no." Kasey clenched the steering wheel. "This time you're Alpo, buddy." She didn't veer from the center of the road. The car shuddered as it passed through heat waves stirred by the horse's thrashing forelegs.

It had to be environmental, some combination of heat waves, reflection, and imagination. Before Kasey could look back at the apparition, two raps, like hard-thrown rocks, cracked the glass behind her. A fist-sized boom buffeted her ears. A hole opened in the front windshield.

Kasey stared up into her rearview mirror. A colt, real, substantial, and terrified, ran with outflung legs and scarlet nostrils. It careened by her rear bumper and onto the open white plateau.

Kasey braked to a stop. She lowered the rental car's window and switched off the air-conditioning. The colt's hoofbeats clattered as he launched his rough-coated body over a clump of sagebrush. He had the scrappy conformation of a Nevada mustang. *That,* unlike her recurring fantasy, was a fact.

She'd found half of what she'd come for. With luck, the colt was being pursued by the menace that had killed a hundred of his brothers, and Kasey Wildmoon was here to ensnare that killer.

But the colt hadn't caused that other sound. Kasey studied her cratered windshield. The glass hadn't been cut by a hoof-tossed rock. Any cop's daughter ought to recognize a bullet hole.

An overtaxed engine snarled behind her. She was a sitting duck, stationary at the roadside, ignition turned off, when th tan truck passed her, spitting sand.

Kasey stabbed the window button. A skinny-armed boy standing in the truck bed yodeled a rebel yell. A tattoo showed as he gripped the cab frame while the open passenger's door rocked wide on its hinges, but she didn't make it out until he pumped a rifle over his head. Then, she saw it was a swastika.

Another boy lurched up from the truck bed. He fought for balance, swaying from side to side before he launched a beer can her way, then dropped his jeans and mooned her.

The truck careened forward and the boy stumbled. Hobbled by his pants, he clung to the cab. He howled skyward, as his pal flipped her the finger.

"Cute," Kasey muttered. Still, drunk kids and guns didn't add up to slaughter.

Puffs of smoke drifted back from the truck, followed by the rapid popping of the rifle. These ranch kids played rough.

Kasey cranked the key so hard the ignition switch screeched, then she slammed the car into gear. It stalled. Damn all automatic transmissions.

"Come on, come on!" Kasey whispered as she pumped the accelerator. Her car jerked forward, spinning a beer can under its tires.

At least the colt had escaped. Kasey steered around gray-green sagebrush crushed by the truck's passing and fumed at the delay caused by the wannabe juvenile delinquents. By now, she should be driving into Gold Canyon, where the Bureau of Wildlife had their headquarters. They were expecting her. Although she despised such a breach of professionalism, she also had an aversion to bullets racing past her skull.

As the tan truck slowed, so did Kasey. Hang back, stay patient, and applaud research for getting you this far, she thought.

Research was all she'd had to go on, once she learned

McDermitt's case had been dismissed the same day she'd made her wager at Magnifique.

McDermitt had fled L.A. the instant the gavel quieted, so there'd been no chance for an interview. She did her best work on-site, anyway, and McDermitt's absence had forced her to prowl electronic and hard-copy archives first.

Investigation led her to wonder who *didn't* have motive and opportunity to kill Nevada's wild horses. Hunters said mustangs scattered game animals. Ranchers swore horses ate grass needed to fatten cattle for market. Paiutes claimed a sovereign nation's right to solve the horse problem their way. And kids like these considered public lands their own private shooting gallery.

Telephone interviews had been a bust. Except for the Bureau of Wildlife's congenial PR man at Gold Canyon, her calls led to dead ends. Conversations with ranchers and members of the tribal council had been thick with one-word answers and the silence reserved for outsiders.

Not that reluctant sources were a novelty. Once she talked her way into a kitchen and bummed a cup of coffee, they'd respond. Face-to-face, she had the knack.

Not only was she a good reporter, she had a lively interest in the lives of others. She'd gossiped with gang girls and Yukon hermits; she could crack the reserve of lonely ranch folk.

Except Gabriel "Bronc" McDermitt. A spool of nerves cranked tight inside Kasey's chest and she cursed the shooters' truck for dawdling. Regardless of the verdict which freed McDermitt—topped-out rodeo rider, dropped-out college student, burned-out bad boy—she didn't trust him.

But *Dare* had sent her to search out answers and McDermitt was her contact. K. D. Wildmoon was too professional to be sidetracked by teenage betrayal.

It had been ten years since a gangly young cowboy had

kissed her, promised to reveal all he knew of her birth mother, then stood her up.

Still wincing from that lesson, she'd let computers clear away the secrets surrounding her adoption. Data bases and Web sites were more efficient than huddled whispering in a corner booth at Hannah's Hen House. In hours, she'd discovered that Leticia Wildmoon, who'd given her up for adoption, had once been Leticia Buck. Sitting in front of a computer terminal in Los Angeles, Kasey discovered she'd been within minutes of the Buck ranch when the Toyota broke down.

But she'd never gone back and her only acknowledgment of her birth mother was using the woman's flashy name for a byline. Her only inheritance was the necklace she'd worn on the day of her adoption.

Dawn-colored shells threaded on doeskin were interspersed with five blue beads tied on at random. A tiny cowrie shell, gray speckled with blue, hung at its center.

Irritated with the kids' sluggish progress, Kasey slipped the necklace inside her shirt and squinted past the windshield. Bullet holes weren't covered by standard car-rental insurance and *Dare* hadn't anticipated expenses much beyond airfare from L.A. to Reno. This story had better start earning its way.

With one hand, Kasey grappled for the point-and-shoot Pentax she'd snagged from the photo department. She slowed and, steering with her knees, raised the camera.

"How are you going to like showing your butts and beer cans on a glossy cover nationwide, fellas?"

She focused on a cyclone of dust, judging it two city blocks away. The tan truck canted up on two wheels, then jostled down, springs squeaking. Kasey zoomed in on the white splotch of butt. She took three shots before the lens's magnification cut through dust and distance and showed her the colt hadn't escaped after all.

The fallen colt scraped the desert floor with forelegs no thicker than her arm. Kasey lay the Pentax on the passenger's seat, clicked the ignition off, and eased the car door open. Softly, she closed it behind her.

At her approach, the colt tried to heave himself up. He failed.

Breath huffed through a hole in his neck, spraying blood. "Shhh." Kasey inched closer.

The colt's long-lashed eyelids lay closed and its nostrils flared red with exertion.

Kasey glanced at the truck idling a quarter mile past. With their thrill kill over, why didn't the kids run?

Before she could guess, a tumult behind her announced an intruder. Static spiked the skin under her necklace. A look over her shoulder showed no spirit horse, only another truck, faded blue as old jeans. It parted heat shimmers on the road as it came her way.

When the blue truck braked, the size of the driver convinced her: skipping Mom's self-defense class had been a mistake.

This man was big. Standing, his hat brim passed the level of the truck's rooftop. The cowboy left the truck door ajar. Scratchy strains of country music mixed with the sound of his boots' approach.

"Don't touch him!" Low and curt, his voice reached her without agitating the colt.

The man emerged from behind the truck and walked closer. Lanky, you'd call him, until your eyes rested on those shoulders. And his blue shirt looked fresh-pressed. Hardly threatening, but something in the first glimpse had warned her.

Kasey backed up two steps, but it was the horse he watched. He lifted his hat to smooth the hair underneath, then settled the

Stetson, shading his face.

"Coyote bait." He shook his head.

The colt huffed. A twang of steel guitar floated from his radio into the desert stillness as Kasey walked back to the rental car. It was nonsense to think that with each step away from the man, the charge thrumming through her necklace faded.

Coyote bait. The boys had killed it, then. Soon the colt's wound would stop whistling.

Kasey climbed back into the rental car and focused on the tan truck still idling up ahead.

Even if they weren't mass murderers, even if that weapon didn't look like the limited-edition automatic that had led the law to McDermitt, the kids were up to something. They sat there gloating, waiting for her to give chase. She wanted to give them the trouble they deserved.

"Lady, don't even—"

Kasey raised her window and ignored the reprimand. Ahead, the rifle-toter gulped another beer, dropped the can, and aimed.

Kasey sat watching. Drunk as he was, he probably couldn't muster the coordination to pull the trigger.

A muffled pop and whine turned her back toward the cowboy. He hadn't moved, except to shake his head at his shattered side mirror.

Ahead, the skinny-armed kid celebrated by crowing and turning his rifle on Kasey's Taurus. She ducked beneath the dashboard and waited. Sweat crinkled the silk beneath her arms. She closed her eyes and listened.

If she'd counted right, Swastika Boy had run out of ammunition. When Kasey peered over the dash, the kid shook the rifle and flung it to the truck bed. The boys whooped as the truck pulled away.

Kasey followed. Dust boiled before her, but she could almost read white letters on the blue Nevada license plate.

"M-O-N, and three numbers," Kasey memorized. If she got the rest of the plate, they were done for. "And I've got lots of gasoline, boys."

She tailed them until the truck bumped off the road ruts. "M-O-N-L ..." Or was it a one? Were there six digits or seven? Under the thick dust, she couldn't be sure.

Possessed by deciphering the next number—an eight? three? Kasey wasn't prepared for the sand dune that appeared before her.

"Keep your foot in it," she recited, but the technique for driving in mud apparently didn't apply to sand. The Taurus wallowed and fell behind as the truck drew away.

For a heartbeat, near the dune's top, it tilted.

"Please dump it," she begged.

But the wide tires gripped. Hooting and jutting their middle fingers, the boys drove on. Kasey pounded her steering wheel and swore.

§§ ⅔

WELCOME HOME. Scolding Rock never let a man forget who was boss. The desert dizzied newcomers by spinning them round, from grandeur to danger. Today he'd lowered his guard and the desert had done the same to him, spreading the alkali flats with white sun, a dying colt, and two minutes full of a woman so gorgeous, Bronc McDermitt forgot to breathe.

The colt's head lifted, wobbling on its delicate neck. He should shoot it.

Two months ago, he would have. Now, he couldn't. Couldn't, because the feds might confiscate his rifles, along with his last few dollars and what was left of his good name. Couldn't, because courts carved lessons good and deep. He smelled fear-soured sweat, urine-yellowed underwear and felt marrow-deep cold just remembering jail. Better to be careful than kind.

"Whoa, there." The colt's eyes rolled white.

Stroking the beast would intensify its fear. He'd like to chase that gun-toting kid, jerk him through the window, and see how he enjoyed feeling scared.

Hell, yes, McDermitt. Assault charges look downright puny to an accused felon.

Bronc frowned at the red car jostling back this way. That meant the long-legged beauty with Indian-black hair had failed to catch them and she'd returned to give him hell. When she quit calling him every kind of coward, maybe he'd wink and tell her real cowgirls didn't tuck their jeans inside their boots.

Bronc squatted beside the colt. Wind lifted flaxen wisps of mane and the colt shuddered. Over the oil cooking on his truck's exhaust manifold, Bronc caught the wet-leather smell of the colt's fuzzy hide. Beyond that, he detected a whiff of milk. Still nursing. The kids must've spooked a band and this baby split off in panic.

"Where's your mama, little guy?"

Bronc's fingers itched to examine the bullet wound, but some primal warning energized the colt. Fighting off man-scent, the mustang's nostrils sucked closed, then flared as he lunged to his feet, wheezing. He stood spraddle-legged and blood sprayed from his windpipe before his legs gave out.

Pretty lines and plenty of grit. With anesthesia and a needle, Bronc thought he could suture that trachea, stitch the hide, and have a decent saddle horse.

Bronc stifled a bitter laugh. That dream was dead.

The only doctoring this colt would get would come from Dr. Winchester. Bronc took his rifle from the cab and slammed the truck door. Another slam echoed his.

Her hair, glossy and black, played peek-a-boo from behind her hips as she strode toward him. His dad would say she looked mad as a peeled rattler. She hadn't caught the kids. Never had a chance to, but her sort didn't take advice from dumb cowpokes.

She'd want something done for the colt. Bronc scrubbed the back of his hand across his brow. Sedated, the little stud colt might survive a truck ride to Gold Canyon. Not likely, though. He was thin as a bed slat and scared.

Bronc dug for a way to avoid all this. He came up dry and chanced another look at the woman. A silky, adobe-colored shirt drifted over her like smoke. If she wore a bra, it was a danged flimsy one.

Underneath, something else rippled the silk, there at the points of her breasts. Jewelry, maybe.

She stopped about two feet away and met him face-to-face. Bronc felt a flare of memory before he thought to hold the rifle behind his leg, out of her view.

"Can we get him someplace—?" Then the woman snatched off her sunglasses. She'd recognized him.

"You're Gabriel McDermitt. Bronc McDermitt."

"Ma'am." He took off his hat. A mannerly woman would have introduced herself. This one's eyes feinted to the rifle and up, but she didn't show one blink of fear. She measured him. Waiting, he figured, for him to do something criminal.

"The colt's still alive." She touched the back of her neck, adjusting the necklace hidden inside her shirt. "I thought you said he was coyote bait."

"Another few minutes, an hour." Bronc shrugged.

"Can't your truck beat that? It's not thirty minutes more to Gold Canyon. And he's not bleeding much."

Bronc considered it. No one could accuse him of murdering mustangs if he went rumbling hell-bent across the playa for help. And this woman might rethink things. Might see him as a hero.

She leaned over the colt. It thrashed, misting the desert floor with blood.

"I told you not to touch him." Bronc gentled his voice when she flinched back. "Bleeding's not the problem. The bullet creased his windpipe. He can't breathe right. It's an old mustanger's trick and it works."

She crossed her arms, unconvinced.

"Even if I was to hog-tie him"—he knew he had rope in the truck bed—"and throw him in the back, he'd beat his brains out against the side of the truck."

"I'll hold him."

Her weight shifted onto one long leg and she crossed her arms. Approaching from the car, her stride had looked athletic and competent. Inside that fancy silk blouse, she was strong.

"You're on, lady." He unchained the tailgate, shoved his saddle to one side, and grabbed his rope. "Get in and get ready." He turned to give her a hand up into the truck bed.

"Don't help me."

Well, hell.

"Okay?" she added, as if she needed to salve his manhood.

"No problem."

Even blindfolded with a bandanna, the colt fought. Twisting with squeals that'd tear the heart from most women, it tried to run. Bronc threw the colt, tied it, and hefted it high as his belt buckle, turning his face from its snapping tail.

"Get in," he grunted, just jerking his head toward the truck this time. The colt must weigh two hundred pounds. It reminded Bronc his back hadn't healed from the last time he'd had a horse on top of him.

With a long step, she climbed in, sliding her jeans across the powdery white dust until she braced her back against the truck cab.

"Gonna have to—" Damn, the colt was heavy. Sweat stung Bronc's eyeballs as he tightened his grip. He used his head to motion her closer. "Come this way, grab him, then scoot back."

Her arms no sooner encircled the colt than it commenced a life struggle. Bronc knew his knots would hold, but he wasn't so sure about the woman. If the colt squirmed loose and fell, it'd be the end.

Bronc tried to vault in, but the colt yanked her around like a puppet, blocking him. Its hooves hammered dents into the sheet metal.

"Hold on!" he urged.

She nodded, effort hardening the muscle at her jaw joint. Then Bronc was up. The colt's head flailed against Bronc's shin before he got around behind. He tripped, lost his hat, then managed to sit. This time, the woman didn't squawk when he tried to help, forming himself into a chair, aligning his arms to hers, helping her cradle the frantic colt.

What a fighter. The colt simmered down about the time Bronc thought his own panting drowned out the frantic horse's. Then Bronc heard her voice, crooning.

"There, it's okay, baby." She leaned forward, taking Bronc with her as she pressed her cheek to the colt's.

No. This baby was no stuffed toy, but a wild—

Bone snapped on bone. The colt's head smashed into hers before it lay still, and Bronc heard her gasp between the colt's shallow pants.

"Did he hurt his nose?" Her voice clogged as she coughed. Bronc felt the spasm through to his spine.

Her face wrenched around and Bronc's unshaven chin

rasped her forehead. He leaned back to see that he'd been wrong about the tears.

"No, but he mighta broke yours."

She sniffed and lifted a shoulder to wipe a drop of blood. She only made it worse.

But the horse was fine. Where the blindfold had slipped, Bronc saw the colt's eyelids close. It shuddered, slumbering soundly as a babe who'd cried itself to sleep.

The woman sniffed again. With her head tucked up under his chin, Bronc couldn't help breathing the meadow-grass smell of her hair. Now that the colt had nodded off, there wasn't much reason to have his arms—let alone his legs—around her.

Slow, so as not to wake the colt, he parted from her. He'd eased his legs away and started peeling his chest off her back-bone, when the woman fixed those strong-coffee eyes on him.

"The federal government accused you of killing—" She cleared her throat.

On his knees beside her, trying not to wake the colt with his own clumsiness, Bronc thought the red smears on her face looked like war paint. Why couldn't she let this horse thing rest? He flat was not in the mood for wrangling over it.

"With blood runnin' down your throat, maybe this could wait." Bronc got his boots under him and stood, searching his pocket for another bandanna so she could blot off.

"—over a hundred wild horses."

More nerve than good sense, he decided. Her eyes aimed up from the level of his knees. His belly twisted at her expression. Again, Bronc felt the flicker of memory, of something harsh and bleak.

He jumped down from the truck bed, plucked his hat from the ground, and dusted its brim. He jammed it back on, flat-handed it low over his eyes, then shook his head.

"If it looks to you like I'm fixin' to hurt this colt, you need to open your eyes, hon."

With one finger, she fished a loop of necklace out of her blouse. Thinking, still cradling the colt's head in the crook of her opposite elbow, she rubbed the smooth strand of shells against her bottom lip, giving Bronc a jolt of the most potent temptation on earth.

Feverish certainty that he'd have her clamped him from gut to groin. Bronc looked directly into the sun and squinted.

"The *Los Angeles Sun-Times*—"

"Who you gonna believe," he demanded, "your own eyes or the lyin', godforsaken press?"

"Pardon me if I can't shake your hand, Mr. McDermitt. My name is K. D. Wildmoon and I *am* the godforsaken press."

THREE

FANGS BARED, the dogs erupted toward Kasey.

She jerked her boots into the truck bed and watched McDermitt. Arms laden with the colt, he crossed the dirt parking lot and passed the government-issue sign identifying this clutter of fences and buildings as Gold Canyon Holding Corrals, Bureau of Wildlife.

Of course the growling pack had parted like lambs for McDermitt. Since he didn't glance back to see what all the snarling was about, she wouldn't call for his help.

Sniffing with satisfaction, the dogs bumped shoulders, wagged their tails, lost interest in Kasey, and tagged after McDermitt. Kasey gave them a minute to move away, then reached for the notebook and pencil in her back pocket. As soon as she did, a volley of barks announced her movement.

The apparent leader of the ragtag pack, a gray and black Aussie with yellow eyes, darted forward. When the others followed, Kasey decided to stay in the truck and make notes while she outwaited them.

She tapped the pencil eraser on her notebook. Her greatest insight—that gangly "Shep Fontana" had certainly grown up—didn't belong in her notes.

It hadn't taken a trained observer to notice the way his shoulders spread beneath the blue shirt as he moved away from her. She'd felt his strength, there in the bed of the pickup, when he'd made himself an all-encompassing chair for her and the colt. His chest had felt solid behind her back. His body was like an athlete's, fit torso tapering to slim rider's hips.

Moving only her eyelids, so she wouldn't aggravate the dogs, Kasey watched McDermitt's efforts. He'd managed to open the gate to a pipe corral without dropping the colt. His contortions while doing it proved her first assessment: no man had a right to look that good in jeans.

Too bad Nature had wasted such form on an unconvicted felon.

Certainly she'd remain objective, but she knew why McDermitt had been arrested. Forty dead mustangs had been found on McDermitt's struggling cattle ranch—bringing the number of horses who'd died in that area last year to more than a hundred—and the prosecution had lacked nothing but a witness to make the charges stick.

☙ ☙

ACCORDING TO KASEY'S RESEARCH, Rainbow Bend ranch had been handed down through four generations of Mc-Dermitts. His parents, sister, and brother lived there now, but Bleek County tax rolls indicated they were far behind on property taxes.

The penalty for one hundred years of overgrazing, by domestic cattle and wild horses, had come crashing down on Bronc McDermitt's family. Soon, they'd lose the ranch.

Kasey drew a deep breath. She wouldn't enjoy exposing him.

Even Mom, who loved her job as a cop and rejoiced in cornering bad guys, hated handcuffing a man in front of his family.

If Kasey documented Bronc McDermitt's last-ditch effort to save the ranch, she'd feel the same. Not that her feelings mattered. Only the story did.

"Okay, guys, I'm coming down." Kasey dug a granola bar from her other pocket and tossed it over the dogs. The Aussie vaulted past the others and snapped the treat into crumbs.

Kasey squinted skyward as a sound from above caught her attention. With a knife-edge glint, the helicopter vanished. As the afternoon advanced, thin clouds had clumped into fat gray balloons. The copter's drone deepened as it burst from the clouds, then hovered.

Kasey eased one leg from the open tailgate, then checked the dogs. Heedless, they gulped the bribe. Finally down, Kasey backed away from the landing site and dogs, then walked toward the trailer whose sign announced: "Office."

She glanced at her watch. Damn, a full hour late.

A man shouldered through the wind-worried trailer door. Hand clamped to his cowboy hat, head bent against the sandstorm stirred by the helicopter, he almost rammed into her.

"Ms. Wildmoon." He shouted over the rotor's racket, one hand cupped to his mouth, but he gave the helicopter no other notice, as if its arrival were routine. "I'm Tate Evans."

Evans's red hair and beer-barrel body made him an unlikely looking administrator. The sun-aged skin around his eyes crinkled with genuine pleasure.

"Glad you made it." He motioned Kasey to follow him away from the helicopter.

"See you met up with Bronc." He nodded at McDermitt's truck.

"I did." The sudden hush of the blades amplified Kasey's

dubious tone.

Tate nodded. "Guess the cowhand survived the big city."

Over Tate's shoulder, Kasey saw the khaki-clad helicopter pilot dismount and give her a quick once-over. Kasey realized she hadn't seen another female in Gold Canyon.

She ran her thumb over the spiral wire at the top of her notebook as her mind returned to McDermitt. Her best move might be to catch Tate off guard.

"If McDermitt returns to work here, won't the charges against him compromise the Bureau of Wildlife's wild horse program?"

"Cut to the chase, don't you, ma'am?" Tate gave a chagrined smile. "BOW's doin' okay. Bronc didn't shoot those horses. Boy hasn't got a cruel bone in his body."

Kasey recalled McDermitt's roughness in tying the foal.

"I said it on the phone, and I'll say it again," Tate continued, "we know how it looks—like Bronc used his job to spot horses, then went after them with a gun."

As Tate led her toward the corrals, Kasey matched him stride for stride and listened to his defense of McDermitt.

"We believe in him. We believe this program is the best chance for balancing the needs of mustangs and all the folks that want horses runnin' free *anyplace* except their land. That's why we're helping you out with this story. Come to that, we're sort of hopin' you'll be our backfire."

"Pardon me?"

"You've done stories on fires, I bet." Tate waited for Kasey's nod. "Haven't you seen 'em light a backfire? They're harmless because fire guys *decide* where to set them. They send them burning toward the big blaze, then there's nothing but blackened ground between the fire and the houses."

Why had he thrown down such a challenge? Kasey stared

at the pronounced creases in his earlobes, trying to ponder their significance instead of reacting.

All the same, she blurted, "You expect my story to be harmless?"

That's *just* what he should expect. He probably hadn't read any of her investigative work and she'd purposely misled him on this. By phone and fax, she'd outlined a happy-face piece with informative sidebars.

"I expect you to dig." Tate bumped back the brim of his hat. "I expect you to skip the sexy sound bite and ask questions. Might even go so far as to hope you'll listen to folks' answers." Tate's smile tipped freckles into the sun lines around his eyes. "Tell the truth. That's all it'll take to save the man. And the program."

"You're expecting a lot from a personality feature." Kasey tried to backtrack. "My editor wants a story that'll bring in home-and-garden readers who don't already buy *Dare. Soft* news," she emphasized, "about a cute cowboy."

Tate craned his neck to see the corral. "Think he's cute, do you?"

"My readers will." She gambled on the likelihood he wasn't a *Dare* subscriber. "Most coo over anything with eyes bigger than their thumbnails, Mr. Evans."

"*Tate*," he corrected. "And I don't believe I greeted you properly." He offered a gentle handshake. "Welcome to Gold Canyon."

Kasey shook, then withdrew her hand as Tate noticed blood marking his palm.

"Sorry," Kasey apologized. *Smooth move, Lois Lane.* "The colt—" She gestured toward the corral. "But since we're practically blood brothers, you may as well call me Kasey."

"Kasey," he echoed and had the decency to ignore her hasty

scrubbing of her fingers along the seam of her jeans.

Colt's blood. Her hand felt warm and sticky all over again as she thought of the gun-happy kids slipping farther away each minute.

"Tate, on my way out from Reno, I caught some kids shooting wild horses from a tan pickup. One of them hit that colt."

If she'd walked into an L.A. newsroom with that revelation, she would have started a riot. Tate's lips tightened in irritation.

"Bronc's taking care of the colt and he's good as a vet. Don't worry," Tate assured her.

"That's nice, but I got a partial license plate." Kasey flipped her notebook open. "We can notify the sheriff."

"We'll tell him when we see him. God willin', that won't be soon."

"But—"

"'It's not a priority' is what he'll tell you. If no one's hurt." Tate shrugged. "I wish it were rare, but it's not."

"Look, the police can run this plate in CLETS and find out who registered the vehicle." Kasey brandished her notepad. "It's time-consuming, but it can be done."

"CLETS?"

"It's an acronym. It stands for—well, I'm not sure, but it's like a data base for California license plates," Kasey faltered. This was not California. "Nevada must have a similar system."

"I wouldn't bet on it."

"You're kidding, right?"

"Don't tell me you're a reporter *and* a cop?" Tate frowned at the dogs' renewed bristling and shooed them away.

"A cop's kid," Kasey admitted. "Two cops, actually. Both my parents are in law enforcement."

Tate slapped his palms on the front of his jeans and chuckled. "Some bloodlines! By a cop, out of a cop."

Boots scuffed behind her. There must be two dozen pair of them in this patch of desert, but Kasey would bet her laptop that the boots she heard belonged to McDermitt.

Tate straightened his hat, put his hands on his hips, then added, "Truth be told, the sheriff won't follow up."

Kasey's stomach tightened, not because of Tate's statement, but because McDermitt stood so near.

Before, this awareness had felt like static crackling from her necklace. This time, a wave of magnetism urged her backward, toward him. Kasey could swear her hair lifted and flowed back to lick McDermitt's shirtfront.

For crying out loud, he hadn't spoken a word. He probably wasn't even there. And what had Tate just said about the sheriff? "Okay, he won't follow up." She didn't ask why. It was too soon. Just the same, she'd keep the license number. Maybe Tate barred the law from Gold Canyon to protect McDermitt.

Soon, she'd talk with Sheriff Glen Radich, the lawman who'd testified against McDermitt. If Tate thought she'd mosey around Gold Canyon watching his choreographed rodeo, he thought wrong. She'd write the story she found. She'd make it so strong, Mark Savage's shareholders would read it in *Dare* and howl because he'd let her go.

First, she had to clinch the deal with Tate.

"I appreciate your cooperation, and your offer—when we talked on the phone—to lend me a horse. In addition to interviews, I need to scout photo sites."

Kasey inventoried the sand and sage landscape, hoping Cookie's artistic eye would see more.

"My editors are sending out Cookie Hodges, one of the finest news photographers around."

Kasey paused as Tate held up a finger and tilted his head to listen.

" 'Scuse me." Tate jogged off to answer a telephone ringing in his office.

"I've met Cookie." McDermitt's words cracked like a slap.

Kasey's necklace lay quiet. As she turned, she felt neither startled nor shy. She felt ready for a fight. Tossing her hair back over both shoulders, Kasey faced him. *Okay, cowboy, you're on.*

§§ ⁊⁊

BRONC WANTED TO RIP K. D. Wildmoon's composure right up the center.

Instead, she confronted him with eyes level, hip aslant, chin up. She dared him to make something of knowing the photographer.

Bronc let her stew a minute. He didn't admit Cookie Hodges had caught him as he'd left the courtroom. Wearing cameras like bandoleers, she'd ducked into his path as two deputies hustled him, handcuffed, down the hall.

"Show me your pretty white teeth, Cowboy," she'd wheedled, "and I'll make you look like an honest man."

Embarrassed, he'd glanced away, and wound up looking shifty. That picture made newspapers nationwide, and made his mother cry.

K. D. Wildmoon still waited. He couldn't think what to say. That picture hadn't been the worst of it. First Cookie, then his attorney, had urged him to sit down for an interview with K. D. Wildmoon. Champion of the underdog, they'd called her, and a veteran reporter. They'd delighted in retelling her award-winning stories, "Ninja's Boy" and "Mamma's Girl."

He'd refused because he was no whiner, because he only knew two Wildmoons—one dead, one just a girl, and both trouble. Finally, though, a phone call from his father had convinced him.

"Do what ya gotta do, boy." Mac McDermitt's throat had

sounded sore. "Don't much matter. The wolf's been at the door so long, the bitch's gone and had pups."

Then and there, Bronc decided he'd submit to anything if it would end the trial in his favor.

So he agreed. His lawyer passed the word to the *Sun-Times* and Bronc settled down to wait. He'd figured K. D. Wildmoon for a stocky crusader in a mannish suit. With wire-rimmed glasses, probably, and thick calves slumping into sensible shoes. No matter, all he wanted was a smart gal the feds would hate to tick off.

Sitting in his cell those long evenings after court, after pasty potatoes and gray gravy that arrived every damn dinner, he waited for K. D. Wildmoon. She never showed.

He'd given in and she'd stood him up. Now he had her alone. K. D. Wildmoon pushed her sunglasses up to crown herself and tried to stare him down.

Stubborn, both of us, Bronc thought. Neither willing to break the silent standoff.

Objective reporter or not, she wasn't buying the not-guilty verdict. She'd come to cause him more grief, but Bronc McDermitt was wise to her. Wise as a tree full of owls, honey. So watch out. Then, before he could help it, he winked.

She gave a short surprised laugh. He had to admit, for that instant, she didn't seem to take herself quite so seriously.

"You're one cocky son-of-a-gun, McDermitt. I'll give you that.

Her laugh rippled the filmy thing she wore as a shirt. Hell, it could pass for lingerie. She looked down and held it out from her ribs, grimacing. She thought he'd been staring at the smear of blood.

"Oh, man." She drew the second word out so long, he figured she'd calculated her dry cleaner's bill, plus tax.

K. D. Wildmoon and her fancy blouse wouldn't last long here. She'd have the devil of a time interviewing folks whose great-grandparents knew his. None would brand Bronc McDermitt a horse killer.

As if the shirt reminded her of the colt, she asked, "Is he all right?"

"He's in there."

She lowered her sunglasses, then wandered toward the corrals. This gal was a strange one. First, she'd squared off, ready to fight over that colt. Then she'd forgotten him.

Must be convenient, having such quick-flare feelings. In her line of work, it probably paid off. Fuse short as a birthday candle—short, bright, and burned out when the party's over. Damned convenient.

Before he got morose staring after her, the screen door to the office opened and one of his oldest buddies emerged.

"Welcome home." Tate shut the door to his office. He clapped Bronc's shoulder, then snatched a pack of cigarettes from his shirt pocket.

He lit one, glancing both ways, reminding Bronc of the drifter Tate had been the day he tried to tempt Bronc with the habit.

Bronc and his pal Calvin Buck had scored big in their first season of high school rodeo, so they'd come to the pro rodeo in Reno, strutting. Tate, years older, home after chasing a barrel racer as far as Calgary, had been loitering around the chutes and offered the boys a smoke. When they balked, he challenged them to something else: entering bareback broncs. Cal Buck, Paiute calf-roper extraordinare, had said sure, if Tate went first. In the end, only McDermitt had ridden, and found another wild thing to love.

Tate, Buck, and Bronc had been partners until Jack Flynn

intruded. Tate, older and less tolerant of fools, had drifted off again. Now, he was boss to Bronc and helicopter-flying Flynn. Only Buck worked elsewhere—if you called sitting in an air-conditioned office, pushing papers as a mine supervisor, *work*.

Tate blew out a breath and coughed. "We sure were glad the way things turned out."

If he forgot the humiliation, losing his vet scholarship, and beggaring his parents with court costs, Bronc guessed he agreed

"Yeah, life's looking just fine."

Bronc glanced toward the corral, where K. D. Wildmoon squatted and offered her fingers through the rails to the colt.

"It's over." Tate made a dismissing cut with his hand, then took off his hat and slapped it against his jeans. Bronc saw a lecture coming. "It didn't do the Bureau any good, either."

Bronc held his peace and watched Tate act like a boss.

"K. D. Wildmoon," Tate lowered his voice, "is offerin' us a chance to mend fences with the Bureau and keep us all employed."

Bronc studied his boot's scarred toe.

"Washington's about to send out some slicks to 'do the job right,'" Tate said.

"That's bull, Tate. You know it."

Tate ignored him.

"Now, Ms. Wildmoon wants to write a personality feature, she says." Tate shook his head. "I got my doubts about how upfront she's bein'. I pulled up a couple of her *Dare* stories—"

"*Dare*—that's a magazine, right? Doesn't she work for an L.A. newspaper?"

"Used to." Tate said it with emphasis.

So, the smooth lady reporter had gotten herself fired. That might explain her delay in showing up at his cell.

"Now," Tate continued, "she writes for *Dare*, sort of a political magazine. I pulled, as I was saying, some of her stories off the Internet—"

Bronc laughed and Tate pointed his finger like a revolver.

"Yeah, go ahead and snort, but I live in the real world, where computers are common as pencils. That girl could save your neck. Her stories make folks want to jump up and do something—about poverty, gangs, hydraulic mining—whatever the hell she writes about."

Bronc sighed. Tate was probably right.

"So, I'll behave." Bronc glanced back at her, still squatting by the corral. "Is that all you want?" It sure wouldn't kill him to be nice to Ms. Wildmoon.

"No cotton-candy interview with a 'cute cowboy' would include meeting Delaney or the Bucks," Tate mused, "but I told her to go ahead. She wants to camp in the sagebrush, too, so watch for snakes and cook her some real cowboy grub."

It rankled, thinking of her talking to his friends behind his back. He imagined her asking sly questions that couldn't be answered fairly. Then Tate's rambling sentence clicked.

"Watch out for snakes?" Bronc asked.

"... instead of that air-conditioned car. And she says she can ride. Since the damned drought's delayed roundup, you won't be missed takin' her around."

Takin' her around? Was he supposed to watch her trip up his friends and make them crucify him? "No. No way."

"Just let her interview people about BOW—"

"No."

"—Indians ... what?" Tate halted. "What'd you say?"

"I'm not going. If that's why the Bureau took me back, they can shove this job. My standards are pretty damned low, but you just dug deep enough to hit one, Tate. I won't be her babysitter. And I won't watch her make notes pointing me up as a half-brained buckaroo who let himself be framed."

The pulse pounded in Bronc's neck as Tate stayed quiet and let him run down.

"What she oughta do," Bronc added, "is find out why the feds spent thousands of dollars tracking me down and trying me, when the real horse killer's still out there."

The rusty-hinge call of a starling filled the silence. Tate juggled his cigarette while he dug a brown plastic bottle from his pocket and thumbed the cap off.

"Sorry to hear you so bitter." Tate popped a pill into his mouth.

Nitroglycerin tablets. Tate's first heart attack had happened at thirty. He'd had a couple "episodes" since. Bronc cussed himself for causing Tate more stress.

"Sorry for being so contrary." Bronc watched the pills disappear back into Tate's pocket, then wondered why talking had wrung more out of him than wrestling the colt.

He glanced over at K. D. Wildmoon, still crouched by the fence. She'd best mount up in other jeans. Those clung tight enough to strangle them both.

She opened a button on her shirt, twisted her hair up, and coiled it off her neck. When she felt his look and stared back, her arrogance looked a lot like embarrassment.

"The Bureau needs you to do it." Tate's tone hardened.

"Or I can take my saddle and head on down the road, huh?" Bronc kicked dirt and kept his eyes down. "Let my folks lose the ranch 'cause I'm too proud to earn a paycheck. 'Course, they already sold every last steer to pay my court costs."

Tate made smoothing motions. "It's only for two weeks. Less, if she gets what she wants right off."

Bronc knew what she wanted. Conviction in print, if not in court. Let her see what she could write when he kept his mouth shut. He had no patience with "assertive" women. Females were either tough, or they weren't.

"I'll answer her questions, but I'm not orchestratin' a Girl Scout campout."

Tate's smile turned mocking. "Don't let yourself go thinking about how many men'd like to switch places." He jerked his head toward the chopper, its engine still pinging as it cooled. "Think Flynn would turn down a chance to go camping with K. D. Wildmoon?"

Something clamped like a claw on the back of Bronc's neck, and it wasn't jealousy.

Bronc imagined K. D. Wildmoon wriggling into her jeans at daybreak. Flat, tanned belly, legs that went on forever, and Flynn watching, in concealment.

"No, sir."

"So, quit feelin' sorry for yourself and go."

"I can always count on you for sympathy, Tate. Gives me a restful sort of feeling," Bronc answered.

"How're your folks?"

When Tate swapped topics that way, it made Bronc jittery.

"They hate living in town. Mom's doing secretarial work for a cement company. My dad's mixing feed for dairy cows. Callie cries because kids at school call her a redneck and Josh still thinks I should have shot it out with the feds. Too much TV, I guess."

With every word, Bronc realized he had no business quitting over self-respect.

God knew, his folks wouldn't insist he take a job riding herd on a girl reporter. Mom always put the best face on things, even when she'd call him in jail, her voice faint over the jail-house phone.

"I go out and check things at the ranch every chance I get

Champ runs over from the Albrights' just to see me off," Tate told him.

Bronc felt sick, picturing that useless collie defending an empty barn and ranch house.

"They're coming down soon. My dad said he stays away because he hates driving off at the end of a weekend, when there's still fence to mend, shingles to patch, work that shouldn't have to wait."

"Yeah." Tate nodded.

Far thunder made Bronc edgy, even though there was no herd to keep from breaking up in panic, no crop to protect from hammering hail. Just thunder, a warning.

Long as he was feeling soppy as an old dishcloth, he might as well finish up. "Thanks for testifying at my trial."

"Least I could do." Tate shrugged off Bronc's thanks, then ground out his cigarette, exhaling loud and long. "Thing is, when I left, when I was coming down the courthouse steps, one of the suits from Washington followed me out."

Bronc felt the hair on his neck bristle.

"He seemed sure you wouldn't get convicted, since the ballistics were off and all. He said BOW could use a tame outlaw like you to find the real killer, on the quiet. Unofficial."

Tame? Bronc felt like he'd been kicked in the chest.

"Now I told him"—Tate held up a hand—"he'd picked the wrong cowboy, but he trotted out a few blackmail items like malicious mischief, driving without a license, drunk and disorderly—"

"All juvenile stuff." Bronc went hot at the betrayal. "Those records were supposed to be sealed."

"—contributing to the delinquency of a minor?"

"Hell, Tate." Bronc closed his eyes against the desert glare.

"It was my twenty-first birthday and Shannon turned

eighteen a couple weeks later. We were necking under the bleachers—"

"Necking?"

Bronc sighed. "Nobody pressed charges. I was a wild kid, and I drank too much. I haven't had a drink in months."

"Buy ya a cold one in my trailer."

"Yeah, that's just what I need." He could feel the noose tightening. "They tell you to get me skunked and make me sign something?"

"You won't be putting nothing in writing."

"What is this? A bunch of deny-all-knowledge, the-truth-is-out-there crap? After they framed me?"

"It wasn't BOW. They just took the tip. This is how it went: somebody called in the location of those shot horses and framed you. Whoever it was didn't claim the reward."

"Then why—?" Bronc stopped dead.

"That's what they want to find out. Why take the trouble to frame you, but not take the ten-thousand-dollar reward?

"If you find the killer, BOW will give you the current reward and the unclaimed one, too. For information leading to arrest and conviction."

Bronc listened to the panting of Tate's dog pack. Gold Canyon had accumulated too damn many canines. They'd dug a cool summer den under Tate's trailer. From there, they kept watch on the dumb humans standing in the sun. Bronc wanted to crawl on under with them, out of the glare of responsibility.

Truth was, he could go panting like a hound after that reward money. Twenty thousand dollars would go a long way toward easing the McDermitt family miseries.

"They gonna put me in the Federal Witness Protection program, too?"

"Criminy, Bronc, you think we're dealing with the mob?"

"I think someone who wipes out a hundred horses won't balk at plugging a rodeo bum who's been arrested more times than he's paid his taxes."

"Don't get skittish on me." Tate looked him in the eye. "The point is, you'll look a lot less suspicious than some dude from law enforcement."

Bronc studied Ms. Wildmoon's backside for a couple minutes more. What was he agreeing to, really? A paycheck for following her around, letting her flush out potential bad guys, while he protected the real culprit.

Unless the truth turned out way different than he had it figured, he couldn't collect the reward. What would be the point of saving the ranch if the one who loved it best went to prison?

Tate stretched and gave a yodeling sort of yawn. "So I can tell them you'll do it?"

"No. Give me some time."

" 'Til daybreak. Then you ride out." Tate clapped his hand on Bronc's shoulder. Then shook it. If it had been anyone else, Bronc would have resisted. Instead, he let Tate jolly him into being a team player.

"Look at it this way." Tate sounded philosophical. "All those things that got you in trouble are gonna bail you out. All except for fooling with females."

At the scrape of boots on sand, both men watched K. D. Wildmoon stand and dust the seat of her jeans.

"I'm advisin' you to think of her as . . . your partner," Tate muttered. "Treat her like gold and she's gonna save your sorry hide."

FOUR

Kasey closed the door and felt it sag on its hinges. Scented with pine cleaner and coffee, walls decorated with wrinkled black and white photos autographed by rodeo champs of the past, the shack apparently served as Gold Canyon's kitchen and bunkhouse.

It was no palace. Kasey crossed the creaking pine floorboards, wishing the five silent cowboys hadn't taken her arrival as an eviction order.

Riding in on brown horses, they'd looked just like movie cowboys. Ruddy-faced and young, they'd welcomed Bronc with nods that, once they dismounted, turned into back slaps and grins.

Once Tate introduced her, they'd all vanished with their bedrolls.

Kasey passed a couch cluttered with magazines, a canvas bag, and spurs, to peer into the bathroom. A mirror-fronted medicine cabinet hung over a pedestal sink. Inside the shower stall, a window opened out to darkening sky.

⌇⌇ ⌇⌇

THE SECOND ROOM held three bunkbeds. Her duffle bag sat on one, and Kasey wondered who she had to thank for jimmying the rental car's trunk. Inside the cave of the lower bunk, a sketch of a coyote was tacked beside small Polaroid shots faded to watercolor blue. One showed a cowgirl with a blond braid. Glare had bleached her face, but she sat relaxed and buxom on her horse.

Kasey unzipped the duffle and burrowed for a replacement blouse. With a place to sleep, a helpful support staff, and her main source at hand, she only needed a few days on the range, to gather colorful details. Her story's framework could be hammered together right here at Gold Canyon. It should be a cinch.

It would be, if she could dispel her pulse-stuttering response to McDermitt's nearness.

Kasey glanced at her watch. She'd left Tate promising McDermitt a cold beer in his trailer. That meant she had time to rinse the silk blouse and change.

She'd run the sink full of water before she noticed the bathroom had no door. At least she could pull the shower curtain to block the window. She did, then shed the blouse and held it poised over the water.

Either way, the blouse was ruined. This way, she wouldn't have to haul it around stiff with blood.

Kasey felt exposed, standing before the mirror in her bra and jeans. She listened. The only sounds were mechanical humming from the refrigerator inside, and a generator outside. Clearly, she was alone.

As she sluiced the blouse in the basin, water splashed onto her chest. Even though she wore a no-nonsense ivory bra, it framed her necklace.

Twice it had *seemed* to sound an alarm. Ten years ago, it had warned her of the flat tire—or had it been the hallucination horse? Today, she'd felt the heat and heard the shrilling before she saw the real horse and kids with guns.

"Forget it," Kasey muttered to her reflection.

Reared in a household of cops, she evaluated every odd situation in terms of motive and opportunity. Neither existed for a necklace, so maybe she should blame her own guilt. She'd fiercely ignored her heritage and the legacy of this necklace.

And she'd continue. She had work to do.

Kasey wrung water from the blouse and emptied the sink. If she hurried, she'd have time for a shower.

Afterward, Kasey tucked a white tee shirt into her jeans and exchanged her boots for Nikes. She double-knotted the laces, remembering the loophole Tate had left her.

"If you find it awkward riding out alone with Bronc," Tate had said, "we can figure something else."

Awkward? Many of her best assignments had required her to live in desolate settings with men. Excluding one hang-glider pilot who'd taken too many blows to the head, all the men had heeded her natural reserve.

Awkward was not the problem. She felt off balance because she'd arrived with a bloody nose. She felt touchy because a journalist should have no opinion of her source, and not only did she know McDermitt for a liar, she *wanted* him to be guilty. McDermitt talked little and never smiled, but he knew the terrain and the people of Bleek County. If these cowboys were an example, she'd need McDermitt as an interpreter.

So what if he had absolutely no memory of their first meeting? It wasn't as if they'd shared a torrid love affair. Twenty teen-aged minutes in a truck shouldn't interfere with two adults' abilities to do their jobs.

Just before Kasey closed the shack's door, something

moved behind her. She whirled and stared into the main room. Nothing. She heard a faint patter. Probably her shirt, dripping in the shower.

⚡ ⚡

TWILIGHT WIND WHISTLED around Tate's trailer, bringing a male voice and a squeal. McDermitt and the colt. Intent on catching a glimpse of him before he saw her, Kasey didn't hear the dogs burst out from under the trailer.

"Back off." She batted aside a black muzzle and kept walking. In a swirl of teeth and saliva, the dogs slashed her. "No!"

Kasey held her wrist, staring at the bloody rip across her palm. The dogs retreated, blinking in pained sensitivity.

It hadn't been her shout that shamed them.

"Bite ya?" Bronc McDermitt's hands were sticky, his tone casual as he tilted her hand side to side, examining the tear.

For a moment she wondered how he could have appeared beside her so quickly, then she blurted, "I've never been bitten by a dog."

Face shaded by the black hat brim, his expression was hidden, but one of them was leaning against the other for support. Good thing she wasn't the sort to cry.

"I love dogs." She clamped her jaw shut, straightened, and told herself she didn't need McDermitt. She hadn't asked for his help, certainly hadn't required rescue.

"If he'd meant to hurt you, he would've bit down and hung on."

Was that supposed to console her? Or maybe McDermitt was siding with the dog.

And then she felt the trembling. Furious, Kasey tried to jerk her hand free. It hurt, but she'd already let him see her bleed. She'd be damned if she'd fall apart.

But the trembling was *his*.

Kasey took a chest-filling breath and glanced back at the corral. Vaults over eight-foot fences took something out of a guy. She tried believing that, then did a double-take. At the foot of the fence lay a giant-sized baby bottle.

She came up with three possible explanations: the climb had taxed his obvious toughness or he'd feared for the colt's safety. Or hers.

Kasey focused her reporter's objectivity, gritted her molars, and decided Bronc McDermitt was shaky from low blood sugar. She extracted her hand from his.

"Scrub that, irrigate it for five minutes, and get it covered," McDermitt urged.

"Since we'll be riding together, you should know I don't take orders."

McDermitt's head jerked up. "And I don't ride with folks so stubborn they'd tempt infection."

"Thanks for your concern." She knew there was no sense arguing. He'd be a great help with this story. "But it's no big deal. I imagine you get banged up in your line of work, too, right?"

The brim of his hat shifted, marginally, back toward her. "Fair amount," he said.

"So do I, but let's not compare scars." She saw him shake his head, amused in spite of himself.

"No, ma'am." McDermitt rubbed his jaw. "Let's get you a horse."

He walked away. Dusk lapped in behind him and the clatter of dry juniper applauded. One raindrop, then three all at once, splattered the dust at Kasey's feet.

Damn. These strong, silent types were more attractive in fiction. Still, a reporter didn't earn her check by staring after a man's denimed backside. Kasey followed.

Arms slung over the top rail of another corral, McDermitt

watched several horses and a mule mill around. Had he missed them while he was in jail? Swiveling ears said the horses were alert for his intentions. All except the black nuzzling McDermitt's neck.

"The buckskin's off limits; he's Tate's rope horse." McDermitt pointed. "Rook is mine." He pushed the black's lips from his collar. "The gray's your size, but wily. He'll roll if you let him, bite your knee, hump up and buck of a morning, but he's not mean."

The gray—actually he looked white to her—surged toward the other horses and they scattered.

"What *would* you consider mean?" Kasey wondered if McDermitt had chosen homicide-by-horse to shake her off his trail.

He shrugged as though he'd already rattled on interminably. "Tate said you could ride some."

"He wasn't lying. I'm used to horses that are more mannerly, but—"

"Men, too, I bet."

"—I can handle him." Kasey's words tangled with his, but she heard every one.

Skittering hooves stood silent, wind stopped, and rain tapped McDermitt's hat brim as he choked out an apology.

"Sorry. Swear to God, I don't know where that came from." Finally he looked up. In spite of his hat's shade and the twilight, she saw McDermitt's embarrassment.

In a flash of crystal-and-brass-tinted memory, Kasey saw Mark in evening attire, in a hotel ballroom, lying on national television without a brush of shame.

Bronc McDermitt couldn't have devised a more potent defense. He'd found her weakness. Kasey had a soft spot for a strong man who could still blush.

⧗ ⧗

RAIN AND THUNDER PURSUED THEM into the gloomy shack.

Kasey leaned against the closed door and inhaled something delicious as McDermitt's boots crossed the creaking floorboards to yank the string dangling from a bare light bulb.

Whatever was cooking now hadn't been when she'd left after showering.

"Mutton stew." McDermitt hung his hat on a rack, walked to a propane stove, and lifted the lid from a black iron pot.

Kasey inhaled the aroma of garlic, peppers, and meat.

If McDermitt didn't put the lid back on the pot, she might lose the battle between hunger and manners.

"Sheepherders brought us a trough full, knowin' we were between cooks," he explained.

And why were the sheepherders so considerate, she wondered. Because the BOW kept mustangs off their land?

"It smells wonderful." When Kasey moved close enough to watch its thick bubbling, McDermitt left the room.

"While your appetite's up," he called back, "come pick your week's feed. Then I'll go over Tate's checklist while we wait for the rest."

She didn't want to wait for the others. The combination of bullet-holed windshield, colt-inflicted thrashing, and dog bite had her starving. Her stomach lining felt as if someone had worked it over with an emery board.

McDermitt sidled between two bunks and vanished into a closet she hadn't noticed before. Kasey stood in the doorway of the makeshift pantry.

Light washed over canned food labels and McDermitt's face. As he squatted to study the cans, Kasey considered his blood-stained jeans and the intensity with which he ignored her.

Kasey peered over his shoulder. McDermitt seemed to take up air as well as space.

Sitting behind her in the truck, his legs had outlined hers, but that had been for the colt. And he'd held her hand to examine the bite, but that had been for her safety. Some brazen part of her wanted McDermitt to touch her and *remember*.

"Limas in barbecue sauce?" Holding a can, he turned and his nose almost grazed hers.

Before McDermitt pulled back, she saw his eyes were blue. Almost turquoise in his sun-browned face.

Kasey bit the inside of her cheek to keep from laughing at herself. Romantic exaggeration had never been her style. "Ugh," she managed.

"No limas." He snatched a dozen cans down from the shelf. "Any problems with chili, hash, refries, or corn, ya might as well keep to yourself. There's a bag to put 'em in, out there."

Together, they stood to retrieve it and their bodies filled the cramped closet. Kasey tried to edge ahead of him and they ended up face-to-face. Or would have, had she been taller. When she turned sideways, his shoulder collided with her eye.

"Quit dancin'." he directed. "I'll get the bag."

Kasey sucked in a breath and waved him ahead. Once he'd gone, she stared at the shelves. Her pulse felt like a bird's rapid pecking. Lucky she hadn't opted for police work. Suspects in close quarters made her skittish.

Outside the pantry, bedsprings creaked. Kasey gathered an indiscriminate bunch of cans and swaggered out to drop them on the bunk across from McDermitt.

Hunched and stiff, he'd fit himself onto the edge of a lower bunk and sat poised with pencil and clipboard.

Kasey released a huge green can last. He ignored its crash. "I need coffee," she said.

Bronc glanced up.

"My solitary vice," she promised.

"Mm-hmmm. Be wanting some every morning?"

Kasey sized him up. She'd only shared one man's bed, but she'd shared campsites with dozens. Going on instinct, she'd bet Bronc McDermitt, with his rock-angled cheekbones and black beard shadow, wasn't a man who took morning sips of chamomile tea.

"Don't worry, I can make my own."

He nodded and her stomach growled.

Too keyed up to sit, Kasey stood in the alley between the beds while McDermitt recited what she'd need for their ten-day ride.

She'd done pretty well, but wished she'd anticipated every single item. As her hands fisted, pain from the dog bite sizzled up the nerves to her shoulders.

Then a pang, hot as an electric needle, lanced from her necklace, into her breastbone.

Kasey started for the bathroom, set on banishing dog germs. She'd be damned if she'd let pain impede her. It must be the bite and not some imagined warning from the necklace. No mustangs galloped in the distance, no gun-toting delinquents bore down on her. She was safe and snug, with dinner on the stove.

McDermitt watched her lift the necklace over her head. She moved out of his view, lay the necklace on an edge of the pedestal sink, and left the bathroom without tending her hand.

The shack's door swung open.

"I see they're making a sorry-ass dude wrangler out of you, McDermitt."

The stranger's military-short silver hair, leather flight jacket, and mirrored sunglasses jarred Kasey more than the insult. She might have laughed at his *Top Gun* attire, if he hadn't tilted his head with a watchfulness that made her feel like prey. He removed the glasses, one side at a time, and she recognized him as the helicopter pilot.

"I'll stand in line for my turn, if this is the caliber tourist we're getting."

Before she thought of a snappy rejoinder, his eyes swept to her. He looked boyish. "I'm Jack Flynn."

As their hands met, she noticed Flynn carried an animal pelt in the crook of his elbow. That, she thought, was downright weird, but she didn't recoil. His hand felt surprisingly soft against her injured palm.

"Ms. Wildmoon is a reporter." McDermitt stayed seated on the bunk. "She's tryin' to make a story out of the Bureau's horse program. Jack's a government pilot. He'd probably make great 'local color.'"

Flynn had forgotten her long before he released her hand. While his eyes stayed hooked on McDermitt, Kasey studied the pilot.

Flynn probably had the steadiest nerves in Nevada, but she'd balk at climbing into his cockpit. With luck, he wouldn't bed down in this bunkhouse. But she couldn't imagine him sleeping under the stars with the boys, either. Maybe that animal skin was a Western futon.

"Looking at this?" Flynn's smile was open and easy as he draped the pelt over her arm.

She didn't own a fur coat and objected to them on principle, but her hand passed over this thing as if it might purr.

"Coyote pelt." Flynn pronounced it *kye-oat*. "Even in summer, it gets cold in the chopper. A jacket feels too bulky." Flynn's hand followed hers as she stroked the pelt. "Coyote's fur is designed to keep him comfy, even in the deepest snowdrifts. Each hair is hollow, so it warms the air."

Kasey's eyelids drooped. She could barely follow Flynn's words for her sudden drowsiness.

"You probably disapprove of wearing fur . . ."

How did he know and why was she letting him drape the fur over her shoulder?

". . . but when you're alone, its warmth is better than goose-down, better than body heat, for sleeping."

She let him arrange the fur, resisting the female instinct that recognized his slow, easy movements.

" 'Scuse me, Jack."

McDermitt might have clapped his hands and released her from a trance. Flipping the clipboard aside, he stood and crowded Flynn back a step. Once past, McDermitt clattered in a kitchen drawer, took up a spoon, and dabbed at the stew.

Maybe her lethargy was a result of shock, but her hand didn't hurt. She flexed her fingers, remembering she'd been about to go scrub it when Flynn arrived. Holding up a just-a-minute index finger, she slipped away from the men and into the bathroom.

First, Kasey splashed cold water on her face. Better.

Alert and eager to eavesdrop, she heard Flynn's voice turn clipped.

"Shannon said you were on your way home."

"Yeah?" McDermitt sounded bored.

Kasey kept her face in her cupped hands. Who was Shannon? Listening to the sound of crockery being unstacked and thumped down at individual places at the table, Kasey tried to remember if she'd come across that name in her research.

"Truth be told, you were the last thing she was worrying over." Flynn paused. "She was downright irate at Radich. Seems he pulled her over for driving her cattle truck too fast."

Kasey remembered that name. Radich was the sheriff who'd arrested McDermitt. She wiped beads of water from her eyelashes, then ran cold water over her palm, but just for a minute. She couldn't hear the men's voices, so she shut it off.

"...Radich just as ticked off. Said Shannon barely took time to peel the cigarette off her lip before telling him to go to hell. She's going to court over it."

"Sounds about right."

Kasey felt compelled to wear the necklace, but each time it grazed her skin, static spiked her. It must be something in the desert air.

As Kasey returned to the room, Flynn tore a piece of bread from an unsliced loaf and began chewing. "How long's Tate had this? It could chip your teeth."

Flynn grimaced and McDermitt kept silent. The wooden spoon churned half a dozen rounds of the pot and rain dripped from the eaves outside.

Old tension rattled between the two men. Over this Shannon, maybe? Or McDermitt's arrest? As a pilot, Flynn would be in a position to see the entire range. Maybe he knew the truth about McDermitt, and maybe he could cause big trouble.

"What makes you great local color, Mr. Flynn?" Kasey wished the bare bulb shed more light. Something flared in Flynn's gray eyes.

"I fly for Predatory Animal Predation Abatement."

She'd run across PAPA in Montana. The wildlife biologist she'd been interviewing had squared off over the timber wolves PAPA had destroyed. It turned out feral dogs, not wolves, were the monsters who'd mauled dozens of lambs, but by then the wolves were dead.

Kasey saw no reason to share that anecdote. Instead, she joked, "Even for a government agency, that title's kind of redundant."

"Long as they send paychecks, I don't care who signs them."

She laughed, playing along, teasing out the truth of his involvement with McDermitt. "You must be a good shot, to take down animals from the air."

Flynn didn't respond. He unzipped his jacket in one move. His silver crewcut made her wonder if he'd flown in Vietnam, like her dad.

Then Kasey chided herself. She'd let the prematurely gray hair fool her. Flynn was too young for Vietnam.

"Predators." Kasey considered the forgotten fur. "Even out here, there can't be many predators left."

Boots stomped the front porch, interrupting her. Tate, followed by a flock of cowboys, entered with sights set on the stew pot.

Kasey forgot her inquiry until the men departed after dinner. Last to leave, Flynn stopped in the doorway.

Kasey crossed her arms and smiled. At dinner, she'd determined Flynn wasn't part of this story, but as long as he didn't insist on claiming one of these bunks, she'd listen to whatever he wanted to say.

It wasn't much.

"I'm one helluva shot, Kasey." Flynn looked at her with gray, gunfighter's eyes and she believed him. "And there are enough predators out here to keep fuel in the chopper and me out from under the thumbs of fools. That's all that matters."

⤲ ⤲

AN HOUR LATER, KASEY PACED. McDermitt had warned her to bed down early, but she couldn't. She tried sitting in the overstuffed chair, reading, but her eyes kept wandering to the couch and that damned skin.

All day she'd kept her mind on business. Now, leaving the deceased coyote behind, she stared out the shack's kitchen window into the darkness and allowed one personal thought.

In a day or two, she'd meet the Buck family. She had no choice. They were part of the story. And part of her heritage.

At best, she'd meet Leticia, her birth mother. Kasey knew her first question would be about the necklace. She imagined Leticia—would people call her Tish?—laughing and revealing some odd chemical property that contributed to the necklace's legend. Some ability to emit static electricity, perhaps.

At least, she'd meet Becky Buck, who was married to Kasey's uncle, Calvin. Becky Buck was a sometime tribal activist who'd testified at McDermitt's trial.

Kasey pressed her forehead against the cold windowpane, then stepped back. The rain had stopped, and outside something moved.

How could she have stood there, oblivious to the fact that she was backlit, outlined for anyone who looked? Kasey jerked the light bulb's string and stood in the dark.

Outside, wind taunted a campfire, stretching, then calming it. Beside it, a solitary figure tossed kindling. She didn't ponder why she knew that silhouette, cloaked by a dark duster.

She stopped in the doorway. Snow wind from a far mountain made her grab a jacket. The sight of McDermitt, alone in the firelight, still chilled her with a feeling she'd lost long ago.

As a little girl, Kasey hadn't questioned soundless calls to wild places. She'd known that something—her Indian blood, the necklace, or the wordless chants haunting her dreams—made her different. But, by the end of sixth grade, she'd taken control. Each time mystical nonsense beckoned, she made it stop.

Kasey raised her collar against the wind. Scents of sage and sand had stirred up her reporter's intuition. That was all. Kasey closed the door behind her and walked to the fireside.

࿇ ࿇

BRONC WISHED SHE'D STEP OUT in the open. Eight hours ago, Kasey Wildmoon had ripped the thin peace he'd pulled around himself. Now it was payback time, but he had no itch to fight.

Ms. Wildmoon was a beauty, but no nervy high-stepper who could be spooked into running away. A man could find more than her looks to admire. At dinner, she'd jawed just like one of the boys. She'd had Tate, Flynn, and the cowboys eating out of her hand like it was full of lump sugar.

She'd been damned clever, scraping out secrets even he didn't know. Her lips had pressed together in frustration at their short answers, but she'd had Tate calling her Kasey and telling the story of why China, the horse she'd ride, turned gun-shy. Flynn admitted his flights into Namibia and Bosnia.

Everyone had wondered where Flynn had gone off to after that bar fight was declared an accident, not manslaughter.

She'd cleared up the mystery over dinner, and her interest seemed real.

Yeah, she'd talked to every one of them, except him. Each time she glanced his way, she went stiff. The lady planned to bag Bronc McDermitt, horse killer, and didn't want to get too friendly.

But she wanted something from him. He'd seen it twice, strongest of all there in the pantry. Her eyes had tried pulling something from him. Some words, some feeling, some action. She probably wasn't asking for his arms to cinch around her or his lips to close on her sassy mouth, but that's what had nearly happened.

And now, how long would she stand in the shadows? Inside the denim jacket, her tee shirt glimmered white, giving her away. He'd watched that shirt get wet, raindrop after raindrop, out by the corrals. Over dinner, he'd watched it dry.

The fire shrank from the wind, reminding him it'd be cold tomorrow night when he slept out, with her.

How far would Ms. Wildmoon go for a story?

Bronc tamped down his smile by thinking of the bluff he had to pull off. How would he manage to protect the guilty without siccing her on an innocent?

Only luck and lack of manpower had kept the feds from finding the rifle he'd ditched down a mine shaft. If K. D. Wildmoon was as scrappy as Tate said, she'd shinny down into the shaft herself at the first whiff of a clue.

Nobody would give it to her. Only Josh knew, and Bronc trusted his kid brother with their dad's life.

Bronc stared into a sky milky with clouds. If he'd stayed in school, this never would have happened. On the other hand, without his paychecks, the ranch would have long since been sold.

Abruptly, Bronc lost patience with her skulking.

"You didn't inherit your people's stealth, Ms. Wildmoon."

She didn't move or speak. Hell. His shoulders ached from hefting the colt and wrestling it to the bottle. His hand ached from the fairy-fine stitching he'd done on its neck. He didn't have the energy for much of a squabble.

He watched her hair follow the wind. She stood stone still, eyes steady as a she-cat's as she watched him through the fire. "Boots on the ground at four A.M., Ms. Wildmoon."

"I'll be ready."

Her lips remained open, but before she started prying, Bronc forced his boots to walk away from the fire, back into the dark.

FIVE

Starlight sifted from the cone's peak, losing all brightness by the time it reached her. A black glimmer fell on the living, insinuating weight across her ankles. Pulses, thick and carnal, kept her waiting and ashamed. She looked down. Tawny eyes glowed, vowing guilt was a small price to pay.

A match scratched, propane belched into flame. Under the covers, Kasey hugged her ribs and scuttled lower in the bunk. The torrid dream wafted away as a wet nose probed her armpit.

Bronc McDermitt. Wild horses. Gold Canyon.

Got it. She had the who, what, where of her story. The *why* and *how* made her brain burn. Too groggy for dream analysis, Kasey pulled the pillow over her head.

"You said four a.m. It's only . . ." As a yawn stretched the sentence, Kasey focused on her travel alarm, then rubbed her cheek against the pillow. ". . . three-fifty. And cold."

Metal pinged and a scoop grated. The wet nose returned. At the sound of whining, she raised her eyelashes. The yellow-eyed dog who'd slashed her palm panted fishy-flavored breath.

"Get away." She burrowed beneath the blankets. "You don't even like me, so don't kiss up."

"I'm making coffee. None of those lazy cusses wants theirs before five."

Kasey sat up, pulling the blanket around her like a shawl. Wind and rain had churned her dreams, but now it sounded as if the storm had passed.

She blinked the cowboy's blurry image into focus. Enough blue chambray to stretch over the ribs of a covered wagon spanned those shoulders, and he wore no hat. As he passed under the bare bulb, McDermitt's hair glinted tar-black and crisp.

As he walked her way, Kasey pulled her knees up under her long red jersey. Her left hand tugged down the hem. Her right gripped the blanket and pain arced across her palm.

"Hand still sore?" he asked.

"It's fine." She released the blanket, rippled her fingers in flamboyant display, and didn't even whimper.

Clearly unconvinced, McDermitt stood next to her bunk.

"I could take a look." Spirals of steam rose from the pottery mug he pushed toward her.

"Smells great." She took it with her left hand and made her voice breezy. "Do you have a doctor out here?"

"No doc and no phone. You get an infection raging, and we'd have to load you in the chopper and fly you to Gully, where there's an airfield, a phone, and a fax. He added, "But no cappuccino."

"Savages." Even though she was the butt of his unsmiling joke, she had to admire humor that rose before the sun.

"From Gully, you'll be flown by AirCare to the medical center in Reno."

"No, I won't." She touched her necklace. Playtime was

over and she needed her primary prop to be K. D. Wildmoon. Sometime around two o'clock, she'd blamed the absent beads for her inability to sleep and retrieved them from the bathroom.

Reaching up to touch them made her wince. McDermitt noticed.

"You gonna let me take a look?"

"You know—" She stopped. Women who protested they could by-golly take care of themselves sounded prissy. Besides, Tate had declared McDermitt was as good as a vet. "I'd really appreciate that."

Kasey offered her palm for inspection. The bed dipped as he settled beside her and she forced herself to concentrate on the tin coffeepot shimmying on the stove.

This time, his hands didn't shake. His fingertips pressed the area around the rip, exploring with a sureness that made it hard to ponder how bad that overcooked coffee would taste.

"You should've washed up with soap and warm water and covered it with a soft dressing, not this." His forearm supported the length of hers. She noticed the press lines on his shirt sleeve and his hair, wet and smelling of soap—*at four o'clock in the morning.* Then he zipped off the Band-Aid.

"Ow!" She yipped.

"Looks fine." He tilted her palm side to side, judging the swelling, then awarded her shoulder a pat that might have rocked a horse.

Just like she was one of the guys, Kasey reasoned, and though that was fine, the movement reminded her she wore nothing under the jersey.

"Use the gauze and tape I left out in the bathroom. And wear gloves," he ordered. "Then let's get moving. We'll eat in the saddle."

"Thanks," Kasey managed. It came out grudging and

ungrateful. More than his commands, she resented the fact that this man, hatless and near, was a major distraction.

"Kasey? I'm not bluffin'." He called her mind back. "Let this get infected and you're out of here. I'll conduct the tour and help you get what you need, but I won't babysit. Got it?"

With a suddenness that nearly capsized the hunk, he stood, called for the dog, and left the cabin.

She kicked off the covers and almost knocked her head on the upper bunk as she stood. So what if he'd called her Kasey? There was no way on earth she'd call a grown man Bronc.

§ §

SUN-PATCHED MOUNTAINS ARCHED on the horizon. Kasey slipped a map from her saddlebag and unfolded it.

"Careful," Bronc warned. He rode beside her and his horse's ears flattened as the paper crackled. "China's gonna have your chin knockin' holes in your chest."

For all McDermitt's warnings, China showed no inclination to buck. The gray planted each hoof deliberately, as if he expected an earthquake.

Now, the horse bobbed his head and pulled, reluctant to approach her abandoned rental car.

McDermitt had to be irritated that they'd backtracked for her laptop computer before riding toward the Buck ranch, but he gave no sign.

"Do you mind?" she'd asked.

He'd merely shrugged. The man had the communication skills of a rock.

"If we're going to be together for ten days, you're going to have to tell me what you're thinking."

"When I'm riled, you'll know it."

That was the last she'd heard, since sunrise.

Pointedly, Kasey snapped a crease out of the map. China

plodded on without flicking an ear and McDermitt pretended not to notice.

"Calico Range," she muttered.

From this scatter of peaks, they'd ride to White Wells, where Bronc guaranteed she'd see a band of mustangs. Then they'd cross onto reservation land to interview Becky and Calvin Buck, then Shannon Delaney.

Once he'd mentioned her last name, Kasey had figured out that the Shannon of McDermitt's conversation with Jack Flynn was the foreman of the Diamond Q, a witness quoted in the court transcripts.

China shied as Bronc lifted a hand to point.

Far off, a rider and cattle circled the red Taurus. Bronc extended his mount's trot, and China bolted after. Kasey kept her seat and pulled the gelding to a head-tossing stop. She reined him in circles, using hands and legs to give him a stern lecture, and hoped Bronc didn't notice their battle of wills.

She needn't have worried. As she rode into earshot, Kasey decided Bronc and the cowgirl wouldn't have noticed if she'd fallen facedown in the sagebrush half a mile back.

In the shade of his hat brim, Kasey saw him smile before the other woman even spoke.

"Hey, Bronc."

The Diamond Q brand marked one thigh of short. fringed chaps slightly darker than the Rapunzel-long braid that followed the cowgirl's spine before brushing her horse's hindquarters.

As she talked, the woman kept the cattle gathered. While the horse pivoted on his haunches, the rider swayed with unconscious grace.

So this was Shannon Delaney. Flynn's jabber yesterday had led Kasey to expect someone coarse and crusty. Everything about Shannon Delaney—her palomino horse, her hair and skin—was smooth and golden.

"What are you doing all the way out here?" Bronc asked.

"Nice to see you, too." Shannon's warm jibe was underlined by an instant's creasing around her eyes.

Then the lines vanished. Kasey would bet the woman had ridden the high desert most every day and never used a fingerful of sunscreen. It made her doubt everything she'd read—and written—about the ozone layer.

Like a snapping dog, the palomino lunged at the cattle. They stood still, waiting to be ordered elsewhere.

"I got an empty cattle truck parked at Sheep Camp, but I saw these two with late calves"—Shannon gestured—"and decided I'd best not crowd 'em, just bring 'em along slow. So, I unloaded Jim," she said, giving the palomino's neck a pat, "and here I am."

Kasey watched McDermitt nod. He seemed about to introduce her, but it was a false alarm.

"Heard you rubbed Radich the wrong way. Again," Bronc said.

" 'Sakes, lover, he's dreamed of seeing you, me, and Buck behind bars since we were in sixth grade." Shannon's palomino shifted, bumping McDermitt's horse. "Thought he was halfway home and now you've busted loose."

Kasey considered the calfless cow. She took out her notebook, set her molars hard, and wrote about the cow's brindle coloring and the mudline running along her side.

"Lover," was it?

Not that she cared about Bronc's love life. She was only curious about the identity of "Buck." Was he her uncle, Calvin Buck? Or another nicknamed cowboy?

She didn't ask. A breeze ruffled pages and China tensed. She rubbed his neck, stowed the pad, and waited. Experience had taught her she could learn a lot through silence.

When Shannon Delaney turned, Kasey saw McDermitt's face over the cowgirl's shoulder. His expression looked a little queasy.

Kasey squared her shoulders. Darkly aware she'd never ride well enough to even parody the cowgirl's grace, she made the first move.

"K. D. Wildmoon." As she extended her hand, China shied. Damn. Kasey reined him around, trying to bridge the gap. Arm still outreached, she failed. Damn it to hell. She wasn't used to looking foolish, especially before someone who seemed to enjoy it.

"This your car?" Shannon asked.

"Yes—"

"*You* make friends fast." Shannon's laugh accompanied a nod at the bullet hole in the car's back window.

McDermitt stood in his stirrups to get a better view.

"Hell." One long, denimed leg swung down from his saddle. "You didn't say they hit you."

Bronc ground-tied his horse. At his ringing stride, Kasey realized he wore spurs.

"They were aiming at the colt," Kasey explained.

Bronc walked to the front of the car and ran a hand over the windshield.

"Then I'd say they'd been drinking," Shannon observed.

"They had," Kasey agreed.

Shannon and McDermitt stared as if there was something this dumb city girl just didn't *get*. China struck out with a rear hoof as the palomino sniffed his tail.

"Careful of Jim," Shannon said. "I married three Jims and annulled 'em all. This is the only one who's stuck by me."

Kasey gave a token smile as McDermitt stalked around like a watchdog scenting an intruder.

"*This* is no prank." Bronc frowned. "We've got to ride back and tell Tate what's up."

About time, Kasey thought, but she kept her features serene.

"I already have." She lowered her voice. "Help me understand, Mr. McDermitt, why you'd consider it a prank if they'd hit 'only' the mustang."

McDermitt stared at a patch of ground between his braced boots. Except for the steady swelling of his chest, he stayed still as if he hadn't heard.

Sulphur fouled the air as Shannon struck a match. Cigarette lit, she snapped her wrist and let the spent match fall to the desert floor.

"Quick work," Shannon congratulated. "Looks like you got him green-broke already." Through a veil of smoke, she squinted at Kasey.

"Go to hell," McDermitt sighed. Studying the ground, he walked in widening circles around the Taurus.

"Shannon Delaney, right?" Kasey confirmed. "Owner of the Diamond Q ranch?"

"Foreman," Shannon corrected, closing her teeth on the cigarette.

"Foreman," Kasey said while McDermitt squatted in front of the Taurus.

Kasey recalled Shannon had testified as an expert witness at Bronc's trial, detailing the destruction caused by wild horses that roamed their adjoining ranches.

While half her mind stayed on China, bunched and nervous beneath her, Kasey stripped off her gloves and tucked their cuffs into her back pocket.

When we were in sixth grade, Shannon had said, so she was McDermitt's age. Nearly thirty. No girl, certainly, but still young to run a ranch.

Kasey watched Shannon pick a flake of tobacco from a lower lip that could have been sculpted with collagen, but probably wasn't. Then she noticed the oval glittering at the woman's waist.

Shannon Delaney looked like the perfect mate for McDermitt. Not only did she run the neighboring spread—always a selling point in Western movies—she was gorgeous, smart, and a rodeo athlete.

"Is that a trophy belt buckle?" Kasey asked.

"She's not just nosy," McDermitt's voice came muffled from where he lay on his belly, reaching under the car. "She's a reporter."

Bronc stood and slapped his dusty hat on his jeans. He waited for Kasey to thank him, then gave up and surveyed the scrub. "I'm writing a story about the wild horse—"

"*Wild.*" Shannon hooked a leg around her saddle horn in a contortion that shouldn't have looked natural. "They're just trash horses set loose to feed themselves. Good for nothing but chicken feed and fertilizer." Shannon rested her elbow on the knee of her chaps. "Write that and see what you hear from the Sierra Club."

"It's not my job to please the Sierra Club. Or the Cattlemen's Association or"—Kasey nodded at the rifle butt jutting from Shannon's saddle scabbard—"the NRA."

Shannon's accusation put Kasey at ease. Through repetition, the charge had become familiar ground. Many people wanted to believe journalists were part of an international plot. Kasey rested her palm on her saddle cantle and leaned back. It hardly hurt at all.

"Maybe not, but it's no secret the media backs tree-huggers, not ranchers. Take Bronc, for instance." Shannon faltered as

McDermitt waved her off.

"Not me." Bronc approached a stand of mountain mahogany and dug at the bark with his pocket knife. "I'm out of this, girls."

Kasey didn't let him end the one battle she was winning.

"If you believe in a media conspiracy," Kasey said, "it's because you've never worked in a newsroom. Two reporters can't agree on where to have lunch, let alone how to run the government."

"Oh, *ain't* she sassy," Shannon muttered, then McDermitt caught her attention. "Whatcha got, Bronc?"

He strode closer, rolling something in his palm.

"Worthless little slug of lead." He caught his horse's reins. "We'll be out to see your spread, Shannon. We'll go by the Bucks' first, though."

"And your folks."

"They got in, then?"

"Day before yesterday. Josh rode over to see me." McDermitt bumped back his hat brim.

"Yeah?" While he studied Shannon, searching for something left unsaid, Kasey recognized his expression.

In Los Angeles, she'd seen a hardened gangster, skin as warm with scars and prison tattoos, arrive at an accident scene. The sight of his brother's twisted car laid his fear bare, exposed for anyone to see.

Quick as he felt her stare, McDermitt covered up, cursing K. D. Wildmoon as an emotional vampire whose eyes latched on to signs of weakness and drained the feelings right out of you.

"My kid brother," he explained, then slid his hand between the black's belly and the cinch.

Pretending to check the fit gave him an excuse to avoid her soul-sucking eyes. The cinch lay smooth and snug. And why not? His life was nothing but saddling, unsaddling, riding, and roping. With a little left over for family.

"Josh have much to say?"

"Not much," Shannon answered, though he still faced his horse. "Champ was with him. They were just playin'."

"I'm not sure fifteen-year-olds play." Not after waking with a four-cell Kell Light glaring in your eyes. Not after being hustled home to face your weeping mother. Not after sawing a bowie knife over your own tender wrist.

" 'Course fifteen-year-olds play, and now he's got this obsession with"—Shannon's cigarette left a blue trail as she gestured—"potato cannons."

"The hell you say." His gust of laughter was followed by hope.

At the creak of saddle leather, one of the red calves bawled. Shannon did, too. He knew what she'd say and wished she wouldn't, not in front of Kasey.

"You gotta quit blaming yourself, Bronc."

Yeah, yeah, yeah. He pulled down the shades in his mind and pretended she hadn't said a word.

"If you talk to 'em, Shan, say we'll pay 'em a call in a couple days. Meantime, study on this: you're one of the ranchers she'll interview." He jerked a thumb toward Kasey. That'd get her back up all over again. "If you don't behave when the tape recorder's rolling, you'll make us all look bad."

Kasey fiddled with her necklace, looking chagrined. He figured she'd let herself forget a thinking man lurked beneath Bronc McDermitt's aw-shucks manner.

"I can show you some range that looks bad, and it's not from overgrazing cattle, either," Shannon told her, wanting to get another lick in.

"That would be great," Kasey answered, "if I were doing a

longer piece, but this is just a splashy feature about the BOW mustang program. Controversy will be a minor point."

You'd have to be blind as a post hole not to see Kasey was lying. Shannon smirked a little, matching his own disbelief. Bronc wished he'd never screwed himself out of Shannon's friendship. Shannon used to have sweet dove-gray eyes that matched the rest of her. A couple of tumbles from him had turned them anxious. His apologies and backsliding had turned them sly. Each time she called him "lover," he winced.

"I still need cooperation from the experts." Kasey clearly didn't know what to make of their silence.

Her p.s. sounded hollow and Shannon made sure Kasey knew it.

"About this." Shannon tipped her belt buckle so sun danced on sculpted silver. "I won it barrel racing. Yes, ma'am, I did."

Shannon spoke over Kasey's approval. "Being from L.A., you might not know the awful reputation us barrel racers have with cowboys."

Shannon brushed the end of her braid across her lips, pumped up her I'm-a-tramp pout, and made sure he didn't miss it.

"Hey, Bronc, have you heard this one?" Shannon tilted her head and he felt sure he didn't want to, not here and now. "What's a barrel racer's idea of safe sex?" She waited through a couple beats of silence. "Give up? Hooking the tailgate on the pickup truck!"

Shannon chortled, head back like a coyote, while he jammed a boot in the stirrup and remounted.

In a flurry, her palomino jumped to land beside Rook. The black shuddered, but obeyed Bronc's orders to stand.

"Shannon, you're lucky that pony doesn't bust your ass."

"No luck about it. Just pure skill, Bronc. Quit pursing your lips like a preacher's wife and give me that bullet. *I'll* report the shootin' match to Tate and you can be on your way."

"No need." Bronc patted the pocket where he'd stashed it. If he planned to rustle cash out of the feds, he needed hard evidence. "You just be ready when we come callin'."

Jim jumped at the prick of Shannon's spurs, then gathered the cattle in one swoop.

"Nice meetin' you, Ms. Wildmoon. You come by 'long about dinner time, end of the week. Branding'll be done and you can down a *cerveza* and sink your teeth into a few calf fries."

Bronc shook his head and glanced at Kasey. Her polite half-smile said she had no idea Shannon had offered her a plate of testicles.

Shannon's smirk said Kasey already had a taste for them. He held up two fingers, cautioning her not to make a third joke at his expense.

"Don't push your luck, *lover*," he cautioned. Shannon's snipe about Kasey having him green-broke had rubbed him like a burr for about twenty minutes now.

Shannon didn't apologize, just wheeled poor Jim like a stick horse and herded her cows, getting the last word even when she said nothing.

"She'll make an interesting interview." Kasey pretended Shannon hadn't given her a run for her money.

"Yeah, you got along like two pups in a blanket," he said. "Let's go."

She had her godforsaken computer and Tate would send someone for the car. His job was riding.

If only this bullet didn't mean all bets were off on Kasey's safety. Still, she'd be okay if he kept her in the dark. A cowboy could lead a pretty little mare through fire if he kept her blindfolded.

He snuck a quick look. Profile pasted against blue sky, she looked proud. Too elegant to be involved in something dirty as horse-killing.

If things got hot, he'd make Tate pull her out.

Bronc touched his heels to Rook's sides. One thing he could do was get past Abner's stronghold before sundown.

No telling what the old coot had booby-trapped since Bronc's arrest. Feds snapping up a buckaroo had confirmed every conspiracy theory seething in the old man's brain. But Abner owned the land that formed the shortcut to Scolding Rock Reservation and the Buck ranch. Bronc had permission to use it and he planned to.

Riding by his side, Kasey matched her gray's gait to Rook's. Her hair was stuffed up inside a flat-brimmed black toreador hat. It would've looked phony on just about anyone else, but the stampede strap crossing her cheek, and the ends blowing back across her neck, made him imagine her dressed for dancing, a black velvet bow tied around her throat.

All part of the act, no doubt.

Bronc concentrated on the view between Rook's ears. Tate had said Kasey wrote hard-edged stories and Bronc would bet that took more than skill. *Fraud* was the term that crossed his mind. Kasey probably knew more than she was letting on.

Bronc changed leads, sending Rook off at an angle. Her horse followed. Yeah, she was set on turning Bronc McDermitt and China into a couple of well-mannered geldings, all right.

Bronc sat down hard on Rook. The black halted and Bronc's arm snaked out. Before China could pass, Bronc's fingers closed near the bit. The gray squealed and tossed his head, more surprised than hurt. Then Bronc shifted his grip to Kasey's rein arm.

"You just stay put, Ms. Wildmoon. Bronc felt every tendon

in her arm go hard, but he held on. "I want to know who's been shootin' at you."

For an instant her anger tripped over puzzlement. "Those boys—"

"No way. The kids had .22s. I saw them."

He used his size, looming with narrowed eyes, to look threatening. She tried to set up. On foot, she'd be fixin' to defend herself. On horseback, she didn't have the leverage to do more than smack him, and it made her furious.

"Just settle down," he said. "And tell me why the bullet that went through your car is the same kind that blasted through those horse skulls out on my ranch."

Six

Right at the gap, where Bronc kept the manacle of his fingers gentle on her wrist, Kasey jerked loose.

"You tell *me* who did the shooting, McDermitt. Besides those kids, only one vehicle was following me."

Between her words and his next heartbeat, Bronc wondered who was leading who through fire. Blindfolded. Kasey's sharp mind had already done an analysis and concluded the blood trail led back to him.

But her brown eyes didn't accuse him. She wanted him to convince her that her conclusion ran contrary to the facts. That ounce of faith took a half-hitch in his tongue.

Her hat had fallen back on its strap. She took it off, looking thoughtful, and her hair came tumbling down.

"The only gun in your truck was a Winchester," she said, "and you had no motive to shoot me."

"That's right. We hadn't been introduced."

A flick of her eyelashes was the only indication his jibe had hit home.

"Not to mention you're probably such a stud with a rifle, *you* would have drilled me faster'n I could spit and holler howdy," she drawled. "Right?"

"What?" He guffawed like a mule.

"My roommate is a John Wayne fan. Cookie," she clarified. "Some of that awful dialogue stuck to my brain cells, even though the man couldn't act his way through 'The Itsy Bitsy Spider.'"

Her loose hair and smug smile left him mute, but if he didn't talk quick, she'd turn all business.

"You don't like the Duke?"

"I'm more of a Kevin Costner–cowboy kind of fan."

"The hell you say."

Just a second ago, she'd been watching him like he had a chance at holding her. And he was a far cry from a scrawny Costner cowboy.

Faster'n I could spit and holler howdy. Bronc reined in his laughter, but, God, it felt good. Jokes had been in short supply in the Washoe County jail.

"Okay." The last chuckle left him. "So, you don't believe I was plinking at you. Thanks."

"You're welcome." She set her teeth against her lip. "But that's not all."

"I didn't figure it would be."

"I've been manhandled by worse men than you—" She broke off.

Bronc blanked his face. *Manhandled.*

"You didn't hurt me and I'm sure you didn't mean to, and I know how to take care of myself. Both my parents are cops. I've had some instruction." She looked up from the hatband she'd nearly picked loose from the hat. "Is any of this sinking in?"

"Who manhandled you?"

"That's not the point."

"Your dad take care of him?"

"No doubt." She shook her head in irritation. "I couldn't file charges if I didn't want to go public. Even small-timers like me have paparazzi stalkers, and the kind of stories I do—well, the buzz says K. D. Wildmoon is tough. If word spread that I'm not, I'd be out of work."

Again. He didn't press for details. He'd bet her cop-dad had handled the situation just fine, but thinking of that bullet made him worry over her belief she could take care of herself.

Kasey's hair shimmered blue-black as she plaited it. Her right hand still moved stiff. She pulled her hat back on before the braid unraveled, then raised one brow.

He liked making her wait, but he was damn poor at it.

"You want me to keep my hands off. Until you say otherwise."

She took it for teasing. "I'm agog, Mr. McDermitt." She put a hand over her shirt front as if pledging allegiance. *"Agog,* at your conceit, but yes, basically, that's it."

He nodded, and set Rook to trotting.

He'd like to outwait her. He was patient with dogs, horses, and usually with women. But this one wanted to play boss, and he was the foreman of this outfit. He could convince her of that and make her like it, if he could just sidle past that buttoned-down sex appeal and drive her out of control. He imagined her eyes dazed and full of him, her arms raised to hold him.

All the high-tech clutter in her saddlebags would be useless then. He could hardly wait.

It was McDermitt who found the first water hole, but something had told her he was thirsty and hinted water could be found over the next ridge.

Kasey held China's reins while he stretched down to drink. Ten minutes ago, McDermitt had angled east, followed a crack in the desert floor until it was crowded with wispy weeds, then grass, then a spring. And Kasey had felt it coming.

The horses drew noisily as Kasey admired McDermitt's skill. He'd ridden to a pool that was clear and pure—free of giardia and other internal parasites. In an emergency, she wanted this sort of partner, one who could find fresh water in a wasteland.

Mark Savage, on the other hand, couldn't find a decent taco in Los Angeles. *Los Angeles,* for crying out loud. Once, she'd heard him ask his chauffeur—*Wait.*

"I didn't tell Shannon I was from Los Angeles." Kasey turned to McDermitt. As always, he'd been staring across the sagebrush. She stepped between him and the horizon. "When she talked about barrel racers, she said, 'Being from L.A.,' I might not know their reputation."

"Naw, I let that drop."

"No, *you* said I was a reporter and I talked about working in a newsroom. Neither of us mentioned L.A."

McDermitt rubbed the back of his neck. "Glad we got that settled."

Kasey led the gray a few steps from the water and knelt to check his hooves for stones.

"It might not matter. It's just the sort of thing I notice."

"Shannon didn't used to be so—cantankerous."

Kasey glanced up from the hoof balanced on her knee. McDermitt's tone said he would have used a stronger word if Shannon weren't a friend.

"Ever since she took over running the place, after her dad died, the owner's been baiting her. If she has it running in the black by the end of next year, the owner—a Las Vegas orthodontist—will make her a full partner. Fifty-fifty."

A frisson of nerves alerted her. Kasey touched her necklace, but it lay still and cool. Knowing Shannon Delaney wanted that partnership, big time, wasn't superstition. It was instinct. Good cops had it and so did the best reporters.

China swung his head around and whuffled her neck with wet lips. With the backs of her fingers, she stroked the soft skin between his nostrils.

"No tickling, big boy." She set down his hoof.

"That's a good thing, checking China's hooves. Could save you some walking. Lets him get to know you."

As the simple praise swelled through her, Kasey cleared her throat. "I'm not totally devoid of kindness, McDermitt."

"Then use my name."

She didn't want to. Nor did she want to explain her technique of handling forced intimacy with men. Call them by their last names and you were a teammate, one of the guys.

Besides, though the cutline under Cookie's photo had identified him as "Gabriel McDermitt," she hadn't heard anyone call him that.

Kasey waved away a gnat. She rubbed her nose. His easy blue stare made her restless.

"Your name. Let's see," she mused, "that'd be 'Lover'?"

Kasey felt her mistake as he grinned, then gave a laugh that cracked his make-my-day glower. And curled her toes.

"No?" She pressed on. "Well, then, what's your mom call you?"

" 'Bronc, honey'. "

"Okay." If she kept resisting, he'd make too much of it. "I'll do it, but I don't like it."

"I bet you say that to all the guys."

He wasn't a bit funny. She pulled China close enough to remount. As her leg swung over the saddle, she felt the first pull of muscle strain and caught his sympathetic look.

She didn't want sympathy. McDermitt must learn he was

dealing with a professional. An achy place where saddle struck skin didn't count when sundown meant one day down and only eight left to get her story.

"Lead on, Bronc, honey."

&s &s

THE EXPLOSION CHANGED BRONC'S MIND about introducing her to Abner Bengochea, mad gunsmith of the American West.

"Get back! Right out the way we came." Bronc's voice was pitched so low and calm that for a minute, Kasey didn't worry.

"Can you back that horse up, or do I have to jump off and do it for you?"

"He's backing!"

"Quiet. You're gonna have your hands full if you panic him. Get down on his neck. That's it. Get all over him. Let him know he's okay and keep backing."

They'd both heard the sputtering, but Kasey was scanning the ground, still searching for rattlesnakes, when Bronc shouted. "Fuse between those rocks, not—Hang on!"

A fountain of dirt sprayed from the bomb.

China reared and came down with his legs braced like a four-poster bed. He trembled, but he didn't buck, even when Rook's hindquarters struck him in the chest.

"Good boy." Being left afoot in this minefield would compromise her air of competence beyond repair.

"It's me, you loco old coot!" Bronc bellowed.

"Who are you yelling at? It's mined, or if someone's there, it's radio controlled."

"Radio controlled, my ass." Bronc slapped at his saddle-bags, then peered inside them. "He's there," he muttered, then returned to roaring. "It's Bronc McDermitt, you lunatic!"

"What are you looking for, McDermitt?"

"Binoculars. I knew we should've brought the mule."

"I've got some." Kasey slipped a tiny pair from her pack.

"Never mind."

Because he'd convinced her to travel light, without the mule and, apparently, his binoculars, McDermitt was acting noble.

"Bronc, *take* them."

He gave her a hard look, as if he found it significant that only exasperation had made her use his name.

"Shrew."

At least she thought that was what he said. Her ears were still ringing from the explosion.

"It was just an M-80." Bronc's rein hand soothed Rook while his other dwarfed the binoculars. "He buys 'em over the hill. Fireworks're legal on the reservation." He glanced at her, keeping his explanation quiet, settling the horses. "Like a cherry bomb, you know? He used to do this with a trip wire attached to sandpaper, which rubbed a match head and lit the fuse. Gives you plenty of time to get away."

"Or gets your confidence up before he kills you." Kasey shifted in the saddle. She wanted out of here, now. "This isn't part of my story and I'm not going closer. You're a fool if you do."

"Abner's pretty much all bluff." He lowered the binoculars and really looked at her then. "Are you scared?"

"You're damned right I am. Fear, McDermitt, is a survival instinct. Normal people experience fear when explosions detonate practically under their—Look." She pointed at a pinwheel, spinning and spewing sparks in a spindly cottonwood tree.

"All just warnings," Bronc said. "Abner fancies himself an antigovernment survivalist. He lives alone and listens to a lot of talk radio. Believes the government'll swoop down in black helicopters and take his guns any day now. Custom guns, like the Storm Hammer, are his livelihood."

"Okay, and for that reason maybe he figures into the story. I'll give him a ring. I'm sure he's got a telephone."

"No."

"A prison record then. Sorry, but there's no way I'm sticking around."

"What's got you so spooked, Kasey?"

His trust-me tone should have annoyed her, but Kasey looked at Rook standing there hipshot and drowsy, and she realized Bronc's voice was designed to soothe. It almost worked.

"When we've got a little more time, I'll tell you a story."

"I got time," Bronc dismounted and handed her Rook's reins. He didn't depend on ground-tying his horse as he had before. "I'm going to walk in."

Kasey swallowed. "Why are you so determined to go where you're obviously not wanted?"

"Abner's not only old, like I said, he's a paraplegic. In a wheelchair since he flipped his jeep on the playa. Said he listened to Scolding Rock moan all night long until some woman coming from Gully with groceries found him. I like to check on him."

Kasey felt sheepish and small, but she owed Bronc a warning. This cowboy probably had no idea what explosives did to a man.

"Short version of the story, okay?" She stayed mounted, looking down on McDermitt, afoot. "One of my first assignments in L.A., when I was still with the newspaper, was to cover a disturbance in Jacinto Terrace, a rotten neighborhood where a group of small-scale anarchists called Rand's Family was having a standoff with Social Services and then the police.

"Word was there were explosives and children inside, so I followed the bomb squad and the SWAT guys out there.

"On that hot summer night, June bugs had pattered against the screens of evacuated houses in the neighborhood. Cops joked and smoked, soothing each other just like you had the horses, until the hostage negotiator arrived.

"When he got there, it turned out to be Jim Pinto, a guy my parents knew. He'd been to our house for cookouts, stuff like that." Kasey's throat tightened. "He congratulated me on my newspaper job and then started walking up to the door, without a bullhorn, just talking like he'd come to borrow the lawn mower, and one of those"—Kasey motioned to the mound of dirt where the cherry bomb had exploded—"went off. He kept going, even when somebody yelled from the house."

Rook rolled his bit. Bronc crossed his arms. If he spoke, his words were overshadowed by Kasey's memories of that rusty voice at Jacinto Terrace. An educated voice, she'd thought at the time.

"A man shouted, 'That was just foreplay, asshole!' and then Jim went up. My face hit the street. The explosion had that much force. Then there was fire." She shook her head.

"And your friend didn't make it." Bronc squinted up at her.

Jim had been black, crisp, the inside of his mouth an ungodly pink as he called for Nancy. And no one, even later, knew who she was.

Kasey took a long breath, trying to clear the charred stench from her nostrils. "No," she told Bronc, "he didn't."

"Okay. Promise I won't make you do that again. The real firepower's under the house—old, sweating dynamite—no way in hell I'm going into the basement."

"Why does he live there? Why do they let him?"

"Who's they, Hollywood? You're in the wild West, where we let folks do as they please, no matter how wrongheaded they are."

Hollywood. Had he called her *Hollywood*? She wasn't gaudy, flashy, or phony. Kasey fumed, until she noticed the satisfied firming of his mouth. McDermitt didn't do much by accident. A nickname that corny had to be a distraction.

"Abner knows the dynamite's too unstable to move and he likes it that way. He figures when the feds come for him, it'll go up like the Fourth of July. He'll die here, instead of in some veterans' hospital."

Kasey considered the distance to the wide front porch with wheelchair ramps on each side. It was about a city block away.

"Hey, Abner, you old renegade." Bronc strode forward, eyes down, navigating a path impossible for her to see. "C'mon out and be sociable. Man goes to jail and can't get anyone to say howdy, is that how it is?"

"... a ranger?"

Kasey jerked straight in her saddle, startling both horses. The thin voice came from inside. China snorted and stamped and Kasey kneaded his withers, but she didn't talk.

"Naw, just my new girlfriend, Abner, and your cussed firework display scared her a little."

Apparently, the men were going to chat awhile. Since her trembling hands were making China skittish, Kasey dismounted and sat, back propped against a tumble of boulders. She should have checked for snakes and she really wanted a sip from the canteen hanging from her saddle, but her legs were shaking too badly to stand up again.

She pulled her hat brim low over her eyes, seeking shelter from the glare and the sight of Bronc walking into ambush. She held China's reins in one hand, Rook's in the other. The horses dozed, casting a little shade. She sighed. It had been a long hot time since four A.M.

Kasey forced her eyes open. Bronc still stood by the house. Now he propped one boot on a porch step. He looked down and his Stetson moved as if he were nodding.

She'd close her eyes, just until Bronc came back. The horses had no interest in wandering away. Rook rolled his bit. Over and over he rolled it, lulling himself to sleep like a child sucking his thumb.

As Kasey dozed, a feeling, like the plucking of harp strings, strummed through her. Behind her eyelids, there flashed a vision too keen for a dream.

"I thought you'd be more clever." Black braids, flushed cheeks, and impatient brown eyes marked the girl resting her chin on crossed arms. The waft and waver of her white buckskin dress indicated she was floating. Nose-to-nose with the apparition, Kasey stirred.

"Heed me, Wild Moon. You won't get what we need by pretending I'm nothing but a dream."

Kasey roused enough to wet her lips. Weird dream. Something in it reminded her of her necklace, throbbing now like a second heartbeat.

"Last night's dream was prophetic. Those golden eyes, that irresistible, guilty lust, remember?" The impish maiden drifted upright, leaned against the neck of a silver-blue Appaloosa, and plaited its mane with idle interest.

Kasey recognized the mystical stallion who'd appeared to her in the desert.

"Listen and learn, Wild Moon." The maiden snapped her fingers. *"You are smart like your mother, like me, but we all share the same weakness. That's part of Fox's game, and we play until we conquer him or confine him."*

Kasey fought her heavy eyelids, trying to wake. She didn't need lecturing from her imagination.

"Why must you be so very dense with signs?" The maiden tossed her braids in exasperation.

"That first day in the desert, Fox was so weak we could have

defeated him in a blink. But you couldn't be bothered to believe the necklace." As she stamped her moccasined foot, the shell-studded buckskin dress tinkled. *"I thought you'd be different from Letty, more like Blue Rain."*

Behind her the Appaloosa stallion pawed the desert floor. Silver with blue roan spots. Was he "Blue Rain?"

"You modern women won't heed visions and you're worse than most. But, since you have a passion for proof"—the apparition giggled, and brandished three fingers—*"I'll give you three predictions."*

"First, you'll be accused of talking to horses. Next, you'll be welcomed by my wild desert band and third, you'll embrace the desert's greatest gift. You'll learn to be a water-giver and thirstslaker for all creatures." A rattling like beans in a gourd, a whiff of something green and herbal, and the maiden vanished.

"Thirst?" Kasey pronounced the word and lifted one eyelid.

Across the desert minefield, Bronc sat on the steps of the hermit's house. Sunlight glinted on metal spokes behind him. A wheelchair. *That* was real.

"I'm a journalist, so I do need proof." Kasey rubbed her face, then muttered, "And I am talking to myself."

Warmth thrummed through her. The necklace throbbed as a breeze whispered past, carrying the voice.

"More proof than your necklace shocking you with small lightning each time Fox comes near? More proof than shrilling flutes? Than me?"

Kasey opened her eyes and stretched. To hell with this. "Hey, China, hey, Rook. You had a nice long drink, and *you're* not hallucinating, right?"

Still woozy, Kasey stood, lifted her canteen from the saddle, and deliberately rubbed her sore palm over the canteen's khaki covering. The twinge of pain, smell of hot horseflesh, and trill of birdsong from the cottonwood tree grounded her in the reality that was the Scolding Rock desert, Bleek County, Nevada, U.S.A., planet Earth.

Once she reminded herself exactly where she was, Kasey looked around, then closed her eyes for one, simple test. "If you're real, appear. Right here, right now."

Silence, but Kasey remembered the whirling, flame-bright cone that had appeared before her old Toyota, the first night she'd seen the spectral horse and rider.

Kasey sipped from her canteen, then screwed the top back on. It must be nearly dinnertime. Bronc had promised they'd stop once they navigated the pass. They didn't want to arrive at the Bucks' just in time for dinner, so they'd spend this first night camped on reservation land. The tribal police weren't likely to notice them, or roust Bronc McDermitt, if they did.

Renewed shrilling, the song of the bone flute, startled the horses, but Kasey clamped her hand hard on China's reins and Rook stopped after a few steps. Eyes rolled white, the black nickered over his shoulder and she snagged him. As before, the whistle heralded the vision.

"Back again?" Kasey tried to muster a tone of acid skepticism. Before, the maiden had appeared as a watery image. Now, she was a vivid teenager whose radiance fell somewhere between angel and imp. Her Appaloosa stallion was heavily muscled beneath silver skin strewn with indigo spots.

Whoever had spun this apparition had borrowed from a mishmash of Indian cultures. Appaloosas were Nez Percé. The white leather gown appeared to be a Plains creation. The otherworldly

"Spirit, Wild Moon, I'm a spirit." The voice chided.

Who. What. When. Where. Why. Motive. Opportunity.

Kasey doubted her daily guidelines were up to the task of analyzing this mystical pair. But she tried.

"Who are you?"

"I already told you: Blue Rain." She wrinkled her nose. *"Actually, I've gone by many names. White Shell Woman, for instance."* She awaited recognition.

Kasey shook her head.

"White Buffalo Calf Woman?"

Kasey forced an apologetic smile. She couldn't fake this one.

"Those are my best-known spirit names." She tapped a moccasin impatiently. *"Blue Rain is this."* Her hands skimmed her gown. *"I stay in the guise of my first failure, to remind me that I'm due for a victory."*

Kasey scanned her spare trove of historical knowledge. 1800? 1900? When did tribes dress like this, ride horses like that one?

"When was that failure? Do you know the year?"

Blue Rain bobbed her head from side to side. Clearly she thought the question frivolous. *"Do you remember the blue warriors?"*

"Blue." Kasey took another sip from the canteen.

"Not blue-skinned." The spirit tittered and rolled her eyes skyward. *"Uniforms. With yellow, um . . ."* She held a thumb and forefinger a small distance apart. *". . . rounded strings of cloth."*

"Like cording? Cavalry uniforms? Or Union soldiers. Is that it?"

Blue Rain shrugged. *"Blue Rain allowed herself to be tricked by Fox. He can assume any shape. His favorite is the last shaman, a man so wicked, he destroyed all other shamen for recognizing his evil."* She put a hand on her hip. *"My power, and yours, flow from the necklace. It's brimming with enchantment, of course, but the longer my spirit exists, the less women believe in magic."* Blue Rain sat sideways on the Appaloosa, crossed her knees, and jiggled her foot.

"As a blue warrior, Fox tricked a maiden into falling in love with him and calling the wild horses. Then a blue rain of soldiers came down on the People."

Kasey's mind boiled with sounds of galloping hooves, screaming women, and the thud of clubs and rifle butts on skulls. She pushed past chaos to the single element that made sense.

" 'Blue Rain,' then, was a name she—you—got after a massacre. The name was a punishment."

"Yes."

Bad as a scarlet *A*, Kasey thought. You'd hear it daily and picture the carnage you caused.

"I was a good girl before that and a good woman for ever after. I brought rich harvests. Every seed I planted grew. Every appeal for showers brought rain. When I was very old, children didn't know the other stories. But at this age"—she flicked fingers toward her teenaged torso— *"I had a weakness: men."*

Kasey felt the start of laughter. A weakness for men was not one of her flaws.

"Don't look so smug, Wild Moon. Each woman who wears the necklace shares the weakness he's learned to use against us."

"Me?" Kasey shouted as Blue Rain disappeared and China snorted. "A weakness for men? You must be joking."

She'd lost track of Bronc's return. Now he stood beside her, chuckling.

"Have mercy, Kasey," he drawled. "That poor pony don't know much except giddy-up and whoa. He shore don't know nothin' about some fast city gal who's come out West to shake her loop at a lonely cowpoke."

SEVEN

Heat waves rippled around Bronc McDermitt, obscuring everything but his smirk. Kasey wondered if he'd still be smiling after they pumped his stomach for the teeth she wanted to knock down his throat.

"Don't do that." She separated the words with deep breaths. "Don't pull that down-home, thank-God-I'm-a-country-boy crap with me. I happen to know you were one semester short of graduating *with honors* at U. C. Davis."

"I prefer to think of my language as colorful, Ms. Wildmoon, not crap." As he moved toward Rook, the horse sidestepped, flaring his nostrils at the spot where the Appaloosa had stood. "Okay, boy, you're safe."

She couldn't combat his teasing, not with the real threat on her mind. "How was Abner?"

"None too pleased. From a distance, you have an official set to your shoulders. He thought I'd sold out and brought a federal agent to his doorstep."

When they were both mounted her horse followed his. She wished for a few silent moments to ponder Blue Rain. Even if she suspended her disbelief, the experience made no sense. Except that the spirit's first prediction had just come true. Kasey *had* been accused of talking to a horse.

Still, an ancient visitor from the spirit world would be somber, not sassy. She'd speak a primitive dialect, not modern English.

She would not select a skeptical journalist as her errand girl. And the part about a last shaman named Fox was just too bizarre.

"Tuck in close, now." Bronc's black started up the trail and over the pass. After Bronc's lecture on not being put afoot and not becoming a burden, she'd stay right on Rook's tail.

Kasey considered the risks of an adventuring journalist. Last spring in Alaska, she'd braved thin ice and polar bears. Shooting class 5 rapids with Brian "Berserker" Armstrong had made her eyes bulge and heart thunder. Even the ritual beating she'd endured as she was "jumped in" to Las Gatas paled next to the prospect of explosives, a deranged hermit, and a bossy apparition. And then, there was emotional sabotage by Bronc McDermitt.

"How did you navigate that path to the house without more fireworks?" Her voice didn't sound a bit tense.

"Remembered what Abner said." Bronc rode loose, but his hat moved side to side as he scanned the trail. "Even all stove-in, lying in the hospital, Abner figured on using a wheelchair to lay booby traps in a spiral."

She flinched at a sudden sound and he must have caught her movement from the tail of his eye.

"Just a rock." Bronc gestured to the trail. "Abner said he hasn't changed anything and I've been crossing this way to Buck's since I was a kid."

He pointed out a few traps half obscured with sagebrush

and explained the pits they covered were only two feet deep, but spiked with pungi stakes. The trail edges crumbled from the traffic of knowing travelers who'd stayed away from the center and danger.

⚞ ⚟

BRONC CHECKED HER TWICE with glances over his shoulder. Warned how the trail was mined, Kasey probably could've crossed alone. In spite of her upbringing, she kept her mouth shut, her ears and eyes open—pretty much the keys to cowboying.

He heard her murmur in awe as a golden sweep of range opened below them. From this height, clumps of sagebrush looked as smooth as a meadow. Black volcanic rocks appeared to be late afternoon shadows. It was a long, steep way down.

Alone, he could've pushed Rook and been at the Bucks' by now, listening to frybread sizzle in a cast-iron skillet. But Kasey had been rattled by Abner's explosives and her muscles would be seized up after she climbed off China. Better to camp at Towerdown and let her get used to him tonight.

No telling how that would go. His usual well of patience was sucking sand.

One minute she was all business, next she was reeling him in with a cop story that was better than watching TV. And that talking to China about men . . . Hell, he'd been known to grumble or sing to his horse, but she'd been haranguing the poor animal.

And the way she'd looked while she was doing it—stripped to a black tank top cut low in front and high on her shoulders, showing off bronze arms with just the right sort of female muscle—what a sight. Those tight jeans, dirty and pulled *over* her unpolished boots today, nearly wrecked his whole plan to watch her and keep her from sniffing too close to the truth.

He'd been lucky she'd turned on him, yellin' and setting those gold hoop earrings dancing, instead of noticing his zipper was lying nowhere near flat.

"Something came loose here." Kasey's voice snatched him back.

"Sure enough." He considered the shaley decline. "Looks like someone set off one of Abner's toys. China's sure-footed though. Keep your weight centered and let him pick his own way."

She did fine. All the same, he'd be relieved when they reached level ground. From there, it was only two miles to Towerdown, a semicircle of black rock columns that sheltered a spot where generations of campers had pitched tents and kindled campfires against lonely desert nights.

Before he could expect to see the outcroppings of volcanic rock that signaled Towerdown, they should come to a water hole. In fact, that was it, dead ahead, but it looked like hell.

The rim of the water hole was bare of reeds and grass. Either somebody had driven a hungry herd through, or the mustangs were harder pressed than he'd figured. Damn, he'd planned on refilling their canteens here.

China knew where they were headed. The gray picked up his hooves, pulling abreast of Rook, inciting him to a race. Kasey glanced over, asking permission, but just as she loosed her reins, he saw the band of mustangs. Rather than speak and send them high-tailing, he flipped out his right arm, making a barrier like he did when he was driving with one of his younger siblings and had to make a fast stop.

Two bays, a black, and a steeldust Appaloosa flowed toward Towerdown. They seemed to have no leader.

"A bachelor band," he whispered to her. "The stud kicks them out when they get old enough to steal mares. Then they hang out together." Belatedly, he dropped his arm. "That's water, there where it looks like mud. Just some of the boys out for a drink."

When he looked, Kasey was smiling, her pink lips bare of the stuff she'd worn this morning. They curved into the gentlest expression he'd seen on her.

"Aren't they just great?" she said and fingered the necklace with a reverence that made him wonder.

Then, unsettled by his stare, or because hard-boiled reporters didn't succumb to the desert's enchantment, she cleared her throat and raised one eyebrow as she watched the horses play.

With the scent of water in their nostrils, the young stallions feinted kicks and snaked necks at each other, practicing battle moves for fun.

The water was sweeter at Towerdown, but stone formed a random wall around the campsite and the wild ones preferred open range.

At the edge of the water hole, they lifted their heads in a last check for enemies. A breeze licked their manes, and then they lowered their heads.

"We'll let them drink now," he said. "Once we're camped, they'll stay away."

Kasey stood in her stirrups, though he knew that from this distance, she couldn't see much.

China neighed and the mustangs' heads popped up.

"Aw, shoot." Rook's cry, a vibration that shook through Bronc's knees, joined China's. "They're gone now."

With the steeldust in the lead, the mustangs stretched into a gallop with bellies nearly skimming the ground. A bay vaulted a clump of sagebrush and then the whole band entered a ravine and vanished.

Kasey watched them until they were out of sight. Bronc had

to agree with her expression of wonder. All horses were great to watch—powerful, graceful, unpredictable—and wild ones were even better, with no man telling them how and when to use it all.

"Incredible."

As Kasey turned toward him, Bronc wanted to curl an arm around her waist and tug her close, but then her dreamy smile faded and shutters covered her brown eyes.

There she went, remembering why he'd been arrested. Bronc clucked to Rook. They might as well go ahead. The magic had ended.

ᔐ ᔑ

THE WATER HOLE, deserted by the mustangs, was a muddy mess. Obviously other animals had watered here.

Rook and China whuffled at the edge, then backed away. Bronc rode Rook a few yards off.

"Might want to get off here, let them investigate on their own." Bronc dismounted.

"There's water further on, though, right? Where we can fill our canteens?"

How in hell had she known?

"Should be," he said, "but I'd hate to count on it and have 'em go thirsty."

Kasey backed China, but not enough.

"He's gonna go down that thing like a slip and slide," he warned, "if you don't back him a piece more."

Kasey ignored his advice and dismounted. Once her boots hit dirt, she wavered on unsteady legs. "Here boy, are you thirsty? Good boy, China," she crooned to the horse and ignored Bronc's advice.

Fine. It was slick as snail snot at the edge and she was welcome to it.

She was holding China's reins when the gelding decided to lunge to the middle of the water hole. For a second, it looked like she might water-ski behind him. Bronc yelled for her to turn loose, but she didn't, even when her feet slipped out from under her and she landed seat first in the slippery mess.

When the wave of China's charge sloshed back, cresting at Kasey's chin, Bronc almost went after her. But she flopped over on her belly against the slippery side of the hole, did a slurping pushup, and came upright looking spitting mad.

Bronc kept his distance and tried not to laugh.

Gray-beige mud plastered the black tank top from her nipples down. There was no other way to put it. The line ran straight across the tips of her breasts.

With a squelch, she got one boot free of the muck. She tried to maintain her dignity, but as Kasey slogged ashore, the smooth dun coating was setting up like concrete on each ridge of her jeans. Then she fell again.

This time, Bronc went to her, lifted her elbows, and held her steady. She stared up from the level of his collarbone with a glare that said she wished *he'd* go down into the muck, face-first. Before he could joke her anger away, Kasey's expression softened and there was nothing funny in her eyes.

His hands took over, ignoring his mind's warning. They slid up the insides of her elbows to her biceps and down again. Tender flesh, so soft beneath that slick coating; his hands must have tickled, gliding like that, because she shivered.

"I'm dirty," she said and her pupils pooled as if she thought he'd kiss her.

Surprise revived his judgment. *No way in hell.* Finger by grudging finger, he released Kasey's arms and bowed her ahead.

She splashed away from him and China followed like a poodle on a string.

He ought to be sainted for his self-control. Bronc could only watch Kasey's muddy backside. That flicker in her eyes had been warm and sweet as melting candy and he wasn't likely to forget it.

"I can ride." The mud on her pants had started hardening. She had to lift her boot, by hand, toward the stirrup.

Willing. That's how she'd looked and he hadn't done a thing about it.

"That might ruin the saddle. The mud. All I'm sayin' is it's BOW's saddle, property of the federal government, and with the national debt bein' what it is . . ."

"You're suggesting *what*?" Kasey's glare couldn't convince him he'd imagined her softness.

"If you want to shuck those pants and put on some others, I won't watch," he promised. "Lord knows I'm a gentleman."

"What you are is pathetic."

"I am, huh?" Damn, is this what he got? Scorn, instead of credit for not rolling her in the mud when she would've gone down smiling.

Once she levered herself into the saddle, he rode Rook alongside.

"Right." She made an extended process of gathering her reins.

"Pathetic?" he repeated.

"Absolutely."

"Okay then, honey, explain this." He sat close enough to hear her swallow. Though he wasn't about to let her off the hook, he lowered his voice. "How come, when I was giving your arms a mudbath, you said you were dirty—instead of tellin' me to stop?"

Kasey's breath caught before she slammed her heels against China and galloped ahead. Smiling, he let her go, pleased with the fact that it was pretty hard to backtrack on playing hard-to-get.

⚜ ⚜

CHINA AND ROOK HAD DRUNK their fill at Tower-down. Now Kasey squatted on the other side of the stone posts, where Bronc couldn't see her. She dribbled water over toes that curled at the thought of returning to wool socks and boots.

She wanted to stay here, where a locust tree and a couple spiky saplings shaded a spring the size of a truck tire.

Of course, as a "water-giver" she'd guessed it would be there. That, and Blue Rain's other predictions had come true. Bronc had accused her of talking to China, then she'd seen the mustangs—including a wild Appaloosa—and now, she'd turned psychic over water.

Maybe she could unravel the paranormal after dinner and sleep. Bronc had refused to accept her help with cooking, so she'd worked every speck of mud off her saddle, picked up her saddlebags, and slipped between two black stone pillars for a bath.

Now the aroma of hamburger, frying onions, and some sharp spice, maybe chili powder, mixed with the scent of sagebrush.

"Better get your rear in gear, unless you want these charred black."

A "gentleman," he'd called himself. Kasey squeezed a bit more water from the tail of her french braid. He hadn't spoken since he'd accused her of— Her eyes clamped shut and her stomach dipped in remembrance. Animal attraction.

Another one of Blue Rain's pronouncements, but it made no sense at all, and she'd smother it.

"They smell great." She gathered her shampoo and washed-out jeans. "I can't believe you hauled hamburger out here."

She kept her voice level, offering a truce as she replaced items in her pack.

"No big trick. Just froze 'em overnight. Glad you're not a cussed vegetarian." His eyes homed in on the spot her hair had soaked through the white tee shirt.

"I usually am a vegetarian. But when I'm on a story, I eat whatever I'm served. Do you mind if I interview you a little while you cook?"

He jammed the spatula under a burger.

"That's why we're here."

Start easy. He's edgy and you're the professional. Stay one up on him. She lowered herself on the other side of the cook fire. "What's your job, really?"

He smirked without looking up from the frying pan. "When I'm not shooting wild horses?"

She waited out the chill from his sarcasm.

"I'm head wrangler for this gathering district, meaning I spot horses and send out riders or aircraft to round them up."

When she stayed silent, he seemed to think she needed clarification. "Tate could supply the payroll number and that gives you my official job description, but mainly I locate herds in areas where they appear to need gathering and notify the experts, who assess the condition of the land and make final determinations regarding the horses' impact on the environment."

In spite of himself, Bronc McDermitt sounded like the U.C. Davis honors student he'd been.

Kasey resisted a smile. "Coming from three generations of ranchers, I'd think you'd know the land well enough to make those determinations."

He loaded the meat and onions onto slabs of sourdough bread that had also made the saddlebag trip. Her mouth watered.

"Not well enough to remove horses. It's illegal, besides." He drew a breath. "Our hands are tied, even if they're starving or dying of thirst."

She put aside her notebook and juggled the paper plate as he settled it into her hands.

In the story, how would she describe him?

The paper plate bowed under the weight of the sandwich and a little orange pyramid of carrot sticks. She could describe the meal, but she couldn't study Bronc long enough to picture him for her readers.

His left temple wore a crescent scar she remembered from that day ten years ago, in the truck. Her fingers longed to touch it.

"Once the determination has been made to remove them, I call in the choppers." He regarded his own plate, then met her eyes. "There are only a few chopper pilots I'll work with."

"Flynn?"

"No, he's with PAPA. Just uses our airstrip. He's good at what he does, but I won't have him working horses anymore."

If only Cookie were hovering behind her with a camera. The set of Bronc McDermitt's jaw, more than his voice, said *my horses.*

His thumbs rubbed the fluted edge of the paper plate. "If it's the right time of year I supervise the roundup, make sure it's done right, that the horses recover, get their vitamin shots and all."

One of his hands shielded his sandwich. He sighed and continued. "If this had been a normal year, we'd be in the midst of it now."

Without staring, Kasey used her foolproof means of jump-starting her description of an interview subject: she counted things. Three coffee cups and three hamburger patties.

Was he expecting company or was he just hungry? His hands

fidgeted with the plate, so she couldn't tell how many buttons lined his shirt cuffs, but starting at his throat, where the first button was open, numbering down his chest, over the flat belly intermittently shaded and spotlighted by the fire, she counted seven buttons. The snap on his jeans made her falter, made her mind circle back to the mud hole, to the way he'd slid his hands up her forearms in gentle possession. . . .

Description. Blue eyes, black hair, about six foot, two inches. But that wasn't her kind of description. It sounded like a police blotter. And then her imagination took over.

Across the fire, she saw a desperado who'd ridden into town to hide out. And broken a few hearts in the process.

He wouldn't encounter many women, but as he rode away, each one would hold a memory. The boardinghouse mistress would pause in throwing dishwater out her back door when she saw his black gelding pass. The whore rising from bed at dusk would see dust from a dark horseman headed out of town. The schoolmarm, waving a last pupil down the path, would touch her breast, pretending to check her clock brooch, as he rode past and grazed the brim of his hat in farewell.

One remembered his long rider's body, folding into a bench for a supper of chicken and dumplings. One remembered blue eyes watching a schoolyard of children with longing. One remembered the desperado's mouth and wondered if it was deceptively cruel or kind . . .

Kasey almost dropped her plate at the crack of his voice.

"You gonna start eating that? I'm trying to be polite, but I'll tell you the truth, Kasey, I'm hungry enough to eat a cow, two calves, and chase the bull for half a mile."

EIGHT

Kasey didn't drop her plate. In fact, she was confident she'd handled the moment nicely. "Go ahead and eat. I got side-tracked thinking how to help my readers visualize you."

By the time she finished explaining, he'd finished his hamburger, the night had turned pewter, and she'd given up on an interview that had dwindled to words and gazes that deflected each other like opposite poles of magnets.

"Think you could get a coyote to howl so I can punctuate your words with its mournful cry?" When Bronc chuckled, his suspicious frown cracked into boyish pleasure.

"Our fire." She tugged down the cuffs of her jeans to cover her bare feet. "Is it big enough to burn all night?"

"It'll last if I wake up a couple times to tend it."

Kasey rolled her shoulders, heard her vertebrae creak, and felt comforted by his competence. Literally bone-tired, she knew she wouldn't wake to tend the fire, even if the temperature dropped to freezing.

"You know what they say about campfires." Bronc kept his eyes on the flames. She shook her head. "White man build big fire, sit far back. Indian build small fire, sit close up."

"Is that what they say?" She wasn't insulted, exactly, but he must have noticed she was half Indian. Last night, beside that other campfire, when he'd scoffed that she hadn't "inherited her people's stealth," he probably hadn't meant investigative reporters.

Since the records from his trial were full of character witnesses surnamed Buck, Winnemucca, and Spirit-Hair, he probably knew more about being Indian than she did. Still.

"You don't seem terribly respectful of my ethnic heritage, McDermitt."

He shook his head. "Forget that downtown racial diversity crap and tell me how I've insulted you. If I didn't notice you were Indian, wouldn't that be insulting?"

Sometimes you gained a source's confidence by admitting you were wrong. She'd give him this one.

"Maybe."

"Should I be worrying if you don't have your notebook open? I'd sure hate to be labeled a *racist* horse killer."

"I'm not—" She stopped.

Deadline for a fifteen-thousand-word story—double the usual *Dare* article—was three weeks away. She couldn't swear she wouldn't label him a horse killer.

"Bronc, any time you want to talk to me as a person, not a reporter, just say something is 'off the record.'"

"And that'll do it, huh?"

"Absolutely." She waited for his sarcastic rejoinder, but it didn't come.

After they'd rolled out sleeping bags on opposite sides of the fire and crawled inside them, the only sounds were the horses whuffling and a night bird's far cry.

"Bronc?"

"Yes, ma'am. He sounded relaxed, but not sleepy.

"With so much college, what made you decide to do this?"

"Too lazy to work and too nervous to steal." Bronc recited he answer like a man who'd faced the question too often. Kasey turned her back on the satiny orange flame and concentrated on the upright rocks and dark shapes of horses.

Her heart bucked when Bronc's sleeping bag grated on the ground. When the sound stopped, she knew he'd probably only raised up on an elbow. She waited.

"Off the record," Bronc said, "what'd you and China decide about your weakness for men?"

In the midnight darkness, she heated with a blush he couldn't see and Kasey pretended to sleep.

ॐ ॐ

BLUE RAIN WATCHED KASEY DREAM. With a spirit's deftness, she blew tales one direction, tugged them back when they strayed. Finally, she coaxed Kasey into a second rendering of the vision she'd seen before.

As before, Kasey's dream began in darkness. *Her dream-self felt weight, smooth and warm as a fur robe, over her legs. But that comforting illusion was spoiled by golden, slanted eyes looking up through the shadows.*

A tent flap lifted to show blue sky outside. The village sounds of children, yipping dogs, of mothers stirring breakfast, came to Kasey as her vision moved out of the tent.

The shameful bulge of her pregnancy showed in the sunlight. Stunned, a bare-chested man dropped his drinking gourd as he stared at Fox, trotting beside her. Clearly, her mate.

Kasey battled images vibrant as oil paintings and thrashed in her sleeping, fighting the dream's demand that she take the role of the disgraced woman.

Through that woman's eyes, she saw villagers' hands reared in

anger and children hidden. Banishment lashed her from home. A
club struck her, struck Horse. Blood trickled down his silver-blue
legs, while Fox gamboled ahead, out of harm's way.

ᔥ ᔥ

BRONC HATED TO WAKE HER. Kasey had finally quit
tossing and turning. Her cheek snuggled into her palm and she
looked almost childlike, except the white tee shirt had slipped
down to bare her shoulder, and the shell necklace gleamed
against her skin.

The coffee had started perking, but daylight was an hour off.
If he mashed a few frijoles and heated them on the griddle with
jalapeño cheese, they'd give her a little punch of protein. And
she could rest a while longer.

Last night, watching campfire smoke settle around her
while they talked, he'd felt strangely satisfied by her strength.
She hadn't said a word when he didn't pitch a tent and she'd
refused his offer to lay a *reata* around her sleeping bag to ward
off rattlers.

Skeptical behind her yawn, she'd shaken her head. Even
when he told her lots of old-timers, his dad included, never slept
in the desert without using that old vaqueros' trick, Kasey was
willing to take her chances.

She should've slept like a stone after yesterday's ride, but she
hadn't.

Bronc poured a cup of coffee and looked toward the horizon. He wasn't much for analyzing folks, but he thought he'd
figured out Kasey's willingness to let him touch her.

The lady was a predator. No, that wasn't quite right. She was
a *professional*. Reporters, far as he was concerned, were professional vampires. They sucked dry the best and worst experiences
of a man's life for profit.

He'd like to believe she wanted him. Or even just the kick

of kissing a cowboy. A little something for her résumé: climbed Mt. McKinley, ran before the bulls of Pamplona, mud-wrestled a true Nevada buckaroo ...

She wouldn't be the first woman to manipulate a man via his hormones. And he wouldn't mind being manipulated, if he weren't aiming for a bigger target just now.

Since he hadn't killed those horses, it was only a matter of time before the real killer grew cocky and more horses died. He fingered the spent bullet in his pocket. If a second carnage had started already, some federal go-getter might uncover the truth. If they tied hard evidence to a custom Storm Hammer rifle this time, his dad would be well and truly screwed.

⚡ ⚡

THE NUDGE MADE HER START. Yesterday's dog bite, the symbolic dream, and reality swirled together before her eyes opened on gray morning and a denim-covered knee.

"Boots on the ground."

Kasey rolled over and smelled the rich aroma of coffee beckoning. "Okay."

"I want to do most of this ride before noon. We pushed these ponies hard yesterday and it's going to be another scorcher."

Kasey dressed inside her sleeping bag, pulling up jeans she'd left crammed down by her feet, maneuvering a bra under the shirt she'd worn as a nightie. She was so quick, she wished he'd timed her.

After one bite of the crusty tortilla and spicy filling, she blurted, "Can you do this for me every morning?"

She waited for his all-or-nothing smile, but it didn't come.

"Suppose I could." No smile, but Bronc's blue eyes speculated.

Silence sizzled between them, leaving entirely too much time to consider mornings. And the nights before.

"This is really good. Thanks." Kasey sucked breath over a tongue seared by peppers and coffee. She considered the scorched tin coffeepot suspended over the fire, the folding grill, and lightweight frying pan. "I'll take the next turn cooking."

"Suit yourself."

It was the last she heard from him until they'd cleaned up and packed up.

"Watch him," Bronc said as she mounted China. "He's just waitin' to put on a rodeo."

Again, she looked for Bronc's smile, but he was all business this morning.

"Okay."

The gelding felt limp and lazy beneath her, oblivious to Rook's shying at a prickly poppy and sidestepping away from a hole that might have belonged to a rabbit or ground squirrel.

Other than those, she saw few signs of wildlife, but her head ached as her mind tumbled over her second, torrid dream. She didn't need a degree in English literature to decipher this one. It was a reflection of the story Blue Rain had begun—with a few tawdry embellishments. It reminded her of the dreams she'd had on her return to L.A., after her first, teenaged trip to the Scolding Rock desert.

Garish and fierce, those dreams had frightened her. Waking from the first one—a mélange of sex and shifting scarlet shapes—she'd felt convinced someone had slipped drugs into her Coke.

The dreams had continued and, for the first time, she couldn't confide a major problem to her parents. It would mean telling them about the trip to find her birth mother. Although it was only curiosity, she knew it would hurt them. So, she kept the journey and dreams to herself, and spent the nights she was afraid to sleep, writing.

But she was an adult now and the headache and dizziness

she felt from a restless night were liabilities she couldn't afford. She'd come here to work. Unless she got Blue Rain's voice on tape or image on film, the "spirit" didn't exist.

Kasey realized the rock formation she'd thought was miles away was really just ahead. She needed to focus on reality.

Kasey touched the necklace and swallowed against sudden dryness. She rubbed the largest shell with the pad of her thumb, tried to ignore the thirst Blue Rain had wrapped around her as a supernatural I-told-you-so, and wondered when Bronc would stop for water.

He drew rein in the shade of the rock formation and pointed. At first she saw a mere shadow on the rock face, then Kasey heard the quarreling yips of pups. As she watched, a dark mustard-colored coyote considered the riders, before vanishing. The pups fell silent.

A hawk followed the updrafts overhead. Bronc took a long drink from his canteen and motioned for her to do the same. Kasey shook her head. The hawk's movements made her a little dizzy.

She didn't know he was watching, until she licked her lower lip and he swore.

"Damn." He leaned over, lifted the canteen strap from her saddle, and pushed it into her hand. "Don't even think of going dehydrated on me. Drink."

Kasey sorted through the survival information stored in her brain. Headache, dizziness, and stomach cramps *were* symptoms of dehydration, but she did half her work in the outdoors. She knew better than to let herself become dehydrated. On the other hand, she'd never battled a show-off spirit before.

"You're going dry just so you don't have to stop and drop your britches to pee."

"What?" She didn't dare tell him the truth. "You're wrong."

"Fine, then drink up."

She hesitated. She didn't want him developing the notion he was in charge. But she'd had a single cup of coffee, and a cup of water last night with dinner. She'd drink more than that if she were riding her bike across town, so she drank.

"You can depend on me to find you a damned rock for modesty." He rode ahead, then called back over his shoulder. "And if I can't, it wouldn't be the first time I saw a girl's behind."

I just bet it wouldn't. Kasey screwed the lid back on her canteen, hung it on her saddle, and sent China loping after Rook.

They rode side by side, straight ahead.

Kasey pictured an Arctic glacier, imagined tinkling ice in a frosty glass, remembered the scent of snow on granite. Then, she pitched her voice in imitation of such cold.

"You're way out of line, McDermitt."

When he didn't answer, Kasey sneaked a look at him. He hadn't shaved. Black beard shadowed his hard-set jaw and he kept his eyes forward until he felt her looking. Then, he smiled.

NINE

A mile from the Buck ranch, Kasey decided she wouldn't tolerate this one-down position with Bronc McDermitt. There was nothing like doing her job right to put her back on top. Kasey pulled her necklace from inside her shirt, putting it on display for the interview ahead.

She wouldn't hide who she was. Her aunt and uncle lived here. And maybe dead-end Internet searches didn't mean her birth mother was dead. Maybe Leticia Wildmoon lived here, too.

What a test that would be, to take down data on her reporter's notepad, like she would for any story. She had a thing or two to teach Bronc McDermitt. Foremost was the fact that K. D. Wildmoon didn't flinch.

Dust from a vehicle's passing hung on the long graveled road. The driveway's border of half-sunk tires created a scalloped effect. A tidy bit of recycling, though a clutter of uprooted posts and chicken wire detracted from the effect.

A late-model Land Rover, waxed to a champagne sparkle, sat near blood-orange poppies. They quaked on spindly stems in front of a tiny house with green shutters. Off from the main house stretched a structure reminiscent of a longhouse, Indian council chambers built of redwood, with skylights and wide windows of double-paned glass.

She recognized Calvin Buck immediately. That one day in the Scolding Rock desert, long before she'd learned memory tricks vital to a reporter, she'd latched on to one for him.

She'd been scared of the other guy, and though Bronc had gravitated to her, right off, she'd wanted it three-against-one. Cal Buck had looked brown and shy, and she'd imagined herself coaxing a wild buck to eat from her hand.

Ten years later, Cal Buck had traded jeans for Dockers, and long hair down his back for a crewcut over his wide, lined brow, but that shy restraint remained. Until he and Bronc began sparring.

"Still driving this foreign piece of crap?" Bronc squinted at the Land Rover. "Hell, sell this thing, spend more time at work, and you might be able to afford an old Airstream trailer."

"Yeah, and you're still making that horse take up the slack for that fine piece of American machinery you drive. Where's it?" Calvin Buck slid his eyes her way, but briefly.

Kasey didn't take either of them seriously. Starting with her parents' largely male colleagues and continuing through her job, she'd learned that insults, among guys, could be a form of affection.

"Still can't go through a mud puddle without killing the engine, huh?" Bronc cast an eye toward a gathering cloudbank. "That why you're home?"

"Naw, the old woman said we might have company today."

Kasey wished for a mirror. Not just to check her disheveled appearance, but to see if the necklace was really glowing like sun-warmed honey. Not the electric jitter it had made before, but something cozy. Maternal.

Her throat closed with choking rigidity the necklace couldn't soothe. What if "the old woman" was Leticia Buck?

"Guess she got her wires crossed," Calvin said. Then Bronc pounded him on the back and Buck's lips jerked in a painful smile. "How ya doin', Kemo Sabe?"

Bronc shrugged. "Sober, free, and riding with a pretty girl." For a feather-thin slice of time, the men's eyes met and Kasey saw Bronc's arrest, imprisonment, and humiliation played out in the desert air between them. "Pity you can't say the same, Tonto."

Tonto? Kemo Sabe? If the affection between the two hadn't looked genuine, she might have thought she'd taken a wrong turn in time.

Kasey dismounted, told herself she wasn't nervous, and looked for a place to tie China.

"Introductions," she reminded Bronc, and then watched Buck, waiting for a reaction to the name she'd taken from his sister.

"Introductions," Bronc said. "Ms. K. D. Wildmoon, Calvin Buck."

Buck's gaze might have sharpened fractionally and his chin might have lifted as he extended his hand, but his grip and smile were merely polite.

She'd always wondered if the name Wildmoon was a fake, an alias fabricated by her shady mother.

"Cal's some kind of mine supervisor. Ms. Wildmoon is a reporter covering the mustang situation. She thought you and Becky might help with the Native American perspective."

"Nothing nearly so formal," she said. "I'm just picking up a few quotes to go with a photo story *Dare* plans to run in a few months. I noticed Mrs. Buck's name in testimony about a sovereign nation's right to deal with wild horses." Kasey shrugged.

"You'd better talk with her then." Cal Buck brightened, openly pleased he wasn't on the hook. "She's over in the studio." He gestured at the redwood longhouse. "You want to go over, just let yourself in; I think she knows your work. Or I could walk you over."

There. Kasey caught uneasiness in the man's expression.

"Don't bother. I'm used to talking with strangers," she joked.

Cal Buck reached for her reins. "I'll be glad to get your horse some water."

"You're a helluva host to horses," Bronc said.

"Becky keeps tea and stuff out there," Calvin Buck nodded toward the studio, then turned to Bronc. "Guess I could rustle up a beer for you."

Kasey checked her back pocket for notebook and pen, and set off toward the studio.

"Sure you don't want me to walk across with you?" This time Cal Buck's tone was clearly solicitous.

"Enjoy your beer," she said.

⚜ ⚜

THE BUCKS' BACK PORCH was partly shaded. Occasional sprays from a lawn sprinkler blew over chairs pulled up to a table that had once held telephone cable.

"You gotta explain." Calvin popped the tabs on a grape soda and a beer and handed the latter to Bronc.

"She's a crusading journalist here to screw me, is what I think."

"You wish."

"Don't I just." Bronc took a long pull of the beer, then tapped the can. "This doesn't bother you?"

After too many sad and stoned Sunday mornings, Buck had kicked booze, completely. Bronc felt a twinge of guilt drinking in front of him.

"Warrior to the core, man. I can take it." Cal licked the purple soda from his top lip. "You don't want to talk about jail, do you?"

"No." Bronc leaned back and watched the sprinkler spray across his boots, dotting the dust. "What?" he asked when Buck laughed and shook his head.

"You don't recognize her."

"Might come as a shock to you, buddy, but I don't read many magazines besides *Western Horseman* and *Newsweek*. Just can't seem to get rural delivery on *Gentleman's Quarterly*."

"From before. You have no clue."

"When you're done showing off, would you mind telling me what the hell you're talking about?"

"Remember high school graduation and that girl that was stranded? The girl in the baseball cap? You were loco for her for years."

"Wasn't her name Cathy Harrigan? I mean—" Bronc felt poleaxed. His head leaned against the chair back and stared into a sky scattered with thunderclouds. "You know, she's acted like I should be apologizing for something ever since I met her."

"Like that's a new experience for you."

Bronc thought of that kiss, meant to be a fake, but he remembered it as the most genuine, knock-his-knees-weak kiss of his life.

"Shit, it is her."

"You know, Becky's followed her career, ever since Mom saw a picture of 'K. D. Wildmoon' accepting an award, wearing that necklace. In *Native American News,* maybe." Buck worked the pop top back and forth. "It looked like that 'family treasure' Letty gave away with her baby, Mom said." Cal broke the pop top loose and squinted at it. "Supposed to be a big medicine item."

Bronc had seen Buck's expression, or lack of it, before. When it came to spirits, Buck was absolutely noncommittal.

"That'd mean you two are related," Bronc mused, but that fact faded under the return of the ache.

For years after he'd met her, pain curled under his breast-bone. He'd tried to track her down, even taking his first pay-check, cashing it into quarters, and dialing every Harrigan on the L.A. phone book page he'd photocopied in the library.

"You're right." Bronc felt the heat of their attraction. It had been instant—a couple days ago on the playa and yesterday in the mud. "Think she recognized me?"

"Can't you tell?"

"I guess not." He and Kasey had a history. He'd gotten her flat tire patched. And saved her from a bad guy. Soon as he reminded her he was a real, live hero, she'd drop any go-for-the-throat story she'd been planning.

Cal Buck stood and crushed the soda can under his heel. "So, by the time Becky gets through with her, she'll know everything. Then what do you plan to do?"

Bronc felt a slow smile lift the corners of his mouth. "Make up for lost time, buddy. Starting tonight."

§§ ٪٪

"HELLO?" KASEY LEANED a palm against the studio door and it swung open.

The longhouse was half gallery, half workspace and clearly set up for public viewing, so she stepped inside. Potted yuccas and three lacquered chairs with coral cushions formed a con-versation area. Kasey heard a woman humming as she ran water behind a closed door.

Kasey strolled between a loom and a spinning wheel toward a clutter of easels, hangings, and vivid canvases.

The smell of turpentine was missing, but there was no lack of color. Collage, Kasey thought, taking in layers of cloth and leather, beads and feathers. Many were Native American women—joyous, somber, dancing, dying.

Was one her mother? Could her mother be the artist? She imagined the bathroom door opening on a Paiute Georgia O'Keeffe. Wide-striding in a split skirt, with a gray braid streaming down her back, she'd rush to greet the daughter who'd taken so long finding her.

One of the smallest works was a frame covered with white leather cut into eyelash-thin strips. Kasey studied the smoke-blue design that had apparently been etched on before the leather was snipped. Maybe it was only an abstract pattern.

A gust of wind from the opening door and the window beyond set the leather ribbons aflutter, defining the image with such realism, Blue Rain might have ridden into the room.

The laughing Indian maiden wavered before her, shell necklace moving with her breath as a spotted horse shifted behind her.

Kasey wished for something to grab to steady herself. Blue Rain appeared so tangible, Kasey had overlooked the woman who'd entered the room.

Now, Kasey squared her shoulders and prepared to meet the artist.

Becky Buck stood about five feet tall. She had short, shingled hair, wore glasses and yellow denim shorts, and was at least a decade too young to be Kasey's mother.

"Is he still mad?" The woman whisked past and stood near the open door.

From here, Kasey could see Calvin Buck and Bronc at the back of the small house.

"He didn't seem mad." Kasey drew breath to introduce herself, but the other woman was quicker.

"He got an espresso machine so I could make him cappuccino every morning." The woman leaned against the doorframe. "He thought it would save money, because when the coffee cart comes by the mine, he can't resist."

It had to be intentional, Kasey thought, the way Becky Buck prattled without looking at her. It created a strange sort of distance—being chatty, before they'd really met.

"I don't drink coffee," the woman continued, "but I've done fine with the machine—lots of foam, no grounds—then, this morning, I accidentally put curry power on top instead of nutmeg." She left the door ajar and motioned Kasey toward the chairs. The studio suddenly felt cool as a cave.

Aware the other woman waited, Kasey said, "Curry powder on coffee. I'm afraid I would've sputtered all over the kitchen."

"Spewed," Becky corrected.

Then, Becky Buck faced her. Fingers fanning the air, she imitated the shape of Kasey's necklace. "It really is you."

Kasey imagined the necklace responded. The pulse that had been thrumming behind Kasey's knees spread to her entire body. Her heart seemed to sing, while her mind recoiled.

She could not work surrounded by magic.

Her logical mind dictated this solution: she would not discuss their family relationship. If she let Becky Buck pour out a lifetime of secrets, the interview wouldn't happen.

Still, she couldn't deny the connection.

"I'm K. D. Wildmoon. Kasey," she added. "And you're Becky Buck?"

"Do you know how cool this is?" Becky said. "I wish Cal's mom hadn't moved to Santa Fe."

"It really *is* interesting." Kasey didn't sit and she kept her eyelids at half-mast, detaching herself from Becky's excitement.

"And I would like to talk about—" She hesitated, then retreated into the sarcasm that always served her well. " —my long-lost family, but first I'd like to discuss Nevada's wild horses and their effect on your ancestral lands."

"Our," Becky corrected.

"Pardon me?"

"Our ancestral lands. You're half Paiute."

Behind her back, Kasey heard the chuckling flutter of ten thousand leather strips; Blue Rain mocked her.

Kasey tilted her head in wry acknowledgment and saw Becky's expression shift from welcome to incredulity to nothing.

"Ask away." Becky settled into one of the chairs and took up a willow basket filled with tissue paper and rough cloth.

While Becky gave a crisp public-relations recitation about a sovereign nation's right to choose how to handle environmental, social, and economic issues, she ripped sheets of aqua- , teal- , and adobe-colored tissue paper into ragged clouds of color. When she looked up, light glazed the lenses of her glasses, hiding her eyes.

While Kasey noted names of legislators and tribal activists, she felt the quaking of her heart, or the necklace, or maybe some reaction to a couple days in the harsh Nevada sun. Regardless, she took down Becky's statistics on forage, vegetation, and BOW encroachment on reservation lands and property owned by Native American ranchers.

Although Becky made no attempt to veer from the topic, Kasey thought the woman's colorless delivery was a reprimand. She had what she needed, but she could have gotten most of it from a library. She'd broken her cardinal rule, to establish rapport with a source first. In fact, she'd purposely avoided rapport. She hoped it wasn't too late.

"Can you tell me a little about your art?" Kasey braced herself for a shrug. "I'm woefully ignorant, but I'm educable. What would you call this form?" Dropping her professional bearing, making Becky the expert, Kasey ventured a guess. "Collage?"

"Sort of. I call it pastiche." Becky's fingers unraveled a metallic copper cloth with the texture of burlap. "It's not making me rich and neither is my storytelling, but I'm giving kids a taste of their heritage. At least they can breathe in a few tales from the old folks, along with *Beavis and Butt-head*.

"When you do your work where I do—at libraries, fairs, and in canvas tents at powwows—you're glad to break even. Calvin and I get by."

Kasey's fingertips grew cold. Why had Becky interpreted her question as a financial query? Lord, she was losing it. She needed to get out of the desert and back to L.A. Something here was leeching her skill.

"Let's take a break." Becky stood, brushing all her materials from her lap. Sunset-colored confetti floated in her wake as she opened a hinged screen to reveal a tiny refrigerator.

"Okay." Kasey didn't close her notebook. She ran the pad of her thumb over the spiral binding at its top as she glanced back to the image of Blue Rain.

Kasey grappled for a simple explanation. Perhaps, in her teenage research, she'd run across a legend describing Blue Rain. That could have happened, except she wouldn't have forgotten and Blue Rain's three predictions had come true.

Kasey stared at the portrait and felt it happening. Spidery fissures cracked through logic as she realized Blue Rain was real.

Kasey heard far-off men's voices, but the words were blurred. She felt a breeze, neither warm nor cool. Becky asked her something, moving closer, but Kasey's only link to reality was a small pain from the metal spiral atop her notebook.

"Okay, so I won't put sugar in your iced tea."

A cold glass bumped the back of Kasey's hand and then she heard Becky sigh. "Why don't you ask me about your mother?"

"Okay," Kasey said, as they both settled into their chairs again. "When—?"

A look of professional detachment must have returned, because Becky held out a stifling palm. "I'm the storyteller. Listen. Then ask questions if I haven't filled in all the blanks."

"I don't want a story," Kasey said. "I want facts, to go along with *that*."

Becky followed her gesture. "Blue Rain? She's a prevalent gal in legends around here. Clearly an archetype, though, since she crops up in Southwest and Plains stories, too, and we were never a horse culture."

Archetype. Such a cool, clinical word. Kasey felt her neck muscles loosen.

"But Cal's mom says the Bucks are Blue Rain's descendants. And Letty believed it."

"Believed it?" Past tense, Kasey thought. "She *is* dead then, but I knew that."

"Absolutely. She stopped short of saying she'd had a vision. Bad enough marrying two white men, you don't want to be called crazy, too, but—" Becky turned her head as if she'd heard Kasey's heart breaking. "You knew she was dead?"

"I was pretty sure. It hardly matters now." Kasey used the fingernails of both hands to skim tendrils of loose hair back into her dusty braid.

"She wasn't crazy when she put you up for adoption. In fact, she was incredibly sane. What she did was illegal. She had to subvert the entire system. Twice."

Kasey's ribcage expanded. She crushed it back to normal with her arms. Twice?

"The tribal elders almost went after you, but then Letty died, and with Billy gone, too . . . There were other things to spend money on." Becky smiled. "It was a big year for scholarships. Calvin got one of them."

"Good." Kasey could imagine her adoptive parents fighting to keep her in just the same ways, legal and illegal. "Who's Billy? Not—" Kasey saw the answer in Becky's eyes. "My birth certificate said 'father unknown.'"

Becky clucked her tongue. "She did that in case you ever wanted to claim government money as a full-blood, but they were married. She took Billy's name. He'd had it changed from something Italian. He was a trick rider, followed the rodeos in buckskins and feathers." A little puff of a laugh came then. "An Indian wannabe."

"I'm half Italian?" Kasey heard the childish query in her voice. When Becky began to laugh, she joined in.

"All the Italian jokes to deal with too. Sorry, Kasey." Kasey laughed harder than the revelation warranted.

"I'll tell you about your mom. Some stuff from Cal's mother —your grandmother—some from Cal, and what I remember of Letty.

"She was a very sickly kid. She had migraines, but for a long time, they didn't know what was wrong. Kids weren't supposed to get 'sick headaches.' And not only did she see flashing lights and reflections, she heard"—Becky nodded toward the portrait of Blue Rain—"a voice. So, she was home-schooled. Didn't know how to act around other kids. But she read constantly and Calvin played school with her, even though he was younger.

"Then, when she was about fourteen, the headaches stopped. She bought a tee shirt that said 'Custer Died for Your Sins' and exploded into Indian activism. She helped occupy Alcatraz. You've probably read about it. Adam Fortunate Eagle? She was with him when they commandeered a Canadian sailing ship and used it to seize control of Alcatraz Island. She stayed in San Francisco for a while, driving her parents crazy with worry.

"Then she got arrested for helping to scalp Columbus. Kind of ironic when you think she married an Italian later, but there was a beach reenactment of Columbus finding the new world, and Letty decided to do what the People should have done in the first place. She ran out with a rubber tomahawk and lifted the guy's moth-eaten gray wig off his head. He pressed assault charges." Becky shook her head.

"Great days, huh? Now all we've got is bumper stickers. Have you seen that one: 'Before Christ, Columbus, and Costner, there were Paiutes'—or Shoshone or Iroquois?... just fill in the blank with your favorite tribe.

"Anyhow, Letty was really something. First, she married some teaching assistant from Berkeley, and that lasted about six months. The rumor was that she had a baby down there, but she swore she didn't. And I believed her, because there's no way she would've left it. She was such a good mom after—to you. But she was kind of a mess, when she came home."

"Drinking?"

"No, not much. Really, she never did. She got sad a lot, and the headaches returned. She spent a lot of time with the elders, talking about spirit world stuff. That's when Blue Rain came back to her.

"Then she met Billy. For a while she was happy. He had a good heart and he was handsome enough, I guess. I was already hung up on Cal, and Billy was definitely not my type. Tall, thin, and stoned a lot of the time—but never around the horses. Never. He loved his horses, wouldn't let people smoke in the same county in case of a barn fire.

"You know what he could do, though? Play basketball. He

was a beautiful player. . . ."

Kasey thought of high school, of the coach who'd called her a natural.

". . . boards just loved Billy. It was like the court tilted any direction he wanted to go. Once in a while they used to play down in the gym in Gully. Ask Bronc, he must've seen Billy play."

Kasey felt a jolt of reality at her mention of Bronc's name, but Becky circled back to Letty's story.

"After Billy died, she started obsessing over the necklace again. She didn't say it was giving her directions or making visions appear. Letty remembered too well what it felt like to be the weird one. But the headaches came back, and people knew."

As Becky looked up, Kasey felt her face being scrutinized for skepticism. She didn't allow a single nerve to twitch, but she couldn't keep her heart from vaulting. Blue Rain had taunted her mother, too.

"The week before she died, we talked about Blue Rain."

Kasey pretended it was merely an interesting fact. "Is that when you did this?" She pointed to the leather-stripped portrait.

"Oh, no. I just did that six months ago. But I did take the concept from Letty." Becky smiled. "She convinced me Blue Rain could just as easily be young, as an old lady with a corrugated face."

Had Blue Rain stood beside Letty as she died? Had she felt comforted? And how had it happened, her mother's death?

Kasey reached into her reporter's core for the strength to ask. "Was Leticia sick?"

"No. Not drunk, either, if you're asking about when she died. They checked, of course. A lone Indian, walking along the roadside just outside Pahrump? They did a blood alcohol test before they called her next of kin."

Kasey answered her anger with a reporter's solution. Instead of wondering how different her life would have been if she'd stayed with her mother, she vowed to write something about that kind of prejudgment.

"They said she died of hypertension." Becky's voice held a shrug. "And it does run in the family. Cal's already on blood pressure medicine."

As it had before, at the unprovoked mention of money, Becky's eyes changed from welcoming to blank.

Was her sudden reticence linked to Cal? Or did she blame Kasey for wearing that protective necklace when Letty died, walking alone at a desert roadside?

"Where was she going?" Kasey asked. "Did she drive to Pahrump? Did her car break down?"

"You never know." Becky shrugged and Kasey was about to press her, when she shifted the conversation. "So, how did you meet Bronc?"

The truth was too close to the scene she'd just pictured. If Bronc hadn't driven up ten years ago, Kasey might have been wandering a desert roadside. Her half-Paiute body might have been screened for alcohol before her parents were called to claim it.

"Bronc's my business contact." She put on a cool smile. "Tate Evans at BOW set him up as my escort."

"He's cute, isn't he?" Becky asked.

Kasey laughed. She'd never been good at being "one of the girls." Her social life was a zero and usually she liked it that way, but most women couldn't resist meddling.

Becky stood, without mentioning Kasey's lack of an answer.

"We've left them alone too long. Leaving Cal and Buck together is like locking two big, clumsy dogs in the house. The pack mentality takes over and next thing you know, they're marking territory and howling at the moon."

HE TELEPHONED THE SAME MORTAL he'd called before, dropping his coins into a pay telephone hundreds of miles away from the one he'd used in Los Angeles.

"The reporter is still prying. Did you do as I said?"

He waited. Because the mortal denied his powers and tried to resist, he conducted conversations while the woman was entranced. He savored her struggle against belief, though her slow responses tested his patience.

"Yes," she answered at last. "The bullets hit her car. She's just too stubborn to back off."

"And the boy, you used him?"

This time, the woman all but groaned. "Josh went along."

Winning meant destroying Horse and the reporter. Losing Josh would damage both, leaving them defenseless against the last shaman's dark magic.

"Get rid of her. If I must do it for you"—visions of black feathers, smoke, and blood filled his laughter—*"let's just say, you won't like it very much."*

"I KISSED YOU ONCE, RIGHT?"

For two hours, since they'd left the Bucks', he could think of nothing else. Buck had told him to leave things alone, and he'd agreed that would be the smart thing to do, but once they'd stopped to water the horses, the words just came spurting out.

He might have *thought* the words, for all the impact they made. He and Kasey stood shoulder to shoulder at the water hole. No chance she hadn't heard him.

"Don't deny it," he said. "Don't even try."

"Oh, that's not it." She brushed away his suspicions. "I was thinking you had a faulty memory, McDermitt." She took off her black hat, brushed a little dust from the brim, and smiled like a bored debutante. *"I kissed you."*

He'd by God fix that.

Her waist felt narrower than it looked as his arm caught her to him. She held China's rein like a lifeline as she came to him, belly flatter than he'd thought and head lower. Just before their lips met, he looked down. Her knuckles shone white from clutching the rein. Her thumb worked across it, again and again. Then his mouth closed on hers and he heard the rein fall and scuff the desert floor.

Her hat crushed between them as their chests met in a kind of confrontation. His lips held hers as he touched her cheek, her neck, and—God, this was how a kiss should feel. Surprise, then her mouth yielding, opening.

He'd wanted to punish her for disappearing that day, but he couldn't. Kasey turned soft in his arms. A sigh ran through her whole body.

Then she stopped. Cold and stiff. When he opened his eyes, hers stared back at him, one brow raised.

He let her go. She stepped back, arms crossed. Icy and objective, she tried to erase that head-spinning second in which she'd melted against him, and he fought back.

"Just how far would you go to get a story?" he asked, then waited for her to laugh, to wallop him across the face, anything to keep him from lowering her to the ground, fighting her frigid reserve with hands, lips, and whatever words it took to rekindle their bodies' unfinished business.

TEN

Bronc watched as Kasey cinched her arms tighter across her ribs.

Quick as a rattler, her chin jerked up. "How far would you go to hide a secret?"

That sleepy, giving-in look must've been his imagination. Kasey was sizing him up, for fair.

"I've got nothing to hide," he lied.

Kasey laughed and retrieved sunglasses from her saddlebags before remounting. She backed the gelding from the water and rode.

Damn. He'd blown it. If only he'd led up to it nice and slow. He swung aboard Rook and caught up.

"Best kiss of your young life, though, huh?" He said it cocky, making her smile, just as he'd planned. He couldn't think of much he wouldn't give for her to say yes.

She pushed her dark glasses up her nose before she answered. "First time I've ever been stood up, I'll give you that much."

She'd been stood up? Bronc thought of the sweaty hours

he'd waited in the county jail, hoping his attorney was right, that the hotshot reporter would save his ass. It had been no stocky, sensible do-gooder who'd spurned him. All along it had been Kasey.

"Yeah, well, you sure returned the favor, now, didn't you?"

"What are you talking about?" Her words snapped like a lash. "I sat at that—that—friggin' Hannah's Hen House—with grease suspended in the cigarette smoke—for an hour! Don't tell me—" Cool K. D. Wildmoon sounded on the verge of sputtering when she clamped her lips together.

She had waited. She *had.* Joy squirmed in him and, though it was cruel to leave her fuming, it kept him in charge.

"We can talk about it later, Ms. Wildmoon." He glanced up at the full-bellied clouds. "Just now, let's see if we can ride away from this storm."

⚡ ⚡

THEY COULD HAVE, BUT IT would've meant pushing the horses hard and the storm wouldn't amount to much. Besides, Kasey's sweet kiss and tart words had proven her to be down-right unpredictable. He didn't want to loose her on his family. Not that she'd scorn his parents to their faces. But mince them up in print? He figured that was a definite possibility.

A line of cottonwoods fluttered up ahead. There, they could pitch a tent against the rain and, if she wasn't so proud she'd sit out and get soaked to the skin, the tent would force some staked-at-four-corners intimacy.

She had no way of knowing they were only an hour from his folks' house or that he planned to pick her brain and find out what she knew of the Storm Hammer, before he took her near his dad.

At the pattering raindrops on his own hat brim, he looked to see how hers was holding up. A little worse for being crushed between them, but serviceable. It reminded him of the last hat he'd seen perched on Kasey's glossy black hair. That baseball cap, with her ponytail stuck through the back. He wondered if it was still hanging where he'd left it.

"It sounds like the tide rising." Kasey stroked China's neck as they rode. "The wind through those cottonwoods," she added.

"Wait 'til nightfall." Torn between the dangerous paths his brain could pursue, he asked, "How the hell old were you, when you drove out here in that broken-down Toyota?"

"Sixteen. I'd had my license for all of two weeks."

"Jeez, and your parents let you—They didn't know did they?"

"I was spending the night at Cookie's house." Prim and wide-eyed, she might have been telling the lie for the first time.

And that oughta be a reminder. Kasey had lied as a kid and she lied now. That didn't change with a kiss.

"And you a cop's kid."

"They tightened up later," she said, "but by then I'd already gone to the dogs."

"Aren't you ashamed of yourself?"

"I never did anything bad."

"Dangerous, though."

She made a throaty sound that conceded that much. Danger. That sound made him take self-control one notch tighter, made him search for words to distract himself from thinking how he could make her repeat that sound, just for him.

"I bet you're going to be one of those permissive moms, yourself."

"Are you kidding? My daughter won't be allowed to watch PG-13 movies until she's eighteen, drive 'til she's twenty-one, and as for dating…" Kasey's eyes narrowed in a tough-love glare. "As long as she lives in my house, we'll have none of that."

He tried to imagine her as a mother and only came up with the act that would put her there. "We need to pitch a tent before the wind comes up."

She helped him clear a site of rocks, lay out a ground cloth, and unroll the tent. In minutes, she sized up the design, slid tent poles together, and threaded them through the nylon channels.

She'd told the truth about camping. He hurried to say they should trench around the tent, before she could suggest it.

"Don't want you having to call nine-one-one in case of a flash flood." He scraped out a channel with a fold-up entrenching tool.

"Tent looks pretty watertight." Kasey brushed dirt from her jeans as she stood from hammering down the last stake. "I'm going to set up my laptop and type in some of my notes."

The idea wrenched his gut, though he couldn't say why.

"I should check my e-mail, too. Cookie said she'd keep in touch."

"Have at it, Hollywood. Don't mind that promise you made me." He loosened Rook's cinch and swung the saddle off.

Her eyes processed his jibe faster than any computer.

"Oh. Cooking. I can do that."

He imagined her serving a morning-after breakfast and munching a strawberry that matched her kiss-swollen lips.

Buck had told him about the millionaire she'd been engaged to—Mark Savage. Now *there* was a phony name. But she'd probably cooked for him. And more.

"Naw," Bronc thickened the accent she hated. "You take your little machine, and—"

"Bronc, don't be a pain."

She'd gone from "McDermitt" back to "Bronc" and he had no idea why it warmed him.

"All I was going to do was heat up some chili I bummed off

Buck."

"So, I get off easy. While you go into the tent and take a nap, I heat chili someone else has already cooked." She crossed her arms and flicked her fingers toward the tent.

"I have the horses to take care of."

"Okay, that'll give me five minutes in the tent, then you can doze to the sound of someone else working. That always puts me to sleep."

Damnation. Bronc could just see Savage unloading a five hundred-dollar briefcase or working out with weights, pumping iron while Kasey dozed on a velvet couch, waiting for him.

Rook sidestepped as Bronc slipped his bridle. He squatted to hobble the horse to keep him around, and wondered what Kasey was doing inside the tent. She was too smart to change clothes, with this drizzle coming down. Might be getting a slicker or making sure his sleeping bag was smoothed out and comfy.

He snorted at his daydream. She might be slipping into a fire-engine red teddy, too, but it wasn't likely.

He heard clicking. What was the little sneak computing? What was so important it couldn't wait?

And then Kasey was back.

"Scat," she said and Bronc allowed himself to be banished.

Once inside the tent, he wasn't sure what to do. One thing for sure, the six-by-six-foot space would keep them tucked close together. The two times he'd slept in this tent he'd ended up practically eating his knees.

When he heard Kasey humming and clattering utensils, creating quite a racket, he looked at the little gray computer. It was so small, he didn't see how it could have all the letters. Telling himself it was only curiosity about the machine, and not her correspondence, he reached toward it. After all, it probably wasn't one of those little jobs that automatically brought up the last document you'd been working on.

He heard the partially frozen block of chili hit the hot skillet. Then heard her rooting through packs and wondered if there was anything embarrassing there.

Not condoms. Lord knows he'd have to get new ones, if, *if* . . . No use making those plans.

He shucked off his boots, determined to make a real nap of it. He laid back on his sleeping bag, then tilted his Stetson over his eyes. Even with no sun to block, it'd put him in the mood for sleep. He took two deep breaths scented with sage, cumin, and beefsteak. And kept seeing the computer.

This could be a life-or-death situation. K. D. Wildmoon might be writing notes on something that'd get him thrown back into jail or worse, something that might get his dad thrown into jail. He needed to know. Pure and simple.

He opened the computer. Sure as sunrise, there it was, addressed to *LAPD.com*. That had to be the Los Angeles Police Department. Suspicions confirmed, he started to close the lid without reading further. But he'd already burgled her belongings, might as well be hung for a sheep as a lamb.

Oh yeah, real hard-core stuff. Bronc grabbed the bridge of his nose and squeezed.

"M&D," it read, "Sorry I didn't write sooner. Got here fine. Easy flight into Reno, pretty drive out to Gold Canyon, nice people, good horse, and easy interviews. Feel like I'm stealing *Dare's* money. Could you call Cookie & tell her to check her modem? Whatever she sent arrived blank. I love you guys. K."

Bronc lowered the lid and closed it with a nearly silent click. He rolled back onto his sleeping bag and tried to see the note as further proof she was a liar.

"Pretty drive"? What about the bullet-pocked red Taurus?

"Nice people"? No mention of the gunfire from Abner and the explosives-mined trail to the home of her long-lost relatives. And when her primary source was a lockjawed man still living down his bad-ass teenage reputation when he'd been arrested, how could she say her interviews were easy?

Eyes closed in the dark cave of his hat, Bronc smiled. The smell of wood smoke reminded him he hadn't bothered to start the campfire for her, but dinner was underway. This was the life.

〜〜 〜〜

MOVEMENT BROUGHT BRONC AWAKE.

"Hey there!" His own words echoed through his skull. In the darkness he grabbed an ankle.

"If you don't want a chili-pepper shampoo, you'd better turn loose." Her voice came from above and the savory smell of dinner meant she was balancing his meal.

He opened his fingers and she stepped past him.

"Don't move, or lean against the walls of the tent, either. I put on the rain fly, but it's coming down really hard."

Good thing he'd thought to pack that rain fly. He imagined Kasey digging through the pack for the extra sheet of tenting. He envisioned her shirt turning wet as she staked out the second barrier between them and the rain.

She smelled damp, flowery, and girlish enough to hug, but he didn't say so.

"Is that you that smells like a wet dog?" he asked.

"Mmm-hmm, but if someone had heated my dinner, cleaned my camp, and left nothing to wash but two dinner bowls, I'd be mighty sweet."

"Yes, ma'am."

"I'm going to try to sit without scalding you." As she said it, one of her kneecaps caught him in the chin. "Sorry. I couldn't find a lantern."

"I didn't bring one, but there's a flashlight—"

"In my pocket."

"If you want me to, I can get it." Bronc swallowed hard. Groping in the darkness, inside Kasey's pocket, was a prospect that made his gut buck in anticipation.

"Not if you want to keep all your fingers."

She knelt on the tent floor beside him. Her nearness sent out currents of warmth.

"Hands out," she said and placed the hot bowl of chili squarely in his palms.

Buck's chili stopped conversation. Propped against the saddle, the flashlight cast dim illumination.

"Do you know what this reminds me of? Did you ever read under your covers at night?"

"No, my parents had this incredibly open-minded attitude about reading. As long as I got up on time, I could read as late as I wanted."

"Well," Bronc paused at the slap of her wet braid as she tossed it back over her shoulder. "I had to sneak. My dad wanted me up by five, doing chores before I went to school. One morning, he knew I'd been up late reading the night before, I lollygagged around in bed so long I didn't have time to feed the horses. I lied, said I had fed them, and ran down the road to catch the bus.

"When I got home, I found out my parents had fed the horses, then conspired against me. *I* didn't get fed until breakfast the next morning. I swore it was child abuse, but Mom wouldn't even give me a slice of bread."

"I guess it didn't stop you reading." Kasey sounded downright pleased with him.

"No. My dad bedded down early, and I found out that if I put more blankets on my bed, and crawled under, the light didn't show." Bronc yawned, thinking of sauna-hot summer nights under the down comforter his mother had finally given him because he kept asking for thicker blankets.

"My mom knew. She'd mention the dark circles under my eyes and cookie crumbs in my bed."

Kasey's silhouette shifted as she leaned her chin into her palm. The necklace swayed, catching the flashlight's beam, but it was nothing compared to the black and bronze contours of her face.

Lit from beneath, her cheekbones looked even higher, her brow smoother beneath the ink-black hair. Her eyes remained in shadow, unsettling him until she leaned forward.

"When did I stand you up?"

"You just can't resist fighting, can you?"

"I don't want to fight. I'd apologize if you'd let me."

"Outside, the wind had slacked off. The only sound was the sodden snapping of sticks that had been hot with fire and were now drenched.

"Okay. When I was in jail, waiting for trial, my attorney told me there was a hotshot reporter who wrote for the *Sun-Times*, and if she wrote a story that, uh, 'flattered' me, things would go better for me."

The uncertain light made the crease between her brows deep as a knife cut. "And that reporter was me?"

"K. D. Wildmoon."

"But I haven't worked for the *Sun-Times* in months."

"There you go."

Her fingers interlaced and he heard her set her jaw.

"I was in Los Angeles. If your attorney had called the *Sun-Times* and they'd called *Dare*, you could have gotten me." Her fingers seesawed back and forth. "For crying out loud, who's your attorney? How did he try to reach me?"

"Now, why do you assume my attorney was a 'he'?"

"Because a woman would have tried harder." She paused,

regathering her outrage. "How was I supposed to help you if no one told me?"

"Hey." He grabbed her hands between both of his. "It's all over. You didn't know." He shrugged and thought he was loco to be comforting *her* over this.

"Your attorney was right. It's my kind of story. That's why *Dare* sent me." She sat quiet for a moment, but she didn't pull away from his hands. "I bet he did call the *Sun-Times* and Mark—He sent Cookie, didn't he?" She shook her head. "He's such a..."

"Son of a bitch?" Bronc felt pleased to supply the appropriate words.

"At least."

He pulled her toward him, certain he could kiss that lopsided smile into passion. In this tiny tent, there'd be no excuses, no interruptions.

She almost came to him.

But then she leaned back, weighting herself against his pull. At first he thought she sighed, then he realized it was a long, intaken breath and it shivered.

"C'mon, darlin'. One little kiss."

She glanced around the tent pointedly and came to the same conclusion he had. A kiss would lead to a lot more.

"I think..." Her voice was low. He wanted to believe desire tightened her throat, making her vocal chords irrelevant compared to other parts of her body. "... we better keep to business."

Light as he could, he touched the backs of her hands and stopped when he felt the tender risings of her veins. He couldn't think of a single thing to say.

"In fact—" She stood, pulling away, ducking so her head didn't collide with the tent top. "I'm taking our bowls out to wash."

"Leave 'em, Kasey. Or just stick 'em outside the flap." He realized he was using the same soft voice he'd use with a spooked pony. Only the quiet seemed to agitate her.

"No. I know you probably don't have bears, but—" She groped for a sensible excuse. "Coyotes! I don't want to leave them out to attract coyotes. Once they start thinking people are feeding them, next thing you know, they're looking for people and then some tourist shoots one, or something.

"I'll tell you what else. Just, um, while I'm outside, why don't you get ready for bed? That way, there won't be two of us thrashing around in here."

He lifted the flashlight to hand it to her, since she was so hellbent on escape, and its beam picked up the tee shirt clinging to the undersides of her breasts. Christ, it was like an offering.

"How 'bout if I wait for you to tuck me in?"

"Don't," she said. "Just don't."

෫ ෫

RENEGADE THOUGHTS wouldn't let her sleep. Kasey tried to lie still. Even with the rain pounding outside, she heard every restless movement of his legs, every fitful crossing of his arms, each stifled breath.

For a few minutes after they'd doused the flashlight, she'd turned her back on him. That was even worse. She imagined his gaze gliding down her spine, from nape to tailbone. She imagined scooting back against him, pretending to sleep, so that his arms would go around her and hold her all night.

She tried a screwy sort of meditation, using his breaths as her mantra, matching her exhalations to his. It didn't soothe her. Especially when his breath caught and she thought, just maybe, he'd decided to call her bluff. But he hadn't. He'd finally fallen asleep.

෫ ෫

THE FACE OF HER WATCH said she'd waited a full hour.

He'd been asleep that long and his breathing had gone peaceful as soon as the storm outside stopped. Surely he hadn't heard her slip out of the tent.

China greeted her with a whicker. Rook raised his head and shook it.

The moon shone bright as hammered silver. *A horse-thief moon.* Where had she heard that? The words flowed like a snatch of song, perfect for this Western desert and the outlaw she was supposed to be sleeping beside.

Her parents agreed people did weird things during the full moon. And who'd know better than a couple of cops? But they'd expect the accused felon inside the tent to be the one committing the weird act. Not their daughter.

Blue Rain, more contrary than a spirit who wanted help should be, had deserted Kasey just when she'd started believing. Kasey replayed the moment in Becky's gallery when she'd felt the medicine woman's power. In that moment, she'd surrendered.

Hearing from Becky that Blue Rain had come to her mother, too, had intensified her belief.

Once before, Kasey had summoned the power of the necklace. She glanced back toward the tent. No sound. Not even the rustling of Bronc's sleeping bag.

She knelt and held the necklace in her outstretched hands to catch the moonglow. She stared at the central shell and the tiny blue trade beads lit like cobalt fire.

This was her heritage, white Europeans bringing beads blown from molten glass to red men who'd gathered shells here, when the desert was still the bed of a great lake covering this state and several more.

She felt the wonder of the necklace's age, but no magic. Kasey slowed her breathing. *Blue Rain, I'm ready.* She listened to the faint wind, imagined it lifting the horses' manes, fluttering the rainfly against its tethers.

Heaven help her if Bronc McDermitt swaggered out of the tent while she was in this posture, a postulate to the moon, a vesta offering up her simple adornment. A pagan.

The necklace warmed in her hands and the shells seemed to swell, gathering the glow and electricity it used for warnings.

Both times she'd come to the desert, Blue Rain had crackled power through the necklace. Now, she needed Blue Rain's guidance to know just what the electricity meant.

Still staring at the smooth central shell, Kasey pictured Blue Rain's face framed with braids. Childish, but she'd confided a weakness for men which hampered them all. Kasey focused. Nothing existed except the necklace and Blue Rain, its protectress.

Come on, girlfriend, let's have a little paranormal activity.

This was rich, like the First Lady consulting an astrologer. If anyone saw journalist K. D. Wildmoon begging for a spirit guide, she'd never work again.

Once before, the necklace had responded to her plea, instead of arcing its energy into her in random bursts. Beyond doubt, beyond self-induced hypnosis or meditation, help had come that night she'd been betrayed by Mark.

Bereft and steeped in tequila, she'd unplugged the nonstop sympathetic voices coming through her telephone answering machine and wandered into the adobe brick courtyard of the apartment she shared with Cookie. She'd sat on the edge of the central fountain and held the necklace in both hands. Unsteady, she'd slipped to the well-tended grass and knelt. And the necklace had spoken.

"Let him go," the voice had commanded and Kasey hadn't questioned it.

Now, as if the northern lights had changed address, a curtain of radiance wavered around her. No amount of staring could pierce the light, and yet she heard drums, horses, bone rattles, and shrilling flutes beyond the wall of brilliance.

"I've met your tests. I've given you all three knots on this story string: you, Fox, Horse. You know all three. You've touched all three. Our victory must be your doing."

Fingers pointed at a medicine woman who'd believed the vows of a cavalryman who wanted wild mustangs tamed. He wanted them saddled and ridden into war on muddy battlefields. Like film from a reel, blue and silver images slipped past her mind's eye until, slowing, she saw a face that looked almost like hers, a face she knew for her mother's.

Letty Wildmoon pointed to the last frame on the film, the last box of color printed on plastic. In it, Kasey saw herself, but only from the back. Legs bare, muscular, and braced on each side of an animal pelt, she stood and stared. Cresting a distant mountain, disappearing into mist, rode a man.

"Don't let him go," said Blue Rain's voice, and then, as if she'd flipped a switch, the necklace turned cold. Beads and shells were no more than baubles.

Kasey stood with stiff knees. Blue Rain was a cryptic wench.

Kasey had thought herself pretty talented at deciphering symbolism in English literature, but the stakes had never been this high.

Kasey looped the necklace back over her head, let it settle across her chest, and rubbed her eyes. The magic curtains had been drawn back, then yanked closed. She stood under the full moon, alone but for two dozing horses.

Kasey crept back into the tent. She drew in the scents of lingering spices, saddle leather, and sleeping man and listened for sounds that didn't come.

ELEVEN

"How long 'til we reach your ranch?" Kasey felt eager, rested, ready to interview anyone about anything.

Finally, she'd received an e-mail from Cookie bemoaning Mark Savage's decision to play Clark Kent on a news story in Salt Lake City. He'd insisted Cookie come along to do the photos.

The upside to the trip, Cookie said, was that she would break away from Mark and piggyback her secret *Dare* shoot onto the trip. Keeping in touch via e-mail, Kasey would direct Cookie to faces and places to shoot, and they'd work out a rendezvous.

Kasey could hardly wait.

Cookie hadn't mentioned the other plus to her excursion. Mark would take a giant nosedive on this story. His topic was polygamy. Always a publisher, never a reporter, he saw nothing wrong with jetting into Salt Lake City, waltzing up to the Temple, and asking a list of sensitive questions. Kasey rubbed her forehead in embarrassment, glad she wouldn't be there. Country club–reared Mark needed to stay in his air-conditioned office.

Kasey pushed a lock of wind-blown hair from her eyes and glanced over at Bronc. After a couple days of neglecting that black beard, he'd decided to shave. She hadn't meant to startle him this morning, but when she'd walked behind him and he'd caught her reflection in the mirror he'd hung from a cotton-wood, he'd nicked his chin.

It didn't make him less handsome.

Self-indulgent and immature as it sounded, even inside her own head, Kasey couldn't smother her delight over reintroducing him to Cookie.

But blue eyes, black hair, that skeptical squint, and a jaw that looked seven sorts of stubborn until he loosed that great laugh made him just the sort of renegade male she and Cookie targeted in the game they'd designed as teenagers.

If she'd had to give it a name, Kasey would have called their exchanges Not Him. Only tough, reckless, not-hungry-for-love-but-maybe-just-a-taste males qualified.

Even in fantasy, the breed was difficult to find. She and Cookie had agreed on Daniel Day-Lewis, hair streaming against a fiery background in *Last of the Mohicans*. They'd agreed on Harrison Ford and on Tom Selleck—but only in *Quigley Down Under*.

Kasey couldn't defend Cookie's choice of Bruce Willis any more than Cookie understood her nomination of Brad Pitt.

Now, riding beside Bronc next to a stream trying to become a river, Kasey decided he qualified. Cookie would definitely agree.

Soldier Creek, Bronc had told her for her notes, and the footing was steep. Saplings formed thickets and riding took so much of her attention that Kasey was almost startled when Bronc finally replied.

"Rainbow Bend is about an hour, hour and a half away."

"We could have slept there last night," she said.

She didn't begrudge him his silence. She knew why he'd stopped in that lonely place. He'd seen through her cool exterior to the family curse. Too bad it hadn't worked out for him.

Feeling smug, Kasey straightened in her saddle and guided China after Rook as the black forded a thick stand of saplings. She lifted her right boot from the stirrup, keeping a particularly thorny bush from ripping her jeans.

Sexist as it was, Kasey reveled in Bronc's pursuit and his buckaroo etiquette. His sure touch and sexy small talk beat the heck out of the crotch-grabbing moans dispensed from city street corners.

Ouch. Kasey flinched silently as a sapling whipped the back of her hand and drew blood. Bronc glanced back and frowned as if she'd screamed. She hurried to retrieve the gloves she'd stripped off because the warm weather made her hands sweat. She wasn't fast enough.

"That's it." Bronc reined Rook hard right and motioned for Kasey to follow. On a gravelly downhill, he rode to the relatively clear riverside. "Get off and put these on."

Bronc yanked a pair of chaps from his pack.

Chinks, Kasey reminded herself. They were the short version of his chaps. This morning he'd settled his chaps low on his hips, fastened them at the waist, then reached behind him, buckling the leather in a gruff ceremony that would have aroused a nun.

Kasey had taken one look and blocked out Bronc's lecture on utility. Chaps might protect her jeans from ripping brush and dust. Chaps' fringe might direct rain to drip off so she wouldn't spend another soggy evening in wet pants. Even so, their crotchless, leg-hugging fit didn't suit her sense of style.

"Same thing as the gloves—" Bronc stared at the crimson scratch. "Damn it to hell, Hollywood. Think you could use the brain God gave you, just for a couple days?"

She could hear McDermitt's babysitting lecture brewing, so she took steps to avoid it. Still, even as she dismounted, Bronc yanked her gloves from the loop on her saddle, tucked them under his arm, and slung the chinks around her waist.

"You know," Kasey said, fighting her breathless tone, "if we're that close to your house, maybe I could tough it out."

"Yeah, that's a great idea." He turned her to face away from him. "How many pairs of jeans did you bring?" He hauled back on the leather strap around her waist as if he were fastening a saddle's cinch. "Five or six, I hope, because they're going to get ripped to ribbons between here and Rainbow Bend." He tucked the strap end through the buckle and gave it a satisfied jerk.

Then he knelt behind her.

"This is really too much." Kasey stared back over her shoulder. Even though it was covered by denim, the leather curved away, covering only her legs and showcasing her seat. Each leg was fastened by two buckles, one just behind her thigh and one near her knee. "I can do this."

"Steady there, girl." He awarded her the same pat he'd give his horse. Not, lucky for him, on her flank. "I'll have you harnessed up in just a minute."

He was enjoying this entirely too much. When he'd finished the first top buckle, he trailed his open hand down her leg to the lower one. To a horse, it might have been a soothing movement. It didn't have that effect on Kasey.

A *source*. He's a source for a story.

A damn good story that's going to knock Mark Savage on his butt. Don't think butt.

Kasey told her mind to focus, to remember the stakes she'd chosen. If she failed to nail the horse killer, she'd be back writing drivel for Mark.

ﻻﻵ ﻹ

WIND HAD KICKED UP by the time they broke from the cottonwoods and onto a plain. Kasey felt a strong uneasiness, although she should have felt relieved to be free of the uneven footing and slashing saplings.

She could make out miniature ranch buildings, far ahead. It had to be Rainbow Bend, Bronc's home, but a sheet of white dust partially obscured it.

Just as she was trying to count buildings, a sizzling jolt arced from the necklace against her collarbone. Kasey swallowed the gasp, pressed her lips together, and clenched her stomach muscles. She'd wished for a visitation from Blue Rain, but this wasn't a convenient time.

She didn't allow her legs to tighten against China as she scanned the terrain, searching.

Blue Rain and her spirit horse were invisible, but foreboding mixed with the familiar jangle of alarm. An intermittent drone made her look skyward. Half-hidden by dust, silver glinted and a rippling red ribbon floated down.

Squinting against particles invading her eyes, Kasey turned to Bronc and pointed. He nodded, tight-lipped, and reined Rook closer to speak over the wind's whistling.

"Flynn. The guy from PAPA."

Kasey nodded. She concentrated on the helicopter in spite of the necklace's demand. Why would Flynn fly in this dust storm? As the electric intensity tapered off, leaving her mind free to think, Kasey decided the skies above the Scolding Rock desert must be clear. Flynn would be safe flying above it.

"The marker means a kill." Bronc's face stayed so nonjudgmental, it had to be intentional.

As she arranged the necklace outside her shirt, Kasey decided the marker was probably plastic tape similar to that used to designate a crime scene.

Maybe she'd read about the process and filed the fact deep in her memory, so her sympathy for a beast fleeing death had stimulated the necklace.

No. Both horses shied, but even Bronc's soft, "What the hell?" didn't lever Kasey's eyes from the image ahead.

Blue Rain was garbed in heartbreak. Afoot and alone, her shoulders slumped. Her garments were blurred, but her face was real. Tear trails wandered over gray ashes scrubbed into her cheeks. Then she vanished.

Kasey was left to deal with China, switching his tail, shifting from side to side. She glanced up at Bronc's calming word to his horse, and he met her eyes.

Kasey had no answer for Bronc's inquiring, unsettled look. China kicked a rear hoof and Kasey checked the pack tied behind her saddle.

"Funny they'd spook at the helicopter."

Bronc had seen something. Maybe not Blue Rain in the throes of despair, but something.

Put your reporter's head on. Kasey checked the knots binding her sleeping bag to her saddle. *Blue Rain wouldn't appear to a down-to-earth cowboy. You're the half-breed recipient of this uncertain magic.* Satisfied the bag was centered and comfortable as possible for China, Kasey gave herself one last mental shaking. *This is your mad mission. Don't go looking for company.*

Satisfied she'd swept the static from her mind, Kasey met Bronc's eyes again.

The shadow in his sureness made her want to grab his face and kiss him. Instead, she did what she'd trained to do.

"Why's this called Soldier Creek?"

Bronc lifted one shoulder. "Some Civil War catastrophe. Union soldiers rounded up a band of wild horses for cavalry mounts. Local tribe took exception to it."

He set Rook to a ground-eating lope.

Kasey blamed her shiver on a damp shirt and the breeze, but her modern reality and Blue Rain's had just meshed again.

§§ ⌘

RAINBOW BEND RANCH WAS AN oasis in time. It was the ranch where grandparents in children's books lived to raise puppies, bake cookies, and tuck you in at night. It was the place moved-away adults came home to, where they shucked off high heels and walked barefoot through soft grass.

A squeaking windmill pumped water into a stock tank while a cowboy stood in the bed of a pickup truck, working on it. "Hey, Mac," Bronc called to him.

"Hey, yourself." He waved a pair of pliers. "The sucker-rod's loose again. I'll be up to the house in a few minutes."

As they rode on, a Lassie-colored collie streaked past meadow oaks and split rail fences to greet them with joyous, body-curling barks.

"Champ, you idiot, you'll spook the horses."

Bronc's soft scolding and the idyllic setting made Kasey set her teeth together. Hard.

Get a grip. This isn't your homecoming from prison. You're not a member of the family. You're a reporter. Act like one.

Still, she didn't retrieve her notebook. Because the situation called for sensitivity, she set her mind on "record" and continued her observations.

In books, ranch entrances were marked by squared-off wooden arches tall enough to admit a cattle truck. Rainbow Bend was the same. The name, capped by two curved lines, was burned into the crosspiece. Another rectangle of wood hung from slightly uneven chains, showing off a motto engraved in almost illegible script, "Better to Live Rich than Die Rich."

Kasey's research and the rambling brown ranch house said the McDermitts weren't likely to do either. Not if "rich" included dollar signs, but that sort of journalistic analysis came later. Now, she needed facts.

Kasey smiled at the yellow rural delivery tube for the local newspaper nailed to one of the posts. Then she noticed the duct tape X closing off its portal. Had finances or a dispute over news coverage caused the McDermitts to slam the door on news? Or was it the simple fact that jobs in town only allowed them to come home on weekends?

A neigh floated on a breeze spiced with wet sagebrush. In response, China gathered beneath her. For an instant, Kasey wondered if Bronc was right. The gelding might be biding his time for a display of equine fireworks.

A screen door slammed open. A woman, with two gangly adolescents in her wake, vaulted off the front porch. Bronc cleared his throat.

"Get ready for a real tearjerker." In spite of his hard-set jaw, his tone was half dread and Kasey knew she was the cause.

"You've been giving me Buckaroo 101, and it's time I returned the favor, with a class on journalistic ethics, but not right now."

He nodded.

"I'm reporting on a problem." Kasey reached out in time to grab Bronc's arm as he rode past. He halted. Questions still filled his eyes as she tugged him closer, threaded her fingers through his.

"I'm not here to smear your family, McDermitt."

When she released his hand, Bronc kept riding. Kasey felt a hollow knell beneath her breastbone.

Then, he glanced back over his shoulder with a boyish smile and said, "Thanks, Hollywood."

⤳ ⤳

BRONC HARDENED HIMSELF AGAINST SENTIMENT and dismounted.

Josh, looking gaunt and not nearly thirteen, stood aside, holding one of Rook's split reins, while Mom and Callie wrapped Bronc in hugs.

"I'm so glad—" Bronc's hug ended Mom's words. Her shoulders felt narrower than Callie's, but she kept fighting not to cry. "You look *just* fine. Why didn't you call and tell us you were, you were—"

Bronc felt her tears against his shirtfront. His own eyes stung, but he was damned if he'd put on a show.

"Hey, Mom, I'm fine. I'm never going back, so it don't mean nothing."

"Bronc." Callie, hand on one hip, rolled her brown eyes skyward and pulled his name into a reprimand for the grammatical lapse. "You don't have to talk like a redneck, gee."

Over his mother's shoulder, Bronc saw Josh flush and give a half-hearted thumbs-up. Bronc took it as a gesture of manly support until he noticed Josh was staring at Kasey with undisguised craving. Rotten little sucker.

"Callie," Bronc mimicked. "You don't have to be such a lady, geeeee."

As Bronc caught his little sister in a headlock and ruffled her heavily moussed hair, Josh piled on. He wrestled Callie away from Bronc and she shot an elbow to Josh's ribs. He retaliated. Too hard.

"Ow," Callie yowled.

"That didn't hurt." Josh pushed a forelock of matching hair from his eyes.

"You don't know that! It's my rib you about broke and it did too hurt." Callie curved an arm around her middle. "Mom, he just ruins everything."

"Josh, take it easy on your sister." His mom's reprimand was a little too good-natured as her smile included Kasey.

Bronc watched Kasey study the encounter with an intensity that didn't look journalistic. Hadn't Kasey said she'd been an only child? Maybe she missed family life and that—not her yearning for his young ass—explained her gentle touch and promise.

Welcome to the real world, Bronc thought. *You try being in high school when your mom pops out twins.*

"Oh, sure." Josh's grin faded into a sneer. "She can take a shot at me, but I'm not allowed to do anything back." Arms crossed, weight on one leg, his eyelids closed to a menacing slit. "Later."

"Oh, like I'm so scared—"

"That's enough," Bronc said and the twins settled at his bark. "Kasey Wildmoon, I'd like you to meet my mother, Wendy."

Recognition of the name Wildmoon made his mom's eyes widen as she shook Kasey's hand. Bronc kicked himself for being dense. He'd been a kid when Billy Wildmoon shacked up with Buck's big sister, Letty, but his mom remembered. By the warm and curious looks passing between the two women, he could be sure they'd have a long talk over it.

"And my sister, Callie, and brother, Josh," Bronc said, long schooled not to designate them as twins.

Instead of shaking their hands, Kasey gave the kids a wave of recognition and launched into a conversation.

"I'm from L.A., where there's a school every couple miles." Her lips twisted in sympathy. "I sure haven't seen many here and I couldn't help wondering where you go to school."

True to form, Josh stood silent while Callie responded for them both.

"In Fallon. It's a little middle school. How many people?"

Callie lifted her shoulders as she stood next to her mother. They were just about equal in height and Callie gloried in it.

"Close to two hundred." Mom gave a tug to the hem of Callie's shorts, which barely covered her bottom.

"I hope you don't wear those to school," Bronc grumbled. His baby sister's sun-tanned legs had started looking like a woman's. Callie stuck out her tongue, before continuing.

"It's kind of a redneck little school. I wish I could go to school in L.A. I bet you share lockers with, like, movie stars' kids and stuff."

Redneck. Twice in ten minutes, she'd spouted off with that. "This horse belong to anyone 'round these parts?"

Shit. Here came Mac leading Rook. Bronc felt caught, like a guilty kid all over again.

"Josh was supposed to be holding him," Callie answered, then sighed in a long-suffering gust. "But I guess I can take him to the barn, and your horse too, Kasey."

"Miss Wildmoon," Wendy corrected, gesturing for Josh to take China's reins and help his twin.

" 'Kasey' is fine."

"Kasey Wildmoon, meet my dad, Mac McDermitt."

"Mr. McDermitt." Kasey's surprise underlined his dad's name. "I'm glad to meet you."

She took Mac's greasy, scabby hand, seeming unaware of the finger he'd lost to a careless dally around his saddle horn as a ton of steer hit the end of the rope.

"Ma'am." Mac gave Kasey's hand a quick wringing. "I didn't know it was you—" Kasey gestured.

"No reason you should," Mac said.

"—out working on the windmill."

"Somebody's got to do the work around here."

Bronc rubbed the back of his neck, feeling the tense urge

for combat.

"I'll help you," Bronc said, believing all over again that there was a good reason young stallions split off from the main herd into bachelor bands.

"That figures, don't it?" Mac nodded toward Mom. "I work all day and he rides up to take the credit?"

Bronc held a breath and replayed the softness of Kasey's hand against his. She might not have come here intending to smear his family, but Mac might make it irresistible.

At six foot, two inches—a tall man for his day—Mac reminded Bronc of a lone pine tree, burnt black and bitter.

He shouldn't compare Mac to Abner. Mac wasn't crazy, but he'd turned into one paranoid son-of-a-gun, accusing his son of "taking all the credit" instead of acknowledging he'd taken the blame for shooting horses, just to throw them off the track of his old man.

"No, sir," Mac said. "Don't think I'll be needing your help.

"Okay, Mac."

Bronc remembered a time when he'd called him Dad. At about thirteen, he'd tried calling his parents by their given names. Mac accepted it for himself, but he hadn't taken to Bronc calling his mother Wendy.

Now, gray threaded Mom's brown ponytail, but she'd been sixteen when she met and married Mac, seventeen when she bore Bronc on the long drive to the hospital. Mac swore he'd nearly lost his teenaged bride. Ever since, he'd demanded absolute respect for her.

On the day Bronc had called her Wendy, Mac had grabbed Bronc hard enough that some would call it child abuse.

"Your mother's not your buddy," Mac had hollered. "Instead of hanging out with your pals this weekend, you stay home and babysit while *Wendy* puts up tomatoes. Sitting in that hundred-

and-ten- degree kitchen with two whining brats might help you remember why you call her *Mom*."

Now, Mom interceded.

"Kasey, tell me you wouldn't turn down a glass of iced tea." She guided Kasey toward the house with a sweetness that reminded Bronc he hadn't explained Kasey's presence.

"That sounds great." Kasey lifted her saddlebags over one shoulder.

The bags carried her computer, notebooks, and every incriminating memo she'd made about him. He needed to correct Mom's impression that Kasey was a girlfriend, needed to warn Mac that she was a reporter set on solving this horse thing.

Before he followed them into the house, he turned at a creaking sound. Not the windmill, but the swing.

How many days had he waited, a bored child watching for his father and the hands to ride in at dusk? Every time, he'd begged the man, face grimed with sweat and alkali dust, "Swing me, Daddy. Swing me!" And Mac had.

How could he tell Kasey that hard times and worse luck had molded this mean-spirited Mac McDermitt—a man absolutely capable of killing animal intruders on his land—from his daddy?

TWELVE

*W*hat in God's name was I thinking? Kasey slipped from the McDermitt family bathroom, wishing they'd offered her the chance to shower. But she'd only been invited to 'freshen up' before joining them in the cool, woodsmoke-scented den. Kasey heard steps on floorboards overhead and wondered if Bronc still had a bedroom here.

Kasey slid aside an Indian blanket draped over the leather couch. She tried to study the room, instead of brooding over what she'd done.

I fondled a source. I rubbed my fingers through his. No man would interpret that as a simply friendly gesture.

Polished copper glimmered throughout the room. A kerosene lantern on the mantel, a dented bucket holding a nasturtium on the windowsill, harness decorations threaded on a leather strap next to a collection of faded blue ribbons and old photographs.

In the kitchen, she heard Bronc talking to his parents, but the hum of an open and overtaxed freezer kept her from discerning the words.

I led him to believe—shoot, I practically promised—I wouldn't write anything negative about his family, when Mac's bitter words have already cast him in a bad light. Ice cubes tinkled and boots clomped on hardwood floors, but she was still alone with sepia photographs in unique frames.

Several were hammered together from scrap wood to frame favorite horses and family outings. Grammar school pictures of the twins—gap-toothed and grinning—sat amid glued-together Popsicle sticks.

Kasey stood and walked closer to a photograph framed by the arching neck of a copper horse. In it, two young cowboys wore chaps and held coiled lariats. White smiles shone from the shade of their hats.

Kasey considered the chimney, counting ten bricks before she allowed herself to study the photo of Bronc McDermitt and Calvin Buck. They looked younger than the day she'd met them in the Scolding Rock desert, but she forced herself to look past their apparent innocence.

As adults, they might be taking payments from ranchers to kill wild horses. What if they were partners in crime?

"It's so warm in here, why don't I turn on the fan."

Wendy McDermitt juggled a tray and flipped on a wall switch with her elbow. Overhead, a huge ceiling fan began to spin. It looked like it had come out of an Old West saloon instead of a Sears catalog.

Kasey loved it. She loved the entire room and the cozy, cantankerous feeling of family. If she hoped to maintain an ounce of objectivity, she needed to get on the next jet bound for Los Angeles.

But maybe that wouldn't be necessary.

Callie settled at the far end of the couch and slid a sidelong glance toward Kasey. Josh and Bronc bracketed the mantel. If she hadn't felt attention leveled at her with firing squad intensity, she would have smiled as Josh adjusted his stance to mirror Bronc's.

He'd told them she was a reporter. That explained Wendy's fluttering. She jostled a spoon from the sugar bowl, centered a plate of cookies on the coffee table, smoothed wrinkles from a paper napkin, and retreated to a chair halfway across the room.

Mac took the offensive, pulling up a chair to face Kasey across the coffee table. At least it was a posture she knew how to handle.

"Gabe says you're here to write a story about wild horses."

Kasey's mind stuttered before realizing Mac referred to Bronc.

"That's right, in a way." Kasey lifted her iced tea and made a sip last long enough that she could conjure up the horror of working for Mark Savage again. "But he's being modest." Time to get down to business. "I work for a magazine that covers controversial topics in a way readers can understand."

"Sugarcoats 'em, you mean."

"Not at all. *Dare* wants to consider the mustang troubles via a personality piece on Bronc."

Kasey paused, expecting the twins to interject sibling jibes, but they both stiffened. Kasey heard Callie's teeth grit.

"There'll be pictures—of the horses, the land, the people involved—and interviews with folks willing to tell me what they think about Bronc and BOW's wild horse program."

Callie twisted to face Kasey, but Josh spoke first.

"Did you plan to tell us you were spying—"

Bronc bristled as Mac silenced his son with a gesture. "Spying wouldn't get me anywhere." Kasey lifted her saddlebags. "My reporter stuff is pretty bulky."

"No little espionage tape recorders?" Josh sneered.

"Son, that's about enough."

"Dad, I've read about this surveillance stuff." Josh swept an index finger before him. "That's how they get big stories."

"I'm kind of old-fashioned," Kasey said. "I like paper. Tape recorders can malfunction. If the tape breaks or I get into talking and forget to flip the tape over, I return to the office with no story.

"Not that I don't have one." Kasey sorted through her saddlebags. "It was a gift, a little voice-activated thing. I've just never had a need for it. Here." She extended it to Josh. "Take a look."

Kasey took out her notebook and a ballpoint pen and laid them on the table. "These," she said, "I can trust."

Mac leaned back, arms crossed over his chest.

With her fingertip, Kasey drew a wavy line on her frosted glass of tea, then claimed one of Wendy's oatmeal cookies and tried to keep the shower of crumbs over the paper napkin. If she kept this low-key, Mac would come to her.

Over the mantel, a bevel-edged mirror reflected rainbows. Kasey resisted the urge to swivel and search the room for their source. Her necklace lay quiescent and ordinary around her neck.

"So, what d'you want to know?" Mac growled.

"Anything you want to tell me. I've explained what I told BOW to get out here with your son as my escort." Kasey glanced at Bronc. His stillness said he was waiting for a misstep. "Maybe, instead of talking about Bronc—since I'd have to quote you as his father—you could tell me about the wild horse program. Explain the best and worst of it and I'll use it as background."

Her hands did a little shrug. "Just a suggestion," they seemed to say.

"There ain't no 'best,'" Mac said. "The government put this thing together without considerin' facts."

Kasey groped for her pen, keeping her eyes on Mac as he began to number points on his fingers.

"The fact that this is open range means they can't keep horses off private grazing land. The fact that these stinkin' bureaucrats still don't know much about horses' reproduction rate, and worst," Mac said, pressing down his ring finger, "they won't face the fact that Nature goes by her own timetable. If there's a drought or a wet season, it's all the same to them assholes in Washington."

"Great, Dad." Callie rolled her eyes toward the rafters.

"You know," Kasey said, still writing, "that's an incredibly succinct evaluation of the problem."

"For a broken-down buckaroo."

She met Mac's skeptical eyes. Nothing would keep her from believing the horses had been mistreated, but Mac's few sentences had acted like a magnifying glass on the problem.

"For anyone." Kasey tapped her pen against her notebook. "It's a complex situation."

"And cowboys aren't exactly known for their brains," Josh said.

"Neither are cops," Kasey said, "and yet both my parents are good at things besides pounding heads and writing tickets." Kasey enjoyed the twins' looks of astonishment. "And journalists don't exactly have sterling reputations these days."

Mac swirled his glass of tea. "Cops, they got a real job to do, like ranchers. Reporters, if you'll pardon me sayin' so, don't do much besides paw through other folks' dirty laundry."

Kasey's heart lifted at the dare.

"You're gonna wish you never put that burr under her blanket." Bronc said. "She'll tell you how she's a pit bull for the public—"

"A watchdog," Kasey corrected.

"—how you can't be in Congress watching politicians vote wrong or in Brazil seein' what they spray on your bananas."

"You'll do well leavin' my banana outta this, boy." He wheeled back to face Kasey. "I'll tell you I'm as shy of politicians as an old maid skinnin' a skunk."

"Mac, it's a mighty good thing she isn't using that tape recorder," Wendy said when her laughter subsided. "You're suffering from heat stroke, is all I can figure."

"Write this down," Mac said, pointing. "Those roundups are useless, even if they're Gabe's bread and butter. He and the local hands BOW hires know what they're doing, but it's not enough. They oughta harvest those horses like a crop."

"Because of the overpopulation," Kasey said, nodding. "But the vasectomies they tried on stallions, they worked, right?" She caught Bronc's nod and continued. "But they were too expensive."

"Lead's cheap."

Damn. It wasn't as if she hadn't heard the same sentiment expressed by cops about criminals. But cops didn't say it on the record, to a reporter.

She caught Bronc's despairing expression before he hid it, and suddenly this twisted story made sense. Bronc's tough talk about wild horses, and his "ahhh" of disappointment as the mustangs galloped out of view from the water hole. Bronc's gentleness prying a stone from Rook's hoof, his kindness toward old Abner Bengochea, whose front yard was a minefield. She hated the obvious conclusion: Mac had killed mustangs and left Bronc to take the blame.

"I bet you think that's harsh," Mac said. "But let me tell you how heartless BOW is about those horses.

"For years I worked on a water system—ponds, pipelines, and whatnot—to bring river water to my range cattle. Sure as sunrise, the summer I finished up, a hundred horses moved in on me. Why shouldn't they? There was plenty of water and grass and the cattle wouldn't stand up to them.

"So what did I do? You tell me, Ms. Wildmoon. Put yourself in my place. Over here." Mac said, stretching one arm far to the right, "you got hundreds of thirsty, starving cows and calves which have kept this ranch afloat since the Civil War. Over here"—he extended left hand—"you got hungry, thirsty horses who're no more use than an infestation of rats. What would you do?"

Until now Kasey had refused to see the rifle hanging over the mantel. Now, as Mac turned abruptly and stared at it, she wondered if it was the Storm Hammer, the distinctive weapon implicated in the horse deaths. Did Mac's question amount to a confession?

Victory sat inside her laptop. Facts were falling into place, eager to be written. The story would mean victory for her, humiliation for Mark Savage, ruin for Bronc McDermitt.

"Why, you're quiet as a feather duster, Ms. Wildmoon. Speak up."

"Mac." Bronc pushed away from the mantel.

"No, it's okay." Kasey held out a hand, but she didn't look at him because she felt a confusing certainty Bronc would have taken on Mac for her. But why? "Mr. McDermitt, in journalism, everything's supposed to be black and white. It's my job to stay objective. It's kind of like being an emergency room doctor. I find the wound, stop the bleeding, and move on."

"You're not there for the healing," Mac said. "Or the infection."

"I guess not."

Dozens of headlines and lines of type rained through her mind. *Snow.* The horses' bodies had been found in the spring thaw. The state of decomposition—she should ask her father to look at the autopsy reports—something had indicated most of the horses had been shot in the snow, and Mac McDermitt had had trouble with them in summer.

Mac was still waiting. Her gut said he'd come up with a solution besides violence.

"I don't have the experience or the knowledge to guess what'd be the right thing to do," she said.

" 'Least you admit it. Those bureaucrats don't. See, what I did, I reported the problem and asked BOW to do something about it. Nothing happened. So, finally, I turned off the water."

"There was nothing else we could do," Wendy said, and both she and Mac looked pained.

"Those damned broomtails wouldn't move along. There'd been water, so they expected there to be water. Pea-brain idiots." Mac squinted and rubbed the back of his neck in a gesture she'd seen Bronc employ when he fell victim to some unwelcome emotion. "I started finding them dead in waterholes, especially colts." He grimaced. "They tried to drink the mud and it turned to cement in their bellies."

"An awful death . . ." Kasey began.

"No, really?" Josh asked with fake incredulity. "Ya think so?"

"Josh, you may leave the room," Wendy snapped. "On second thought, wait. Wait. Go to the linen closet, get fresh sheets for the hide-a-bed and for Bronc's bed, and—"

"We're not staying, Mom." Bronc didn't look at Wendy as he said it. He fixed Kasey with a glance so heated, her mouth felt dry.

"—get busy making them up." Wendy turned her glare, briefly. "Bronc, honey, this is not the time to cross me. Josh, do it now or skip that rodeo. Your choice."

Josh flung himself away from the mantel. His pout approximated a man's scowl as he turned, but he went.

RESTLESS AND JUST GENERALLY PISSED OFF, Bronc stood before the barn, facing the ranch yard. It was nearly midnight and he was spoiling for a fight.

It was hot, still, and darker than the inside of a cow, in the house. Out here, moonlight silvered everything and made you wish it was day, so you could get on with your business. Maybe he hadn't been working hard enough.

His dad had been sawing off snores when Bronc walked down the upstairs hallway. At Josh's door, he'd heard faint music and stepped inside to find his little brother had fallen asleep with headphones on. When Bronc removed them, Josh's head fell sideways, as if his neck were broken. Callie slept decorously on her back.

Maybe it was the thought of Kasey sprawled on the hide-a-bed in his mother's sewing room that had him itchy, but it could be the fact that the ranch night sounds—windmill creak, night birds, Champ trotting on his rounds—were the same, except for one. He heard no far-off lowing of cattle.

Champ saw her first. He gave a soft woof that made Bronc turn. Kasey's silhouette separated from the front porch. She wore something swirly and long. A skirt, unless it was a night-gown. No, a skirt, but he'd be damned if he could figure out why she was dressed up.

She picked her way out from the house, walking in the gingerly fashion of someone barefoot. Or maybe her legs were abraded from wearing jeans and riding for two days. And there was her hard-headed insistence on riding through the thorn brush without chaps.

But she wasn't the sort to complain. Over dinner, she'd been friendly, but something had been wrong. It went beyond that buttoned-down sexuality he wanted to rip loose. It was an intellectual tension, but he couldn't read her mind any more than he could guess why she couldn't keep her hands off that cussed necklace. Or why twice today, she'd offered him a glass at the same time he felt thirsty.

Champ bounded across the yard, set on investigating as Bronc tried to figure it out. No one else had seemed to notice Kasey looked tense as she coaxed them into talking about the upcoming state fair. Mom nearly confided the recipe for her bake-off-winning Zebra Bread. Callie offered to display the pottery she'd made for 4-H competition and asked Kasey if she could "mess with her hair."

"Yes, but only if I can wash it first."

That had sent Mom into a frenzy of apologies for not offering the shower earlier.

Callie talked right over Mom, saying there was a pink-ribboned Guinevere braid—whatever the hell that was—she'd seen in a magazine and really, really wanted to try on someone, and since all her friends were off at camp, well, Kasey's thick hair would be just perfect.

Skilled as she was, Kasey had drawn little from Mac or Josh. Although Mom had told him later that Mac admired Kasey's "sass," he'd mostly watched her. And Josh . . .

Across the yard, Kasey crooned to Champ. Useless, anteater-headed mutt was getting his ears rubbed and yodeling with pleasure. Bronc couldn't blame him.

All the same, Kasey better keep her distance from Josh. For everyone's sake. Josh's adolescent unpredictability had been magnified by the night Bronc was arrested.

Mac had made a mistake, not getting a counselor or psychologist to talk to Josh. A kid scared into wetting his sleeping bag, then mocked for it by strangers, had to be filled with impotent fury. And that fury had to go somewhere.

They'd been "lucky" Josh's childhood fear of guns had bloomed into an abnormal aversion. Afterward, he hadn't shot up a school or shopping mall. But that fury had to go somewhere and Bronc was afraid Josh had turned it on himself. He just couldn't figure out how.

After dinner, Bronc had asked Josh to show him his latest cannon. It didn't take much talking. The kid was obsessed with potato cannons. They'd done precious little talking, as they spent the long summer dusk shooting off things that almost deafened them. But once they finished, Josh had seemed more like the boy he'd been before.

Bronc ceded the first shower to Josh and managed to walk past Callie's bedroom. Girlish laughter and the smell of fingernail polish seeped under the door. It did something to his innards, making him think of Kasey in a way that was tender and sweet, not horny.

Now, across the dark ranch yard, Kasey spotted him. She walked toward him, skirts flaring on the wind, then flattening to her stride. Even in feminine garb, that walk said she had no time for nonsense.

Yeah, if this was the kind of attention she lavished on her interviews, no wonder she was a prizewinner. He dreaded Callie had let slip some fact that might turn up to bite him on the ass in Kasey's article.

Bronc flipped a stick in her direction, tempting Champ to career away from her.

"Hi. What are *you* doing up so late?" Kasey's voice was breathy, surprised, and pleased to see him. The braid had unraveled and left a ribbon flapping in her hair. The wind brought the scent of the baby shampoo Callie insisted on using and Bronc felt downright shamed by his suspicion.

"C'mere, Hollywood, I want to show you something." He led the way to the barn and pointed.

"What?" she whispered, maybe trying not to scare off the critter she imagined he was showing her. "I don't see anything."

"Right there over the door."

She leaned toward him, following the line of his arm, his index finger, and then she saw it.

"That hat?"

"Your L.A. Dodgers cap."

"Oh," she said. Obviously mystified, she kept staring, then she jumped back a step. *"Oh, wow!* How did you get it? Where did I—?"

"You left it in the truck."

"Boy, I was so lucky you guys came along. Do you know how cold I was, sitting in that Toyota all night, trying to sleep? I could've changed that tire, but not in the dark and not without a jack handle." Her voice trailed off. "Really, thanks."

Bronc thought of what Flynn'd had in mind when he'd pulled over his new truck. "Don't mention it," he said, then added, "You want it back?"

"No, thanks."

"I nailed it bill up so the luck wouldn't run out."

A moth the size of a sparrow coasted past the cap and Kasey sobered. "Jim Pinto gave it to me."

"The guy—" He stopped.

"—that got blown up," she spoke quickly, minimizing the pain like ripping off a Band-Aid.

"I sure have a way of stirring up your bad memories."

"There are worse ways for a cop to go."

Bronc wondered if she kept staring at the hat to hide tears, then wondered—and damn, it was beneath even him—wondered what Jim Pinto had meant to her.

"Was he your boyfriend?" He gritted his teeth at his own weakness, but Kasey didn't turn on him.

"No, a friend of my parents, but he was a college graduate, Navajo, and a hostage negotiator. He starting showing up at our house about the time I told my folks I wanted to drop out of college. A positive role model."

God knew he felt sympathetic, but He was not making it easy to be a comforting soul. Kasey's tee shirt was tucked in tight. Moonlight glimmered on her collarbones and the night wind chilled her, bringing her nipples to attention.

Something creaked. Not the windmill.

Bronc turned a full circle, searching for the disturbance before Kasey pointed.

"The swing," she said. "That's the tallest swing I ever saw in my life."

He didn't tell her why.

With its long ropes fluttering, it was hard to imagine Mac had detached the swing seat and ropes, slung another rope over the top beam, and used the frame as a place to drain blood from a slaughtered steer. Of course, it hadn't been used that way for a long time.

"Want a push?" he asked, walking toward it.

Kasey's hands came to her hips, considering. "Yeah," she said, then lifted her skirt a few inches, hurried over, and plopped down on the unfinished plank seat. She looked back over her shoulder as he approached. "Please."

Since he did better when he didn't talk at all, Bronc pushed. For a minute, he only noticed the wind in her hair, then he adjusted his hands' position.

Pushing Kasey's back dead-center was seemly, but it didn't

give her much altitude. He lowered his push to the small of her back. She sailed high enough for a good view of the plain and her skirt blew back like wings.

THIRTEEN

From a soar so high the swing's ropes went slack and rippled, Kasey looked back at him, earthbound. As she fell closer, she said something that was muffled by the pink ribbon fluttering across her lips.

He kept pushing, and the next time she came back, closer to the ground, she tugged the ribbon free.

"So, what've you been doing for the last ten years?" she shouted, floating up and away from him once more.

Bronc found it easier to answer with Kasey facing away from him.

"Pretty much the same thing I'm doing now. Workin' for horses' behinds, chasin' horses' behinds."

Even in the dark, he saw disapproval in the tilt of her head. He gave her a hearty push and added, "Tried to go to vet school, but I flunked out."

"I don't believe that." Kasey's words drifted behind her.

He got a charge from the fact she didn't think he was dumb. Still, Bronc pretended not to hear. When she turned to look over her shoulder, he cupped a hand to his ear and shook his head.

"I don't *believe* that," she bellowed.

"Want to wake the folks in Winnemucca?"

Moonlight caught her smug smile as she turned away again. My God, she was pretty.

From behind, Bronc set a hand on each side of her waist and stopped her.

A little breathless, Kasey asked, "Your turn?"

"Naw. Just figured if we're going to have ourselves a conversation, we shouldn't invite everyone to listen."

She nodded, then insisted, "You *didn't* flunk out, did you?"

"Good as." He took his hands from her waist. As he moved around front to talk to her, his palms felt cold. "Too many trips home, to help out. I finished a couple classes by correspondence and I still might go back."

Kasey kept a grip on the swing ropes as she scuffed her bare toes in the channel plowed by a generation of McDermitt feet. The ease with which Kasey accepted dirt amazed him, especially after he'd seen the jubilation with which she sprinted to the shower. She hadn't complained over not having a makeup mirror on the trail, either, and she knew how to keep quiet.

Thing was, he didn't want her quiet.

Bronc listened to Champ chew his stick a minute or two before he nudged the swing with his knee.

"What about you?" he asked. She peered up, still clinging to the ropes. "*You* didn't drop out."

"One summer during college I worked for the *Baxter Beach Bugle.* I covered the police beat and a labor strike. After that, writing editorials on the sad state of meals in the dormitory dining commons lost its thrill." She shrugged. "But, I might go back, too. Sometimes I think about being a teacher."

He pried her right hand off the rope to check the dog bite.

They both knew it was an excuse to touch.

Hers was a strong, capable hand and both sides were scuffed from where she should've been wearing her gloves. But then he explored the soft, hidden surfaces of her fingers. First, barely touching, he felt the inside of the little finger, then both smooth sides of the ring finger.

Kasey gave an involuntary start, but didn't pull her hand away as he touched the smooth flesh at the base of her thumb. The slash had drawn closed, but the instinctive contraction of her fingers told him it was still sensitive. He traced the area around the tear and wondered what she'd do if he raised it to his lips.

"Don't kiss me," she said.

Well, he figured that answered that.

"Okay." Bronc curbed his impulse to sound offended or cocky. He relinquished her hand, and took hold of the swing ropes, which felt darn near as prickly as he did. "Mind if I ask why?"

"I like you . . ." she began, but then they both laughed.

"Aw, now, Kasey. There you go, startin' to talk like a female."

"That's just it. At the newspaper, I had to work twice as hard to get half as far."

Getting hired was easy, Kasey said, because she fulfilled two minority quotas for her employer. But her publisher blamed her first misstep on her gender and soft heart.

Soft heart, my foot, Bronc thought. Agitation, like an engine winding up and whining when you needed to shift, gripped him. *Jealousy.* It felt like high school all over again. He wanted to hear all about his girl's old boyfriend, and yet didn't want to know. And Kasey wasn't his girl.

"It took five years to build my reputation as a hard-hitting journalist and he took ten seconds to demolish it."

"He?"

"Mark Savage, the bastard who was my boss."

The *millionaire* bastard, according to Buck. But damn, he felt silly with relief that Kasey felt no lingering love for her former fiancé.

"The thing is," Kasey said carefully, "he dished out one teaspoon of truth with the bucket full of b.s."

"You might learn to talk like a cowboy yet." He wished she'd stop talking. He didn't want to hear what she said next.

"I tend to get too close to sources, and that can backfire."

Too close to sources. Didn't that just sum up what was happening between them all nice and neat. Bronc bent, snatched the stick coated with dog drool, and hurled it for Champ to chase.

"I know what you mean," he said. "Reminds me of Mac's Angus steer Toro. When you raise cattle for meat, you don't treat them like pets, but damned if Toro wasn't the most personable steer ever created. He'd mosey up to any rider crossing his territory, even rub his knotty old head against your saddle, if you let him. He drove the horses crazy, but Mac got a real kick out of him, right up to the day he had to shoot him.

"I'll show you something in the barn, tomorrow. A wooden flap opens out over a feed bin. That's where you pour in grain to bait in the animal you want to butcher. Just above that, there's another opening. That one slides open and when old Toro came snuffling over to eat, Mac put a bullet in his brain pan. That steer fell without a sound, 'cept his chin hit the wooden manger and he looked kind of surprised. Least that's what Mac said. And you know what?" Bronc mused. "I don't think he's ever named another one of his beef cattle, heifer or steer."

Kasey didn't take a minute to be teary.

"Nice metaphor, McDermitt. You might be wasted in

veterinary medicine. But I won't put a bullet in your brain pan."

Not unless it's a dynamite story, he thought, a prize-winning bit of investigative journalism.

"What's this dog doing?"

Champ bowed before her, hindquarters up, tail wagging as he made a long *grrr*ing sound.

"He wants you to run around so he can herd you. He's a frustrated sheepdog, aren't you, boy?" Bronc rumpled Champ's ears, and the collie gave his tail a courtesy wag.

"Can't he herd cattle?"

"Naw, Champ's a home boy. He doesn't get out on the range. Even if he did, there's only one or two head left."

Bronc crossed his arms hard, when the dog continued to ignore him. He'd said about everything he could think of to tick her off and ignored the opening to get her talking about what kind of a lover she'd found in old Mark Savage. Maybe he should've gone ahead and pursued rodeo as a career. He'd apparently been dumped on his head so often he wasn't much good for anything else.

But she was still sitting there, sifting her fingers through the collie's white ruff. "What about you? How'd all this affect your reputation?"

"Off the record?" he asked. Two could play Kasey's objectivity game.

She exhaled a long, growling breath, which fascinated Champ. His pointed muzzle jerked up and he licked her on the lips.

Kasey ignored Bronc's chuckle and rubbed the back of her hand across her mouth. Then, with sugar and strychnine sweetness, she said, "Of course, Bronc, honey."

"Well, you might say folks are waitin' to see if I'll strike out.

I had a bad-boy rep as a kid. Just the usual stuff—fighting and drinking and playing stupid pranks—but I pretty much erased folks' irritation over that by coming home when I was needed. And I quit the serious boozing. It was easy for me, harder for Buck." He grimaced. "Your, uh, what is he? uncle?" Kasey nodded.

Bronc held up two fingers. "Strike two was the arrest, but folks here don't have much use for federal agencies of any kind, and I didn't name any names."

She fidgeted and he knew she was aching for names. As if he knew anyone with the firepower to mow down a hundred horses.

"So, I figure to keep my eyes open for the real bad guy who's got the feds digging in everybody's business, and maybe I'll be set for life. Plus, that twenty-thousand-dollar reward would go a long way to putting Rainbow Bend back on her feet, and the more ranchers who stand and fight, the better it is for all of us."

Kasey's lips softened, the lower parting from the upper one. Her head tilted until her hair brushed the swing rope, and her hand gestured toward him.

Bronc grabbed it and nuzzled his lips against her knuckles. "Change your mind about that kiss?"

"No." She said it kind of plaintively. "I just . . ."

"What're you trying so hard not to tell me, Hollywood? I'm pretty sure I don't want to know, but you may as well spit it out."

"Josh was one of the kids in the truck," she blurted. "One of the kids who shot the palomino foal."

He held his hand up for her to halt. He'd known what she was talking about even before she clarified it and there was no sense asking if she was sure. Kasey appeared to be shrinking inside her skin, trying to pull back from what she'd said. She wouldn't have said it if she weren't sure.

Bronc needed to sit.

He lowered himself to a tuft of grass at the base of the swing. He oughta roast that boy. Weren't they all in trouble enough without chasing after more?

Bronc had almost buried his face in his hands when he felt her watching. Sympathetically.

"It wasn't him with the gun."

"I haven't developed the film yet."

"I know it wasn't. Not saying he wasn't along for the ride, but Josh's always been scared of them, and that night the feds rousted us—that about cinched it.

"That night, I'd actually taken him out shooting. You know, pinecones off a rock, with the Storm Hammer. Mac and I thought that between us—the big brother and the custom gun—I might gentle Josh to handling a rifle."

He saw her recoil, up there on her swing-seat throne, and pointed a finger. "I know, you don't see the need for it. But this isn't the city and I'm not talking about shooting rival gang members or 7-Eleven clerks. I'm talking about an animal hurt beyond help and way out there on the playa. Believe me, a quick gunshot is one hell of a lot pleasanter for everyone than cutting its throat.

"I had precious little success, but Josh was glad to camp out overnight. He was scared to fall asleep, kept thinking he saw something, but I told him it was imagination and firelight." Bronc cleared his throat against the knot tightening. "Then the horses tossed up their heads; Josh grabbed the pistol and started to shoot."

Bronc ran a hand through his hair. The sight of Josh slinging around the pistol had scared him more than anything that followed.

"What the hell else you going to do when guys come out of the dark and surround you?" Bronc demanded. "But one of 'em, in camouflage, kicked the gun out of his hand and Josh peed his pants.

"I was on my feet, holding both hands out, trying to get them to hit *me*, cuff me, just calm the hell down, but—well, that part doesn't matter."

Damn, but the night had turned chilly. Bronc wrapped his arms one over the other and wished he had a bottle at hand.

The sympathy in her silence reminded him of Buck. Her quiet understanding didn't need waterworks nor words. Even rich and city-reared, Kasey'd had her own hard times.

The wind flirted with the edge of her skirt, baring her ankles, but Kasey kept her hands folded and her eyes down as he told her.

"After they took me off to jail and we couldn't afford the bail, Josh made a half-assed attempt at suicide. He wanted to die for being such a wuss."

Her clasped hands came up against her breastbone. His felt like it might crack and maybe she felt the same. He knew somebody'd killed those horses and he knew somebody had to pay. And he'd been as good a suspect as any other loner on the range, but he'd never forgive those men for terrifying Josh.

"They let you go for a lack of evidence." Kasey let each word drop as if it were scalding hot.

"That's a fact."

Then she was off the swing and sitting beside him, skirts puffing up with scents of girl and powder. "You've got to countersue. That's all there is to it." She was nodding and numbering charges on her fingers. "Malicious prosecution, loss of personal freedom, emotional and physical pain, loss of . . ."

"Simmer down. You're about to run out of fingers." Bronc

felt ready to burst at her eagerness to get revenge on his behalf. "My attorney was just a public defender, but he wanted me to do the same thing. Still, it's a pretty pricey process and I just wanted to put it behind me."

Kasey hadn't stopped talking.

". . . know a hungry storefront attorney—a tall, leggy blonde"—Kasey leered at him as if that would clinch his decision—"who'd take this case on contingency. I can e-mail her tonight." Kasey lurched to her feet, in spite of her entangling skirt. "As soon as we get back into the house."

"Not right now." He had a hard time getting his boots underneath him, too. "Maybe later, if I don't find the horse killer and get that reward."

She was a tall girl, but he was taller and in that moment, when she looked up from the level of his collarbone, Kasey's mind was as clear to him as water. She believed it was Mac.

Bronc couldn't tell her she was wrong. But yesterday he'd been sure and tonight he wasn't. He needed time to go back over everything Mac had said in his jabbering this afternoon. Something didn't jibe with him being guilty.

Bronc felt a chill, which had nothing to do with Kasey and less to do with the wind. What if he and Mac weren't the only owners of Storm Hammers?

The ballistics tests had been inconclusive and the decomposed bodies a total loss, except they kept insisting the horses had been trapped in a box canyon and shot from above.

That was a joke. On their entire spread, there was no canyon the horses couldn't climb right out of.

Still . . . the rifle. Abner was a queer old duck. Bronc wouldn't be surprised if Abner had fallen in love with the Storm Hammer pattern and made another.

He needed to get out to Abner's stronghold and ask.

Without *her*.

"I better go in. I guess you're going to have me on the trail to Shannon's bright and early."

"You guess right, but not too early. Mom misses cooking for hands. She won't let us ride out without stuffing us full of breakfast."

Kasey stood within about three feet of him. Not out of reach, but she was considering and he didn't want to rush her. The wind lifted her skirt in a wheel of muted color and she didn't push it down in time to hide two-thirds of her legs.

That first day in the desert, she'd been wearing shorts and he'd judged her an athlete. Basketball tall, he remembered thinking. He'd give every penny of that twenty-thousand-dollar reward and judge it money well spent to have those legs locked around him.

Kasey darted forward then, laid a hard, loud kiss on his lips, and jumped back.

"For old time's sake," she said in a rush, and then she was running toward the ranch house, with Champ at her heels.

⚡ ⚡

BLUE RAIN WAS WAITING in Wendy McDermitt's sewing room and she was mad.

"Men! It's always men with you, your mother, and all your grandmothers before you!" White leather fringe, white feathered braids, and bleached bone beads fluttered in a virtual snowstorm around the flush-faced maiden as she paced.

Without looking, Kasey reached behind her for the open door and eased it closed. The latch settled into place with an oiled click and her necklace hummed with energy, which had been building since her lips touched Bronc's.

"What are you doing here?" she whispered.

"I warned you: this family failing might as well be fatal. If you

could look back over centuries as I do and see it strewn with the dead, you would listen."

Through Blue Rain's slender torso, Kasey saw an elderly Singer sewing machine and a button box. Nine-tenths of Kasey's mind belonged to the spirit of her ancestors, but one fraction remained dubious. Especially about Blue Rain's language.

"As if you would comprehend the tongue of the People?" Blue Rain loosed a torrent of smooth and incomprehensible words.

"It's odd, is all." Kasey bowed her head as energy swirled around her. She felt humbled by an ancient dialect spoken with such facility. Her humility seemed to calm Blue Rain.

"Do you know what I gave to learn my lesson? I gave up my dignity and opened myself to the Great Ones. I lost myself and became spiritual so that I might pass my wisdom on to you."

Martyrdom was so often a smoke screen; Kasey resisted. "Wait a minute. You're the one who started this. I'm only trying to put it right."

"How hard can that be, with me to guide you?"

Smoke rose from the floor. Tiny tendrils slipped between the floorboards and curled through the braided rag rug. The sound of chanting rose with the shrilling of an ancient flute.

"Stop." Kasey made a reckless move toward the spirit and a buzz of static crackled before her.

Smoke coalesced into a waving curtain. The clack of shells dangling from the dress crowded Kasey's hearing. She recalled dreaming of Bronc riding into a fog and thought, with terrible foreboding, that it had been smoke.

Kasey clasped her hands behind her back and lowered her voice. "This is your fault."

"No." The spirit maiden settled onto the hide-a-bed. Her movement banished the cloying sweet smoke and once more the room smelled of laundry dried on a clothesline in the sun.

"You have me confused with my incarnations," Blue Rain said. *"*Yes, I took on the appearance of Blue Rain and you may address me so, but her betrayal came from the cavalry officer. Mine came from Fox."*

Kasey listened to the house sounds and wondered why no one had come to see what all the shouting was about. Not Bronc, not edgy Mac McDermitt, not even the vigilant collie.

"Sit beside me. It's all right."

Kasey steeled herself and settled beside the apparition. Far from feeling terrified, she felt comforted. She sighed, imagining Blue Rain smelled of Christmas trees.

"Would it soothe you if I took the form of an elder?" Blue Rain inclined her head and the tips of her crow-black braids began to gray.

"No!" Kasey shouted and in that moment realized she hadn't turned on a light. But she could see. "No," she whispered. "I'm just getting used to this . . . form. Please."

"Very well." Blue Rain rocked back and forth, humming a minor-note tune. *"Do you think you might concentrate on finding Fox?"*

"I've been preoccupied with business. With this story, I know."

"You have been preoccupied with it, yes, but I promise all stories will fall into place once you have found Fox and beaten him."

"How?"

"By ramming his fat red tail, of which he is so vaingloriously proud, down his throat."

"Are you speaking in—parables?"

"Of course." Blue Rain's eyes were half-lidded. *"He's in human form. You have touched him, spoken with him, allowed him to read the uncertainty you feel in the power of your necklace.*

"He grows stronger as he talks with each human you've encountered. He bleeds each one for information that will make your defeat easy. And you will not go down alone. Your body may not die, but others will. Let me warn you, living with the deaths of others is hard. Listen."

Hoofbeats shook the room like thunder. Kasey closed her eyes but the screams pummeled her from a hundred directions. Screams of horses gashed by sabers, horses falling on blood-slick battlegrounds. Screams of mothers running, lifting toddling feet free of the ground, and wishing for flight before they cowered, beseeching, covering children with their own backs, vulnerable spines slashed by the swords of the raging blue-uniformed men.

"You may bring all that forward to your time." Blue Rain extinguished the onslaught as if pinching out a candle. She vanished, but her voice twined through the darkness. *"Do not weaken yourself by falling in love."*

The warning stayed with Kasey through the blackest hours of the night, twisting like smoke after the flame has died.

FOURTEEN

China picked the next morning to prove he was no milquetoast lady's mount.

As Kasey buttoned her sleeveless white blouse, Wendy called that breakfast would be ready soon. Kasey tucked in her blouse, zipped her fly, and fastened the tooled leather belt before slipping out the front door toward the barn, where she'd spotted China and Rook, already saddled.

Instinct told her she'd be happier if she worked him a few minutes before they set out; after last night, she believed in instincts. And omens. Not to mention portents and premonitions. She had a job assignment from the spirit world.

As Kasey approached, China's ears tilted back, showing his foul mood.

"Bad night, boy?" Kasey smoothed her hand between the cinch and China's furry belly to be sure it didn't pinch. She repositioned the bit and checked the chin strap to see that it lay flat. "I know just how you feel."

In answer, China's ears flattened to his neck and he raised his lip to show threatening teeth. Rook sidled as far away as his reins would allow.

"What's your problem, China?" Kasey slid her hand down the gelding's neck. His head snaked around with teeth bared.

Kasey stepped away, keeping watch on his swiveling hind-quarters.

She studied China from all sides, glanced back toward the house, and tried to think like a horse.

Warm barn, familiar food, equine company. Hadn't she longed to stay in bed this morning, and thought with dismay about rolling out her sleeping bag on the hard ground tonight?

"Sorry, boy." Cautiously, Kasey untied the reins and mounted. "Let's get this over with before we have an audience, okay?"

Ears still flat, China took two stiff-legged steps away from the barn. Kasey heard her own breathing and felt the hump beneath the saddle. She urged the gelding into a trot. He swished his tail, shook his head, and continued the slow, stilted walk.

"Let's go, China." Kasey gathered her reins and applied her legs harder.

China stopped. He struck out with a foreleg and before she could reprimand him, kicked out with a rear one.

For an instant, Kasey's attention wandered. The ranch house door slammed. Bronc stood on the porch, sipping coffee. And then all hell broke loose.

China reared and launched himself skyward. Kasey clung to his neck in time to feel him drop back to all fours, lower his head, and kick both hind feet. His neck formed a steep slide and she was about to slip down it. Beyond her hands, gripping hand-fuls of mane and reins, she saw dirt.

As he began whirling and kicking and bucking all at once, Kasey discarded technique for a single goal. Bronc wouldn't see her fall.

When China finally stopped, dust swirled around them.

The gray gelding sniffed and trotted prettily in the circle she'd asked for three spine-shattering minutes ago.

Not until her trembling hands had retied China to the rail did she brush the dirt from her shirt and hazard another glance toward the porch. With flailing arms and shifting shoulders, all the McDermitts were trying to shove in through the door at once. Except Bronc.

He stood waiting as she took a staggering step toward the house. She stopped, commanded her knees not to wobble, and blessed him for not offering to help her.

"Well, if it's not the sweetheart of the rodeo."

If the sun hadn't been rising behind her, Kasey might have thought Bronc's squint and nod hid a proud smile.

She made it up all three steps to the porch before the morning chill made her rub the gooseflesh from her arms.

"Ms. Wildmoon?" Mac's voice boomed from inside. "I don't ask any of my hands to smooth out the rough stock before breakfast. Get on in here and see what this wife of mine's cooked up."

The smell of foods absolutely forbidden to a woman with a public persona wafted to Kasey.

"You bet." She answered Mac, but her attention clung to Bronc.

Last night, she'd learned more than she wanted to know about his loyalty. And he regarded her with admiration. She reached for the front door. Bronc reached past her, opened it.

As he leaned close, his fresh-shaven cheek grazed her ear. "Nice work, Hollywood," he mumbled, and gave her a congratulatory pat on the butt.

The maple table wore a red gingham cloth, but Kasey could hardly see it for all the dishes, bowls, and platters. Only Mac and Josh were seated and Kasey couldn't remember which of the empty chairs she'd used last night.

"That was so-cool." Callie made the last two words flow together as she carried a fruit bowl toward the table. "Mom, where am I supposed to put this?"

"What'd you feed him, Bronc, locoweed?" Josh's shoulders tightened as he looked past Kasey to his brother.

While Kasey hesitated, Wendy smiled a grin that took the place of teammates' hail-the-hero hand slap. She motioned Kasey closer on the pretense of handing her a glass of juice and spoke quietly, "I always admired Letty. Her eyes alone—You know they say Thoroughbreds have the 'look of eagles'? That's what Letty had."

Kasey sipped the juice as Wendy poured cream from a flowered pitcher into a skillet of scrambled eggs. Kasey knew she should have been thinking calories, but her mind boasted, *the look of eagles.*

Kasey sank into the chair Bronc pulled out. She surveyed baskets of blueberry muffins and corn muffins studded with red peppers. At her elbow sat a tiny pot of honey, a rack of toast, both white and wheat, and a yellow platter stacked with bacon.

Mac offered Kasey a tureen of fried potatoes. Wendy turned just as Kasey declined.

"Making hotcakes would be no trouble." Wendy frowned at Kasey's empty plate.

"Oh, no, really. Don't make anything else." She took a muffin and a dollop of fruit and arranged them to cover half her plate.

Sunlight slanted through the kitchen windows by the time Wendy allowed Kasey and Bronc to push away from the table. First out the door, Bronc crossed to the loaded horses while Kasey thanked the McDermitts for their hospitality.

Wendy gave her a hug as Callie rolled her eyes and waved. Josh managed a gruff "See ya," but it was Mac who followed her down the steps, rubbing his chin, as Bronc approached.

"Eight years ago I was fined sixteen-fifty apiece for three of my quarter horses getting caught grazing on public lands," Mac said without preamble. "I refused to pay the fine, since those welfare mustangs had been eating my grass for years. And then BOW went and auctioned my prime horses off for chicken food. To cover my debt. Some folks say that gave me an ax to grind." Mac checked a pearl-snapped cuff. It was already fastened. "Just in case you run across that, I wanted you to hear it from me first."

"I appreciate that, Mac."

"No reason you should." Mac turned his critical glare on Bronc's mount. "Now ain't that a slick, grain-fed lookin' cayuse." Mac shook his head, but Bronc refused to rise to the bait. "You two have a safe ride. And, Bronc, since you're riding over that way, tell Shannon I saw one of her danged experimental heifers looking mighty springy. Ain't natural, what she's doing."

"Okay, Mac." Bronc turned Rook toward Rainbow Bend's front gate.

"You tell her I said so. Don't forget, now."

"I won't, Mac. See you in a couple weeks."

⚡ ⚡

THIS TIME, THE LAST SHAMAN called a different mortal, for a different reason. Curiosity was his sole weakness.

Gully's single telephone booth afforded him little privacy but Hannah's Hen House café was nearly empty at midmorning.

"She came and dug into your business, just as I warned you."

"Girl doin' her job, is all I saw. A sleazy job, but didn't seem personal."

"Young Josh is a fair judge of character, now, what did he think?" The uneasy silence inflamed the last shaman. Of all mortals, he'd thought he could count upon this one to see K. D.

Wildmoon's threat. *"Watch your back, Mac."*

He replaced the receiver with reptilian silence and stared at it. Time to face her directly. If he came to her as the last shaman, K. D. Wildmoon would sweat like a mare in heat. All her grandmothers had. But that meant a revelation he didn't care to make. And he could do well enough in this guise. Well enough.

⚞ ⚟

AT FIRST, KASEY BLAMED a shaley hillside for the invisible sparking from her necklace. The hillside soared up, covered with shale, the size of dinner plates balanced in slick, overlapping layers. Coming down was suicidal, but Bronc didn't ask if she could do it. Once they were at the hill's crest, she had no choice.

"Easy." Bronc looked after a rock that shattered as China fought to keep his hooves beneath him. "Let him find his own footing."

"Hush." Kasey needed every ounce of concentration to keep her weight balanced.

Once they reached level ground, Rook surrendered to his nerves. Fighting Bronc's firm hand on the reins, the gelding squealed, begging to bolt, but Bronc kept him to a jog.

Kasey rode alongside, resisting the urge to ask Bronc if she'd earned her horsemanship badge. She settled her hat firmly, hoping she looked more assured than she felt. Clammy and careful, she didn't need the necklace arcing electricity into her sternum.

I've got the message. Blue Rain might have picked a better time for a reminder. *I'm looking for Fox, now knock it off.*

Unable to escape the needle-sharp pain any other way, Kasey jerked the necklace over her head and crammed it into her saddlebags.

She gave China a pat for not exploding at her contortions and then, surreptitiously, wiped away perspiration that had gathered above her upper lip.

"Sure you should be taking that off?"

His lazy inquiry made her wonder if he had seen the spirit horse, that day at Soldier Creek.

"Why shouldn't I?"

"No reason," he said.

Bronc raised a hand as if holding off a storm of complaints, then set a faster pace toward Shannon Delaney's ranch. Kasey glared at the terrain surrounding her. Sagebrush and pinon pines stretched toward a blue horizon. How could she have believed she was growing to understand this desert and this man who was just as spare with clues to who he really was?

Give her a nice dark alley and gang-bangers, anytime. She understood those threats and she knew how to be careful.

§§ �

A BELLOWING BULL HERALDED their arrival at the Diamond Q ranch. "Wait 'til you see that fella," Bronc said. "Silver Dollar. He's Shannon's Longhorn bull."

Kasey sorted through her mind for an image. "You mean those big, old-fashioned cattle, like you see in cowboy movies?"

"Exactly. Descended from Spanish cattle and driven down the Chisholm Trail. I sure hope he works out, 'cause I'm the one who convinced Shannon to spend her boss's money on him."

After Blue Rain's warning, Kasey had counted herself past jealousy. She was here to interview Shannon Delaney, who just happened to call Bronc "lover." That didn't matter. Kasey noted white fences and irrigated fields. They signaled this was a prosperous working ranch. Besides, cow advice couldn't be judged much of an intimacy.

"Yeah, the Herefords—these white-faces you see out here?—are meaty, but they're British-bred, and still better suited for calving in barns, with human help, than on the range.

Especially the first-time mothers.

"Longhorns, they're just the opposite, too muscled to be good beef cattle, but they drop calves easy as can be.

"When I told Shannon what I'd read about successful crosses, breeding Longhorn bulls to first-calf heifers, she decided to give it a shot. But she's trying for summer calves, so she doesn't have to go looking for them in the snow. I'm not sure that's such a good idea."

He *should* be a vet, Kasey thought, but she didn't say it, only hoped she could find the horse killer and help Bronc get his chance.

Though it was near noon, a rooster crowed as they rode in. They passed several white outbuildings, including a rambling barn with an adjoining pen of cud-chewing, tail-switching Herefords.

The sky vaulted blue and cloudless overhead, so she couldn't blame the weather for her uneasiness. When they approached the silent house, Bronc swiveled in his saddle, surveyed the barn and ranch yard all over again, and she knew he felt the tension, too.

Shannon Delaney didn't seem the sort to let folks ride in unnoticed. And where were her ranch hands?

"There's Dollar." Bronc indicated the corral of a gray bull with wickedly curved horns.

"He'll be a tough interview."

From the corner of her eye, Kasey caught movement just past the bull pen. She'd already unbuckled the saddlebag, determined to pull the necklace back over her head, when she heard a throat being cleared. Turning, she saw only a hen.

Chickens scratched outside the ranch house. Maybe inside too. The screen door was ripped open in a three-cornered tear and, as Kasey watched, a red biddy hopped inside. A black and white hen hopped out.

Though she wasn't the most fastidious of housekeepers, Kasey decided she'd draw the line at having fowl as house pets.

"Hey!" Bronc shouted. "Anyone home?"

"Warn me before you try to wake the folks in Winnemucca, okay?"

They were both laughing, remembering the swing, the moonlight, and that fleeting kiss, when Shannon Delaney swaggered around the corner of the house.

Shannon was the same palomino beauty Kasey remembered, but this time she didn't wear smooth buckskin chaps. Flushed and sweating, wearing a support belt of the kind Kasey had seen on truck drivers and pro football players, Shannon looked as if she'd been running. But no one in her right mind would run in cowboy boots.

"Over here." Shannon motioned them to follow, but Kasey tethered China first and Bronc, looking edgy, ground-tied Rook.

He stayed especially close, shortening his strides so Kasey stayed beside him. Such consideration made her nervous.

Hands on her hips, Shannon looked down on a man skinning an animal. It was Jack Flynn, the gray-eyed PAPA pilot she'd met at Gold Canyon. He knelt astride a dead mountain lion.

Turning away was a weakness. She knew it the instant she stared in the other direction, toward a giant satellite dish, and felt their eyes on her nape. Let them sneer. She wasn't auditioning as a ranch wife.

The sound effects proved worse than the sight. Cutting, ripping, and a slither-bump that sounded a lot like birth, but was surely its opposite.

When she turned back, the cougar was bare. Deprived of its luxurious pelt, the animal looked sorrowfully small.

As soon as her attention shifted to Flynn, Kasey relaxed. A drugging lethargy flowed over her.

"How's your dude working out?" Flynn aimed the question at Bronc and a spur of jealousy pricked her.

"Just fine," Bronc gave his small smile to Shannon instead of Flynn. "She sure took her lickin's this morning."

If he elaborated, Kasey didn't hear.

Flynn still straddled the cat's pelt and scraped the inside of it with what she could only guess was a bowie knife. And then he looked up, at her.

A tug of desire surprised Kasey. And appalled her. How could she could feel attracted to Flynn, with his butcher's hands?

Alarm pulsed weaker than curiosity, but Flynn must have noticed her revulsion to the ugly business of skinning.

Flynn shook his head as he staked the skin to dry. She heard him tell Bronc and Shannon about a minister who hunted and ran trap lines in answer to God's order that men hold dominion over beasts of the field.

Who? Which religious denomination? When did you last talk to him? Where does he live? Why were you having that conversation in the first place?

All the questions she should be asking rained through her brain, but Kasey stayed quiet. She felt hypnotized, vaguely apologetic, and most of all detached. She had a very real vision of standing outside herself, looking at her silent form with its sun-browned arms and untidy hair straggling from under a black, flat-brimmed hat as she listened to the voices drone.

All at once, Kasey knew the droning came from the ascending helicopter, not voices. She jerked at her stampede string, removed her hat, and breathed. She opened a button at the throat of her blouse.

Bronc squeezed her shoulder. "Lookin' a little peaked there,

Hollywood."

"I'm fine." Kasey shook her head and noticed Shannon's half-smile. Time for K. D. Wildmoon to buckle down and act like a reporter. She fanned herself with her hat and laughed. "And not genteel enough to swoon."

"C'mon inside." Shannon opened the door and a tumult of hens burst past.

"If you've got a hammer, I'll fix that."

"Hammer, hell, I've got a whole new screen, but not time to install it."

"Do I look like a handyman? I don't do fence and I by God don't install screens. Just thought I might keep the animal-rights folks from claiming you're keeping chickens in an unwholesome environment."

Magazines and mail were mounded on the recliner facing a big-screen television. Overflowing ashtrays shared the floor with stray popcorn kernels and plastic containers from microwave dinners.

"Feel like some lunch?" Shannon taunted Kasey.

"Actually, in spite of Wendy's best efforts, I do."

When Kasey ignored the state of the house, Shannon gave a grudging smile and gestured with an all-encompassing hand.

"I'm a rancher, not Betty Crocker, but I've got a cleaning service that comes out from town once a month to muck out the place." Shannon pretended to look at a wristwatch. "Due any day now."

"Speaking of things that're due, we need to talk about your heifers," Bronc said.

Then they were off and gabbing about Shannon's Longhorn-Herefords. She had ten heifers penned at the house and expected two to calve in the next twenty-four hours.

"Dollar covered an even dozen," Shannon said, "but I keep

coming up two short."

She opened a can of chili, dumped it into a saucepan, and prodded it with a table knife. That done, she turned to a cupboard and stemmed an avalanche of paper plates.

"Mac said to tell you you're committing a crime against Nature, cross-breeding, but it don't mean he's unneighborly enough to ignore the Diamond Q heifers that wandered over our way."

"Great." Shannon extracted three small packages of corn chips from the cupboard and split them open.

Kasey prided herself on being a connoisseur of dishes from gourmet to pure junk, but she couldn't guess what Shannon was creating.

"Better not watch," Bronc said as Shannon snagged a bag of pre-shredded cheese from the refrigerator, opened it, and sniffed.

He pulled his hat down over his eyes, plunged his thumbs into his back pockets, and turned away.

Kasey stifled a smile. She'd eaten stew steamed in a hubcap and she knew you didn't get close to a source by spurning her cooking.

Shannon divided chili and cheese over the chips. "Frito Pie," she announced. "My specialty."

"Wow, not bad." Kasey gave an okay sign with thumb and forefinger.

"Thanks." Shannon drew on a moisture-beaded bottle of beer. "But don't go getting all filled up." Shannon rolled her eyes toward Bronc. "For dinner, I'm makin' prairie oysters."

Oh lovely.

Kasey saluted Shannon with a fork. Since her last conversation with the blond rancher, Bronc had educated Kasey on Western cuisine and she wasn't at all sure she could choke down a plate of calf testicles.

FIFTEEN

W hy in hell hadn't he kept her out on the range? Bronc scrutinized Kasey's washed-out blue work shirt and khaki pants and racked his brain for the cause of this ache.

She'd dressed like a man. She strode out onto Shannon's porch as purposefully as a man. Hell, she even smelled of a man's soap, having begged a shower after lunch and used Shannon's gritty bar of Lava.

But the sleeves rolled to her elbows exposed smooth forearms and she'd brushed her hair until it made a night-black cloak around her shoulders. She looked as Indian as if she'd been decked out for a powwow. Her heritage was in her bones, those fine and fragile wrists he remembered holding.

Tucking her tidy butt into one of the willow chairs on Shannon's porch, Kasey fidgeted with her pad and pen.

Shannon took a pull on her fourth beer, a skunky brew that shouldn't tempt a soul.

The women ignored him. Bronc watched them balance and upset each other like two kids on a playground teeter-totter.

Kasey asked about horses and Shannon gave her contradictions.

"Hell, mustangs are destructive as those fools who drive out into the Scolding Rock and scorch their tires trying to set land-speed records."

"You don't approve of that," Kasey said.

"D'you know, *do* you, that there are bugs and lizards out there? And wildflowers the size of your little fingernail."

Clearly amazed at Shannon's concern for bugs and lizards, Kasey wet her bottom lip as she scribbled. He thought of last night's kiss, then wondered if she'd picked that shirt on purpose. It lay open enough that he saw the shine on her sternum and a dusky shadow between her breasts. The top button she'd fastened dangled from a single white thread.

"It's not a dead land. You just got to look hard for what's there."

Kasey got more frustrated as Shannon got more drunk.

"So," Kasey said carefully, "you object to all the big animals, deer and antelope and others, being out on the playa."

"Hell, no. I'm running a thousand head of cattle. And feeding antelope."

"Oh, really?"

Bronc recognized Kasey's dull tone as a setup. When he saw her stare across the yard where dusk was creeping in, he knew she meant to provoke Shannon by pretending boredom. Kasey was darn good at reeling folks in.

Except Shannon wanted another beer.

"Bronc?" Shannon stood and stamped her jeans down over her boot tops.

"Naw, I'm full up." Better stay stone-sober in case he had to deliver a calf. Or make love to Kasey.

"Tell me about the antelope," Kasey urged when Shannon

returned.

"Aw, you know." Shannon leaned toward Bronc.

Warning slid through him. In the old days, when Shannon got drunk, she'd turn weepy or horny. He hoped to hell she'd mellowed with age.

She hadn't.

"Antelope." Shannon rolled the syllables on her tongue and circled the fingers of one hand in the air. "Chestnut-colored bodies with white rumps."

Even though he was sitting, Shannon reached around and trailed a finger down Bronc's back pocket.

"Knock it off, Shan. You know I'm ticklish."

"And white bellies." Shannon skimmed her hand down the front of his shirt.

Hell's bells. He shifted in his chair and frowned. Shannon didn't seem to notice.

Kasey stood, flapping her pad against the opposite palm. Then, as Kasey started pacing, Shannon tapped the beer bottle against her front teeth. Intent with concentration, Kasey watched the board porch.

"I've seen antelope. But what've they got to do with you?"

"I sow crested wheat along the highway. They chow down on the stuff. Supplement my cattle money." Shannon rubbed her brow and this time it was she who stared across the yard, where long shadows spilled from fence posts, where Dollar's horned head made demonic shapes.

These two females made his gut hurt and Bronc couldn't even say why.

Kasey paced on and he thought of seacoast mansions whose widows' walks had paths worn into the wood from captains' wives pacing and staring out to sea.

Kasey gazed at the Calico Mountains and her expression

made Bronc long for homecoming. To her. Then that top button came loose from its thread. It didn't hit the porch, but it did make Bronc stop thinking with his heart. Although he saw just the edge of her bra, he imagined his fingers sliding along the ivory-colored satin, looking for that lost button.

Keeping her voice casual, Kasey wheeled on Shannon. Half gone with booze, Shannon probably didn't notice that on-the-scent look in Kasey's eyes.

"The antelope supplement your cattle earnings." Kasey left the words for Shannon to pick at.

"Yeah, the tourists love seeing 'em along the road."

Shannon made no sense at all, so Kasey egged her on., "The tourists."

"Yeah." Again, Shannon tapped the bottle on her teeth, faster and faster. "Ever since that road was named the loneliest highway in the world, we get a fair number of gawkers."

What the hell kind of tourist dollars was she getting?

For an instant, Kasey's eyes flicked to his. Without meaning to, he must've verified her belief that this story was not hanging together, because a faint smile lifted Kasey's lips.

He tried to give Shannon a way out. "How come you're in today?"

Kasey glared like she'd about lured Shannon to hand and he'd spooked her.

"Branding's done." Shannon sounded pissed off, not spooked. "And Flynn stopped in."

Something just wasn't right, and now Shannon had her chair leaned over on its two right legs, leering at him.

Then Shannon messed everything up.

He felt bad for thinking it, but she had the same dare-ya look she'd worn the night she blacked his eye. That night he'd come home from college, she'd offered him a roll in the hay and he'd turned her down.

Not now. Bronc tried to shoot his thoughts into hers. *Give me a damned break, Shannon. Not now.*

"Can you believe," Shannon said, dropping her beer bottle on the porch, "that this man used to love me?" She kicked the bottle toward the steps.

Kasey gave the tiniest sound of denial, but he didn't have the time to wonder what it meant.

"Still do, Shan, you know that." Bronc stood, picked up the bottle by the neck. He didn't dare look at Kasey. It was shameful, the way he'd treated Shannon, but he'd just been a kid.

"Not like you loved me in high school." Shannon shook a scolding finger. "Ms. Wildmoon, get this down for posterity: we did it behind the bleachers, under the bleachers, and I wanted to do it right smack dab in the middle of the football field—get it? Foot*ball* field?" Shannon rocked the chair onto its back legs. "But Gabe was too much of a gentleman."

"That's enough, sugar."

"You know, that's why I'm such a fanatic..." Shannon mumbled other, unintelligible words. "I'd do anything for this ranch because..." Her head wobbled his way.

A gentleman wouldn't contradict her. What he'd done—having her, then moving on—was bad enough. But these days Shannon forgot she wasn't trying to impress him. She was impressing her daddy, who'd run this ranch for thirty years before a rank mustang snapped his back as he tried to break it to saddle.

Another beer sat under Shannon's willow chair, but it had been there since he and Kasey rode up. When Shannon reached for it, Bronc stopped her.

"Shannon, it's too warm. It'll make you sick."

"I already feel kinda sick, lover." She leaned against him, so cozy and sweet that he knew she was faking it.

Kasey saw the act crystal clear, and she was pissed.

A blast of wind caught her hair. She lifted her chin and there was the earthiest, most primitive allure to the way she looked. Fierce and a little possessive.

He wanted her out on the playa, flat against the desert floor beneath him, mating like her people and his did a couple centuries ago.

"I'm so sick." Shannon turned toward the moo of a heifer. "If you could see to 'em, Bronc, just for a while, it'd sure be neighborly."

The act faded as Shannon's eyes grew wide. She stared and Bronc remembered Buck talking of times he'd been literally blind drunk. What had Shannon drinking so hard and why had she halted work when Flynn flew in?

"I am so sorry about Josh."

"Water under the bridge, sugar. Josh is doing fine."

Shannon staggered to her feet and he rose, too, slinging one of her arms over his neck.

As he walked Shannon to her room, he felt Kasey's eyes asking all kinds of questions of his back. Come to think of it, he had a few questions of his own, like why she'd seemed so spellbound by Flynn.

He tipped Shannon onto her bed and had about decided to leave her boots on, when she sat bolt upright.

"Don't sleep with her at my house, y'hear?" Shannon shouted.

"Just when things were looking so promising, too," he said. But Shannon didn't answer, just drooled like a Brahma bull and passed out.

Shaking his head, Bronc returned to the kitchen in search of the Coke he'd seen in Shannon's refrigerator. The solitary green bottle had been a reminder of the day he'd met a little L.A. girl in the desert.

Kasey might add a plus in his sensitivity column if he gave her the Coke to sip while she went and snooped around the ranch.

One thing he didn't want was Kasey following him into the calving barn. All the heifers were first-time mothers. They might tolerate the presence of a single human, but not two. There was always the chance she'd go all gooey and get in his way.

As he popped the Coke cap with the red bottle opener screwed to the wall, Bronc remembered Kasey's sole indication of female weakness. The palomino colt. He could still hear her sniffing and talking through her bloodied nose, asking if the colt would be okay.

If baby animals were Kasey's weakness, he didn't want her thinking he was a brute for working his arm up a heifer to extract a calf.

He'd never understood how movies made birth romantic. It was messy, smelly, sweaty work if everything went well. With these first-time heifers, it never did.

On the other hand, there was a solar shower rigged behind the barn. He could imagine a couple romantic uses for that.

She gave an edgy smile as he creaked open the screen door. No woman had ever made his heart bound into his throat every blessed time he looked at her. Bronc blew breath through his lips and wished she'd been a cowgirl from Carson City instead of a cutthroat reporter from L.A.

"Is she going to be okay?" Kasey balanced a notebook on her knees. Though daylight was fading, she still seemed determined to work on the porch.

"Nothing a good night's sleep won't cure, but I'd just as soon be gone when she wakes up."

Kasey's eyebrows rose. "Should we leave tonight?"

She might have read his mind. He wanted Kasey alone.

Every minute he spent with her made him want it more. Now, she'd given him the perfect opening and he couldn't take it.

"She asked me to watch the heifers."

"I always thought cows had babies without any help."

Bronc felt the yearning expand. She was practically begging him to go and all he could hear was that same bawling heifer calling his name.

"Some do." He extended the Coke, making sure no millimeter of his flesh grazed hers. "Here."

She took the Coke and looked up at him with puzzled pleasure. He couldn't get his sensitivity points if she didn't even remember she'd had a car full of Coke bottles the day they'd met. That just about figured.

"For old times' sake," he said, and headed toward the barn.

〰 ⁂

THE BIGGEST OF THE HEIFERS was about to birth. That should make his job downright easy. So why, Bronc wondered, did he keep pacing?

Shannon's barn was equipped with overhead fluorescent lighting, but he left them off. The heifer would be more comfy and he didn't mind watching, waiting, and whittling by lantern light. He could pretty much do this blindfolded, depending on the animals' sounds to alert him to trouble.

He'd gathered everything he could need—a plastic bucket, warm water, antiseptic lubricant, calf-pulling chains, and a set of come-alongs—when he knew something was wrong.

Not with the heifer, nor the calf, but Kasey. Had he been concentrating so hard he'd ignored some sound outside? Not likely. He shrugged off the spider-leg creepiness inside his collar. Usually that signaled he was being watched. The feeling gripped and wouldn't let go.

It had turned pitch dark by the time he stepped out of the

barn. Everything before him was still. The front porch stood empty, but light streamed from the kitchen window.

Bronc lengthened his stride. His heart bounded as if he'd been running. He had no cause to worry. He knew this ranch as well as his own. Kasey couldn't get into much trouble. The old wiring might give her a jolt and the well pump could start sucking sand without warning, but that was about all. If anyone had driven in, he would've heard tires.

The low rumble of a man's voice made Bronc's scalp tighten.

He kept moving, scanning the porch for a club, but Kasey hadn't even left the Coke bottle behind. He kept his steps soft on the porch boards, quieter still across Shannon's living room rug, and took surprise as his only weapon.

Bronc stopped short of the kitchen doorway and used reflections off the kitchen windows to show what he was about to walk into.

It was Flynn. Back and standing behind Kasey while she did dishes. The scene seemed cloyingly domestic, until Bronc noticed the stiff set of Kasey's shoulders and Flynn's predatory looming. She ignored him, refusing to face him while he tried to sweet-talk her.

Whatever allure he'd held for Kasey this afternoon had vanished. She'd given Flynn the cold shoulder, but he refused to understand. Bronc tried to see her face, but the reflection on the window over the sink only showed the top of Kasey's hair. She kept her eyes down on the dishes, avoiding a confrontation. That sure as hell wasn't her style.

"You can't blame a man for asking."

"Mr. Flynn, I'm busy here." Kasey splashed and scrubbed. "Why don't you get the jacket you forgot? Then, if you're looking for company, you might try going out to the barn to talk with Bronc."

Bronc tried to let her handle it. She wouldn't thank him for interrupting, and the tension and threat in her patient voice said this was Flynn's last chance.

Instinct told him Flynn had said something filthy just minutes ago. He knew Kasey could hurt Flynn, so why didn't she?

That made her jerk around. "You were giving me a come-on this afternoon."

"You're wrong."

Kasey faced Flynn with a level look. "I was suffering from a touch of sunstroke." She folded her arms.

"I can tell the difference." Flynn stepped closer.

Bronc felt his control shudder. Since high school, he'd despised Flynn. Scorned himself, too, for hanging with the guy because he had money and transportation. Always, simmering beneath their camaraderie, there'd been the feeling that once he started pounding on Flynn, he wouldn't stop.

These days, Flynn was always armed and he'd beaten a man into a coma only a lazy judge could have ruled manslaughter.

Kasey was trying not to escalate things. He'd give her a minute more.

"Apparently you *can't* tell the difference." Kasey kept her voice light as she gave Flynn a gentle push. A soapy handprint marked the front of his shirt. "Good night, Mr. Flynn."

She turned back to the sink and Bronc saw her startle as she noticed his reflection. While they watched each other, Flynn made his move.

With snakelike speed, Flynn parted the black hair over Kasey's nape and used one finger to lift the shell necklace as if he intended to steal it.

"You oughta get rid of this piece of junk. A female classy as you—"

"That's it." Kasey whirled on him.

Bronc exploded. He saw red, black, a twisting funnel of violence with Flynn at its vortex. He grabbed Flynn under one arm and slammed him against the refrigerator.

"What the hell—?"

Flynn's throat bulged under his thumbs, but even if he deserved strangling, Bronc wasn't ready to go back to jail.

At Bronc's indecision, Flynn wrenched free.

"Back off, McDermitt." Flynn didn't look ruffled. An unearthly calm underlined his words. "This doesn't concern you."

Flynn's gaze shifted. There was no mistaking it. He watched Kasey's necklace. Not her breasts, rising fast beneath the shirt, but the necklace. A "big medicine item," Buck had called it. Maybe he was right.

"Get out of here. Like she told you. Get your jacket and go."

When Flynn shook his head, Bronc felt his fist tighten with a desire to bloody his knuckles on Flynn's teeth.

"Can't you see what's going on, McDermitt?" Flynn's grey eyes flicked to Bronc as an afterthought. "Christ, I was about to get her to show her true colors, but go ahead, let her run you back into prison." Flynn gave a harsh laugh. "You know anything about her background? How she got her big-money job and millionaire fiancé? Start reading the *National Enquirer,* boy. Humping you to get what she wants is just her style."

Bronc hit him, loved it, and did it again.

"Bronc, no." Kasey's voice quenched the roaring in his ears.

He administered the punch like punishment and even though he filled Flynn's face with his fist, even though he blocked the stunned and clumsy return, and shoved Flynn toward the door, he didn't batter him.

All the same, he followed him to the chopper, watched him climb into the cockpit and lift off.

Kasey was waiting when he came back. She jogged down the steps and met him halfway across the yard. When she didn't run into his arms, he figured she hadn't really been scared. Probably could have handled Flynn alone.

Then she slung an arm around his waist and kissed him on the cheek. "Thanks, but won't this make it difficult for you two to work together?"

"Don't matter."

He wanted to ask her what had been going on, what Flynn had against her, but the sound which had been demanding his attention all night, stopped him.

Bronc held up a finger, listening. Kasey tilted her head to one side and together they heard the slow, whup, whup of the helicopter's rotors moving away. Beyond that, they heard the fevered bawling of the heifer.

He'd be a fool to leave either of them alone.

"Come with me." He took in her smirk and made it a request. "Okay?"

"Can't wait to watch you in action, Dr. McDermitt."

She swung into step beside him without one clue how much the christening hurt.

SIXTEEN

Kasey followed. Whatever Bronc McDermitt did next, she wanted to be an attentive witness. She'd never let him sneak up on her again.

He'd scared her. Along with her certainty that she was about to witness a murder, had come the conviction that no smart woman would ever use jealousy to make Bronc McDermitt pay attention. The overflow might get her killed.

Except for the moo of the laboring cow and the crunch of Bronc's boots beside her, the ranch yard had turned still.

Kasey longed to be back home in her apartment. She'd had little enough faith in her ability to handle this man before tonight. Now, he reminded her of the only news assignment so crazy, so completely beyond her control, she'd turned it down.

When she'd just started at the *Los Angeles Sun-Times,* a tremendous storm had borne down on the Carolina coast. Word got out that a few crazies, claiming to be Druids, planned to tie themselves to trees along the shoreline. Together, they and the trees would feel the full force of the hurricane.

Her editor had suggested that if she were serious about making a name for herself, she'd take the story. It hadn't taken her five seconds to decide some actions were too risky even for K. D. Wildmoon.

Now, she looked at the span of Bronc's shoulders, looked down the lean muscles moving beneath the denim, from hip to leg, and shook her head. Tying herself to this man would be no different.

"She sounds scared." Bronc paused at the barn door. "Could be scared of a hundred different things. Doesn't take much to spook these real young mamas."

Clearly, he was warning her off.

"As soon as I finished the dishes, I was planning to come out and ask where I should sleep. If it would be easier, I can go to bed. Just tell me where."

The way things were between them, every sentence seemed a double entendre. His raised brow and considering look proved her right, but his attention was split between her and the heifer.

"Do you *mind* if I stay to watch?" she asked, but by then she'd lost him.

Bronc's attention shifted to the calving stall. He squinted and shook his head.

"Suit yourself," he said, and didn't talk to her again for an hour.

At first, when she saw the cow up walking and the calf in the straw, she thought his job must be over. She imagined strolling back up to the house with him.

But when Bronc continued to study the scene, without moving, Kasey squatted to peer through the bottom rails, staying still so the cows wouldn't take undue notice of her.

In a coat of wet red velveteen, the calf struggled to escape a silver-blue sac. Bronc stared at the mother, waiting.

By lantern light, Kasey saw the cow back into a corner. Her

hind legs, streaked with blood, sagged as if they couldn't hold her weight. Her eyes widened, clearly terrified by the bundle of baby.

Bronc had read the mother's fearful cry from outside the barn, but even a novice could tell the heifer was not ready for motherhood. She wanted no part of this thrashing, snuffling thing.

Bronc ducked into the corral.

"Okay, Mama, work's not over yet." With an open hand, he gave the heifer a gentle nudge toward her calf, but she bellowed and backed into the corral fence like a car accidentally jammed into reverse.

"Gotta lick that off him. He'll look a lot prettier," Bronc crooned as the heifer tossed her head toward the rafters and bawled. "Get his circulation going, too."

The heifer rammed backward again. Twice.

When her hind legs buckled, Bronc sighed. "Okay, Mama, I'll give ya a little help."

Keeping his eyes on the cow, Bronc used a flannel rag to wipe the sac away, to clear mucus from the calf's eyes and nose. Then he rubbed its body with circular motions so brisk, the calf rocked from side to side.

"See, Mama." Bronc watched over his shoulder. "That's how it's done."

Bronc's voice was so low and encouraging, Kasey thought no female could ask for a better labor coach.

And yet those gentle hands had threatened to batter Flynn senseless. And she'd wanted him to do it. Flynn's attention to the necklace, his triangular face, with skin stretched so smooth and glossy from his high cheekbones to his pointed chin, had convinced Kasey that Blue Rain was right. Fox was masquerading as a human. Flynn.

What if Fox could read her mind as Blue Rain could? What if he could appear wherever he liked? Kasey stared up into the barn's shadowy rafters.

"Maaaaa." The calf bleated and blinked huge eyes, begging its dam to come closer.

Kasey caught her breath at the thought that Fox, an embodiment of evil, might come here. She would've brought him.

The cow kicked the fence and ran to the farthest corner.

"This just won't do, Mama." Bronc watched the pair as he unbuttoned his shirt, lay it over the top fence rail, and gathered the calf against him. "Slimy little cuss. All you need is Mama's loving tongue, learning you and licking you dry."

The cow bolted again, leaving Bronc holding the baby, and Kasey heard the first frustration tinge his voice.

"Come on, Mama, stay still. Let Junior have a sip of milk, won't ya?"

She wouldn't. The cow's eyes rolled white with fear when Bronc set the calf on all fours and it tottered after her. Once, she nearly kicked the baby.

Bronc wiped his brow and made a move to pull his Stetson down. Except he wasn't wearing it. He slung his thumb through a belt loop and tried logic with the frightened beast.

"Them teats of yours are going to feel lots better once you let him nurse." He squatted next to the calf and let it lean into him. The heifer shuddered.

"Feel like doing a little heifer wrestling? Hey, you under the fence."

Kasey touched her chest. His mesmerizing voice had conversed with the cattle for so long, she hadn't expected him to address her.

"I'll be glad to help, but you'll have to be really specific and show me. I've only seen kittens born and the momcat seemed pretty much a natural."

"She'll get it here, in a minute." Bronc's voice was low as he came to Kasey's side of the fence and studied her.

The man seemed utterly unaware that he was stripped to the waist and showing off a torso that made her think of power and domination and sex.

"Not feelin' squeamish, are you?"

"Not a bit."

"This is going to seem a mite cruel, but that babe's got a better chance of survival from nursing than being bottle fed."

She nodded, trusting he'd tried every other avenue of getting the reluctant mother to give in.

"This is called a twitch, or a come-along." He displayed a wooden handle with a loop of rope on one end. "I'm gonna take a little twist of Mama's lip in this soft cotton rope."

The cow bawled at this, the final insult.

"Tell you what, Kasey, for all her moaning, this hurts less than wrestling her down, since she's still sore from birthing."

As the cow quieted, Bronc rubbed her sweating red cheek. "There ya go, Mama, there ya go. I know it's tough, giving up the good old days running wild, but this little guy needs you."

Slowly the cow's eyelids lowered.

"There you go." He handed the wooden handle to Kasey. "Keep it nice and tight, now. Tired as she is, when I get the calf around to nurse, she might still put up a fuss."

Bronc carried the calf up close and squirted milk into his gaping pink mouth. There was silence. Bronc squirted another stream. The cow's ears came alert, then the sound of suckling filled the barn.

Kasey closed her eyes. She breathed in hay dust, wet fur, and milk. She hoped she wouldn't have to twist the rope tighter and hoped the cow got the idea as quickly as the ecstatic calf.

The cow stomped and pulled against the rope, trying to get a look at the calf. Bronc nodded and Kasey gave the cow some slack. She swished her tail, stamped again, and blew a breath that filled Kasey's face with the scent of sweet alfalfa. Bronc stepped back from the pair, arms out as if he were balancing on a tightrope.

"Unwind it completely," Bronc said. "Let's see if she's gonna recommence kicking. I can rig up hobbles if she does, but I think she's getting used to him."

The calf butted his mother, tugged back on her nipple, and she didn't protest, just swung her head to look at him and gave him a loud going-over with her washcloth-sized tongue as he sucked his fill of warm milk.

"Bingo." Bronc walked toward Kasey and leaned back against the fence between her gripping hands. He stretched with satisfaction and watched for another ten minutes.

Just when she'd edged her hands closer together, inches from his bare shoulders, Bronc unlatched the gate and came out. "They'll be okay now."

"It's what you're made for, isn't it?" She blurted the words before giving them a second's thought.

He blushed. "Bein' guidance counselor to a ton of thick-skulled teenage cow? Yeah, I guess so."

"You were the same with the colt." Kasey's throat tightened at Bronc's red-faced denial. He wanted so much to be a vet. "Bronc, when you're working with them, even your voice is . . . wonderful."

"Shucks, ma'am, you got me plumb embarrassed." But he couldn't joke over it. His face went hard and he strode toward the door. "There's a shower 'round back. Give me a minute."

〰 〰

HE DIDN'T TELL HER TO WATCH the cow and calf, or order her to stay put as he had a dozen times since they'd met, and when Kasey heard the splatter of water on hard male muscle, the sound pulled her like magnetism.

She liked this grown-up Bronc McDermitt. He might have stood her up ten years ago, but tonight he'd proven himself.

Kasey kept her footsteps light as she followed the sounds of his shower. It was hard to believe Bronc was the same species as Mark Savage, who'd tossed her aside when she became inconvenient. Although he had no part in her vendetta with Flynn, Bronc had defended her, then kept her at hand during the calving, in case Flynn returned.

And just look at him.

Moonlight scattered silver along his shoulders, sheened the long muscles in his thighs. Shadows cast the rest in darkness, and temptation.

It was her movement, trying to see, that tipped him off. "Hell's bells, woman." He turned his back to her, flashing white cheeks so boyish, she turned away laughing.

"Shameless hussy," he muttered. "How 'bout you go get my shirt while I pull on some britches?"

She ran, feeling every bit of shameless, running because she heard the scuff of denim and she didn't want to miss any more than she had to.

He was zipping, snapping, still looking down, when she rounded the corner of the barn. He looked up through his eyelashes and shook his head in disapproval.

"I asked if I could watch," she reminded him.

"And I said to suit yourself."

Vibration marked the spaces between each word, but she couldn't guess what he'd do next.

He sat on a tree stump and pulled on his boots, still watching her. Just as he'd given the cattle his full attention, he gave it to her. The shirt hung dangling from her fingers.

He was a bad girl's dream. A good girl's, too, except for the threat in his walk. Not a personal threat, but an elemental male-female threat she'd never felt with Mark.

Bronc wouldn't take her here and now. But he could. Instead, he smiled.

"I never figured birthing calves was very romantic."

"It depends, I suppose, on your idea of romance." She twisted the shirt around her finger. "Watching you made me admire your skill. And compassion."

Struck silent, Bronc snatched the shirt from her finger, shoved one arm in, then the other.

"You're blushing again." She said like it a dare, on purpose, to see if he'd lose interest in buttoning his shirt. "That kind of skill and the moonlight . . ." She gestured toward the sky.

His arms closed around her waist. His shirt was open and his chest warm as he pulled her against him for a kiss.

His lips touched her mouth three times, advancing from one corner, to the middle, to the other corner. Softer than she would have guessed, given her taunt, but as soon as she thought it, his lips covered hers with a force that rocked her backward, testing his grip.

Last night's kiss worked like an accelerant on tonight's. She felt the bone of his chest grate her shirt buttons into her flesh, just an instant before her arms clamped around him. His mouth slanted against hers, forcing her lips open.

She twisted her arms free and reached under his gaping shirt to smooth her thumbs along his ribs. His breath caught and the sound urged her on, sending her hands apart from each other to follow his shoulder blades. Like flat, beveled arrowheads, she thought, until Bronc's hands destroyed all fantasy.

Under her blouse, to the front of her, forcing beneath the cups of her bra. Once he captured each of her breasts, his roughness faded.

Hers began. Kasey gasped. Her fingernails clamped on his skin and pulled him closer, trapping his hands between them. She couldn't have said whether she resisted his hands' pursuit or trapped them there.

"I don't think . . ." she began.

Bronc arched back into her nails as if he welcomed the pain, and when he kissed her again, tracing his tongue feathery soft, then faster, inside her bottom lip, Kasey's hands skittered down his shoulder blades and curled around his waist.

"Compassion," she said against his mouth. "I said skill and *compassion.*"

"Uh-uh."

"Mercy?"

"Not a chance." Bronc's hand moved to the back of her bra, searching for a hook, then returned to the space between her breasts, seeking a front clasp. "Well, it's damned sure I'm not doing too well on the 'skill' part."

"You're wrong," she told him, laughing.

"How do I take this thing off?"

"You don't."

"That's hardly sportin', Hollywood."

"I don't dress for seduction."

"The hell you don't."

Under her shirt, Bronc slid the pad of his thumb over the satin, teasing the bud of her nipple. "All this no-nonsense, no-lace stuff, but it's so smooth I can feel every bit of you inside it."

His words might have pushed her past thought, if her necklace's rasp on her nape hadn't turned a floodlight glare into her mind. *A weakness for men,* Blue Rain had said. *It ruined the women of her tribe every time.*

"We better stop." Not my weakness. Not this time.

"Naw, we better not." His lips nuzzled her neck, until he felt her stillness, heard her silence, and sighed. "Okay, why?"

"I've got a reporter's objectivity to maintain." Kasey cleared her throat, thinking she'd sound more convincing if she could slow her panting breaths. "Didn't we talk about that before?"

"If you can't remember"—he nipped the side of her neck—"maybe it's already too late."

"Mmmmm, no." She stepped away, but he clung to her hand, and she insisted, "I'm really strong."

"Then, I've got a suggestion." Bronc swung their joined hands as if they were kids. "If you're so strong, how 'bout we just go ahead and get this distraction out of the way?"

She considered it, and that only proved she was sinking fast. Kasey looked at their hands. In the moonlight, his looked darker. As she tried to formulate a sensible response, he squeezed her hand so hard she felt the delicate bones shift beneath his grasp.

"Don't trust me, Kasey. I'd lie to have you." He stared so hard that she thought he hated her, until he said, "And once we're together neither of us is going to be thinking straight for a long, long time."

SEVENTEEN

"*Think now, Kasey.*" Blue Rain glided into her dream with a following of mythic animals.

The silver-blue Appaloosa walked beside her, shoulder to shoulder. A flurry of ravens, scrub jays, and ring-necked doves fluttered over her shoulders like a living cape. Furtive and gray, a fox darted, froze, and followed them all.

"*Think of what I've told you and what you've seen.*" Blue Rain passed moth-light fingertips over Kasey's eyelids. "*Don't wake. You see better in your dreams.*"

The spirit showed Kasey a fantasy where she wore buckskin and followed an uncertain path through terra-cotta hills and turquoise plains. In the dream, her nostrils were filled with the scent of smoldering ceremonial sage.

"*... and there's Horse and that infernal Fox.*"

"No," Kasey's lips moved slowly, barely forming words. "It's not me, it's you."

"*Same thing.*" Blue Rain wafted her hand, but an awful tension followed.

Kasey watched her dream self cling to Horse. Outcast from her people, but protected by the curve of his warm neck, she watched as Fox took revenge for their exile. He stalked the People by night, snatching babies and snapping them into fragments. When the People came to wreak revenge, Fox was gone, but they found Blue Rain and even Horse couldn't protect her.

"Horse will try to guard you, but the battle is yours." Blue Rain's voice drew Kasey from the nightmare, back to the fantasy of bright hills and turquoise plains. *"And you will win."*

Then fissures spread across the perfect plain. They snaked toward Kasey's bare feet, then curved outward and rejoined in a huge heart shape drawn on the desert floor. Where the fissures met, azure water spouted.

"Water." Kasey's fingers moved over her necklace, telling the shell beads like a rosary. "I know when he needs water."

Kasey saw Blue Rain smile. *"Of course. Water is the desert's greatest gift to the People and the shells' greatest gift to wearers of the necklace."* Blue Rain's voice rose over the crash of far-off waves. *"The shells remember."*

Kasey floated with the shells' memory, a memory so strong her cheeks felt wet and her lips stung from windblown salt. Small as seeds, the shells slid on the indigo breast of waters covering a continent. They rode white wave crests tumbling to shore, then spun on fingers of foam, searching the sand with hushed songs humans could still hear if they held shells to their ears and listened.

As Fox's evil vanished, Kasey sighed. Rocked by a sea cradle one million years dry, she slept.

〽️ 〽️

"BOOTS ON THE GROUND, HOLLYWOOD. We're burnin' daylight."

No daylight hid behind the gingham curtains in Shannon's guest room, and Bronc departed as soon as he left a cup of coffee at her bedside.

For a minute, the dream remained. Vivid as these walls, the dream told her the necklace's power was real. And yet

That suspicion, that contempt for the unseen and unbelievable eddied around her and Kasey knew why Letty Wildmoon had given her up for adoption. The stigma of believing in the paranormal and having others *know* you believed would weigh down a half-Paiute, half-Italian child. Letty had tried to hold off Kasey's otherworldly experiences until she was old enough to cope.

Just now, she could barely cope with her real life.

Kasey forced her feet from beneath the blankets and dressed quickly, pulling a denim jacket over a sleeveless white top even before she stashed her nightshirt in her pack. She disconnected the laptop computer she'd recharged overnight. That had been a sop to her sloth.

Last night, she'd planned to work for hours, transferring her notes to a disk, but she hadn't even checked her e-mail.

Kasey stretched like a cat and smiled. She'd felt no desire to work when she'd come back to this room, alone.

Kasey took a gulp of hot coffee and thought how considerate he'd been to deliver it. How long would she receive such treatment if Bronc were hers?

Not going to happen.

Kasey used the heel of her hand to clear a corner of the dusty mirror. Even if she discounted the direction her article had taken—one that might destroy his family—there was the unsettling city mouse and country mouse aspect of their attraction.

He called her "Hollywood." Kasey smiled and smoothed lotion onto a face that hadn't worn makeup for days. Hollywood and Bronc were unlikely names for a couple. But she loved his hard-guy attitude and sweet, sweet seduction.

She looked away from the mirror. Her flush only proved she

needed to resume control. She turned and opened her laptop computer. In minutes, she could reconnect with her real world.

As the electronic screen glowed on, disloyalty knotted in her stomach. She didn't want to talk about this story. Not to Cookie, Mark Savage, or her editors at *Dare*.

Her fingers curved above the plastic keys. Mac and Wendy McDermitt and their twins lived in a way most people thought had ended in the last century. Her story would make sure it did.

She stared at the screen's insistently flashing cursor. Journalism was no place to explore divided loyalties. Her loyalty was to the truth.

All the same, she closed the laptop, slipped it into her pack, and rummaged in her rudimentary makeup kit for mascara and lip gloss. Such props would make her feel like a professional. And she'd check her e-mail tonight.

ॐ ॐ

C.B. RADIO MICROPHONE held in one hand, pottery cup in the other, Bronc stood in Shannon's dim kitchen sipping his own coffee, unaware Kasey watched.

God, he looked good. Standing there in the half-dark, Bronc's hastily shaved jaw and overlong black hair should have made him look like a convict. Instead, his soft flannel shirt and smile made her want to cuddle. With one hard arm, he might hold her against him and she'd absorb his warmth on this brisk summer morning.

"She's a spy." The voice coming over the radio speaker was wheezy and weak. "She followed the codes on the back of the highway signs as far as Gerlach. And then, *then*—"

"C'mon, we've talked about that before. She would've had to drive on the wrong side of the road."

"*You* look, Bronco Billy, and you'll see codes on the back of them signs. Codes imprinted there to guide an invading army."

Bronc held his hand over the microphone and rolled his eyes skyward and confided to Kasey, "An invading army which wouldn't think to bring maps, I guess."

"...wants to find out where every bit of tanglefoot and every trip wire's located and take me in to the V.A. There's nothing wrong with me, but that's what they do with people who know too much, put 'em in with the kooks and pretty soon..."

"Kasey doesn't work for the government," Bronc said quietly. "She's a writer for a magazine, that's all." Bronc cut his eyes toward a closed door off the hallway and tapped an index finger to his lips.

Kasey nodded. It was probably Shannon's bedroom. When she awoke with a hideous hangover, Kasey wanted to be gone.

Now the radio broadcast nothing but coughing and static. Who had Bronc been talking to about *her*?

Kasey flicked on the kitchen light switch. Nothing happened and Bronc shrugged before continuing his conversation.

"Abner, my man, your best friends work for the government."

Bronc talked to Abner Bengochea, king of conspiracy theories and radio-controlled bombs as if he were a favorite uncle, while Kasey hoped Abner's coughing didn't intensify and set off the tons of unstable dynamite in his basement.

"You don't count, boy. I can trust you."

Pity and disgust warred in Kasey's stomach, but she told herself she just needed something besides coffee.

Bronc lowered his voice again. " 'Course I count. The U.S. government pays my salary. And Tate's."

"Flynn's too. Flynn, when he's flying up there, he's seen them black helicopters searching out landing pads."

Bronc's face hardened. He straightened his slump against

the cabinets and stared toward the kitchen sink.

She warmed to Bronc's protective stance, but she resisted. Something about his need to guard her niggled at Kasey's mind. It wasn't just that the notion was archaic.

"Yeah, that Flynn sees plenty. Okay, now Abner, we'll be there by afternoon. You need something, like to go outside and reset something, you wait for us. No sense—" Bronc listened as the voice turned into a garble. He fiddled with a knob on the console, but Kasey felt his eyes follow her hips as she crossed to refill her cup. "No, I don't think we'll be staying."

Kasey looked up, coffeepot poised in midair, halted by the desire in his eyes.

Horse will try to guard you, but the battle is yours. Blue Rain's words came back like an echo, but Bronc's look wasn't sheltering.

Bronc.

Horse.

"Lady has an aversion to sleeping indoors." Bronc set his cup on the counter and walked to the end of the microphone cord. "She likes camping." He reached the empty hand out to her.

Bronc.

Horse.

She could show him who was boss. She could underline her morning resolution and last night's resistance. Instead, she took his hand.

As it enfolded hers, his voice droned into the background and she shivered at the connection her mind had made.

Bronc defended her against Flynn.

Horse was Blue Rain's protector.

While her mind rejected superstition, her heart applauded the primal ease with which Bronc fit into the equation.

And you will win, Blue Rain had promised.

What if it *were* true? What if Kasey Wildmoon and Bronc McDermitt could set ancient wrongs right?

Bronc hung up the microphone.

"He thinks you're real tough, 'cause you like to sleep out." He gave a testing tug on her hand.

"I am real tough." She resisted his pull.

Nodding, Bronc walked toward her, taking up the slack in their straight arms until he reached her and looped her wrist over his neck.

"Horses are saddled," he said, but Kasey only watched his lips. "I've tied on everything but your pack. Time for us to vamoose."

She kissed him quick, before making her getaway. He let her pull back, but he smiled and kept them tethered together by her wrist around his neck.

"You owe me more than that, Hollywood, and tonight I'm going to collect."

"What makes you think you have the right—"

"Save your breath, honey." His thumb played over the tender flesh inside her wrist. "You know I'm not gonna do one thing to hurt you. And I've got my permission note right here."

Bronc kept his eyes fixed on the kitchen clock as he guided her hand under his flannel shirt to a barely swollen line on his shoulder blade.

He didn't say words that would make her blush. He didn't remind her how her pulse had raced, how she'd pressed forward instead of pulling back. How she'd scratched him with her passion. He didn't have to; it was happening all over again.

And then the decelerating roar of an engine invaded the kitchen. Horses neighed, tires crushed dirt, and they heard a plane rolling down Shannon's landing strip.

Flynn?

"You stay here." Bronc pointed his finger as he started for the door. "Please," he added, but it overlapped her refusal.

"No." She shrugged her pack onto her shoulder and followed.

"Fine, but *I'm* going out there to get my rifle off my saddle." He strode through the door, giving it an extra push to let her follow. "If that son of a bitch doesn't have sense enough to give me time to cool off…"

Kasey dropped her pack and beat him to the saddle scabbard. She placed her hand over the rifle's stock. "Bronc, think a minute. An accused felon swinging a rifle around—"

"Accused, not convicted." Still, he didn't push her hand out of the way.

"You said he's always armed. If he provokes you, who's going to take the blame?"

Bronc didn't have to answer. Kasey heard a familiar voice and relief almost weakened her knees.

"… this is the right place…"

The voice belonged to Cookie, but when Kasey rounded the corner, it was just in time to see Mark appear in the doorway of his corporate-logoed plane. A stairway was being lowered by a man in a pressed white shirt and black cap.

Mark looked his golden Viking self in a grape-blue golf shirt, khakis, and aviator sunglasses. After a couple steps, he paused to survey the ranch and put on lip balm.

"I'll be damned." Bronc stood just behind her, hands on hips. His expression would have to improve to qualify as contempt.

Looking like Orphan Annie dressed for summer camp, Cookie appeared behind Mark. "Out of the way, big shot." She clattered past him.

"Kasey!"

China bolted to the end of his tethered reins and Rook sidestepped at Cookie's shout and the energy with which she spun Kasey in a hug.

Clamped against her friend's copper corkscrew curls, Kasey heard Cookie murmur, "My God, Kace, if you're not screwing yourself silly, you need hormone shots. He is gorgeous." The last three words came out in a hoarse stage whisper, which Bronc must have heard.

Not that it improved his expression. Glowering, ill-shaven, shirt hanging from where he'd untucked it to guide her hand over his flesh, Bronc McDermitt was still the best-looking male she'd ever seen.

Kasey sneaked a glance at Mark. All gym-sculpted muscle and styled hair, he suffered by comparison. She smiled at Bronc, hoping he could see his superiority.

Mark couldn't. He looked as if he was trying to marshal amusement to cover his confusion.

"Hey there, Mr. McDermitt, remember me?" Cookie extended her hand and Kasey felt a pinpoint spark of jealousy. "I ambushed you in the courthouse hallway."

Kasey glanced between the two men again, certain Bronc wouldn't want to discuss his courtroom or jail time in front of Mark Savage.

"Yes, ma'am." Bronc's lazy tomcat smile made Kasey want to kick him.

Cookie turned aside, biting her knuckle in a parody of sexual frustration and Mark picked that moment to enter the conversation.

"Looking great, K. D." Mark tugged the lapel of her denim jacket and kissed her with a resounding smack. "Getting in touch with your roots must agree with you."

Bronc bent sudden concentration to lacing Kasey's pack onto her saddle. Mark widened his stance and moved forward, angling for Bronc's attention.

"McDermitt, I'm Mark Savage."

"You want to watch your step, Mr. Savage."

Mark tucked his chin and puffed up with offense, then frowned toward Kasey.

"For crying out loud, Mark. You're standing right behind China." She pointed when he scowled in confusion. "The horse kicks."

"Ah." Mark chuckled with wry understanding. "Hate to get dust on the old Gucciroonies."

Kasey kept from burying her face in her hand, but barely. With pitying fascination she watched Mark take a long step sideways and position himself between her and Bronc. Clearly, he expected Bronc to twirl around and make much of a millionaire visitor. Bronc squatted to check China's hooves.

How on Earth had she ever pictured herself married to this pretentious ass?

"Kace." Cookie shoved her shoulder against Kasey's. "Tell me this little house on the prairie has a bathroom."

"Yes, of course." Motioning Cookie to be quiet, Kasey guided her into the house, but one glance back at the men made her wonder if it was a smart thing to do.

⚛ ⚛

BRONC NOTICED THAT SAVAGE wore "the old Gucciroonies" without socks. His ankles were dark as a Hereford steer and sheened over with sun-bleached hair. Probably from playing tennis. Or sailing yachts. A man didn't get tanned ankles from work.

Bronc knew he couldn't squat here all day checking China's feet, but he couldn't conjure up two words he wanted to exchange with Kasey's old flame.

He'd wanted to upchuck when Savage touched Kasey's jacket and filled his eyes with the white shirt underneath. Then he'd kissed her with an air of ownership.

Savage had slept with Kasey. The fact hit Bronc in the back of the head like a sledgehammer.

She'd worn his ring and agreed to marry him. Bronc rested his palms on his thighs. How could Kasey *not* measure men by Savage, though his every action screamed he was a selfish prick?

Bronc pushed off his thighs and stood, giving China's rump a hearty pat before he turned to Savage. The millionaire spoke first.

"How's K. D. doing, riding all over the countryside?"

"Just fine."

"And the interview? How's that going?"

No wonder Savage had let her go. He sure underestimated Kasey's talent.

"She's done quite a few," Bronc said. "With"—he blew through his lips, estimating—"at least a dozen folks."

"I was asking if she'd been too rough on you."

"She asks hard questions." Bronc shrugged. If Savage thought Kasey's questions were the toughest part of dealing with her, the guy would've been no match for her. "I figure it's her job."

Savage looked at the ground and chuckled. He stuck his tongue in his cheek, shook his head, then glanced back up.

"You don't know, do you?" Savage rocked back on his heels. "She didn't tell you."

"How 'bout cuttin' the crap, Savage?" Bronc walked around back of both horses, warning them with pats. He snatched Rook's trailing reins and clenched his fist around them.

"Oh no. You're not getting it from me." Savage crossed his muscular forearms and nodded toward the front screen door as it slammed. "Just ask K. D. about *the bet*."

Bronc credited himself with keeping a decent mouth, but

Mark Savage made more awful language pump through his brain than the last time a horse rolled on him.

When the two women came off the shadowed porch, Bronc saw Kasey had stuck her hair up under her hat and donned her sunglasses. She was ready to ride.

"Cookie, did you ask Kasey if she wanted to fly up to Lake Tahoe for brunch?"

"Breakfast, Mark," Cookie corrected. "He has an early golf date in Palm Springs, so we had to leave Salt Lake in the middle of the night."

"These photojournalists are sassy, aren't they?" Savage included Bronc in his joking assessment.

" 'Fraid she's the only one I've met."

"They're a sassy breed," Savage repeated. "You're invited, too, McDermitt." Savage didn't even look him over before he added, "I have a private dining room at Chateau D'Argent."

"Sounds like a doozie, but I've got an appointment I can't break." Bronc turned his hand outward, indicating Kasey was free to go.

"I better not." Kasey's voice was hesitant.

Bronc figured he should appreciate that, though she looked like a little haggling might change her mind.

With or without her, he had to go. Flynn's performance last night made Bronc wonder if Abner had made just one more Storm Hammer for his buddy who kept an eye out for black helicopters.

Even if Flynn killing horses made no sense, Bronc had to ask.

Kasey'd probably rather do anything—even eat breakfast with this grasshopper-brained rich boy—than go back to Abner's, where every bush and rock smelled like gunpowder.

Except she had a story to write. And Abner was an interesting source. If last night's passion and whiplash stop had shown him nothing else, it proved Kasey would fight the very devil—at least the one nagging her to mate—rather than compromise a story.

"It would be no trouble to fly you back to McDermitt, after breakfast," Savage offered.

Bronc watched Kasey chew over the possibilities. Then, she shot him an inside-joke smile.

"Actually, I think it might be a little tricky for your pilot to set down at Abner's. I'll pass this time."

Kasey braided a lock of China's mane until Savage ran out of protests, then her voice changed.

Bronc had never heard the tone from *her*, but any man who played poker would recognize it as a bluff.

"Besides, Mark," Kasey said, "we're going to be having lunch together at Glenside, real soon." She pushed her sunglasses up her nose. "I hope you told Beatrice to make reservations."

EIGHTEEN

Bronc watched Kasey's back. Her spine jabbed straight up above the cantle of her saddle and her shoulders didn't sway. China's hooves jittered between a single set of tire tracks pressed into the desert floor.

China tossed his head. The gelding was on the verge of misbehavior and Kasey had only herself to blame. She was wound tighter than an old-time pocket watch ready to pop a spring.

It beat him how Kasey could be so scared. She didn't balk at Flynn's physical menace, at breaking her neck falling from an unfamiliar horse, at facing off with kids who prowled the playa with guns.

Hellbent on making good time, Kasey had refused to stop for lunch. She kept searching the horizon for Abner's place, even though her fear lodged there.

He didn't believe he was leading her into danger.

Trying to defuse her worry, he'd described the pattern of explosives planted in Abner's front yard. Fidgeting with her reins, Kasey had asked him to repeat his explanation. Twice. The last time, she'd closed her eyes as if trying to picture it. He might have stopped to sketch the layout in the dirt, but he knew it would be a waste of time. Facts wouldn't stick on fear.

Shoot, he might as well try distraction.

"Hey!" He whistled through his teeth and she pulled China down to a stuttering trot. "I don't suppose your story's got room for a little history about the playa." He gestured at the flat white basin around them.

"It might." Kasey gave a half-smile and shed her denim jacket. She wasn't fooled, but he got to watch her graceful brown arms tie the jacket onto her saddle as she humored him. "Not the ancient stuff, though. I have notes on that."

"Fine." He'd played tour guide to a couple Washington bureaucrats not so long ago, so he recycled the high points.

"In the sixties, it was used for growing algae as an alternate food source, but that was a real small-scale operation and didn't last long. A little later, there was talk of shrimp ranching, but that fizzled before it started. I hear there was a fly-in brothel," he joked. "And then the dump."

"The dump?"

"There was talk of using it as a dump for San Francisco garbage. That was rejected, but it was approved as a bombing range. Most recently, a couple summers ago some Woodstock wannabes carpeted thirteen square miles with Astroturf, enclosed it with chain-link fence, and set a two-story effigy of a man on fire."

Kasey looked over the playa and he directed his eyes after hers. Faint dust hung in the air, as if whoever made those tire tracks had passed pretty recently. But he didn't think she was studying the dust. She lifted her sunglasses and squinted toward the distant walls of soaring red rock.

"Sacrilege," she said with an unladylike grunt and settled her sunglasses once more.

When had she taken a liking to the desert? No matter.

Thoughts of Abner, multiple Storm Hammers, and Savage's "bet" had his stomach turning sour with worry. What had been dared and what wagered?

Not that he'd ask. This little romance wasn't moving fast, but it was headed in the right direction. He hated to wreck that by asking questions.

Questions were Kasey's game and she couldn't ask one that would cool his desire to have her. Nothing short of earthquake or pestilence would do that.

He glanced over to see her necklace half inside her shirt. If he held it in his palm, it'd feel warm from her skin. He drew a long breath, expelled it. Even an earthquake was iffy.

"I've decided I don't need to go in." She stared through China's pricked ears as Abner's compound came into sight.

He gave Kasey time to lay out excuses while he studied the earth-sheltered house. It had long, narrow windows suited for gunports and dirt berms slanted to halt groundfire.

The place seemed awful still. If he hadn't just talked with him, he'd say Abner wasn't home.

"The government found two Storm Hammers," Kasey said. "Yours and Mac's. The ballistics tests for both weapons were close. Given the condition of the bodies, either could have been used, by you, Mac, or a stranger."

"A stranger?"

"Sure." Kasey nodded and Bronc realized Kasey had struck on an angle that wouldn't hurt a soul. "Either weapon could have been stolen to kill the horses, then returned. The only reason to talk with Abner Bengochea is to get him to verify he only made two."

Damned if she hadn't reached the same conclusion he had. Funny she thought it was unimportant. Or did she? Kasey watched him, waiting for a consensus.

"Bengochea's the only one who'd know for sure," she prodded.

"And *he's* crazy," Bronc said.

"Are you agreeing or making fun of me?"

"Neither," he said with a laugh. "Ol' coot doesn't have enough brains to grease a skillet."

"But he has a basement full of dynamite. Isn't that what you said?"

"That's a fact. And you don't need to set foot in there, but I told him I was coming by."

"And you will."

"Yeah." He bristled at her smile. "Don't go looking all gooey-eyed. I've got some questions of my own."

"Do you?"

He should've stopped talking two seconds sooner. Kasey tried to look casual, but she was as hard on point as a hunting hound.

Bronc nodded and kept riding, hoping Kasey's good judgment was stronger than her nose for news.

⌇⌇ ⌇⌇

ONLY HER SENSE that the story was heating up kept Kasey calm. She kept her mind in the present and forced herself to unclench hands that had started to sweat. She wanted to back out, but something was going on with Bronc.

From a distance, he'd pointed to the architecturally out-of-place dormer windows in Abner's roof.

"To see who's sneaking up on him," Bronc had explained. "And that sandy patch, over there? Keep your eye on the house while I ride over it."

Kasey felt as if someone had taken a stitch in her windpipe. "I don't see—" she began. "Wait."

A whooping siren, like something from a World War II movie, blatted from the house.

"It's an alarm," Bronc explained. "A floodlight comes on in the yard, too."

The horses' ears flicked toward the odd sound, but she was the only one freaking out. Cold palms and queasiness were stress reaction she'd learned to understand, but, for just a minute, Kasey felt light-headed.

Mom would counsel putting her head between her knees, but that contortion was tricky on horseback. Blinking against millions of gnat-sized dots swarming before her eyes, Kasey pulled China to a stop and leaned to one side, pretending to straighten her stirrup leather.

"Everything okay?"

"Fine." She straightened, knowing very well how to squash an irrational fear. "Just wanted to get this."

Kasey reached into her pack, took out her tape recorder, checked the tape, and clicked it to voice-activate. Then she noticed they'd drawn rein at the same place Bronc had stopped last time. The place Blue Rain had spoken for the first time.

"Gonna do some work while I'm gone?" Bronc nodded to the tape recorder as he swung down and knotted Rook's reins to a leggy sagebrush.

It was the first time she'd seen him tie the horses and Kasey knew Bronc was thinking ahead to an explosion that might make the well-schooled horse panic.

"Changed my mind," she told him. "I'm going with you."

The hell you are. She so expected the words, she was startled when Bronc didn't say them. Instead of responding, he dug through his saddlebag, nearly emptied it onto the ground, then reloaded it with slow and dreading movements.

He looked over his shoulder, staring as if he could see

through her dark lenses. Then he made a clucking noise to Rook, pushed the horse aside, and took China's reins to tie him as well.

Bronc cleared his throat twice before continuing his travelogue.

"You hear that generator?" he asked. "Abner doesn't trust the power company, either, so he makes his own. Figures that when the feds come with flame-throwers and such, he'll be able to run the sprinklers on his roof. Keep them from burning him out."

The scene swam before her eyes. This had to stop.

Kasey held up a finger. "I'm taping, but give me a minute." She bent from the waist and pretended to straighten the sock inside her boot. She refused to pass out.

"Okay." She straightened and cleared her throat. "Tell me about the tunnels you mentioned before."

Compassion flickered over his eyes and Kasey hardened herself to resist. "*Are* there any tunnels?"

"Can't say, for sure. Abner does have a trapdoor to the basement and he claims a tunnel runs from there to the barn and the barn has a back exit into the desert."

Bronc ran out of breath at the same time Kasey realized she didn't need a word of this for her story. Unless Abner Bengochea turned out to be the mustang killer. And that wasn't possible.

"This is great stuff and it could come in handy on another story," she said, as if he'd inquired.

Bronc's expression said he didn't believe her, but he kept quiet for a minute. Then his expression turned sheepish.

"Now, I don't figure you'll be coming out of here alone," Bronc said, "but just in case, let me tell you the secret to finding the path to the house. It's never failed for me, so far, and unless we have a few bad drought years, I can't imagine it will."

When Bronc paused, blood roared in her ears. *Alone* in a minefield. She fought down the nightmare and managed to speak.

"Okay," she said.

"Squat down here." He lowered himself, nearly squatting on his bootheels on the desert floor, and motioned her to join him. "Right here, sight along my arm." He pointed. "For cryin' out loud, Hollywood, hunker down and let me show you."

She did, half afraid that if she pressed close to Bronc, she'd pull his arms around her.

"See where the water's run through? Not broad as a creekbed, just a little wrinkly path from rainstorms. Abner doesn't plant any explosives in the water's way. That's where you walk."

Kasey moved her cheek away from his arm and touched her necklace. The necklace remembered the sea. Sudden confidence rolled through her. The necklace would help her find her way. "But isn't there something—some Indian tradition saying you're not supposed to walk where the water does?"

Bronc took off his Stetson, smoothed his hair, then jammed the hat back on. "Don't go weird on me now, Hollywood."

"I'm not—"

"I never heard of such a legend, and unless you got it on higher authority than a Hillerman novel, stick with what works."

Kasey swallowed. She listened for Blue Rain's voice, for some hint from the necklace. Nothing.

"Gotcha." She stood. "Let's do it."

He set off immediately, and Kasey found that as long as she focused on Bronc's boots, stepped in his prints, and refused to think, she did fine. Her concentration only faltered once.

"Tanglefoot's a real primitive alarm system." Bronc stepped over a snarl of barbed wire stretched along the ground. "Those soda cans he's got zip-tied to the wire? They've got pebbles inside, so he'll hear us coming if we knock one."

Bronc's voice broke her self-hypnosis. As she glanced around, Kasey realized she stood in the middle of a very real battleground. "You okay, Hollywood?"

"Fine."

"Do you mean to tell me," he drawled, "that I imagined that little moan?"

"Must have."

"Now ain't that a shame." Bronc stepped clear of the last barbed wire and reached back to steady her. "Just when I thought we were gettin' somewhere."

༄ ༅

THE FRONT DOOR STOOD AJAR. Kasey blinked, trying to focus on anything lurking in the space between door and frame.

"Abner!" Bronc shouted. "Don't bother comin' to the door. We're letting ourselves in." He listened for a minute. "Okay, buddy?"

Kasey followed Bronc into a house that smelled of canned soup and burned toast. From the front door, she saw a living room and a kitchen. Both were excruciatingly clean. The brown shag carpet appeared brushed to attention. The couch was draped with a crocheted throw and an arrangement of silk flowers sat on a low coffee table. Polished glass chimneys glittered around candle-shaped chandelier bulbs that set the diamond-paned china cabinet and white kitchen floor gleaming. A butcher-block table, legs cut to wheelchair height, was scrubbed clean and crumbless.

From her first step inside, Kasey knew no one was home.

"Abner!" Bronc didn't seem to expect an answer. As he walked toward a hallway of random lengths of pine, buffed bright, each step jingled.

"When did you put on spurs?"

Bronc glanced at his heels, then met her question with a dubious smile. "Before you were out of bed."

All the time she'd focused on his boots and mirrored every step, she hadn't noticed.

Bronc opened the single closed door and walked inside. "Loco," he said, reemerging. "The television in his bedroom is still warm."

Bronc sighed, frowned, and rubbed the back of his neck.

The gesture squeezed something in the center of her torso. Kasey went to him.

She meant to wind her arms around him.

"Bronc—"

When he looked down, questioning, she grabbed the front of his shirt and hauled him close for a kiss.

"Thanks." She talked against his neck. "For making me be brave. I didn't think I could do that."

That kiss had been more than a celebration of survival. She knew it, even if he didn't, but Kasey could feel his attention wandering. She held her nerve steady and pulled away from him.

"My pleasure." He scanned the room as if coming back to it. He touched a copper kettle on the stove and apparently found it cold. "Abner knew we were on our way. He said nothing about leaving, but there are tire tracks leading in here. Someone else drove."

Significance sparked from those words, but he didn't clarify his suspicion, just kept checking.

"I don't think he fell down the basement stairs," he said. "The trapdoor's closed, but that's where his gun shop is."

Gun shop. Basement. Dynamite.

"Don't look over there, look at me." He turned her chin back and, though it was a proprietary move, though Bronc's eyes were storm blue and demanding, she felt no threat. "Listen," he said. "Something's definitely wrong. And if something goes wrong in this house, it could go wrong *big time.*"

"I know."

"Promise you won't try to follow me down there."

Kasey swallowed. "A gun shop, down there with the dynamite." Kasey's stomach lurched as she pictured the contents of a gun shop. There'd probably be a vise, a lathe, and a dozen sources of ignition. Electric tools, oils and rags . . .

"I told you Abner was crazy, but he's planned it real well. He's got the upper body strength of a weight-lifter, so he doesn't need help getting down the stairs. He's got a second wheelchair down there." Bronc started to reach toward her, then let his hand drop.

"It's all for show, Kasey. A hobby." He shook his head. "Next to no one knows he's out here, and no one at all cares."

She imagined a white-hot flash in the cramped space beneath her feet. "If I stay up here, you've got to promise to tell me what you see."

Bronc raised one eyebrow.

"In detail," she said. "You're searching for an indication he made a third Storm Hammer, right?"

His slight nod reminded her how much uncertainty coursed beneath their attraction. Why couldn't she have met him in an elevator in L.A.? Or on the track where she jogged after work? Even a chance encounter in the supermarket produce department would have had a better chance of success.

And yet, she trusted him. He'd fought Flynn for her and the battle had been more than a territorial dispute between males. He'd backed her up, like a partner.

Kasey touched his unshaven cheek, rubbed her thumb against its roughness, and prayed for his safety beneath the old house.

Bronc lowered her fingers from his lips, opened them, and kissed the center of her hand.

"And while I'm downstairs," he said, "what will you be doing?"

Had he seen her notice the wooden file box that appeared to hold Abner Bengochea's bills and letters? She couldn't admit she wanted to sort through the box looking for evidence. For that she'd need a search warrant—if she were a cop. Since she wasn't, it was a simple act of burglary. If she took something. And, of course, she wouldn't.

"Now, I'm gonna ask you to please wait out on the porch. I know it riles your natural inclinations, but I swore to Abner that I'd never reveal the location of his trapdoor. I can't think why I need to break my word, can you?"

≶ ≷

HELLFIRE.

As Kasey walked outside, Bronc kicked the rust-red throw rug aside and gazed at the floor underneath. He waited for his eyes to find Abner's trapdoor among the random lengths of polished pine.

He knelt, studying the work of a genius. Right there, a man could just work his fingertips beside a knothole, find purchase, and lift. The door came up on oiled hinges, exposing the irregularly-shaped entrance to the basement.

Down there, the walls were whitewashed and modern and the light switch waited at the foot of the stairs. From here he smelled the dynamite, sweating with a chemical scent like no other. It unnerved him just a little and he knew he'd done right, sending Kasey out front.

NINETEEN

At dusk, they rode bareback down to the water.

Bronc watched Kasey measure up to the challenge. With dinner finished and camp pitched far enough away that the mosquitoes wouldn't eat them, a bareback ride with the sky suffused in rose and purple had seemed romantic.

He hoped it proved a big enough distraction. Kasey was eaten up with a need to know what he'd found in the basement, but she was letting him take his time. Her patience made him a little uneasy, but he could use these minutes to think.

There'd been a disturbance downstairs, but probably not a struggle. It looked more like Abner had wanted to move faster than his paralyzed lower body allowed.

While Bronc thought, he watched Kasey try to get comfy. China looked like a big sturdy quarter horse, but his spine would feel knobby, barely fleshed, and Kasey didn't have much built-in padding.

"Slow down." Kasey held her reins in one hand, but both palms were braced in front of her, just below the gelding's withers. "If I ride him faster than a walk, I'll end up in two pieces."

China stood at the lip of the bank, and Kasey looked ready to admit defeat.

"Give him his head. He's no more interested in taking a swan dive than you are."

When she clamped her legs tighter, so she wouldn't fall, China took it as permission to surge ahead.

Poised at a steep slant, Kasey looked straight down into the pool and shivered.

"Doin' fine, Hollywood."

At once, he knew his voice was too gentle. He heard it on the June breeze and saw it in the way she smiled. But this was no time to weaken.

An hour outside Abner's they'd come upon the skittish little bachelor band of mustangs and galloped after them to Lost Springs, the spot where he'd meant to camp. Of all Scolding Rock's hot springs, it was the cleanest, had the best rocks for perching and the most perfect temperature. So he'd told Kasey to keep riding.

She wouldn't have a bathing suit in that puny pack, and she wouldn't go skinny-dipping, but he'd bet that white no-sleeved shirt would turn transparent as Kasey closed her eyes, luxuriating in the perfect summer night and warm water.

He'd known what would happen after that and he couldn't allow his mind to digress. This thing with Abner could be life or death. So they'd ridden two miles to a far inferior campsite. And safety.

He had told her to wear shorts, so that she wouldn't be soaked if China decided to wade. Those she'd pulled on looked like drawstring sweatpants cut off about one handspan down her lean brown thighs.

When the horses stood side by side, drinking in great

draughts of water in a twilight turned almost lavender, Kasey broke the mood.

"I don't suppose you found anything down there to make you think he'd made another Storm Hammer?"

"Nothing."

Her easy tone made him wonder if *she* had. It could've been the house creaking above him, but he was pretty sure that, in spite of her promise, Kasey had come back inside to sniff around.

He'd only have to ask Abner what she'd done. The old man was forever spit-sticking hairs across doorjambs and devising other homemade alarms. But where had Abner gone? If he'd gone willingly, that'd mean Calvin Buck or Tate, maybe Flynn had come for him. No one else cared enough to take him for an outing.

As Bronc watched Kasey urge a full-bellied China back up the bank, he thought that the old coot might've at least left a note to keep him from worrying.

With the fire built and horses hobbled, Bronc found a stick to whittle while he watched Kasey fidget.

"You oughta learn to whittle," he said as she rearranged the blanket atop her sleeping bag for the third time. "It'll keep you from getting bored."

Dark had come on, and firelight danced along Kasey's high cheekbones. He tried not to look. Instead, he considered the lump he'd snapped from a stick of mountain mahogany. He turned the knot of wood, seeing how it had grown one way, then changed directions and tangled back on itself.

"I'm never bored." She tugged her pack into her lap. "Can I interview you while you carve?"

"Not much more to tell." He set the knot aside. It was too nice a hunk of wood to mutilate.

He grabbed the part of the branch he'd discarded earlier

and Kasey hit a button and squinted as she angled the whirring recorder toward the firelight.

"They're general questions," she explained. "About the differences between cowboys and buckaroos." She ejected the tape and flipped it over. "Or are they just generic terms?"

Bronc set his knife against the branch and peeled a ribbon of bark.

"Hope you're just looking for the facts. If you want a yarn, talk with Mac."

"The facts will be fine." Kasey balanced a notebook on one bare knee. She'd said she wanted to dry out the shorts China had soaked and claimed she wasn't the least bit chilly.

Funny. Since the sight of her bare legs made *him* swarm with gooseflesh.

"Hat, for one thing. A buckaroo doesn't wear some junk straw hat. Windy country like this, you'll pay him to spend all day chasing it."

"What about a baseball cap—?"

"You're the only soul born ever looked good in a baseball cap," he said. "Any hand you see wearin' one is drivin' a truck to do chores he could do on horseback.

"Nevada's one of the last open range states and a buckaroo works outside fence. It's a matter of pride. You can work cattle without squeeze chutes and corrals. All you need is a horse and rope. If the foreman tells you to mend fence, you head on down the road."

He watched her note it down, biting her lip and nodding as the little machine whirred. "And?" she said, without looking up.

"And he presses on. He won't quit, no matter what."

"No, matter, what." She dotted a period on the paper and brushed her hair back over one shoulder. In the firelight it gleamed red-black and he wanted to touch it.

Kasey clicked off the machine. "Off the record," she said, moving to his side of the fire, "have you ever had to kill a wild horse?" She sat so near that her folded legs grazed his.

Bronc held his knife free of the wood. So much for skimming the surface.

Bronc tightened his fist around the knife and cut another curl of bark. "Yeah," he said. "A couple with dust pneumonia. They'd been gathered for a university study, then driven off their home range for release. Flynn's doing, probably. That's why he works for PAPA, not BOW.

"He ran them more than three times the recommended distance on a hot, dry day. Dehydrated and disoriented, they galloped and galloped on unfamiliar trails until they were choking. Forty-eight of them died.

"A dentist flying out to his clinic in Elko spotted some of them. And I found two."

Eyes questioning, Kasey waited.

"When I got there, a couple coyotes were eatin' on 'em."

"But they weren't dead?" Kasey wedged the last word from her mouth, probably hoping she was wrong. When he nodded, she managed to ask the next hard question. "And you killed the horses, not the coyotes?"

"The mustangs were goners . . ."

". . . and the coyotes were doing what coyotes do," she finished.

"When did you start thinking like a cowgirl?"

As Kasey shook her head, the necklace glowed with firelight. It didn't flash or glitter. It suited her. Here.

"We should be working together on this."

"Aren't we?" He didn't want to test her. And though his head wanted to know what Kasey was like in the city, his heart hesitated. "For instance, are you sure you didn't find something while I was downstairs?"

She smiled. "Nothing that would hold up in a court of law." When she locked her arms around her knees, he offered her a blanket from his bedroll. She shook her head and stared at the campfire.

A moth careened by, dodging flames before riding heat waves up into the night and vanishing.

"Let me see your driver's license."

Bemused, Kasey opened her pack. She extracted a wallet and passed it to him. "Why on earth do you want it?"

"See a picture of you," he mumbled.

Blue nylon. Practical, lightweight, simple as the necklace, but clearly its opposite. Factory-made and modern. He opened the wallet and released the breath he'd been holding.

Damn. He wouldn't have recognized the sleek woman in the photograph. Los Angeles was a million miles away from the Scolding Rock desert and a guy named Bronc McDermitt.

Five feet, nine inches tall.

Black hair. Brown eyes.

That part he recognized, but her clothes. He turned the wallet toward the fire.

"What's this outfit?" His tongue turned clumsy as a Neanderthal's.

"That," she said, peering over his shoulder, "is my favorite Carol Little suit. Toast-colored, with an apricot blouse."

The distance between them stretched wider than the miles to the moon, creating an ache.

375 Quail Hollow Terrace. Probably an apartment building with no quail within shouting distance.

Organ donor. The words brought him up short.

"What?" She'd obviously caught his unguarded expression.

She jockeyed to meet his eyes.

"What?" she insisted.

"Katherine Dane Wildmoon." He folded the wallet and recited as if he'd committed it all to memory. "One-hundred thirty-five pounds of rompin', stompin' trouble."

She slipped it back into her pack. "I only showed you because I have a clip file this thick"—she gestured with thumb and forefinger—"on you. Since we're doing first date stuff, would you like to see your dossier?"

"Hell, no. I'd feel like I'd been autopsied and laid out." He decided to torture himself a little more. "If we were on a first date, where would we go?"

"To lunch."

"It's about nine P.M."

She shrugged. "I only go on lunch dates."

"But if it were night and we were in L.A., would we be going to the movies or the opera? Miniature golf? Cruising on Mulholland Drive?"

"Really, I don't go out at night. Oh, I used to be on a city-league basketball team," she admitted. "But I had to give it up. And even though it was co-ed, I never dated any of the guys. I just showered at the gym and went back to work."

Bronc rubbed his palms together. He could imagine Mark Savage watching Kasey bound back into work. Smelling of cheap soap and high spirits in the empty office building, she'd be irresistible.

"Why'd you give it up?" he asked, but he damn well knew.

"Once I set myself on the fast track at the *Sun-Times,* I started working late on special sections. And there were meetings." She met his skeptical stare. "It wasn't so bad. Sometimes Mark ordered in dinner."

"I'll just bet he did. Gourmet picnics for two. And then he

probably needed a hostess for charity events." Bronc worked to keep his scorn down. "Close your mouth, Hollywood, you're gaping like a goldfish. I've got a great imagination."

"It wasn't like that." She took his blanket and draped it over her shoulders.

Aiming for the top and giving all she's got. Bronc set his jaw and shook his head, seeing it like a movie. Kasey had taken Savage's ambush as flirtation, admiration for her work, maybe even love when Savage had come through with a proposal.

"But these other guys . . ." Bronc coaxed her away from the memories making her frown. "How come you didn't go out with them? Except to lunch."

Wrapping the blanket closer, Kasey slumped her shoulder against his. "Because I didn't like leading them on."

The fire nibbled sticks in the windy Nevada night, reminding him that although K. D. Wildmoon lived far away, he had Kasey tonight. A sap bubble popped. Sparks showered orange and bright and he circled her shoulders with a hug.

"So how 'bout me, Hollywood? Are you leading me on?"

Kasey searched for an answer. After only six days together, how could she tell him the truth? Around her, blackness stretched away into the desert. Here, next to the campfire Bronc had built, the night glowed golden.

"I don't know." She turned, shoulder pivoting off his. "Let me help you figure it out."

Even though he lingered in his approach, giving her time to think, Kasey felt dizzy. Bronc's lips were deliberate and soft as he kissed her. At first, they asked for nothing.

"He was the first, wasn't he?"

"Is that an assessment of my competence?"

"You know it's not." Relentlessly, slowly, he lowered her to his sleeping bag. His lips covered hers and his tongue urged her lips apart as his fingertips made small circles on her temple.

If his movements were meant to reassure her, why did his mouth compel her to do something, anything, to ease her heart's pounding?

"Oh, all right." She separated their lips and he allowed it. Firelight washed between them, but she couldn't read his expression. "Yes, he was."

Only his body, half-shielding hers, kept Kasey from covering her eyes.

"It makes me sick," he said. "No, that's not it, either. It makes me sad."

"Why?" She smothered a shocked laugh against his shoulder and wondered if a heart could shrink with shame.

She knew Bronc—who filled a simple kiss with passion—couldn't imagine such detached intercourse and see it had nothing to do with them. She remembered sex with Mark as an observer who'd stood to one side, immune to an act rumored to be a high point of human existence.

"Why?" he said. "Because our mamas were right." He covered her legs with one of his, but didn't pull her closer. "There's only one first time."

Regret settled in her bones, but only for a minute. Bronc's eyelashes cast shadows against his cheeks, making him look young and vulnerable. He looked like he'd give anything to make things different.

"Hey!" She gave him a quick kiss of discovery. "You *were* the first boy I ever really kissed."

"Yeah?" Bronc sounded willing to be convinced. "You didn't forget?"

"How could I?" She pretended exasperation. "I'll tell you something I haven't told anyone else." Kasey placed her lips to his ear and whispered. "When I won the Daybook Award, the judges said I wrote, quote: lucid, stirring prose, *memorable as a first kiss.*"

Bronc rustled beside her, but she kept her lips at his ear.

"Mark made us keep any awards out on our desks, on display so visitors to the newsroom would see them. Every day I looked at that marble and plastic trophy, and every day you might as well have been sitting on the edge of my desk."

Suddenly but softly, his hand claimed her breast, kneading it as they kissed. The world spun around her as his leg tightened over hers, denim grating against her bare leg. The feeling of possession made her ache for more.

If she said she loved him, it wouldn't be fair. Would it?

Beneath her white tank top, his fingers rippled, seeming to count her ribs as if he had the right to. His ownership didn't stop there. Bronc's left hand pillowed her cheek as his right loosened her shorts' drawstring and slid them to bare another span of flesh.

"We shouldn't be doing this."

Deep and familiar, with a timbre that raised gooseflesh along her limbs, Bronc answered, *"This* is staying right here, Kasey. I know I've got nothing to do with your real life."

A silent protest made her arms circle his neck. Hard. She wanted this for her real life. *This.* She pressed against him, closer, filling every hollow with her fullness. Still it wasn't close enough. Before she could widen the kiss, he reassured her.

"We're not going too far. I promise."

She refused to listen.

"Bronc—" She couldn't think how far they *weren't* going when his hand traced a hypnotizing path beneath her shorts, beneath her panties, and she gasped, greeting his touch by moving forward to meet it.

"Hmm?" He didn't stop, but he listened. She felt his caress

slowing and cursed his consideration. "You okay, honey?"

"Yes." Her reply was so breathless, she thought he hadn't heard.

His low chuckle said he had. "That might be the sweetest word I ever heard."

This could not be the same thing. Hot and tender, with the sky swinging in a starry arc over his shoulders—not the same thing she'd done with Mark. And Bronc was only touching her.

The thought accompanied an urgent, panicky pressure. It pulled her toward him. She pulled just as urgently away.

"No." She heard her voice, hoarse and insistent. "Stop."

"Don't shortchange yourself, honey." His breath brushed her cheek before he buried his face against her breast. Somehow it was bared, somehow begging for his lips. "Just stay with me for a little while."

His fingers moved with her, slick and relentless and coaxing, until she catapulted against him. She clung, convulsing and cleaving to him as if he could keep her from flying free of the spinning earth. But he couldn't, nothing could as she closed her eyes and stars continued to fall in frosty fire.

He was kissing her hair when she thought to loosen the fingers she'd locked into his shoulders. He sighed a sound that was half grumble, then kissed the corners of her smile.

An echo, an aftershock, tightened her womb and she burrowed her face against his shoulder. *I'd do anything for him. Anything.* She pressed closer, both sleepy and incredibly alert.

Shifting azure lightning streaked inside her eyelids and the wakeful portion of her mind sensed the trap.

He held her captive. Using the crashing intensity of her own feelings, he held her hostage, no less than Blue Rain had been Fox's. Kasey knew she had the power to escape. But where could she find the strength to want to?

She pressed her palms against Bronc's chest, trying to forget that trembling culmination. It was the essence of what she feared—an explosion out of nowhere.

Blue Rain had warned her.

"Settle down, just a minute," Bronc coaxed her, but she refused to give in. "You're still shaking, just—"

" 'We're not going too far,' you said."

He went still and silent.

If she couldn't erase that instant of surrender, she could brand it a mistake. "I trusted you."

"And I trusted you."

"What are you talking about?" She struggled to sit, then stared down at him, infuriated by the softness in his eyes. "Seems like I'm the one with her pants around her knees!"

He sucked in a breath, pulled his legs up, and sat facing her. "Okay, Hollywood, you wanna fight? I'm your guy."

"Don't humor me."

"Makes you mean, does it? Feeling out of control?"

"I'm not out of control, I'm . . ." Kasey's voice failed under an onslaught of tears.

"It's okay." Bronc rested his forearms on her shoulders and kissed her brow. "It happens sometimes." His lopsided smile came with another gentle kiss. "I still like you."

She twisted away, fisting her hands to stop their trembling. He waited, but she stayed stiff, staring away from him.

"Have it your way." His humoring tone made her insane. "You didn't feel a thing. Not even for a minute."

Then, as if the continued view of her back had managed to spark his anger, his tone turned caustic.

"I see. This is all part of your secret bet with Savage." He struck his head with the heel of his hand. " 'Screw the cowboy.' Shucks, ma'am, sorry to disappoint, but I didn't see no photographers lurking around—"

"Shut up." Kasey stood, but her legs wobbled beneath her. "That bet had nothing—" She tried to lie. She *had* to lie. "Nothing to do with you."

Standing, Bronc faced her. Not a bit unsteady, but he'd turned his drawl on, full force. "Nothing to do with me. Now, how come I find that so all-fired tough to believe? But I guess it could be a bet about sending me back to jail. Is that it?"

Her hands went cold, and then her face.

"The feds didn't do a good enough job ruining my family," Bronc mused, "so you and Savage's multimillion-dollar corporation decided to take a stab at it."

Images of the McDermitts swam before her eyes. "No," she whispered as he caught her against him. "That's not—"

"Shit. Me and old Toro. Is that the way it's gonna be?" He held her chin, forcing her to face his profound sadness.

He kissed her. It wasn't like before, it wasn't love, but he only punished her for an instant.

Kasey felt his teeth graze her lips, but she still opened them. She couldn't stop wanting his mouth or his hands, which were everywhere. Their gasps joined into something both feral and repentant, before he set her apart and folded his arms.

She tried to draw herself up in anger. Her act was a failure, but Bronc apparently caught her intent.

"That's right." His smile twisted. "Better hide it, honey. Even in these liberated times, you wouldn't want anyone thinking you're a woman." He looked her up and down, as if scorning every inch. "Everyone knows K. D. Wildmoon is a cutthroat reporter who'll do anything for a story." He shook his head. "And I do mean anything."

TWENTY

"Boots on the ground."

Bronc squatted beside her, offering a cup of coffee. Kasey, her eyes barely open, saw only his hand.

For the first time in days, she felt a twinge in her own hand, where the dog had slashed. But these were Bronc's hands. Brown and lined, marked with scuffs and scrapes. Last night, she hadn't felt a single one.

Memory made her stomach plummet at how those hands had touched her. She wanted more. Now. But she'd thrown Bronc's magic back in his face.

"Okay," he said, when she failed to move. "I'll just leave it here."

Kasey reached a hand from the sleeping bag and into the chill air, but he'd already gone. She held a fingertip against the steaming cup until she could stand the heat no longer.

The sun had half risen. He'd let her sleep later than ever before.

Today would be their last day together. Three days earlier than planned. She'd worked it out last night after Bronc rode into the night alone. She'd lain tense and mute, pretending not to notice when he finally returned. But—oh, damn, she hadn't planned to waste a single hour of this day sleeping.

She wore her last clean shirt, but he didn't notice, only passed her a plastic spoon and a cup of rehydrated eggs with bacon-flavored soy bits. An uninspired breakfast, but what had she expected?

"What's your plan for today?" He'd already emptied his own breakfast cup. He stomped it flat, without meeting her eyes. "If you've got what you need for the story, it's a long day's ride back to Gold Canyon, but I can have you there by dark."

Kasey prodded the foam-rubber eggs. He'd beat her to the kill. These eggs wouldn't make it halfway down her throat.

"I need a few more quotes." She moved her lips, pretending they hadn't loved his last night. Pretending they weren't numb at all the morning's differences. "And there's a little more research I should do."

If only he'd rage at her, sneer at her or call her a tease. Instead, Bronc McDermitt treated her with the same cool civility he'd accord any stranger.

"Mind telling me who and where?" He flung the contents of his coffee cup onto the fire, dousing it. The wet, charred scent rose sour all around them.

"I need to talk with Becky Buck, and then return to Gold Canyon and interview Flynn if he's around."

At the pilot's name, Bronc looked up, harsh and accusing, but at least she'd caught his eyes.

"Bronc, about last night—"

"Save it, Hollywood." He kicked at the burnt wood and ashes, scattering them so no trace of fire remained. "I'm not a sensitive modern guy. I'm not likely to learn from my mistakes. Just eat and let's get out of here."

She managed to swallow the eggs without gagging. "If you'd ride with me as far as the Bucks', I'll handle it from there." She drained the scalding coffee to make sure they stayed down.

With an awkward nod, Bronc handed her China's reins.

"If that's—Fine." He abdicated all responsibility, except for the horse. "Cal won't mind trailerin' China home. His leg's a little hot. Might have strained that tendon getting up and down to water last night. Nothing to worry over if I were going to be keeping an eye on it." He swung into the saddle. "But I'll be heading on."

֍ ֍

IN A FEW HOURS, they'd come so close to the Buck ranch that Kasey could see the gravel driveway bordered by old tires, and see the longhouse art gallery.

As she and Bronc had ridden in silence, she'd managed to cut free of her melancholy. The desert spread ivory and gold around her, ancient and impartial.

If Bronc wanted her to ride into the Buck ranch alone, she could. She felt professional and determined. Tears hadn't threatened for a good thirty minutes.

"Bronc, could you tell me one last thing?"

They sat stirrup to stirrup. The horses nuzzled each others' necks, sensing a parting.

"Sure." He leaned forward in the saddle, sparing Rook's back, then squinted her way as if staring into the sun.

"When those forty-eight horses died, the ones that got lost—?"

Bronc's wry laugh interrupted her, but Kasey wouldn't stop. She wouldn't allow her throat to close with tears. She refused to ask for a second chance. If he wanted a tremulous apology, he'd picked the wrong girl. And a last kiss would break her heart.

Kasey swallowed and clarified her question. "What happened in the area where the horses had been?"

Bronc pressed his palm against her thigh. She hadn't worn chinks this morning and she felt blood thrumming, through his veins and hers. It was an odd gesture, with his eyes closed and lips set in a hard line. She would have given anything to see the thoughts playing through his mind. Then, his hand was gone.

"The ranchers were happy and the antelope came back. A few deer, too." Bronc shrugged. "Ask Tate. He's got a map with a bunch of little color-headed pins on it. I'm sure it'd look real nice on a magazine page." He backed Rook a few steps and swung the gelding's head south. "You be sure to send me a copy, now."

He tugged down the brim of his hat. That quickly, it was over. Kasey half-expected him to shout something corny, like "Adios!" but Bronc McDermitt rode away in silence.

〜〞 〞〜

CALVIN BUCK'S NEW LAND ROVER was gone. The only car in the driveway was a vintage Datsun parked next to the waving blood-orange poppies. Probably Cal was at work, though she couldn't say which day of the week it was. Kasey bit the inside of her cheek, hard. For a reporter, a lazy mind was a liability.

She clucked her tongue at China, more to keep him company than hurry him down the gravel road. For the first time in days, the necklace was active, radiating the warmth of a childhood nap.

Nothing showed when Kasey looked down at the strand of shell and glass. But when she weighed the central shell in her hand, it vibrated with energy.

Kasey released it as a wing of warmth swept over her. A bit dizzy, she focused on what was normal. Ahead sat the Bucks' small house and a valiant sprinkler trying to reclaim this spot from the desert. But right here, something supernatural and powerful swirled around her.

Letty? Kasey let her mind call out to her birth mother. As she did, she felt a calm conviction she'd never think of setting down in writing. She felt—no, she *knew* some part of Letty Wildmoon was here. Not the girl who'd claimed Alcatraz, nor the troubled single mother, but an essence of Letty Wildmoon rushed out to greet the daughter she'd burdened and blessed with a magical necklace.

As she rode closer, the door to the redwood gallery opened and Becky Buck, not Letty's spirit, crossed toward the sprinkler.

"Kasey?" Her hands perched on her hips. "I've got to get some dogs. People are forever sneaking up on me." Becky shaded her eyes and looked down the road. "Are you alone?"

"Bronc had to ride on and I decided to just stop and sit." Kasey was startled to find it was true. "I hope I haven't come at an inconvenient time."

"I'm glad for the company. I was a little prickly with you, before."

Except for an awkward moment talking about Cal's health, the interview had been friendly and calm. Still, it had been mostly business.

"I didn't expect to be adopted into the tribe." Kasey dismounted.

"Don't have to be. We're sisters-in-law, and probably something else. Cousins of some sort."

Kasey smiled, glad Becky could accept this visit on face value. She couldn't explain why she'd returned. Sometimes, in the midst of a story, she knew she'd missed a vital clue. The only way to find it was to retrace her steps and wait for the facts to fall into place.

So far, the evidence pointed to Mac McDermitt, who had the weapon, opportunity, and motive all over the place. But instinct said he hadn't killed those wild horses. She wanted Flynn to be guilty, but all she had to go on was his tough-guy stance and his uncashed check for $750, which she'd found paper-clipped to a stack of Abner's correspondence. Not nearly enough.

The squawk of a blue jay interrupted her thoughts. Wiping her wet hands against her denim skirt, Becky turned as Kasey did, to watch the bird balance his long tail as he rocked on a fence rail.

"China's limping a little," Kasey said. "Can I turn him out while we visit?"

Becky nodded, but she didn't move immediately. The sprinkler splattered her skirt as she watched Kasey strip China of his saddle. Becky led the way to a small paddock and held the gate wide as Kasey lifted the bridle off and set the horse free.

Kasey closed the gate and leaned against it, fighting drowsiness and despairing thoughts of Bronc.

"You look like hell," Becky said.

"No makeup, no flattering light." Kasey thought of the casual glamour of the picture that ran with her *Dare* column, "Wildmoon Rising."

" 'Fraid this is the real me."

"The last time you were here, you didn't have those." Becky knuckled the spaces beneath her own eyes. "White patches, like you've been crying. Probably allergies, huh?"

"Something like that."

A freshening breeze played the wood and stone wind chimes hanging above the gallery door. They made a chuckling sound, like water in a brook. Kasey stared up at them, trying to figure out how and why, until Becky beckoned her inside.

This time the loom held puffy brown and cream strands and the start of a weaving. A dozen boxes, still sealed by mailing tape, were stacked all around.

"I'm telling stories and doing a craft workshop at the rodeo."

Becky motioned Kasey to a rocker beside a potted yucca.

Becky opened boxes while they talked. First, she took out skein upon skein of thin leather lacing. She inspected each bundle and set it aside in an order Kasey couldn't discern.

"Can I ask you more about Blue Rain?"

Becky had been ranging spools of metallic thread from dark to light. "Sure." Her hands paused, then resumed their work, setting tubes of multicolored seed beads in a willow basket.

"You said she wasn't Paiute. What makes you so sure?"

"The horse." Becky glanced up at her small depiction of Blue Rain. "Horses were part of the plains, early on, but they came late to us. Brought by whites, largely."

"That ties in with the cavalryman who betrayed her." Kasey tried to put a date on the story. Early 1860s?

"You'll have to tell me about that part." Becky sorted through cellophane packages of feathers and Kasey felt a stab of embarrassment. Hadn't Blue Rain told Letty or anyone else that disagreeable detail?

"Blue Rain's related to all Indian cultures, representative of none." Becky removed her glasses, and Kasey could easily picture her at a college lectern. "Her story belongs to the necklace and to all of us."

"Sort of Everywoman's medicine godmother."

"If you like. Women give birth and nurture. Men hunt and kill. How can we expect harmony out of that—even mythological harmony?"

Kasey rocked. Disney movies represented the closest things she had to legend. And the stories of Cinderella, Sleeping Beauty, and Snow White each ended on the page after the wedding.

"Blue Rain's no different than Leda or Europa, or Eve. She's a woman betrayed."

A swan, a white bull, a serpent, Kasey mused. Maybe a desert fox wasn't so unearthly strange, after all.

"But *she's* looking for revenge."

Outside, the wind kicked up enough sand to pepper the side of the longhouse and China neighed.

"Mmmm." Becky uttered a dubious hum and wavered her hand in the air. "Maybe balance." Then she shook her head, lowering the curtain on personal belief. "You know, I've used every kind of insulation I can think of, and this place is still drafty."

Kasey followed Becky's nod. Even with the door closed and the windows shut, Blue Rain's portrait fluttered as if a breeze played upon it.

"You want a real Paiute legend." Becky's voice switched to performance level. "Try Pai'unga. Water babies."

"That sounds cute."

"Anything but. This weekend when I tell tales at the rodeo, I won't mention Pai'unga." Becky blinked at the sound of something moving near the door.

"Tell me." Kasey leaned back into the rocker, certain the sound was only the wind.

Cross-legged on the floor, Becky gestured as she spoke.

"They're fierce spirits who punish poor parenting. Say you're working at the edge of Pyramid Lake, gathering reeds to make decoys." Becky pointed to a green-and-straw-colored shape sitting on a windowsill. "And you leave your babe unattended."

Driving from the Reno airport, Kasey had passed Pyramid Lake. She'd slowed at the sight of a tribal policeman ticketing a motorist, but she would have slowed anyway, to study the strange rock formation and lake in the midst of the desert.

"So, you're singing with your sisters, picking and gathering, and when you return to your baby, she looks the same as always. Chubby cheeks, dimpled elbows. Hiking homeward, she cries. An odd little cry, but you lift her to your breast to nurse." Becky made a cradling sign, for all the world as if she held an infant.

Becky's eyes went wide and her fingers splayed in alarm. "It latches onto you"—she grimaced in agony—"with fangs, and it holds you and holds you, making you pay for your mistakes until a stronger spirit banishes it to the lake."

"Water babies are evil spirits, then." Kasey rubbed her arms against sudden chills.

"Dangerous," Becky conceded. "But what *should* be the price for neglecting your child at the lakeside, where currents shift and predators come to drink?"

Kasey shrugged. The legend's purpose was clear: Paiute parents needed to be vigilant and preserve their kind. But what about Blue Rain? If the legend's job was to warn women off unwise entanglements, from a survival and propagation of the species standpoint, it didn't make much sense.

Becky wrapped a nearly invisible length of fishing line around her hand. "You ever work for an insurance agent?"

Kasey took a minute to wonder if fatigue had clogged her brain's synapses.

"Insurance," she clarified. Becky nodded. "Never. Other than waitressing in college, I've been a journalist my whole life."

When Becky returned to her sorting, Kasey wouldn't let her escape. "Why?"

"Last time you were here, well, someone had called the night before and said you'd be asking about Calvin's health—"

"I didn't, though. You brought it up when we were talking about Letty."

"—cooperating with the mine's insurance carrier. If they found it was hereditary—his high blood pressure—or a preexisting condition, they'd remove him from the company's medical plan."

"Why would someone . . ." Kasey began, then broke off.

"Did he or she—*he*, okay—say me? Specifically me?"

Becky considered. "Not by name. I don't think."

Kasey remembered her arrival with Bronc. Hadn't Cal Buck said his "old lady" had told him to expect company?

She wanted to stop and think for a couple hours. She needed to analyze Abner's disappearance and Flynn's antagonism. Before she wrote a word, she had to know more about the players.

"What do you know about Flynn, the pilot who flies for—"

"Letty thought he murdered your father."

Kasey grabbed the chair's arms as if something had tried to fling her forward. Becky followed the pronouncement by stacking envelopes of yellow beads into a plastic chest.

"She—what?" Kasey saw Flynn's eyes as he'd come at her. As if a handful of spiders had dropped wriggling down her neck, she lifted her hair, tugged at her shirt, then flattened her palms together.

Becky closed the plastic chest with a snap.

The wind shrilled and battered the wind chime against the redwood walls, but outside the sun shone and the light on the long-house windows dazzled Kasey.

"The arson investigator said Letty was wrong," Becky pointed out.

Burned. Her birth father had burned. The chills wouldn't stop, no matter how the sun shone outside.

"They said he was drunk, that he forgot and took a cigarette into a barn at the Johnson County Fairgrounds. And dropped it. But Billy arrived early and settled in his trick horses because he loved them. He slept in the barn. He had the snack bar microwave their bran mashes. Does that sound like a man who'd be so negligent?"

A few seconds dragged past before Becky gave a very slight smile. "He and Flynn had a fight the week before and Billy made Flynn's ears bleed."

Hadn't Tate or Bronc mentioned a manslaughter charge, which didn't stick, but drove Flynn from the country?

"Billy never allowed anyone in the barn with a smoke."

The theory that Flynn had killed both her parents was worse than weak, it was ludicrous, but the possibility struck her like a fist. Uncaught, killers rarely stopped with a single murder.

"Motive," Kasey insisted. "Why would Flynn want to kill Billy Wildmoon?"

Becky stared at her, face blank. "No earthly reason." The door burst open. It slammed flat against the wall.

It had to be wind, since no one stood outside. The sound like Blue Rain's laughter could only be the chimes.

Kasey forced a white woman's laugh.

Becky slapped her hands against her thighs, then rose. "Now, how 'bout some lunch before we try to load China in that horse trailer and tow him with my Datsun?"

TWENTY-ONE

Kasey pressed her lips together. Lipstick felt odd after a week without, but she was on her way in to have an actual meeting with Tate. It was one prop she couldn't do without.

She'd applied it in Becky's Datsun. As they rumbled across the desert, she'd kept thinking she heard Flynn's helicopter. Once, Becky had heard it too, and even pulled over to look, but they'd seen nothing. That constant background sound and the little shocks from the necklace made her wonder if Becky, who'd suggested Kasey might have migraines like Letty, was right.

She refused to consider her head might hurt from fighting back tears all night. Now that they'd reached Gold Canyon, things were moving too fast. A cowboy had already backed China out of Becky's horse trailer and shaken his head in astonishment when Kasey kissed the gelding's gray muzzle in farewell. As the man led China off to a round pen where he'd get dinner and liniment on his sprain, Kasey nagged herself to get a grip on her emotions.

Although the red rental Taurus was parked behind the bunkhouse, Kasey had no sense of coming home. Slowly, she crossed the open area between the sign announcing Gold

Canyon Holding Corrals and the trailer that was Tate's office. Just as she had a week ago. But today, Bronc wasn't here.

Kasey had shut down the part of her that cared. She was closing in on the horse killer and it wasn't Bronc. That made life easier, emotionally, but in terms of her story, it made things more complicated. Bronc McDermitt had the means, motive, and opportunity to kill the wild horses. So did his father. But she couldn't count them guilty.

Flynn had the opportunity, but so did everyone else in this godforsaken state.

If she could block the memories of desert sunrise, of coyotes calling, mustangs running, storm-beaten sage releasing a wild perfume, it would be a relief to return to Los Angeles.

Tate's pack of crazy-quilt dogs squeezed out from under the trailer, barking.

"Hey, guys." Kasey made smooching noises at the Aussie with one white eye. "We've met, remember?" She slowed her stride, squatted, and held out her injured hand, palm up.

Beside themselves at the recognition, the dogs tumbled over one another, tails swinging, tongues lolling, to smear her hand with licks.

Miles and miles of miles and miles, that's all that made up Nevada. A few pretty sunsets and grappling with a handsome cowboy hadn't changed her life. There was no sense thinking it had.

A faint drone made her look skyward, but she saw nothing. Little spikes of electricity jolted her chest and she thought of Flynn.

Kasey flipped her notebook open. *Bullet trajectory*. On the drive from the Buck ranch to Gold Canyon, she'd scribbled notes. Becky hadn't seemed to mind the quiet, and making a list of questions, as she would for any story, had kept Kasey cold and centered.

"C'mon in," Tate called before she knocked.

If *she* looked like hell, Tate looked worse. Granted, they'd only met once before, but his red hair and round body looked limp. The smile flattered by freckles and sunlines seemed weary.

"I'm sorry as can be that Bronc took off and left you to your own devices." Tate, half standing, patted the hand she'd extended for him to shake.

"Don't worry. It wasn't that way. I wanted to hang around the Bucks' before I left."

"Well that's what he said. But did he get you all the interviews you needed? Help you scout picture locations?" He watched her nod. "Seems to me he was in a damned big hurry to track down that old lunatic."

"Abner still hasn't turned up?"

"You know"—Tate took a breath between words—"him?"

"Only by reputation."

"He's a menace, but it'd be a shame to shut him up in a hospital." Tate rubbed his eyes and gave a short laugh. "Yeah, nothing wrong with him 'cept half of him's paralyzed and the other half's loony. Still, I hope he hasn't got caught in one of those tunnels. The place is honeycombed with 'em."

Tate began coughing, trying to catch his breath.

"Are you okay?"

"Summer cold or something." Tate tapped his chest. "Now what kind of loose ends can I tie up for you? Bronc said you were probably leaving tomorrow."

"Probably, but I do have a few more questions and I thought, if you didn't mind, I'd take a shower and go over my notes, be sure there's nothing else I need to do on-site."

"Fine. Use the phone, fax, work late as you want. My bedroom"—he jerked his thumb toward the back of the trailer—

"is practically soundproof. Once I'm tucked in, you could have a party and I'd be none the wiser. Help yourself to the kitchen over in the bunkhouse, too. I'm gonna knock off early and put myself to bed with a tumbler of Chivas."

As Tate yawned and rubbed his hair into a red coxcomb, Kasey considered her notes. To maintain the pretense this was a feature story, she'd question Sheriff Glen Radich later. Or have her parents poke around and see if Flynn had a police record.

"Bronc mentioned something about horses dying during a university study."

Tate fixed her with melancholy eyes. *Et tu, Brute?* they asked. "That dumb-ass cowboy don't know when to shut up, does he?"

Outdoors the dogs made a racket as they burst from under the trailer, barking.

"They're gonna drive me nuts," Tate said, sighing, then added, "It's no secret. I'm just sick of it. Okay, are you talking about the ones that died from the radio-tracking collar infections, or the ones Flynn ran to death?"

Kasey pressed back against the chair. She shouldn't take advantage of a sick man. "This can be off the record," she offered.

"Yeah, please." Tate reached for a bottle of water. "There's more in the refrigerator." He took a swig. "Help yourself."

"Bronc mentioned dust pneumonia."

"He was being a gent. Tell me what he told you, and I'll fill in the blanks."

She did, seesawing her necklace as she spoke.

"So," Kasey finished, "forty-eight horses died accidentally that time. Another time, forty were found dead on Rainbow Bend."

Tate stared. Twice he started to speak. When he did, it was

with exasperation. "I hope you're not trying to say those numbers are something other than coincidence." He regarded her with less respect than he'd accorded her five minutes before.

"I have no idea how this fits together, but let me back up. After the forty-eight horses died accidentally, Bronc said the ranchers were happier and the antelope came back."

"Of course they were. Jeez." Tate looked at her askance. "Kasey, if you're trying to make this some weird range conspiracy, it's not possible. Okay, okay, I take that back. Years ago, when I came to work for the Bureau, there *was* something—let me think."

As he thought, Tate passed her a topographical map dotted with colors representing different varieties of wildlife.

"I think I've got this right. A consortium of hunters wanted to foot the bill for keeping horses, cattle, and sheep off a chunk of land. An experiment to encourage the native species to come back, they said." Tate winked. "So they could shoot 'em."

"The horses that were shot," Kasey began, "is there any chance they could've been hit from the air? Did the Bureau check the bullet trajectory?"

Tate drummed his fingers on his desktop, then rolled his left shoulder as if working out a kink. "Still off the record?"

"Yes." Kasey felt the story crystallizing. *Come on,* she urged silently. *Come on.*

"The bodies were too rotted out to tell . . ." Tate began. "News reports said they were trapped in a 'box canyon' before they were shot, but did you see any 'box canyons' when you were riding with Bronc? 'Course not.

"I think our shooter tried a couple techniques and settled on a time of year the bodies were likely to go undisturbed while they rotted."

Kasey felt the pulse pound in her throat. Of course. Most

murders were foreshadowed. The death of all these horses would be no different.

"A couple months before, we had a dozen horses gut-shot. They were looked over pretty carefully and the Bureau decided they were shot from a truck. Figured some kids out coyote hunting got carried away."

Kasey thought of the kids who'd shot the palomino foal, particularly the skinny-armed boy with the swastika tattoo. And Josh. She couldn't rule them out, just because she wanted Flynn convicted.

"Think of this," Tate was saying. "If you gut-shoot a horse, he doesn't die right off. He runs until he can't anymore, so you don't have a knot of dead horses. They're scattered all over the place. That'd occur to a pilot."

They both knew they were talking about Flynn.

"So why didn't he do it that way? And, why do it at all?"

"Some guys always want to make a buck and they don't much care how. And since mustangs have been eating the McDermitts' profit for ten years, why not kill them on their land? Everyone knew they had a reason."

"But who's signing the paychecks? Ranchers?"

"Haven't got that far with it," Tate said, but Kasey thought he had.

Kasey recalled a public television program in which a celebrity helped relocate a bunch of bighorn sheep. Off private lands, onto public. For their own safety. But these facts weren't coming together like puzzle pieces. They were more like pickup sticks, barely overlapping. She pursued the idea anyway.

"If you had a ranch with lots of deer or antelope or bighorn sheep, you could lead pack trips and charge people to hunt on your land."

"You could." Tate had just brought his fingertips together,

matching them, when the phone rang.

"Yeah? Mm-hm. Just four." Tate held up one finger in Kasey's direction, then swiveled his desk chair to face a shelf filled with multicarboned forms.

The life of a bureaucrat, Kasey thought, then flipped through her notes. First, she'd call Cookie and ask her to fax anything she could find about radical hunter consortiums of the kind Tate had described. It was a long shot. Next, she wanted more background on Flynn. She'd get what she could from Tate, since the two obviously weren't buddies, but she wanted Cookie to check on something she'd just remembered.

When she'd talked with Flynn the night she arrived, he'd admitted being a mercenary in Bosnia. Cookie, with her photo shoots for *Soldier of Fortune* and *Warrior* magazines, could probably find out. If Flynn stalked men for money, why should he balk at killing horses?

What she wouldn't give for an eyewitness.

Tate's voice returned to an audible level. "Yeah, a damned shame. I'll get someone—Okay, go ahead." Tate blew out a gust of breath. "Yeah, I will. You, too."

Tate replaced the phone in its cradle with deliberation. He picked up a pen and held it so hard his fingernails turned white. Kasey scooted her chair away from Tate's desk.

"Tate, I'll be going," she said. Though he met her eyes, he didn't seem alert. "I wanted to ask you one more thing about Flynn."

Like a man throwing a knife, Tate hurled the ballpoint pen across the room. It ricocheted off a bulletin board.

"I wonder," Tate asked, "if it could wait for morning?"

"You bet." She headed for the door. "You bet it could."

Before the trailer door closed behind her, Kasey heard a drawer open. When she glanced back, Tate was tipping a bottle of pills into his open hand.

⚡ ⚡

BY THE TIME KASEY CRAWLED into bed, it didn't matter that her favorite silk shirt had been hanging in the bunkhouse shower for a week, or that the picture tacked over her bunk was one of Shannon Delaney. She had evidence Flynn was a very violent man.

"One thing Mark doesn't mind spending money on is computer stuff," Cookie had said when Kasey managed to reach her in the *Sun-Times* newsroom. "I can access *Warrior's* data base from here—"Kasey had heard computer keys tapping all the way in Los Angeles—"and do this fancy cross-reference thing. I *said,* Moronic Machine, cross-*reference.* Okay, it's thinking."

Then she'd heard Cookie's desk chair squeak as she leaned back. "So, what's up with Bronc 'Be-Still-My-Heart' McDermitt?"

Kasey had stared into the glass of powdered orange drink she'd stirred up for dinner and wondered the same thing herself.

"Shall I take that long silence for evidence of a Wildmoon rebuff?"

"Not exactly."

"Oh, here it comes. Straight out of their archives. Flynn's one of their guys, all right." Cookie's voice was muffled, as if she held the receiver against her shoulder while scrolling down the computer screen. "Oh, yeah."

Kasey felt excitement sing through her. "How dependable is that data base?"

"People are always threatening to firebomb the office."

"Works for me," Kasey said. "Fax everything you can. Now. And I'll probably see you at home tomorrow night."

"That was a major sigh, K. D. How about I don't set the

table until I see your face?"

Cookie's blizzard of faxes was coming in when Kasey called the Los Angeles Police Department and caught her dad, still at his desk at nine P.M. Grumbling over the number of favors he'd have to call in to get the real dirt on Flynn, he took down BOW's number and agreed, but only on the condition Kasey come for dinner Sunday night.

"What's today?" Kasey had asked.

"Find out and be there," her father had barked.

When she'd returned from taking a shower and washing her hair in the bunkhouse, there was not only a sheaf of fresh faxes, a telephone message was coming in.

By the tone of her father's voice, and the fact that he'd tracked down the Golden Canyon telephone number so quickly, Kasey decided she'd be wiser not to pick up.

"Two manslaughter charges. Two. And the name of the second victim—Wildmoon—has not escaped my attention. I want you to get your butt home now, young lady. No excuses!"

Eight hundred miles away, the telephone receiver slammed down so hard, she heard it rebound from its cradle before being jumbled back in. Kasey pushed the erase button before Tate staggered out to inquire about all the commotion.

Back in the bunkhouse, Kasey packed everything she owned except the adobe-colored silk shirt and jeans. She'd go home in the same clothes she'd worn on arrival.

Full circle, she thought, and it was a shame things had ended so badly with Bronc. Knowing what she did, there was no danger of compromising her story or her promise to Blue Rain. Until the story ran, she'd keep the truth about Flynn to herself. If she didn't, Bronc would pull some stupid macho stunt.

She felt a dubious smile at her own poor timing. Now that she'd driven him away and gotten down to the business of investigating this story, now it would be fine to sleep with him, to feel that incredible vaulting delight streak through her body again. If he'd forgive her.

Kasey slipped her necklace between layers of folded clothes before zipping her suitcase. It was like packing away a teddy bear, but now she had real facts and a blistering magazine story that should serve Blue Rain as well as any other vengeance.

Besides, the necklace had been spiking her with jolts like electricity all afternoon. Showering, she'd noticed the skin across her chest was flecked with small red burns. Enough was enough.

When she took things out to the Taurus, she saw the five cowboys who normally slept inside were camped near a stand of meadow oaks. The men returned her wave, refused her offer to share sleeping accommodations, and went back to staring at their campfire.

Back inside, she paced for ten minutes, then returned to the car, unzipped her suitcase, and retrieved the necklace.

Her faith in Blue Rain and the necklace reached beyond superstition. She wouldn't wear it, but it had undeniable powers and she didn't want to sleep without it at hand.

The faxes made lurid bedtime reading. There was no mention of a bar fight. The first manslaughter charge resulted from a bout of sadomasochistic sex. The second detailed the county fair barn fire and subsequent death of Billy Wildmoon, but nothing about Letty.

Drowsy, Kasey breathed the pine cleaner, wood smoke, and bacon scents of the bunkhouse, and wondered if she could do the delicate writing required to skirt libel. Her last waking thought was that government standards for pilots really weren't what they should be.

§§ ⌇⌇

A MAN GOING ON THIRTY shouldn't be hopping around in the predawn darkness, trying to take off his other boot. And a woman Kasey's age shouldn't be so exhausted she slept through it.

Bronc hadn't taken off much, just his hat and boot, but he wasn't about to crawl into bed with Kasey like this. If he was gonna get knocked on his ass, he'd by God deserve it.

When he finally tripped over the iron bootjack and shucked off the second boot, he still had to stir up the nerve it had taken him all night long to gather. When he'd coasted the truck into Gold Canyon and woke neither hands nor dogs, he figured luck was running with him.

Now, bending close to the lower bunk, he breathed the soap and girl smell of Kasey and wondered if he could carry on.

She'd kicked off her covers and pulled her knees up in her nightshirt, tucked nearly to her chest. She faced the wall, leaving plenty of room on the narrow bunk for him. One arm was outflung behind, as if she were running. He caught up the hand, kissed it, and folded it back against her ribs. Then, lowering his weight inch by inch, he nestled behind her.

He heard her breath catch, then resume as he cuddled close to the bump of her bottom. Still holding her hand, he lay his arm atop hers, to hold her steady if she panicked. He worked his lips past the heavy black hair, into the warmth of her neck and higher, up to her ear.

For a minute, her even breaths soothed him. He could fall asleep beside her, if not for the stampede of hands who'd be in after coffee before another hour was gone.

Her hand squeezed convulsively on his. As she sighed and tumbled toward a lower level of slumber, he realized he'd fallen in love with a woman he'd never slept with and it scared him half to death.

Now or never, he told himself. Better come out of the chute, spurring.

"Last chance, Hollywood," he whispered. "Today's your last chance to see me make a total fool of myself. In public."

She sighed and scooted back against him with a ladylike little grunt. "Rather," she said thickly, "see it in private."

"I tried that and you didn't seem to get too big a kick out of it." Bronc felt her tense and come completely awake.

"I know." She freed the hand he held, raised it behind her at an impossible angle, and stroked his cheek. "Forgive me."

He closed his eyes and buried his lips in her hand.

"No forgiving to be done," he said, but Kasey was turning, twisting inside her nightshirt, facing him, and locking both arms around his neck.

He kissed her, starting slow until she made an impatient sound and widened the O of her lips. It was the warmest, dearest kiss he'd ever had. He flat did not know what to make of it, until her bare leg reached over his. That lined them up chest to chest, torso to torso. He knew exactly what to make of that.

"Don't tug on weak rope, darlin'." He reached down and circled her ankle with his hand. "I've used more self-control than any six men you know and it's about used up."

"Mmmm." Kasey uttered a long, purring sigh.

He rolled her onto her back. The slopes and swells of her body, a perfect match against his, made him groan.

"I was wondering . . ." Her whisper came through a smile. He could hear it. ". . . where I'd have to go to witness this public humiliation."

Kasey's leg crawled up him again, only this time it curled around his waist, oh, Lord.

"There's this itty-bitty rodeo today in Kildeer County." He managed to snag her ankle again and hold her still.

"There's some old guy, hasn't ridden in a couple years, who thinks he's going to go out, show off for his girlfriend, and teach the young kids a thing or two about putting polish on saddle broncs."

He still held her ankle. Warm and smooth, it slid through his hand as Kasey pulled away, then pushed forward.

"Showing off for his girlfriend?"

He smiled into the dark, hearing her pleasure.

"That's what I've been told," he said. "She's a city girl, and he wants to send her off with a few memories of the real West."

He heard her swallow. Real and true regret welled up from her and though he couldn't make out her expression in the darkness, he thought there might just be a snowflake's chance in hell that Kasey Wildmoon would stick around and love him back.

TWENTY-TWO

Bronc's arm lay across the back of the truck's bench-style seat. Every time the corrugated dirt road smoothed out for a few yards, his hand rested on her hair, or under it, sketching out letters on her nape, sending secret messages. Most of them were indecent.

His long reach and inventive touch convinced her that if he hadn't continued distracting her with stories of the Kildeer County Fair and Rodeo, she'd probably be sitting in Bronc's lap by now.

A steady stream of pickup trucks—some with horse trailers and most with faulty exhaust systems—shared the road with them on the way to the biggest event held in Nevada's remote "cow counties." According to Bronc, no one from outside Kildeer County would have heard of the celebration if it hadn't been for Miss Marvareen Addison's cherry pie.

A maiden lady and home economics teacher who swore she'd drop dead correcting the baking errors of seventh-graders, Miss Addison had directed the Kildeer County 4-H Club, and helped them bake cherry pies for the fair, for as long as anyone could remember. No living soul had ever seen her without her gingham apron.

"There are rumors," Bronc said, jerking the steering wheel to avoid a rut that might have swallowed the truck to the axle, "that she wears one to bed."

His hand made an innocent curve beneath Kasey's hair and she felt chills that became tremors of anticipation.

"You're incorrigible."

"Yes, ma'am." He captured her hand and laid it on his denim-covered thigh, banishing any thought she'd be driving to the Reno Airport tonight. "That's what they said at the Holahalla Home for Wayward Boys."

"There's no such place." When she turned to face him, Kasey considered his pressed shirt and knew she'd see it thrown aside tonight. She thought of Bronc's muscular arms joining work-hard shoulders. By tomorrow morning, her hands would have memorized skin that, now, she'd never even seen.

"Yes, ma'am, there is such a place."

"Well, your parents wouldn't have sent you there."

"Caught me again." He looked into the rearview mirror, checking to see that Calvin and Becky and the twins still followed. "But it's not for lack of trying. Not by *them*, but by Glen Radich. He'll probably be tailin' me all day today. Man's got a memory like a mule."

"The sheriff?" Kasey resisted the good sense trying to invade her sensual reverie. If she met Radich at the rodeo, she'd pump him for facts on Flynn. "Were you such a bad boy?"

"I was that, but he had dozens to choose from. It was his daughter he worried about. I only went to two Teen Club dances with her, but he caught us necking on his front porch after one of 'em. I was a long way away, at college, when she got in trouble."

Kasey didn't try to stifle her moan. "Maybe you were a better catch and he's never forgiven you for it."

"I suppose that could be it." Bronc rubbed the back of his neck and chuckled. "Jacy's not a bad girl."

"Shall we talk about your old girlfriends all day? I know I'd find that real amusing."

"Not a girl anymore, I guess," he went on as if she hadn't spoken. "She just made one mistake."

"And now she's happily married."

"Divorced." Bronc grimaced. "Twice. And not so happily— uh, available."

"What are the odds I'll meet her out here, too?"

"Well, mainly she likes PRCA events—professional rodeo cowboys, you know—but, I'd say it's a fair bet she'll be here."

"Is she one of the 'buckle bunnies' Shannon was talking about?" At that, Kasey had an even worse thought. Shannon might be here, too.

"Maybe." Bronc gave her a sideways grin. "Or maybe she just likes Miss Addison's pie."

〰 ✿

"C'MON, KASEY!" Callie McDermitt was eager to show her big brother's "girlfriend" her glow-in-the-dark nail polish, and that meant dragging Kasey into the Tunnel of Gore on the midway.

Kasey hesitated. She wouldn't allow herself to have a crisis of nerves while standing in the middle of this field turned parking lot.

No one's forcing you to wear the necklace, she told herself. It lay across her hand; its roughly formed beads and olive-green shells shone with obligation, responsibility, and a heaping measure of guilt. If she left it in the car, she'd feel carefree and girlish, as she had since Bronc awakened her in the bunkhouse.

"Yeah, c'mon, Kasey." Bronc stood behind her, hands skimming up and down her arms. "Once we go through the Tunnel of Gore, I can show you Remedy."

Kasey slipped the necklace into her saddle pack, but she still stood with her hand on the door, unwilling to lock it.

"Sounds like you two got a full day lined up. Buck pushed the alarm button on his keys to secure the Land Rover. "I'm going over to see that Becky's set up okay. Talk to a few cousins. See you at the chutes." Buck shook his head. "Unless you want me to drive back into Gully for some Ben-Gay."

"Only help I need from you is drivin' these two home, later." Bronc gestured at the twins.

"They'll be okay alone?" Buck asked.

"Two terrified teenage kids with all-day passes to the carnival—" Josh snatched his sister's ticket and flapped it along with his.

"God, Josh, grow up." Callie jerked the ticket back from him. "Not 'God'," Bronc corrected softly.

Callie tossed her head, but not enough to disturb her intricately gelled hair. *"Gee willikers,* Josh, try to act more ma-toor."

"Yeah, like I'm the one who can't wait to—"

Kasey slammed and locked the passenger's side door, striking a compromise with Blue Rain. She stowed the necklace safely inside her purse and slung it over her shoulder.

⌘ ⌘

THOUGH BRONC PROMISED THE ARENA was ringed with local booths, the midway—Bill Barker's Carnival of Fun—was a traveling show. After the Mad Mouse, the Death Plunge, or the Egg Beater, you could settle your stomach with funnel cakes, lemonade, or corn dogs.

Kasey loved it. Leaving the tunnel, where she'd burrowed into Bronc's arms and dutifully admired Callie's nail polish,

Kasey felt as young as the twins.

Bronc kept her arm looped through his as he issued strict instructions to his siblings.

"You stay together at all times. I don't care if your friends want to go off into the exhibition hall and look at junk jewelry." Bronc aimed this warning at Callie, who fanned herself as if terribly warm—"or if you want to look for video games." Bronc ignored Josh's low-lidded boredom. "Stick together. Don't leave the fairgrounds or even go back to the parking lot."

"Is he always such a tough guy?" Kasey muttered.

"Only when he's showing off," the two said in unison.

Kasey laughed. She and Bronc had started back toward the arena when Josh came after them. His indifference had cracked and his voice shook. "What if there's, like, an emergency?"

Bronc melted. Kasey could think of no other way to describe the droop in his expression before he hugged Josh. Just as quickly, he shoved the boy away with rough affection.

"Becky's at the storytelling booth." Bronc pointed. "Cal will be at the beer garden with his drinkin' uncles. We'll be by the chutes." Bronc pretended to puff up his chest. "Gonna teach this little lady all she needs to know about rodeo." His humor faded at Josh's still-nervous laugh. "And don't forget Sheriff Radich." Bronc indicated the aqua and white squad car parked between the midway ticket booths. "You can always go to him."

"Right," Josh said, as Callie appeared to haul him away by the arm.

"There's Jessica, Josh, come *on*."

"Yeah, Josh," Kasey tossed after him. The boy waved and gave a long-suffering smile. As they disappeared into a canvas tent, Kasey squeezed Bronc's arm. "They'll be fine."

"I'm not worried." Bronc led her past the Bobby Sox Baseball booth, where frybread sputtered in grease and the scent of honey permeated the air. "Not about anything except that Remedy horse I drew."

As Bronc explained the desirable attributes of bucking horses, Kasey reveled in the signs of small-town life she'd believed existed only in movies.

Here was the Boy Scouts' candy stand, displaying ropes of red and black licorice. Next door, Little Leaguers hawked hot dogs, curly fries, and tried to outshout the 4-H'ers selling Miss Addison's famous cherry pie.

They'd passed the Elks' beer garden, set amid potted shrubs and portable white trellises, and a dunk tank of local celebrities, when something made Kasey look back toward the carnival.

All the rides were lighted, though it wasn't quite noon. Picked out in pink and purple neon, the Ferris wheel's spans glowed against the summer sky. But it wasn't that incongruity that bothered her.

If she'd been wearing the necklace, the feeling would have made sense. She would have felt the annoying electrical prick of warning, and Flynn, or some other danger, would have been there. But she saw nothing.

"Kasey?"

She hiked the purse up higher on her shoulder and stood tiptoe to kiss Bronc's cheek.

"Hey, cowboy, when it gets dark, will you kiss me at the top of the Ferris wheel?"

"Do we have to wait until dark?"

A test of the arena's public address system squawked over her reply, but Bronc clasped her hand and drew her toward the arena, where cowgirls in sequined shirts carried huge satin flags and jostled their horses into position for the grand entry.

It seemed every man they passed shouted Bronc's name or punched him in the arm and took openly approving glances at her. One cowboy, tall as a pro basketball player, told Bronc there was room for old men like him on the "pickup squad." Another, wearing baggy cutoff jeans, suspenders, industrial-strength running shoes, and clown makeup, asked Bronc when he'd be man enough to try bulls.

Bronc's rejoinders were clearly toned down because of her.

Walking next to Bronc, in his lightweight chaps, blunt spurs, and contestant number, she felt part of it. It was fun, until Bronc's number allowed them into a restricted area where, he said, there was a better view.

Neighs and grunts. bellows, blood, and bodies slammed against splintering wood were not her idea of a good time. This was worse than being on the fifty-yard line at a football game. Much worse, when she closed her hand around Bronc's forearm and thought how incredibly fragile even a strong man's bones could be.

"Relax, Hollywood," he said. "All those bucking saddles and the flank straps, they're lined with sheepskin. They don't hurt a bit."

"What?" Kasey drew a breath thick with sawdust, popcorn, and manure. "What are you talking about?"

"Aren't you worried about the animals getting hurt?"

"You idiot!" She punched his arm before she thought how childish she appeared to the three contestants passing next to them. "I'm worried about you!"

"No score, McDermitt," crowed the first cowboy.

"Give that cowboy a hand, folks," intoned his partner. "Your applause is the only reward he's going to get."

The other sang, "Back in the Saddle Again," as Bronc laughed and pulled her tight against him.

"Honey, I've never been hurt bad and I've got nothing riding on this. It's just for fun."

Snugged under his arm with the sun on their shoulders, Kasey might have believed him if he hadn't squinted toward another contestant, hailed him, and asked what he knew about Remedy.

While he talked, Kasey felt it again: a feeling her words and actions were under dark scrutiny. She thought about donning her necklace, but by the time Bronc kissed her good-bye to check in at the chutes, she'd talked herself out of it.

Kasey glanced around to see a cotton candy–haired cowgirl with concho earrings the size of hubcaps give Bronc's backside a pat of encouragement. Jacy, no doubt.

Before Kasey turned away, she saw Flynn. For the first time, Flynn wasn't wearing his khaki pilot's uniform. He wore—well, she might have called it a costume, if his feral gray eyes hadn't looked deadly.

From out of the noisy beer garden, Flynn moved toward her. His bare shoulders wore a gray fur cape decorated with black feathers. They fluttered and twisted, though the day was hot and still. His cheeks and brow were smudged by charcoal. His eyes were ringed with black and white paint.

Kasey had read of paralytic drugs that held one immobile, but still screaming inside. Could Flynn have hypnotized her into a similar state?

He approached with such grace, he appeared to skim above the ground. He stopped so near, Kasey looked for Bronc, and there he was, climbing the rails to the top of the chute.

The crowd sounds surrounding Kasey grew slow, lagging so that their meanings blurred.

Even though others couldn't see the last shaman, who'd ceased his imitation of Flynn, Kasey heard him speak. He promised to meet her at a place called Joker B. He promised to tell her other secrets, too, until a sound intruded. The sound of water dripping.

"Kasey! There you are."

Abruptly as a hand-clap, the last shaman vanished. Calvin Buck stood beside her, indicating the pipe carrying water to the cattle pens had sprung a leak. Water sprayed over the front of her jeans.

"Becky sent me over. Good thing, too. You were watching so hard, you never even noticed. Step out of that mud, Bronc's about to—There he goes!"

Kasey grabbed the fence. The daydream had been so weird. And so real. But Bronc would only ride for eight seconds. She didn't have time to watch anything else.

Remedy turned out to be a "sunfisher." That's what Cal called the big bay's exposed-underbelly explosion from the chute.

"Raked him out," Cal assured her, indicating Bronc's spurs. "Keepin' after it, too."

The bay lowered his head and kicked. As the horse spun end for end, Bronc looked almost lazy. One hand held the halter rope while the other swung for balance. His body swayed in time, as if he and the horse had practiced these moves.

She remembered her conviction when Bronc delivered the calf, that *this* was what he was meant for. She'd found another thing he was meant to do. Neither would work well in L.A.

"Perfect. There's the buzzer." Cal misinterpreted her sigh and pointed out pickup men. "He's on the ground." Cal gave an admiring snort as Bronc walked smiling across the arena, chaps flapping, to pick up his hat. "Man, he's good."

Cal slapped Kasey on the back with such enthusiasm, she staggered a step.

He said something about joining the excitement around the chutes and then she stood alone again. Her elation sagged under the memory of the bizarre fantasy.

Except that it wasn't a fantasy. As if Blue Rain's bone flute shrilled inside her skull, she knew it was real, and dangerous. She felt him nearby, watching and waiting. Keeping her purse close, she rummaged for the necklace and touched it. Before she could slip it over her head, the shrilling intensified. A wavering Blue Rain appeared, arms outstretched in warning, and Kasey whirled at the sound of running feet.

Callie ducked through a security fence. "There's a guy," she panted, "some guys, pushing Josh around!"

"Where?"

"In the—" Callie's arm thrust toward the carnival, but her words were slow in coming. "By the M-M—"

"The Mad Mouse?"

Callie nodded and wiped at her mouth, then her face crumbled. "They were messing with me and Josh tried to—"

Kasey started running, then noticed Callie at her heels. "Where's the sheriff?"

"I don't know, you're the first one—"

She shoved Callie toward the chutes. "Go get Bronc!"

〜 〜

SWASTIKA BOY didn't have much of a gang, but Kasey arrived in time to see one kid thump Josh on the head and call him a "narc." Another pushed Josh down, so Swastika Boy could spit on him.

Kasey crowded close as the spittle cleared his lips. They stood on opposite sides of Josh's prone body and she shot the heel of her hand hard into the kid's chest.

"Get up, Josh." Without looking down, she stepped over him, following the tattooed kid as he retreated a single step.

"She a cop? Is she?" One of the other boys shouted at Josh, but Kasey watched the one ahead of her.

"Yeah, she is!" Josh sounded as if he were up. "Better get out of here while you can."

She couldn't tell what Swastika Boy intended, but when he lunged, she caught his wrist, stuck out her foot, and used his momentum to trip him down.

It worked. Kasey stared at the lanky figure in the dust. *It actually worked.* The shock of hitting him still reverberated down her forearm to her elbow. He moved like a beached fish and Kasey braced herself.

"Stay down." Bronc's voice didn't stop Swastika Boy from rolling to one side. "Don't try it, kid."

And then a uniformed man—one who looked exactly like Richard Nixon—grabbed Bronc and shouted, "McDermitt, you lookin' to go back to jail?"

She caught a glimpse of Calvin Buck, heard Josh and Callie hollering in their brother's defense, but she kept her eyes on the hardcase kid.

"Damn it, Radich." Bronc sounded weary.

She didn't keep the kid from springing upright, but she guarded him as she would in basketball, feeling like she'd fallen into a farce.

"Sheriff, I'm in over my head here," she shouted. "I'm not set up to make a citizen's arrest."

As the kid tried to sprint around her, she put a shoulder into his throat.

"Hmmmm." Cal Buck grabbed the boy's arm and nodded at Kasey. "You play dirty," he said, and it sounded like a compliment.

᪥ ᪥

IT WAS DUSK by the time she and Bronc had filled out incident reports and answered Sheriff Radich's questions about the assault on Josh. Darkness had fallen when Kasey completed a written report and partial license plate from the shooting of the mustang colt.

"That's federal," the sheriff grumbled, but he discovered the truck plate was registered to this kid, Lee Goff, who had a juvenile record involving vandalism and violence.

"Hey, I'm not eighteen," Goff shrugged. "Get somebody on 'contributing.' You can't do nothing to me."

"I can put these cuffs on you if you try and light that cigarette," Radich said.

Even though the sheriff was misguided regarding Bronc, there was, in the old lawman's wry threat, something that reminded Kasey of her father.

"Federal prison," Kasey mused. "Where would they send him?"

Radich faced her with a sniff and a blank expression. "Depends on when he's eighteen." Playing along, Radich flipped Goff's wallet open again. "But I'd say, San Quentin."

Kasey clucked her tongue in sympathy and watched the boy.

"Look." Goff shifted in the patrol car's backseat. "I was paid by the same guy for both jobs. Find him. You can do that, right?" Goff pointed at the sheriff. "He's the one who calls in this scary-ass voice and tells me what to do. I do it and he leaves money in my mailbox. That's all I need to know."

" 'Fraid you got that wrong, too, son."

§§ ⌘

BRONC FELT FINE. Every joint and sinew ached, but it was the first time Kasey'd let him take charge. As they stood together, Bronc held her tight to the front of him, arms crossed over the coat they'd pulled from his truck. His coat. She snuggled against the shearling lining, which stood up against her cheeks like blinders. She shivered as they stood in the parking lot, saying good-bye to the Bucks and the twins.

He wanted to take her back to Gully or his folks' place, but Kasey refused to leave without her Ferris wheel ride.

Before the twins disappeared, he needed to give them credit for acting right.

"Josh, Callie, you guys did real good."

Their faces looked green under the carnival lights and they rolled their eyes heavenward though they enjoyed his praise.

"I'm leavin' it up to you how much you want to tell Mom and Dad," he added.

"I'm gonna tell 'em Kasey kicked some butt—"

"Hey!" Bronc snapped. Sometimes he just barely stopped short of giving Josh a shake. "Don't be talking to Mom like that."

"Bro-onc," Callie drew his name out in exasperation. "Mom will love it. Kasey is the first woman you've dated"—she touched her chest—"in my lifetime—who's got any class. I mean, not only did she kick the guy's butt, she did it in a Fiorucci silk shirt."

Laughing between chattering teeth, Kasey kissed the kids and the Bucks good-bye.

Bronc was astounded. She'd kissed them. Where had he misplaced cool, in-control K. D. Wildmoon? As the Land Rover's taillights faded into the desert night, Bronc gave her an extra squeeze. Without letting their bodies lose contact, he turned her to face him.

"Got one of those for me?"

"Those were good-bye kisses," she said, then lavished him— mouth, cheeks, chin, even his ears—with kisses.

Inside his jacket she felt fragile, with thin shoulder blades delicate as shells. Mouth sealed to hers, Bronc let his spirit pray. *Lord, don't let her leave me behind.*

As they walked toward the carnival, Kasey leaned against

him.

"I don't know what's wrong with me. I'm so worn out." Then she perked up. "Hey, do you think maybe I'm a caffeine addict? Maybe if I had a cup of coffee—"

"Maybe you're so used to being in charge, when someone else takes over, you go all mushy."

"Mushy?" Her tone reprimanded him, but she didn't pull away until one of Becky's nieces spotted Kasey and hustled across the midway to introduce herself.

"I want to be a journalist, too," said the young woman. "I'm going back to school as soon as Angela's older." She pulled back a white blanket to show a baby with shoe polish–black hair and a rosebud mouth.

"Oh, she's beautiful." Kasey gazed at the sleeping baby. "You can hold her."

Bronc saw it coming, even before she nuzzled little Angela's head, but he sure hadn't planned to set off Kasey's tears himself.

Once the cousin and baby left, he was holding her hand, swinging it, when he remembered his prize money.

"Hey, Hollywood." Bronc dug into his pocket and flashed a hundred-dollar bill. "Take a look at this."

Right away, she knew what it was.

"Your purse from the bronc riding." Her last word wavered. "I'm sorry I forgot to tell you. Your ride was wonderful." Her arms clamped around his middle, squeezing out his breath. "You're wonderful. I—"

The next two words were muffled because she plowed her face against him, but Bronc heard them.

I love you.

She'd said it. He'd heard it.

Stunned, Bronc held her and stared toward a square of gold lights flashing on and off and on, outlining a corn dog stand.

Kasey stepped back, hands against her cheeks.

"In charge?" With her windblown hair and blurred eye makeup, Kasey Wildmoon looked like a distraught teenager. "I'm not even in charge of what's coming out of my own mouth!"

He wouldn't forget what she'd said and he wouldn't make her sorry.

"Relax, honey. I'm going to take you up to the top of that Ferris wheel, and if you change your mind—"

"—you're going to throw me off." The pep had returned to her smile.

"No." He pulled her close and rubbed his chin against the silkiness of her hair. "Kasey, you are funny, but no, I won't throw you off. If you change your mind, we'll pretend tonight never happened."

TWENTY-THREE

"Soon as we climb on, start pulling people off," Bronc whispered.

He fingered a hundred-dollar bill crisp enough to give paper cuts and snatched a glance over his shoulder to be certain Kasey hadn't heard. He figured the bill was his license to give orders to the Ferris wheel operator, a feral-looking redhead with tobacco in his cheek.

Bronc peered over his shoulder again. Appalled at her instant of weakness, she'd contended it was her turn to pay. He hadn't argued. He'd never have this woman eating out of his hand.

Now she looked across the garish carnival and met his eyes for one unreadable second before turning back to the ticket window. It was just as well she had no clue what he was up to.

"After everybody's off, run us up to the top." He pressed the bill into the Ferris wheel operator's palm. Easy come, easy go. "And stop it there until I holler to bring us down."

The bill disappeared. The redhead swapped his chewing tobacco to his other cheek. "Ain't planning nothing illegal?"

Bronc thought he sounded a little hopeful, so he joked, "What state is this?"

The redhead was still snickering as Kasey approached, but he tore the tickets in two and motioned them on with a send-off that sounded something like "new upholstery."

"What did he say?" Kasey closed them inside the white metal lattice of a cage that had seen better days.

"I'll be darned," Bronc said, stroking the bench seat. "Blue velvet." It looked brand new and he couldn't help thinking even the most fastidious gal wouldn't mind necking in such luxury.

Faces into the wind, they lurched skyward, spun around and around, then stopped as a couple speaking Spanish disembarked below. Once more, they surged away from the earth, and stopped a quarter turn up.

"I thought they were supposed to have drag races tonight." Bronc pointed toward the lighted but empty arena.

"Maybe they're over," Kasey said. "When we were in the police car, didn't you hear whining engines?"

He'd heard only her, quick and efficient with Radich. She'd even commenced the good cop–bad cop routine that scared the tattooed delinquent into a confession.

Maybe she'd like to be a Bleek County cop or write her column datelined: Gully, Nevada.

As they swung another notch skyward, Bronc squinted at the dust and exhaust hanging in the empty arena. If Kasey did want to stay, what would he do about the scholarship? He couldn't see her living on soup and soda crackers in married students' housing while he finished his D.V.M.

"Hey, we're going to be all alone up here." Kasey leaned forward and the car rocked wildly. "There's only one more family and us, and look," Kasey pointed. "He won't let anyone else on."

Three giggling girls tried to coax the Ferris wheel operator to let them ride. Arms folded, he refused.

"They're younger than Callie." Bronc barely gave them a glance. "Too young to be out this late anyway."

He leaned back against the cold metal lattice, trying not to smile. He snaked his arm under the jacket, around her waist, and pulled Kasey close.

"Thanks for loaning me your coat." She said it briskly, holding herself a little apart as the car vaulted for the top. "I don't know why I couldn't find mine."

She hadn't looked for her coat, hadn't been willing to admit she was cold, come to that. He'd had to guide her arm into the sleeve before she realized that she'd taken a chill.

Now, Kasey closed her eyes and faced into the wind, smiling.

"I haven't done this in years. Thank you."

"We have a date, remember?" He pointed toward the summit.

Before they reached the top, Kasey rubbed her forehead. Not as if she were in pain, but with uneasiness, as if trying to remember something. Or forget.

"Did you see Flynn today?" she asked as if checking a silly lapse in memory.

"No, did you?" He thought of Flynn's hands on her neck and wondered if Tate had the horsepower to get Flynn fired. Flynn had screwed up more than once, but he had a government contract and the feds ground awful slow.

"I thought I did." Kasey shrugged. "But then it turned out to be someone else. It was the same time you were riding." She batted her lashes like a flirt. "And I only had eyes for you."

He would have kissed her, except the last family was disembarking with a crying toddler, and the child wiggled the entire Ferris wheel with her tantrum. Bronc watched the weary parents croon for the little devil to shut up, then remembered Kasey's expression as she'd nuzzled that baby named Angela.

As a career woman, Kasey might not want kids. He let the thought course through his mind a second. He probably wouldn't care much. As long as she didn't mind practicing.

"No sign of him?" Kasey said, still chewing over the idea of Flynn being all the way out here.

"Buck said he bumped into him yesterday," Bronc admitted. "And he left a message for me. Nothing bad," he added, as she stiffened. "Since we weren't on the friendliest of terms—that's how he put it to Buck, like I hadn't thrown him out of Shannon's kitchen—but since he knew I kept an eye out for Abner, he wanted Buck to tell me he'd flown Abner into town to his doctor. A spur-of-the-moment thing."

That sounded like pure Abner, but Bronc still puzzled over the tire tracks. They'd gone in, but hadn't gone out. Even if Flynn had flown—hell, there was probably nothing to it.

"He's walking away!" Kasey leaned forward so suddenly, Bronc's stomach dropped as it did on the first jump out of the chute. "Hey," she shouted, "get back here!"

The red-haired carny ambled toward the merry-go-round, where a few men slouched and smoked. He answered Kasey's shout with a two-fingered salute, and kept walking.

"Coffee break, I guess." Bronc couldn't help laughing when she twisted in the seat, her eyes narrowed with suspicion. "I imagine they're a pretty independent bunch."

She leaned back against the far end of the cage and drummed her fingers on the blue velvet seat.

"So, will we be up here all night?"

"I wouldn't rightly know, ma'am," he laid the down-home accent on good and thick.

"You know I hate that!"

As she leaned forward, ready for a nose-to-nose battle, he

caught an arm around her shoulders and kissed her. She sighed against his lips, then parted hers in warm response.

"How 'bout that? Tell me you hate that."

Her hand closed on his shirtfront, then damned if she didn't lean backward. He managed to keep from slamming his head into the cage as she pulled him practically on top.

The girl was a contortionist. With their lips locked together, she shrugged and wriggled free of his coat. By the glare of pink neon, he saw it bunched on the floor of the cage.

He skimmed a hand over her blouse, testing just a little, and Kasey pressed her breast into his palm. He sucked in a breath, trying to gather his thoughts, but then she bumped his hand aside, plucked at his shirttail, and he was pretty much lost.

His knee clanged against metal, their boots slid on the cart floor, and Kasey made a sweet, low sound of encouragement as he moved to capture her nipple with his lips.

Her hand skimmed through his hair, shaking before it formed to the back of his head, keeping him there. Wanting him there.

"I don't know when I started having this fantasy—" Her sentence broke when he touched his teeth to her nipple. Kasey jerked against him. "—about Ferris wheels."

"Kasey, you're gonna have to put up or shut up." Bronc felt the words jam up one behind the other. "You can't—Don't go telling me about your fantasies."

He barely had room to work his hand between them and his brain apparently had no room for anything except homing in on the snap at the waist of her jeans.

"You only call me Kasey when you want me." She spoke against the top of his head.

"You're wrong, Hollywood." He nipped the skin over her ribs. It was impossible that her skin tasted like cinnamon and roses. "I want you all the time. Just because I've tried being polite about it, don't think—" He couldn't see her flat belly, but the faint snick of her zipper lowering one tooth at a time, dazzled him.

He stopped talking. Was it the movement of his hands, swooping up from each of her hipbones to her breasts, that swung the little cart? Or was it Kasey, moving beneath him, trying not to let her long legs eject them from the cage? Could she feel the blue velvet against her back?

He couldn't ask even one of those questions. The flare of pink neon on her skin had his mouth too dry to say another word.

He kissed her again, trying to tell her. Sex, yes. Of course, now. *Now.* But there was more. She couldn't leave tomorrow. He infused the kiss with what he thought of her and she surged against him. He filled it with why he wanted her to stay and her breath grew shallow and shuddering.

He couldn't tell her outright. Because it had taken a moment of weakness for her to say she loved him, he couldn't just tell her.

Kasey nuzzled her lips to his ear and a rill of shivers shook him. "Take me back to the desert," she said. "Please take me back."

For the last time. She didn't say it because he covered her mouth with his. Not another word. Not a single moan as she wondered what would become of them. Only moans of delight. Her head turned, half trying to break away, but he widened the kiss, until she answered by twining around him with a whisper.

"What you did the other night?" Embarrassed, she closed her eyes, pressed her forehead against his chest, and her hips against his. "I want to . . ." Her voice faded to silence, then came back as a wisp of sound. "I want to do it again."

Fireworks flashed in his brain. He couldn't wait. Her sinuous movements didn't stop. Her hands, firm and tracing each side of his spine, didn't want him to stop.

Lost Springs. The warm pool and soft sands would be paradise with Kasey. It was nearby and there was no reason to refuse her. *Cowboy up, McDermitt.* You can do it.

He'd waited ten years to have Kasey back in his arms. He could wait another thirty minutes for lovemaking that might have to last him a lifetime.

〽 〽

KASEY EXPECTED HER KNEES would be black-and-blue from the gear shift, but she couldn't stay on her side of Bronc's truck. She tried to watch the windshield and consider the lightning storm raging over the Calico Mountains, but her left leg was pressed hard against Bronc's right one, their shoulders overlapped, and she could hardly catch her breath from wanting him. She didn't know how he could drive, she only knew tonight felt like more than sex. It felt like a vow.

She took his right hand from the steering wheel and flicked her eyelashes over it in a silly butterfly kiss.

"Whew." Bronc shook his head. "How can that make my stomach feel like I stepped into the Grand Canyon?"

"How far to Lost Springs?"

"Pretty close. We've crossed out of Kildeer County and into Bleek."

A streak of blue lightning, closer than before, lit the sky. Kasey closed her eyes, but the afterimage shimmering on her retinas looked like a horse. *Oh, no.*

"Heat lightning." Bronc reached across her, arm grazing the tops of her thighs in an intentional caress. "Why don't you put your necklace back on?" He snagged her purse and pulled it onto the seat between her and the passenger's side door.

Had he seen it? And if he had, why had he connected the electric image of a horse with her necklace?

She couldn't enjoy his touch as he probed for the necklace inside her purse, found it, and deposited it on her lap.

"Ladies' accessories are an odd sideline for you, McDermitt." Her voice echoed in the car.

"Y'see what you do?" Bronc's voice stayed infuriatingly level. "Get all sarcastic with me when you're feeling prickly over something else."

"You told me to put on the—" Kasey tried to keep the quarrelsome tone of a child out of her voice. "Sorry."

"Don't be sorry. Put it on before that lightning moves closer." She slipped the necklace over her head, trying to stifle her sigh and sort through what he'd said.

"You say that like you believe it has some sort of power."

"I do."

"Right," she scoffed. "I just ran into the mall to buy a pair of earrings and for a few pennies more, picked up a necklace with magical powers."

Bronc cleared his throat.

"I'm doing it again. Okay." Kasey crossed her arms and turned as far toward him as her seat belt allowed. "Tell me what you think."

"It's not something I mull over. It's like the modem in your little computer. You type in the middle of the desert. Cookie receives your note in L.A. Not exactly magic, but most folks don't really get it.

"Out here, it's still pretty much frontier. When a bolt of lightning strikes one black sheep in a flock, what's that mean?"

In the glow of the dashboard lights, Kasey saw Bronc's eyebrows lift before he continued.

"It happened to one of Abner's Basque buddies. And how

do you explain the cougar that came to Buck's tent, curled up to the canvas, and slept by him all night, purring like the world's biggest housecat? Buck decided it was a sign. He quit drinking and took the cougar as his totem. So, if your necklace keeps off bad medicine, wear it."

Kasey had leaned close enough to kiss the smooth flesh at his temple, when Bronc slammed on the brakes and the truck cab glowed with blue light.

Jagged as barbed wire, bright as a sun-struck mirror, the blue horse reared before them. Bronc stopped in the middle of the road, leaning forward against the steering wheel, filling his eyes, ignoring the shrilling flute, blown until it screeched. Kasey covered her ears as fear mixed with exasperation.

If she, like her mother, failed to accomplish Blue Rain's goal, what then?

The image faded, dispersed, vanished.

Bronc drew a deep breath and slid the truck into gear. On the horizon, Kasey made out dark humps of a few buildings. The faint lights of civilization made them both feel better.

"Friend of yours?" His weak joke didn't pry laughter from either of them.

She didn't say it was the same image she'd seen that night ten years ago, the night before she met him. And she didn't want to ask the question that suddenly clutched her heart.

Nonsense. She was trained to ask any question, no matter how difficult.

"Bronc, that morning I first met you. That other boy besides Calvin Buck, it wasn't Flynn." She made her voice adamant. "I know I'd remember if you called him Flynn."

"I didn't." Bronc glanced her way and Kasey relaxed. "But it was him, all right." He turned back to the road and the little settlement drawing nearer. "He was just a kid like the rest of us, and since we had nicknames he wanted one, too. At that stage, he had us calling him Fox."

A thousand pins might have stabbed her arms and legs. So what? She'd already known and she wouldn't allow this confirmation to distract her from what she really wanted on this last night in the desert.

If she wanted to be with Bronc, she'd better start acting like it.

"You know what?" Kasey blinked back sudden drowsiness. "I think we could both do with some coffee."

"Honey, we're almost to Lost Springs."

"Pull in, right there," she said as his headlights picked out a white sign with black lettering and a poorly cartooned polka-dot horse.

In spite of his long-suffering sigh, Bronc seemed amenable to the stop.

"Well, if you wanted a real cowboy bar, you picked the right place." Bronc steered into a gravel lot and jerked on the emergency brake. "Only one I know's named for a horse."

Kasey fought a flicker of dizziness as Bronc helped her from the truck and held her hand as they approached the bar. Honky-tonk music wafted out as he opened the wooden door.

"Yep, named after one of the great-grandfathers of quarter-type Appaloosas, Joker B."

⚞ ⚟

THE WOMAN WAS STRONG, BUT a novice to magic.

And Horse could be defeated, again. How many times had Horse fallen because he would not hold a woman by ravishment?

Fox imagined the swish of black feathers, the acrid scent of wet charcoal, and the copper tang of blood. For centuries, his simple spells had molded mortal lechery to his ends, allowing him to take women beloved of Horse. Rejected and fooled, Horse usually returned too late to keep Fox from regaining power.

This time was no different. No spirit or amulet could protect them, and the woman's intelligence only made the contest more amusing.

🐍 🐍

THE NECKLACE PLAYED A BERSERK HARMONY against her neck when Flynn appeared. Kasey turned from the jukebox as the coins jingled down the slot. It was impossible that Flynn had the power to thicken air enough to slow her movements. But that's how it felt, as she turned to locate Bronc.

He stood at the bar ordering cowboy coffee—black with a splash of whiskey.

"Red, if that coffee's been here since morning, you better brew me a fresh pot," he joked with the bartender, unaware of Flynn's approach.

Logic, strong as hands shaking some sense into her, told Kasey that she had the skills to handle Flynn on her own.

Opportunity, means, and motive.

Flynn had all the opportunity he needed, flying above the desert alone.

He had means, too, if the uncashed check to Abner was payment for another Storm Hammer.

But why?

In the dim bar, Flynn's sun-creased face looked friendly and his athletic grace drew her. With stomach-wrenching irritation she knew he'd bewitched her before. Now, she felt immune, but he didn't have to know.

In wordless agreement, Kasey let Flynn lead her to the dance floor. The jukebox voice of Willie Nelson sang "My Heroes Have Always Been Cowboys." She'd meant it for a clumsy tribute to Bronc.

Flynn treated it like a waltz. One hand clasped her waist. The other meshed fingers through hers and all the while he watched Bronc.

Motive. What did Flynn want enough to risk punishment in a federal prison?

Kasey leaned slightly away and tilted her head to one side. They danced eye to eye.

"I wonder what makes you tick, Flynn."

Flynn's attention shifted back to her. His eyelids lowered over pale eyes and his charisma wavered bright between them.

"Wide open spaces and pretty women. Just like your cowboy, Kasey, they're what I care about. Only I've never been in prison."

Flynn's words were low, but Bronc turned so quickly, anyone in the bar would have noticed. Kasey tried not to watch him. If she didn't concentrate, Flynn might beguile her like he had the women before her.

"Think how that would hurt your parents." Flynn shook his head. "Mother and father of the bride, both cops, giving their daughter to a jailbird."

She overrode the warning chill. Anyone could have learned that information. Every award she'd won, every profile written of her, had mentioned her parents' work. It was time to let him know what *she* knew.

"I've been wondering what exactly you did in Bosnia."

"Flew." He glanced toward the bar, lifted her hand, and pressed it against his shoulder.

He smiled with such sly pleasure she dreaded looking at Bronc. She didn't, telling herself Bronc knew she was dedicated to getting this story. He'd guess what she was doing. Though he'd be angry and protective, he'd better not feel jealous.

"But that 'soldier of fortune' work pays so well, why would you come back here, to *this?*"

Inadvertently, as she gestured to the little bar, she saw Bronc. Dimness hid his expression, but he had one thumb slung from a belt loop and his coffee cup to his lips. Relaxed, she thought. He looked just as lazy as he had riding a bucking horse, which might have snapped his spine.

No time to fool around. If she didn't want Bronc in the middle of things, she must provoke Flynn into revealing something critical. Now.

She knew how to do it. She wouldn't mention Billy was her father and Letty, her mother. She wouldn't hint she suspected he'd killed them both. Safe behind her coolness, K. D. Wildmoon wouldn't feel one twinge of pain.

"Hmm?" she coaxed. "Why come back to this?" She disentangled her hand from his, pretending to block a yawn. If Flynn turned violent, she wanted one hand free. "Especially when there was trouble—wasn't it a fire?—before you left. Why hurry back?"

He stroked her hair before his thumb jabbed the sensitive flesh beneath her ear. She might have called it an accident, except for the words that followed.

"Maybe I was homesick for a pretty little redskin, like you."

Shock raked from her brows to nape, making her hair bristle like a furious cat's fur. If he'd sunk to racism so soon, she was dead on target. When he pulled her closer, to dance cheek to cheek, she didn't resist.

One more minute, Bronc. She heard the sound of a cup slammed on the bar. *Just give me one more minute.* Boots shifted nearby, restless, reckless. *I'll have all I need to save your macho neck.*

"You learned to be a good shot long ago, didn't you? With

a Storm Hammer, I bet you could shoot from the air." She felt Flynn's face lift in a smile. "Or does someone go with you?"

His grip shifted to her wrist.

You're in over your head, Hollywood. Did Bronc say it, or was it simply a dose of her own good sense?

Flynn's hold tightened and her delicate bones shifted under pressure. She was strong. She could keep from groaning, keep needling him until he blurted out something incriminating. If Flynn broke a bone, Bronc would probably have qualms about making love to her.

"Could you let go of my wrist?"

"I could." Flynn's cheek rubbed hers. Anyone would think he was lavishing her with affection. The sinister caress frightened her more than the pain. "But I want you to come with me and you're reluctant. Leave him behind."

Kasey bent toward Flynn, but this time, she wasn't seduced by his words. How could his finger wedge into such a small niche between her wrist bones? Pulling away would make it worse.

Bronc loomed at the edge of the dance floor, waiting for her summons.

"Leave him," Flynn urged.

"No." Gritted teeth kept her from whimpering. If she didn't break his grip soon, he'd damage her arm.

"Who paid you to shoot the horses?" She ground out the words, but he looked smug, hearing how he hurt her.

Flynn squared his shoulders, giving her leeway to jam her left arm down his and grab his little finger and bend it toward his wrist.

Flynn looked faintly surprised.

It was called a come-along hold. Applied with enough force it would break his finger, but Flynn's other hand, on her wrist, didn't loosen. *It was supposed to, damn it.* She cringed toward his grip, but she still bore down hard, harder, on his little finger. He didn't seem to care.

"Do it." Flynn forked his fingers through the necklace. "You don't have the balls to do it."

She heard the bone snap. His, not hers. She jerked from his loosened fingers.

Even the bravest had to know when to cut and run. It was time. She bolted past Bronc.

"Come *on*." She gave his sleeve a yank.

"Start the truck. Keys are in it."

He spoke like a man with unfinished business, and Kasey didn't argue. She kept running as Bronc slammed Flynn against the wall. She heard the first meaty slap as Flynn, undeterred by his injury, belted Bronc. She heard the second blow and Flynn's grunt as she shouldered through the door and sprinted across the parking lot.

〆 ⅋

BRONC BURST FROM THE BAR JOGGING. He tumbled through the door of the idling truck and made a protective grab at his collarbone as Kasey slammed the truck into gear.

"Always admired a girl who could drive a stick shift and break a man's hand," he said as she slued out of the parking lot, spun the tires in a patch of gravel, and accelerated.

He tried not to tense up. The collarbone he broke in his high school rodeo days might have healed years ago, but today's fun reminded him exactly where the jagged ends had grated against each other.

He was too old for this.

Fire burned at the base of his skull, courtesy of Remedy's jackhammer landings, and he felt darn near disjointed, like his hip sockets had parted company with his femurs.

As the truck skidded off the dirt road and onto asphalt, a

nerve that had plagued him since high school rodeo days started rubbing the edge of a vertebra.

"Slow down, Hollywood. He's not coming after us 'til morning. Not unless someone gives him a ride, and folks were standin' in line to kick his ass when I left."

Kasey glanced his way, but the truck was so dark, he couldn't read her expression. Did she think he shouldn't be joking so about an injured man?

"Don't be feeling sorry for him," he began.

"He made me break his finger." Kasey's incredulity turned to frustration. "*Made* me. And I don't hurt people." She gripped the steering wheel hard enough that she heard it. "He practically admitted he killed the horses. I just have to figure out why."

The nerve gave him a pinch sharp enough to make him catch his breath.

"Are you all right?"

"Jim Dandy. Just out of practice for fighting bucking horses and pilots in one day."

"I'll take it easy on you, cowboy."

She reached for his hand. Though she managed to rub the knuckles he'd barked on Flynn's chin, Bronc didn't wince.

He did sigh, close his eyes, and let the feeling build past comfort, beyond wanting. He needed Kasey. The taunting way she slid her fingers through his, convinced him she needed him back.

"Better stop here." He'd meant to explain, but Kasey—who'd required an explanation for every other damn thing he'd ever asked of her—stopped instantly.

The way she surged against him, he might've uttered the most erotic words ever spoken.

"A little farther," he mumbled and she pressed against him with even more fervor, "down the road."

"Oh." Kasey laughed, restarted the truck, and steered it

behind a tumble of boulders big enough to hide a stack of Cadillacs. Then she waited.

They'd sat like this before, side by side with a variation of the same trouble nearby. That time, instinct had told them to depend upon each other. This time, they'd earned the trust.

"We better walk from here." He wasn't sure why he'd wanted to park a half mile from Lost Springs. Maybe so he'd have the warning of footsteps. Maybe a few minutes for her to be sure.

Lush and green, the smell of reeds fringing the hot springs hung on the night air. He made himself unload the back of the truck before leading her through the darkness to Lost Springs.

He didn't explain the bedroll he handed her. Or the lantern he'd brought along. When he started to shrug both their packs over his shoulder, she took hers.

"Ow," she said, slinging it on. "What a sorry pair. We sound like a couple of old codgers with all our aches and pains."

He smiled as she matched her stride to his. The ground felt springy underfoot. Then she flinched, readjusted her park, and he remembered Flynn's hand on her.

"What'd he do to your neck, honey?" He'd never felt so gentle in his life, not with a calf, a foal, or the twins. He touched the curve of her jaw, forward of where he'd seen Flynn's grip.

"I'm fine. I might not be able to take a punch like you can, but I'm not made of glass."

"Good thing." He walked faster. The night was slipping away. "Those stars are incredible." Kasey walked a weaving path, trying to watch the galaxies overhead.

Diamond-white and dazzling, they could be dead, burned out years ago, and not a soul on earth knew the difference. He shook his head. That wasn't going to be him. If Kasey left him, burned out and alone, she'd by God know what she was missing.

"Here we are."

Steam rose like silver dancers from the hot springs' surface. Bronc smiled at her sound of awe and suppressed his own groan at how he'd welcome that water on his aching sinews.

When Kasey turned practical, laying out blankets, he pumped up the lantern and lit it. When he glanced back, he caught Kasey biting her lip, looking faintly dubious.

"Take off your boots," he told her. "Go on, now."

She did, and let him part the reeds and lead her to a pedestal-sized rock. She sat, dangled her toes, and sighed.

"Cowboy's hot tub, Ms. Wildmoon. Nothing better for saddle sores—"

She was taking off her shirt. Bronc watched her arms cross to grab its hem as she gestured with her chin.

"Turn around and I'll race you."

When he didn't turn around quick enough to suit her, she did. Not that it calmed him. Kasey exposed the long graceful curve of her back flowing into the heart-shaped turn of her hips. He could barely breathe. But then she ducked through the reeds, out of sight, yipped, and splashed.

"Hey! Where's the . . . ? You said there were rocks to sit on. A little mossy, Bronc."

"Just polish it off with your hand." He shucked off boots, socks, and jeans faster than any man alive. When he imagined the warm water lapping at her breasts, he tripped. Then he heard her sigh.

Tender-footed, he followed that sigh. Every strained ligament had turned solid. He was moving like an old man, but not for long.

He parted the reeds, moved to the edge of the pool, and slid through the wavering cloud of steam, into the water. Kasey's hair was loose and she'd submerged to the chin. Her hair floated on the surface, black streams wandering among reflected stars.

He settled low, so the water covered his aching collarbone. A ripple grazed his shins, as she kicked out from the other side of the pool.

"Hi," she said.

"Hi."

"It's practically the middle of the night."

He nodded, because damn it, he didn't trust himself to speak. He wouldn't get all choked up because she might leave tomorrow. He still had a few hours to change her mind. If it didn't work—he still had a few hours.

The footing in the pool's bottom was surprisingly good. He felt a few slick rocks and pond plants, but once he was beside her, he forgot everything except Kasey, warm and willing.

She rubbed her cheek against his chest, purring like a cat. "Come be with me, Kasey."

They left the pool without a slip, without a splash. Shivering, they flattened each other to the ground. They rolled in blankets, lips and tongues warm despite the gooseflesh covering them. Kasey banished the cold with hands hunting up and down his back, pressing him closer.

Patience. Her breasts pressed hot against the front of him. Wait. The dip of her waist beckoned his hand to trace it down, up again and down. He thought of the Ferris wheel and Kasey's whisper: *What you did the other night? I want to do it again.*

He parted her thighs with his and her startled breath urged him on. Then she grabbed his shoulders.

One chance to get it right. He looked up into the black, star-strewn sky and ran his hand, palm flat, over the rise of her hip, down her leg as far as her knee. Steadied, he kissed her, but her mind wasn't on his lips. Her legs made a threshing, yearning movement and she moved the softness of her inner thigh against his hand.

"Bronc." Her voice was clipped, breathless.

"I'm right here, honey." Stupid thing to say when he loomed over her, except it brought her nearer, made her swallow so he heard it, made her head tilt in search of his mouth, taking it as if she'd devour him.

If he watched the tossing of her head or the moonlight painting her closed eyelids, he'd lose it. Bronc closed his eyes, too, but even her voice was temptation.

"How can you do this to me?" Her hands started a thousand streams of liquid warmth and her husky voice ignited them. "I don't believe, I can't—Bronc, how—?"

He edged over her, matching lips and chest and, oh, Lord, right there. He stayed in control, thought of his weight, and shifted, saying, "I'm too heavy," until she locked her arms around him and then, even blind sensation was too much.

"You feel perfect, pressing me down." She made an undulating, urging movement. "Don't go."

"No chance."

He tried to take her slowly, thinking of the black night stretching away all around them, instead of her demanding, thrusting hips. He marveled at her trust, at the eight days she'd known him, before surrendering here, in the middle of the desert. He didn't deserve this woman, but he hoped she never found out.

Bronc rose up. Eyes open, he held himself above her so she'd see his face in lantern light and know who took her. He was the one who ended up staring. Kasey's hair fanned around her, leaving her completely exposed, except where a lock slanted across her brow and one eye.

"Do you know how you look?" she asked.

He shook his head, smiling, wishing he could give back her reflection, cinnamon-rose and gold. She raised her hands to touch his chest, thumbs meeting at his breastbone before spreading out with a restless sigh. "Male, just incredibly—not frightening exactly, but overwhelming—*male*."

He cupped her breast and suckled. Losing it, he was holding one hand under her spine, pressing her to his mouth and losing it. His hand returned between her thighs. No trailing touch, this time, but one which left no questions.

Bold, he touched her wetness. Slow down. Slow down, damn it.

But Kasey said, "No, just—" and this time when she thrust against him, she barely missed. This time when she pulled his lips back to hers, he felt every sinew strain to bring him closer. Her nails raked his back. Her mouth twisted against his, teeth grazing his lips. Her legs and arms surrounded him.

"Please," she urged, *"please."*

"Okay, honey." He dispensed with the protective fumbling as if he'd practiced and then he was above her again.

And then there was no more waiting. Half blind with wanting her, he kissed her as they joined. She looked up, filling her eyes with him and he felt like a king.

"You look," she murmured against his mouth, "so *good*." Her head tilted back, lips parting from his as tremors shook her.

He plunged, entering completely while her climax was full, and thinking, wildly, that nothing on earth was so glorious. Nothing so intense could last so long.

Eyes open, he forked his hands through hers and lowered close enough that his lips grazed hers as he spoke.

"I love you. I *love* you." He couldn't believe he'd said it, couldn't believe the strength of Kasey's arms wrapping around him, passing each other as she hugged him closer. She made him reach for something stronger yet, to tell her.

"I love *you*," she said.

His words had been strong enough.

TWENTY-FOUR

The back booth in Hannah's Hen House café was around the corner from the kitchen and invisible to other diners. Kasey decided it was a good thing.

They hadn't slept. By moonlight, he'd come to her again with slow hands and relentless lips. And when a penny-bright edge of sun had shone over the playa, she'd crept atop him, powerless to stop. It hadn't been his hard strength beneath her or the desperation with which his body drove hers that tipped Kasey toward ecstasy. It was Bronc's voice at her ear, repeating her name with awe as she wrapped around him, melded against him, and wished they could be one.

But Flynn's violence had given Bronc second thoughts about Abner. Bronc's worry that the old man was in danger, paired with Kasey's conviction that this story was about to break, had drawn them out of the desert. Now they sat side by side, wishing they'd been more selfish.

For ten minutes, they'd sat undisturbed by a waitress. They liked the neglect just fine.

"Where do you keep all that stamina stored up, Hollywood?"

Under the table, Bronc's boot hooked over hers. His arm circled her shoulders and his hand spread over her upper arm in a greedy massaging motion, as if the blue cotton shirt could be rubbed away.

Kasey burrowed closer, giving in to a primitive yen to breathe the scent of the man she loved.

Last night should have changed everything.

Given more time, maybe one of them would have mentioned marriage. But neither of them had.

The café's door opened. As breakfast smells faded under the sharp scent of sagebrush, Kasey realized this wild place had claimed her as surely as Bronc had.

This morning, she'd ridden past vivid wildflowers, small as raindrops, which had sent roots through the playa's crust, found some shadow of moisture, and bloomed. Even though flowers pushed through cracks in Los Angeles sidewalks, too, they weren't half so wonderful.

She knew Bronc's answer before she asked. "Come back to L.A. with me, just for a little while."

"L.A.'d kill me, honey." Bronc gave three lingering kisses against her hair. "Don't you know that?"

Kasey sighed. For each brave weed that struggled through the streets of civilization, there were miles and miles of asphalt.

She could picture Bronc nowhere but here, in the high desert, riding the white and gray-green stretches he was born to. She waited for him to offer the mirror image of her request, but he didn't.

"*Dare* makes me travel. I can get back here a lot." Her heart was ripping into two hopeless halves. "I love you."

He turned toward her in the booth and both of his arms held her to his chest. She felt the slow, sad thump of his heart and chanted along. Ask me to stay, ask me to stay, ask me to stay.

Instead, the pungent smell of grease and the squeak of rubber-soled shoes heralded an intruder.

"Hannah." Bronc loosened his arms enough that Kasey could look over her shoulder, but he didn't let her twist loose. "How 'bout some chow?"

Hannah's tomato-soup colored hair and the tattooed rose on her forearm would have made her look like a biker-chick, if she hadn't been about seventy years old.

"Bronc, honey, I don't know what in hell you think you're doin' here in town. Temptin' Fate, I guess. Radich is hot on your ass for them horses and he's half sure you had something to do with Tate."

Kasey's scalp tightened. Please let the woman be another Western nut case.

"Hannah, I don't know what you're talking about." His arm stayed tight and Kasey felt his building tension. "You think I should get out of town? Why?"

"Radich and Buck all but had it out last night. Buck just kept him from goin' out to your folks' place, then Jacy called and said if I saw you, tell you she'd hide you out"—Hannah made an apologetic shrug to Kasey—" 'til you could get outta state."

"What about Tate?" Kasey remembered Tate's speculation about Flynn. *Some guys don't much care how they make a buck.... Gut-shoot horses and they scatter all over the place ... that'd occur to a pilot.* Flynn's cold eyes, his thumb jabbing the nerve in her neck. What if he knew about Tate's suspicions?

"Went and had a heart attack, even though his belly was full of those little pills. He's okay, resting in the hospital in Reno. Only thing is, when they were doin' up his blood work, they didn't find traces of medicine. Inside those capsules of his, what do you think? Filled with coffee creamer, that's all."

"And the horses?"

Hannah snagged a folded newspaper from beneath the dishes balanced on her left arm and offered it. Bronc and Kasey read silently.

Bleek County authorities are searching for cowboy Gabriel "Bronc" McDermitt in connection with the shooting deaths of wild horses near Towerdown in the Scolding Rock desert.

The mustangs were "gut-shot," according to Sheriff Glen Radich, who listed two bays, a black, and one steel-dust Appaloosa among the animals found on a tip from an anonymous source.

McDermitt, 29, BOW wrangler and son of Mac McDermitt of the Rainbow Bend Ranch, was tried and found not guilty because of lack of evidence in the deaths of other wild horses. . . .

⚞ ⚟

THE RESTAURANT DOOR OPENED and though Kasey could see nothing from this hidden booth, she looked up. Hannah moved away to greet someone named Pete.

Not Radich, not yet.

Kasey closed her eyes and pictured the beautiful bachelor band running near Towerdown. Descendants of Blue Rain's wild horses, they now lay dead in the desert. Fox couldn't have offered a more obvious taunt.

But Bronc wasn't thinking about horses.

"Abner's good as dead, unless he's hiding out at home." Bronc tapped the news story. "Flynn's taken out Tate for sniffin' around. He tried to scare you off, after he'd already nailed me by shooting those horses yesterday. If I'm arrested, I won't get off a second time."

If the concrete canyons of Los Angeles were doom for Bronc McDermitt, what would happen to him in prison?

"Look." Kasey took both his hands in hers. "Radich will expect you to hide in the desert, or the mountains or—Wyoming, but we're going to the Reno airport. We'll get on a plane to L.A. I know places to hide which you can't even imagine. Las Gatas take care of their homies." She watched Bronc shake his head at her grim smile. "I'll have my folks follow what goes on legally, until it's safe for you to come back."

"Aw, Hollywood, your big story's just about to break. You can't leave now."

"Shut up, McDermitt. The story's broken. I've got everything I need—except time to convince Radich he's taken a wrong turn by accusing you."

Bronc kissed her, slow and lingering. It was a good-bye kiss and she broke away.

"No, now knock that off." She shook her head and scooted apart from him. "You're not going back to jail, no matter if you have to go"—her hand spun circles in the air—"hide in Jacy's bed. Or Shannon's."

Amid the hissing of bacon and clatter of dishes, Kasey's necklace lay quiet, but something about Shannon bothered her. Why had Shannon looked so clammy and uneasy around Flynn that day at the Diamond Q? Was he using Shannon, too?

"Okay, lady, you're on."

Under the table, Bronc's hand covered her knee. In a slow and lazy move, it slid to the inside of her thigh. When Kasey opened her eyelids, Bronc's were still at half-mast.

"Get on the pay phone, there in the hall by the restroom. Call Reno Air and get us outta here. Then, call your folks and see if they're in the mood to shelter a fugitive. You need change?"

"I have change, McDermitt, and plenty of credit cards." She

lifted her pack and patted it as she stood next to the booth. "You get a little breakfast to go and I'll meet you at the truck."

⚡ ⚡

GULLY'S MAIN STREET only had curbside parking. When Kasey closed the door to Hannah's Hen House café behind her, the space where Bronc had parked his truck stood empty.

She walked a few steps down the sidewalk, away from Hannah's, then looked back over her shoulder. At the gas station, two boys in cowboy hats played with a hackysack. Her stomach growled with hunger as she tried to think.

Bronc McDermitt had run off and left her. Again. At least this time they'd gotten as far as Hannah's, but she didn't need men who abandoned her when things got tough. She'd thought Bronc had changed.

"Damn you." Kasey pushed her hair back from her brow. They'd miss the plane. Except, Bronc had probably never intended to catch it in the first place. All the minutes she'd been listening to her mother's voice mail, then the airline's canned music and recorded ads for flights to places she never planned to go, he'd been making his getaway.

Just because he'd done it to protect her didn't make it right.

Kasey slammed back into the café. Bronc had gone back out to Abner's, to search the tunnels and landmined range for the old hermit. By the time she caught up with Bronc, he was going to need protection *from* her.

Hannah verified what Kasey had already guessed. There was no place in town she could rent a car and Hannah wouldn't lend hers.

"Bronc would skin me alive." The cigarette clamped in the corner of Hannah's mouth bobbed as she talked.

What would convince this woman to cooperate? Kasey's hand strayed to her necklace as she thought. She didn't have time to size her up. She tried the obvious female failing.

"I'm his girlfriend. If he's in trouble, I need to help him."

"Hmph. That boy's got no shortage of girlfriends."

Kasey thought her frustration only proved Bronc had softened up her city sense. Not only that, she was hungry.

She scanned the glass case full of pastry, but her eyes caught on an old-fashioned processor for credit cards.

With one hand, she snagged a credit card slip. With the other she dug in her pack.

"What if I buy your car?" She took a deep breath. Between the bullet-riddled Taurus and this, she'd certainly learn how far *Dare's* number-crunchers would bend on an expense account.

"It's just an old Nova," Hannah told her with a jerk of her thumb toward the rear of the restaurant. "You don't want to be buying it."

Kasey picked up a pen from the counter. "How about two hundred dollars?" Kasey entered the figure.

Bronc was walking into ambush.

"Naw, I just couldn't." Hannah had taken the cigarette from her mouth. Her fingers pressed it flat as she watched the pen.

If Bronc met up with Flynn, he'd be in serious trouble. Bronc was a cowboy, not a cop. He'd need her help.

Kasey added another zero to the credit card slip and turned it so Hannah could read the total.

"Two thousand dollars? The back windows don't even roll up, but—" Hannah crushed the cigarette into an ashtray. "You got it, doll, with a full tank of gas."

"Great." Kasey slung the pack over her shoulder, grateful Hannah hadn't bothered to check her credit limit. "How 'bout giving me that glazed doughnut, too? To go."

⋁⋁ ⋂⋂

LIKE A GLARE OFF WATER, the electric shimmer of Blue

Rain's spirit horse led Kasey back to Abner's stronghold. As the stallion galloped ahead, Kasey felt dazed, and though she tried to blame a lack of sleep, she knew the cotton-clogged working of her brain meant more. In the mystical battle between Fox and Blue Rain, she was merely a pawn.

Too bad. *All* she cared about was Bronc.

Pressure thrummed her ribs like harp strings and the necklace lanced her with shafts of heat. Kasey gasped and lifted it away from her chest. Blue Rain's spiteful image glinted in the seat beside her, frightening her in a way she'd never been before.

"Okay." Kasey gripped the cracked steering wheel and kept her eyes on the trail ahead. "He's not *all* I care about, but you know how easily he loses control." Kasey tried not to jabber as images of Bronc flooded her senses, coming one atop the other. "That night in Shannon's kitchen and last night in the Joker B, he exploded. He refuses to anticipate a gun or a knife or— And if he finds Flynn, especially if Flynn's hurt Abner, Bronc will go charging in, mad as hell and—"

Get himself killed. Kasey couldn't say it, even to Blue Rain. Tears knotted her throat as she chanced a look toward the passenger's seat.

The Indian woman beside her was not Blue Rain. A woman in her prime, buxom and burnished with health, slouched against the car door. She wore bubble gum–pink lipstick on a defiant mouth. A black and white peace sign was painted on one cheek and a mane of black hair fell over the shoulder of a red tee shirt lettered: "Custer Died for Your Sins."

No one, not even Bronc, had ever looked at Kasey with such glad admiration and pride. No one except Maggie Harrigan, her mother.

Kasey tried to talk. *Who, what, when, where, why.* She knew the questions to ask. She just had to say the words. *Who—*but, oh, her heart *knew* who.

"Are you Letty Wildmoon?" She wanted to reach out, but her hands locked on the steering wheel. She wanted to feel the warm skin of the woman who'd nursed her, then given her away.

The spirit wavered, dimmed.

Kasey refused to hear the child in her mind screaming *Mama*. She refused to echo that cry, and it was just as well, because a breath of sound lingered as the spirit faded.

"Don't let him do it," said Letty Wildmoon. *"Stop him."*

᛭ ᛭

STOP WHO? KASEY BRAKED before the last ridge overlooking Abner's stronghold. *Fox or Bronc?*

To keep from announcing her arrival, she'd decided to leave the car here and walk down, behind the barn. Kasey locked her pack in the car and touched her pockets. She'd brought nothing but the single car key Hannah had handed her and her Swiss Army knife. Her greatest asset hung around her neck, but she didn't know how to use it.

Blue Rain's voice tinkled in a fairy-high laugh, *"Don't worry, it will use you."*

No doubt.

Feeling like the worst sort of Indian stereotype, Kasey crawled the last few feet to the ridgetop and peered down. There sat Bronc's blue truck, parked at the edge of the minefield. She saw no helicopter, no other vehicles. Maybe she and Bronc were both wrong. Maybe Flynn wasn't here. Or maybe he'd turned into Fox and didn't need mortal transportation.

Her necklace jabbed heat against her blouse, but she ignored it. She had to; Bronc was here.

Go. She didn't take time to gather her nerve. She came down the steep sidehill quickly, eyes scanning the terrain. She didn't stop until she reached the barn.

Bronc had told her he'd never been in the tunnel rumored to connect the barn and basement, so she'd have to take her chances. Going into a basement full of old, unstable dynamite was suicidal anyway. It didn't much matter how she got there.

§§ ﷼

SHANNON HELD JOSH CAPTIVE in Abner's kitchen.

Hidden in the basement below, Bronc listened as Shannon pretended to be nice. She asked Josh if he wanted chocolate milk. Though the day was warm, Josh said he'd rather have hot chocolate. Bronc heard Shannon run water into a kettle and set it on Abner's stove.

Bronc sat on the top step of the basement stairs. He frowned up at the perfectly jigsawed secret door. If he gave it a butt, it would swing open and he'd emerge into the hall, steps from the kitchen table. But until he knew what was going on, that seemed like a bad idea.

Shannon had no business here and he worried that Flynn was on his way. Damn. He'd cut off his arm and use it to batter the pilot senseless before he'd let Flynn touch Josh.

"Bronc sure must be taking the long way around." Shannon sounded exhausted. Bronc couldn't figure that out either. She'd always been the sort to work 'til she dropped and never give a sign before she gave out.

For an instant, it was so quiet Bronc thought he could hear the water starting to ping and boil in the copper kettle.

"Where's Abner?" Josh asked. "You said . . ."

Where was Abner? If he'd been dead for two days, he wasn't down here. Jaw clenched, Bronc had been scouring the basement for signs of Abner when he'd heard footsteps overhead. Bronc had thought about searching the tunnel, even started down there with a flashlight, working back toward the barn.

But then he'd stopped and, steadying himself against the tunnel wall, nearly put his hand on a black widow spider. About then, he'd lost his stomach for continuing into the darkness.

". . . move some junk into town, but he's not even here. Jeez, I don't know why I had to help and Callie didn't. And now Bronc's not even here."

"He'll be here, Josh. I think he might be coming with Flynn." Josh snorted. "Not in this lifetime. He hates the son of a bitch."

Bronc shook his head and tried to concoct a plan. *Kasey* would have a plan. She was the most premeditating woman he'd ever encountered.

"Shit!" Shannon's tone was astounded. "What in—?"

"How'd he get in here?" Josh's voice soared from surprise to pure fear. "Hey! *Hey!*"

Bronc rammed a shoulder into the trapdoor. It gave with oiled eased as he vaulted into the hall, searching for Josh. He didn't have time to see his brother or the muzzle flash. As he fell, Bronc heard the Storm Hammer roar.

⚡ ⚡

"RUSH DON'T MUCH LIKE YOUR STYLE of writing."

Kasey tried to see the humor in her predicament. Worried every minute that she'd touch something crawly, she'd edged down the tunnel. It smelled of fresh cement. Just as she'd passed a curve, she glimpsed a white-haired troll on the ground and then Abner Bengochea grabbed her ankle.

She hadn't screamed then, but if this conversation went on much longer, she'd be wailing. She'd tried to tell him she was looking for Bronc, for Flynn, for someone who could endanger both of them. Each time Abner hushed her with a prod from his rifle barrel.

"Mike Reagan don't care for you much, either. Says you're a puking liberal Democrat and part of the media conspiracy that's weakening these United States."

Only once had a storm of talk-radio interest broken over her work, but Abner hadn't missed it.

"Mr. Bengochea, I haven't worked for the *Sun-Times* for a while." She needed to get down this tunnel to Bronc.

Kasey tried a different approach. She lied.

"Besides that, neither Mike nor Rush know squat about my politics. You might be surprised to know I'm a member of the American Independent party and I'm backing Howard Phillips as the next presidential candidate."

Abner mulled this over, but he kept his rifle trained on her torso. She could imagine a bullet ricocheting off the sides of this tunnel and ping-ponging through her a dozen times before it stuck.

"A good family man," Abner said. "Kinda short, though." Kasey closed her eyes, trying to remember the press kit on her desk at work. "Nearly as tall as Bronc."

"You being a reporter, how d'you feel about his stand on journalists?"

"Journalists." Her arms faltered from their "hands up" position, until the gun barrel's skyward jerk reminded her.

"Yes, ma'am. Phillips has plenty to say about a liberal, one-world controlled press."

Of course he did. "No one's perfect," she ventured. "Tell you what. I'm not givin' you a gun."

"I don't want a gun. I just want to get into your house and see if Bronc's all right."

"He's fine. Up there stompin' around calling me loco, and whatnot." Abner nodded. "You have any kinda protection?"

"A Swiss Army knife."

"Won't do you a fat lot of good if Flynn's waiting at the other end with his Storm Hammer."

"Do you think he is?" Kasey yearned for her voice-activated tape recorder. Abner had just given her absolute confirmation that Flynn owned a weapon like the one implicated in the horse deaths.

"No sign of him, but that man's got a smell on him. Kind of like a bird that's been taxidermied. Do you know what I mean?"

A wintry breeze might have passed by her. She'd never smelled such a thing, but the image of Flynn and old feathers chilled her.

"Your little knife got a wine opener?" Abner snorted smugly when Kasey nodded. "Figured. You go ahead and rake that over Flynn's knuckles and it'll make him sit up and take notice. It's a shame, damned shame, I was wrong about him. He was all dressed in black, like one of them secret helicopter pilots, comin' toward my house that day Bronc promised to come over. I was right to hide out. He looked, but my tunnels hid me just like they were supposed to."

Dressed in black. Kasey moistened her lips, trying to remember when she'd seen Flynn dressed in black.

" 'Course, there's always a knee in the 'nads."

Kasey took a few seconds to decipher the old man's meaning. *Gonads,* she supposed. "Yes, there always is."

They both stared toward the house-end of the tunnel, at the sound of a faraway thud.

"You go right ahead, now. But watch your step. And don't think of looking at my dynamite."

"I won't." Kasey sidled down the dark tunnel, smiling because she was pretty sure that sound had been Bronc, punching a wall in frustration.

The scenario Kasey had figured out wouldn't be best for Blue Rain, and its open-endedness would drive Bronc mad.

Still, Fox had a history of vanishing and leaving others to deal with trouble.

Kasey decided Flynn had sprung his trap and run away. He'd been here, of course. That's why her necklace still spiked with jolts of power, but she had the calm conviction that the worst was over. Kasey hurried down the tunnel, eager to tell Bronc.

⚂ ⚃

FINALLY. Kasey flattened her palm against the trapdoor at the top of the basement stairs and tried to picture where it would open into Abner's house.

Standing here for fifteen minutes, silent beneath the trap-door, had taken all her nerve. Following Abner's directions, she hadn't looked at the dynamite, but she could smell it, metallic and festering. She'd heard nothing upstairs, except a sound that might have been a cat.

She emerged in the hall and lowered the intricately cut door with utter silence. Gunpowder scented the air, but that was natural. A gunsmith lived here.

She'd changed into sneakers before leaving the Nova and it had been a good idea. She crept to the door of Abner's bed-room. Magazines sat on a square table next to a wheelchair. The bedspread was white chenille with little tufts of yellow flowers.

She sensed movement in the living room and heard a sound as if someone shifted on the couch. A board creaked underfoot as she moved toward the kitchen. She froze, listening. Nothing.

She took a long step over the trapdoor. Halfway through the kitchen, she almost slipped. She glanced to her left and confu-sion made her stop. Bronc lay dozing in the living room.

He wouldn't do that. Not in someone else's house.

Kasey stared at the stove, where a copper kettle boiled furi-ously. She looked down at her shoe, trying to make sense of what she saw. She'd tracked blood into the kitchen.

Oh, Bronc. Before she could run to him, the lost-kitten sound came from the kitchen table.

"It's over." Fox wore black feathers. Face grayed with ash, eyes encircled with white paint, then black, he held Josh against him. A rag-gagged Josh, and Fox's hands clamped a huge rifle into the boy's grip.

Kasey felt all pity vanish. Pity would do Bronc and his brother no good. Her necklace pulsed and cold purpose compelled her to battle Fox.

"You don't look much like Flynn now."

"No." The single word carried magic and it wafted around her like smoke. Kasey thought she might kneel at his feet, if not for the necklace and the revelation that struck.

Using his own damaged hand, Fox held Josh's fingers—and fingerprints—against the rifle. How easy it would be for an outsider to believe that fragile, traumatized Josh had turned homicidal, then suicidal.

As Kasey walked closer, she heard Bronc move on the couch. He wasn't dead! Her heart rejoiced in the simple truth, although she still couldn't go to him. She rushed to cover the sound of his movements.

"The last shaman? Is that what you like to be called?"

As Kasey walked closer she heard Bronc move on the couch. *Not dead,* Bronc was not dead.

Fox shifted, moving Josh like a puppet to keep the rifle trained on her. "Bronc and Buck thought you were just making up your own nickname when you were a kid. They couldn't know Fox was your—what?—familiar?"

Fox inclined his head in condescension. *"We might have settled this then, if Horse hadn't interfered. I'd have the necklace. Your mother would still be alive. And your father."*

She refused to snap up that lure, or notice the lost-kitten

sound that was Josh. She couldn't look at him. Imagining his terror was bad enough. *And Bronc . . .*

Because she needed all of her concentration to keep Fox from sending tendrils of power into her mind, Kasey fell back on what she knew best.

"So, why'd you decide to kill the wild horses?"

"You don't care about their battle with me, only about your story. Ah, what a modern woman. You do know they stand behind you? Blue Rain and that bitch that was your mother?"

Kasey counted her breaths and refused to look back. It was only a ploy to unnerve her.

"Do you know how she died at the roadside? She laughed herself to death. At me. I couldn't force her to tell me where you and the necklace had gone. I'll have the last laugh, Leticia. Now you can watch your precious Wild Moon die. And Horse. He's bleeding to death, you know."

No. Kasey hardened herself against pity.

Josh bucked in the man's hands. Though he didn't loosen Fox's grip, he distracted the shaman, who'd begun a breathy chanting as Blue Rain's power pushed Kasey toward the stove.

"There must have been other ways to hurt Blue Rain," Kasey insisted. The shaman shook his head, feeling her vacillation between logic and magic. "Killing the horses didn't help you get the necklace."

His laugh was that of a man amused by an idiot. *"Their deaths brought you here. Their deaths damaged McDermitt, wounded Blue Rain, and allowed me to line up Shannon as a fall guy in case McDermitt escaped conviction."*

"The antelope." Kasey listened to the water, boiling fast as running hooves.

"I suppose it was too simple. She feeds the antelope, they thrive with the horses' deaths and when she receives money from the hunt-

ers' consortium—not to mention years of business for the privilege of hunting on her ranchlands—and BOW—"

Josh signaled his move before he made it, but Fox contracted in half as the rifle butt slammed back and Josh rolled away. A corona of blue flame surrounded Kasey as she grabbed the kettle and slung it, spewing glorious boiling water.

Fox grabbed his face, hands scrubbing until they were smeared with paint. Then they sprang upward, white-palmed with fingers wide apart, when Bronc shot him.

⚡ ⚡

THEY SAID GOOD-BYE AT THE HOSPITAL, because Bronc wanted it that way. He was just a little too proud and sensible to let her cry at his bedside.

It hadn't been so bad at first. Right after Radich left, she'd kissed him and smoothed his hair and told him she loved him. But now his parents and Callie had come. And Josh was strutting around, proud he'd defied Flynn and the Storm Hammer.

He wanted silence, but first he had to force Kasey to do what was best. Instead of what he wanted.

"Savage offered you a year's salary for one stinkin' story," he said. "So don't be hanging around here."

His parents rustled in incredulity.

"I don't care about the money." Her fingers were forked through his and her throat worked hard to keep the tears from turning into sobs.

"You're in the wrong company to be saying that." Bronc watched her blush. He'd turned pretty cold-blooded, hoping for heartbreak that would last minutes, not days. "Catch the next plane out, Hollywood."

She gave a watery laugh, but she didn't release his hand while she explained to his parents that she'd do the personality profile for *Dare,* but the story of Flynn's plot was hot, breaking news and a newspaper like the *Sun-Times* would pay a lot for on-the-spot coverage.

"Bronc, honey, we'll give you a minute of privacy before Kasey leaves, shall we?" Mom's lower lip was quivering, too. He'd had enough of these damned waterworks. He just wanted everyone to get the hell out.

"Naw . . ." But they were already going, leaving him alone with Kasey, who fell to kissing his face.

"I love you, Bronc McDermitt. Why are you pushing me away?"

"Oh, now—"

"That bullet didn't hit your head, so I can only think you've changed your mind."

"About what?" He watched her turn to stone. "I'm not moving to L.A. and I don't remember asking you to stay." He swallowed hard. Of course he had. Not outright, maybe, but what else could telling her he loved her mean?

"I don't want to go." She looked around the room, as if searching for a motive for his cruelty. "I knew you were alive. I'm sorry I couldn't come to you right away, but he had Josh and I thought—"

"Now, *you* knock that off." He pointed his finger like a revolver. "You did fine."

He set his jaw and prepared to lay it on thick.

"Look, you had a summer fling with a cowboy—one who rides bucking horses and gets all shot up. Lunch gossip doesn't get much better than that."

"Please," she said, but nothing came after it.

She wanted him to make it not hurt. Well, damn it, it did hurt. She might as well shove a knife into his chest and lever it open as leave him. But she would do it.

"Excuse me, Ms. Wildmoon?" A nurse hovered in the doorway. "You have another call at the nurses' station. I can't ring it through, but I think it's that nice Mr. Savage."

"I'll call back."

"No sense dragging it out, Hollywood. I need to catch a nap. Go on." He jerked his chin toward the door. "And don't forget to send me copies of your stories."

"Bronc." She bent over him, hands planted on the sheets. Her hands shook so hard, his shoulder recommended bleeding.

He took a deep breath of Kasey's meadowgrass-scented hair, kissed her cheek, and gave her one last dose of the hayseed accent she hated.

"Adios, darlin', " he said, and turned his back.

Eyes closed, he heard footsteps. Kasey Wildmoon was walking out the door.

TWENTY-FIVE

GLENSIDE COUNTRY CLUB
LOS ANGELES, CALIFORNIA

How could Kasey live in a city where the sky glowed the color of rust? Bronc steered his truck into a "Members Only" parking space, figuring that one way or another, he wouldn't be here for long.

Last night, after three months of chasing horses, buying a new herd of Herefords for Rainbow Bend, and enduring the legal hoopla of proving Shannon a good parole risk and getting Flynn locked up for good, Bronc had cranked up the nerve to drive to Los Angeles.

At a multistoried mall in Beverly Hills, he'd put himself in the hands of a girl with a pierced nostril and stiletto heels. When she had him dressed and standing in front of a mirror, he wore new Levi's and a blue shirt with a little polo player on it, which the girl said she chose because it matched his eyes.

She'd tried to convince him to buy a pair of khaki pants, but they'd looked too much like the ones Savage had worn when he touched down at Shannon's. She'd recommended a pair of loafers, too, but finally conceded he could "get away with" Nikes.

Anticipation had built, making him feel so lighthearted he'd stashed his stuff at a motel near Disneyland. If Kasey wouldn't have him, he'd go on over and be miserable with Mickey Mouse.

It was a Friday afternoon. There was no reason to be shocked when the receptionist at *Dare* magazine, in West Los Angeles, told him Kasey wasn't in.

He'd stood out on the sidewalk, trying to convince himself he could find lots to do in this nice little college area. Then he'd spotted a phone booth down the street. As expected, a celebrity like Kasey wasn't listed in the telephone book.

Bronc spent twenty minutes sitting in the truck, staring at the handwriting on the envelope she'd used to send the articles. If she'd written her home address, he would've found the place and sat on her porch until she got there.

That's when he thought to call Cookie. They were roommates, weren't they? He couldn't guess why his hand shook while he dialed through the *Sun-Times* switchboard. After he asked to be connected with Cookie, he almost hung up.

What if Kasey had gotten back together with Savage? It turned his stomach, thinking of the man's manicured nails skimming over her sweet skin.

"Photo."

Bronc's heart pounded, but he couldn't talk.

"*Sun-Times* photo department. Hel-lo?"

"I wonder," Bronc cleared his throat. "Could I talk to Cookie Hodges?"

"You got her."

"Ms. Hodges, this is, uh—" Even his name sounded wrong

here. He reminded himself he'd just earned a scholarship to U.C. Davis. He was no ignorant redneck.

Three months ago he'd had the class to realize marriage to him would be trouble for Kasey.

Nothing had changed.

Except he couldn't live like this.

"Finally got your nerve up, huh, cowboy?"

Cookie performed a passable Western drawl. It surprised him so much, a woman walking a poodle turned around to see what had him laughing.

"You're right," he admitted. "And she's not in her office. Think I could wait at your place?"

"Oh, no. No, no, no." Cookie giggled like someone'd shaken her until she fizzed. "I know where she is, and you've got to go after her."

"She's not in any trouble?"

"Not exactly," Cookie said. "But your timing couldn't be better."

§§ ⚛

GLENSIDE COUNTRY CLUB WAS EASY to find, and the security guard wore a cell phone instead of a gun.

"Yes, sir, Ms. Wildmoon is here, but I'm afraid you won't be able to join her."

"Thanks." Bronc felt his shoulders loosen with relief. "I'll just wait for her out here."

Maybe she'd be sunburned and sleepy when she left the pool inside. Maybe she'd like to hit some cool sheets then, and work out details later.

"I'm sorry, sir, that won't be possible."

"You're telling me I can't *stand* here?" Bronc rubbed the back of his neck and took another look at the guy. His short mustache twitched like a terrier dog's.

"That's right." The guard fiddled with a red button on his telephone. "It's private property. If you won't go, I'll have to call the police."

"The police."

L.A. cops wouldn't take their cues from a guy like this.

"I'm going on in." Bronc lifted the latch on the wrought-iron gate and started across the concrete toward the pool.

The guy sort of bobbed beside him. "Sir, that's not possible."

"Sure it is. When the cops come, tell them I'm inside. One way or another, it'll all be over by the time they get here."

Bronc closed the gate, latched it between them, and started searching for Kasey.

He passed a dwarf palm and two Joshua trees, and saw kids everywhere, most speaking Spanish and carrying boom boxes. And then, across the sparkling aqua pool, he saw Kasey.

She stood next to Mark Savage. She looked up into his broad blond face, laughing, and she wore a red bikini.

Bronc stepped over a plastic raft and kept walking. He hadn't driven all this way to be charged with a second case of justifiable homicide. But Savage was touching Kasey and Bronc couldn't stand it.

᭟᭟ ᭟᭟

"SAVAGE, you are so full of yourself." Kasey grabbed Mark's wrist, lifted his arm from around her neck, and dropped it. "Wow. ¿Adónde vas?"

"Papasito, qué guapo te vas hoy."

Kasey turned to see the man Las Gatas were praising as "looking good." The man was Bronc.

Not a hallucination this time. This Bronc wasn't the guy in the library who'd actually recoiled from her enthusiastic "Hi!" He wasn't the glowering executive who'd driven past on Sunset

Boulevard or the bike messenger she'd followed for a half block. This Bronc was the real thing.

Kasey's hand raised to cover her lips. She'd thought she was done with crying, but Bronc didn't belong here, all groomed and tame.

"K. D.? I don't think you've given my offer fair consideration."

"Shut up, Mark."

Kasey took two steps toward Bronc. The concrete burned her feet and her necklace hummed. She hadn't taken it off in three months. All that time it had lain silent and still. Now she felt a faint vibration, cozy as a cat's purr.

More than anything, she wanted to run to Bronc and beg him never to leave. But she'd made an awful scene at the hospital.

Worse, on the last day of summer, she'd gone back to Nevada, back to his parents' ranch, and no one could tell her where to find him.

The entire McDermitt clan had tried to help. So had the Bucks, but she'd ended up sitting at the edge of the Scolding Rock desert at sundown, waiting.

Even Blue Rain hadn't come, but then, the spirit had gotten what she wanted: Fox defeated and confined, probably forever.

After a black night alone there, Kasey had flown home to Los Angeles and reached a decision based not on logic, but on distance and desire. She'd sat in her living room, reading the Reno newspapers she'd picked up in the airport. She'd thought of roots and permanence and realized she'd never find them in frantic L.A. She'd decided to move by Easter.

With Bronc McDermitt or without him, that high desert country was home.

"¿Cómo quisiera agararte y—"

Kasey's tolerance snapped. One of Las Gatas was proposing she grab Bronc and do—*what?*

"Hands off, *chica.*" Just saying it gave Kasey hope and made the teenage girls howl in appreciation.

Behind her, Mark begged the girls to explain.

Bronc kept coming toward her. She saw his lips say "Kasey" and couldn't stop herself from rushing forward, but his expression, half reprimand and half celebration for the brief bikini, stopped her from throwing herself into his arms.

He looked taller than ever, tanned; and though his shoulder must have healed, she longed to check it. He looked tired, with the line between his brows carved deeper.

"Bronc, what are you doing here?"

"Oh." He pretended to kick his Nike in the dust. "Just came by to see if you were done with Hannah's Nova."

They were back to that down-home drawl he used especially to gall her.

"I'm keeping it." She crossed her arms.

"Suit yourself. Hannah bought a new Hyundai with your money." His frown line grew even deeper and Kasey knew he'd finished joking.

"Don't talk for a minute."

"Okay," she agreed.

"Thing is, between the scholarship I earned and the reward money—" Bronc's face brightened. "Half that money's yours, by right."

Kasey released a breath. "What if I let you take me out for dinner?" she said, but she knew he hadn't come this far to pay her off.

"It's more money than that, Hollywood."

Her cheeks hurt from grinning, and when he grabbed her hand she felt hope bloom. His eyes searched her face with a yearning and lonely look.

"Do you know how good you look?" She said it hoarsely, glad no one stood near enough to hear her.

"Do you know when you said that to me last?"

A rush of heat reminded her of moonlight and desert and her heart against his. She nodded.

Bronc cleared his throat. He stared past her, but there was no desert for him to watch, only the high curve of a freeway overpass. He swallowed. "Do you want me to stay?"

"No—"

"Well, then—"

"Here? Bronc, you said L.A. would kill you."

He shook his head. "Don't make me say it, Kasey. I am *not* good at this."

"But I don't know what you—"

"I'd rather die than live like this. Without you."

Kasey felt her lips part, felt her hand touch the skin above her necklace. "You would? But—where were you? I came back in August. No one knew where you were."

"Up in the hills, with Rook. I'd just accepted the scholarship, so I could go back to vet school, but I didn't know what to do about—" He tipped one hand aside.

"About—?"

He closed his eyes, rubbed the back of his neck, and pressed on. "I don't want to live here. I'd lose the scholarship and I hate this damned brown sky. But I can't ask you to move to Rainbow Bend, or live in married students' housing on campus."

He waited, but she let him finish.

"Could I? You know, though, you could work from there and I could go to school and maybe we could have a couple good years before you told me you'd had enough."

"A couple good years? Are you asking me to move in with

you?"

"I wouldn't do that." His sigh rocked him forward and he took her hands. "I'm asking you to marry me."

She thought he flinched. This man who hadn't flinched when Radich tried to handcuff him, as his blood streamed and she shrieked about justifiable homicide. He hadn't flinched either when they strapped him to a stretcher and AirCare flew him from Gully to Reno in a mosquito-weight helicopter.

"Honey, if it's that hard a call, don't make it."

"Bronc, hush a minute."

"Just tell me no. I can drive back where I came from."

"Excuse me, cowboy," she interrupted. "Haven't I heard Nevada's famous for something besides sagebrush and wild horses?"

He cocked his head to one side. A make-my-day smile spread across his face, but he stayed silent.

"Like..." Kasey could see she'd have to make the suggestion. "... quickie weddings?"

She stood tiptoe and circled her arms around his neck and he kissed her. With her eyes closed tight and the sun hot on her back, Kasey saw Blue Rain once more. Feather-light in white leather, her braids festooned with bells, the Indian maiden cartwheeled, laughed, and vanished.

Held tight against Bronc's chest, Kasey could almost forget the applauding Las Gatas and the distant hum of a million cars. When Bronc lifted her feet free of the concrete, she was already halfway home.

Meet Author
Tess Farraday

Tess Farraday is a fourth generation Californian. Years after she dreamed of a place where horses ran free, she found it in the high deserts of northern Nevada, where she now lives. She has been writing fiction and non-fiction since third grade and loves researching the historical and contemporary West.

Love to read?
Read what you love . . .
with QuestMark Romances!

QuestMark proudly presents:

Blue Rain
by Tess Farraday

For the Love of Grace
by Ginna Gray

Lady In White
by Denise Domning

Out of the Blue
by Kasey Michaels

Rose of the Mists
by Laura Parker

The **Angel Knight**
by Susan King